"Lessman writ[...] I can't put down—a book that has a heroine with unforgettable spunk, a romance with undeniable sparks, and a family that will remain in your heart long after you turn the last page."

—Siri Mitchell, author of *She Walks in Beauty*

"Capt[...] and
thou[...]ou
breat[...]vel
that [...]n-
cond[...]

[...]ies

"Juli[...]n't
let g[...]rs,
A H[...]lly
satis[...]or
your[...]

[...]*ter*
[...]*tle*

"Juli[...]as-
siona[...]'re
look[...]ce,
you [...]

[...]*ng*,
[...]ies

"I ha[...]ok.
I lov[...]*Un-*
dau[...]n,
all i[...]

[...]*nts*
[...]*nts*

"*A* [...]ss-
mar[...]nd
torn[...]ers
but [...]ok
has [...]

[...]*art*

Also by Julie Lessman

THE DAUGHTERS OF BOSTON

A Passion Most Pure

A Passion Redeemed

A Passion Denied

WINDS OF CHANGE

A Hope Undaunted

WINDS of CHANGE

a Hope Undaunted

A NOVEL

JULIE LESSMAN

Revell
a division of Baker Publishing Group
Grand Rapids, Michigan

Published by Revell
a division of Baker Publishing Group
P.O. Box 6287, Grand Rapids, MI 49516-6287
www.revellbooks.com

Printed in the United States of America

Library of Congress Cataloging-in-Publication Data
Lessman, Julie, 1950–
A hope undaunted : a novel / Julie Lessman.
p. cm. — (Winds of change ; 1)
ISBN 978-0-8007-3415-2 (pbk. : alk. paper)
1. Nineteen twenties—Fiction. I. Title.
PS3612.E8189H67 2010
813′.6—dc22 2010016223

Unless otherwise indicated, Scripture used in this book, whether quoted or paraphrased by the characters, is taken from the King James Version of the Bible.

10 11 12 13 14 15 16 7 6 5 4 3 2 1

To my beautiful daughter Amy—
not only the inspiration for Katie O'Connor, but
God's amazing response to my own "hope undaunted."
You were an answer to prayer then
and you're an answer to prayer now,
and Dad and I love you to pieces!

Each man will be
like a shelter from the wind
and a refuge from the storm,
like streams of water in the desert
and the shadow of a great rock in a thirsty land.
Then the eyes of those who see will no longer be closed,
and the ears of those who hear will listen.

Isaiah 32:2–3 NIV

1

Boston, Massachusetts, May 1929

Now this *is how love should be—nice and neat.* Katie O'Connor sucked the last of her Coca-Cola through a straw and studied her steady beau Jack Worthington with a secret smile. No, siree, no dime-novel notions of love for her. Love requires a focused plan, she thought to herself with certainty. Cool, calm, rational thinking, not a moment in time where one lovesick glance seals your fate. With a loud, hollow noise, she drained her soda and pushed the glass away, assessing Jack through approving eyes. Her lips slanted. *Love at first sight, my foot.*

She noted the dimple that deepened on his chiseled face as he delivered a punch line with a boyish grin, and a satisfied smile tilted the corners of her mouth. Falling in love was for fools—*blind fools*, she reflected with all the mature assurance of her eighteen years. Let other girls "fall" in love with their eyes closed, but not her. No, she preferred to be in control and walk—not fall, thank you very much—into true love. And if she had her way—which she fully intended to have—it would be with a man who was everything on her carefully crafted list.

Laughter disrupted her thoughts, and she found herself grinning along with the two couples sharing their booth as they roared at the finish of Jack's joke. As usual, Jack's buddies made a ruckus, whooping and pounding their fists on the table in glee, and Katie couldn't help but sigh with contentment. *Good sense of humor.* She mentally checked a box on her list and quickly scanned Robinson's Diner with its black-and-white-checked décor, grateful they had it to themselves at this late hour. Jack and his friends tended to get a bit rowdy, but they certainly knew how to have a good time. She settled back against the red-leather, high-backed booth and shot a glance at the marble counter where a lone soda jerk polished chrome mixers to a gleam.

"For crying out loud, Katydid, you inhaled that soda! And I bet I'll have to buy you another, won't I? I'm not made of money, you know." Jack draped a sturdy arm across her shoulder and pulled her close to his handsome face. The glimmer in his dark eyes matched that of his deep brown hair, stylishly slicked back with Brilliantine. "Or maybe I am," he teased.

Wealthy *and* attractive. *Check, check.* She drew in a deep breath and gave him a patient smile. "Nobody likes a braggart, Jack, but if you're willing to put your money where your mouth is, I believe I'd like a hamburger. I'm starved."

"No, you can't be!" Genevieve Townsend said with a moan. "How can you possibly be hungry? We just had dinner before the picture show."

Katie shrugged her shoulders. "That was over two hours ago, Gen." She wrinkled her nose and teased with a ghost of a smile. "Besides, Valentino makes me hungry."

Jack leaned in to plant a kiss at the nape of her neck. "Mmm . . . not only for food, I hope." His wayward tone set off another round of chortles from his friends.

"Save it for the car, Worthington," Warren Sheffield said with a smirk. "The woman's hungry—feed her!"

Katie swatted at Jack and broiled his friends with a mock glare. "I'll take a hamburger and another Coke, please." She glanced at the large Nehi clock on the wall and frowned—9:40 p.m. "You better hurry, though—they close at ten."

Genevieve groaned. "It's just not fair. How do you stay skinny as a rail?"

"I'll bet she starves herself at home and saves her appetite for Jack." Lilly wriggled her pencil-thin brows.

Katie smoothed a tapered hand down the straight lines of her blue, long-waisted dress and carefully crossed her legs, resting her palm on a powdered knee beneath her short hem. "I'll have you know, Lilly Hansen, that I watch what I eat, just like you and Gen."

Genevieve's round face wrinkled into a frown, forcing her cupid-bow lips to pucker into a pout. "Yeah, we watch what you eat too, and sheer logic says you shouldn't fit in this booth." Her sigh was heavy. "I'll take what she's having," she announced in defeat.

Jack chuckled and massaged Katie's shoulder. "Hear that, doll? You're a bad influence—both on Gen's figure and my wallet. Anybody want anything? I'm buying." His gaze flitted to the soda jerk bent over the chrome and leather stools with a rag in his hand. Jack put two fingers to his teeth and let loose with a deafening whistle. "Hey, kid, shake a leg—we have an order."

The "kid's" body tightened as he rose to his full height, revealing both a broad, muscled back and the fact that he was anything but a kid. He turned in slow, deliberate motion, eyeing the clock before facing them dead-on. A nerve flickered in his angular jaw while his blue eyes glittered like sapphire. He forced a smile as tight as the short sleeves of his white button-down shirt—which, Katie hadn't noticed before, strained with biceps as intimidating as the man's penetrating gaze. "Sure thing, but we close in ten minutes. Sorry, sodas and ice cream only." He strolled to their booth with a casual gait as steady and slow as the drawl that coated his voice like hillbilly honey. "What'll you have?"

Katie felt the tension in Jack's manner as he cradled an arm around her shoulders and lounged back against the booth, eyes locked on the soda jerk with deadly precision. "I know it's late, but the lady here says she's hungry. She wants a hamburger and another Coke."

The man's blue eyes flicked to Katie and held, his cool smile braising her cheeks with a rare blush. He nodded a head of white-blond thatch toward a large sign over the jukebox. "I sure do apologize, miss, but as you can plainly see, we don't serve entrees after nine."

Katie blinked. *Excuse me? And the world would end if he cooked a hamburger after nine?* Her stomach rumbled, and she straightened her shoulders with willful resolve. The thought of a thick, juicy hamburger taunted her—just like the annoyingly calm look on the soda jerk's face. Tilting her chin in a coy manner, she gave him the shuttered smile that always worked wonders on Jack. For good measure, she propped her chin in her hand and resorted to a slow sweep of lashes. Her tone softened to a husky plea. "Aw, come on now, mister, you can make one teeny-tiny exception, can't you? Just for me? We'll make it worth your while, I promise."

His gaze shifted to the clock and back, and then he disarmed her with a smile that made her forget she was hungry for food. "I really wish I could, ma'am, but a rule is a rule. But if I say so myself, my true talent lies in making one of the best chocolate shakes in all of Boston."

She stared, open-mouthed, his polite refusal slacking her jaw. Despite the faint smile on his lips, his eyes seemed to pierce right through her. A second rush of heat invaded her cheeks. *The nerve!* A soda jerk *and* a mule! Katie's eyes narrowed. If there was one thing on God's green earth she despised more than not getting her own way, it was pushy, stubborn men who dictated what she could and could not do.

Out of pure instinct and more than a bit of irritation, she

jutted her chin in the air and matched his gaze with a searing one of her own. "Yes, well, it's nice to know you have *some* talent, but no thank you. Not even if they're the best on the Eastern seaboard. Let's go, Jack."

Jack drew her close while his thumb glazed the side of her arm. "Come on, Katydid, settle down. I know you're hungry, but this guy is obviously new and doesn't realize who we are." He cocked his head and flashed a patronizing smile. "We're some of Mr. Robinson's best customers, kid. So, tell me, what's your name?"

Drawing in a deep breath, the "kid" shifted his stance and exhaled. "The name is Luke." He shot a glance at the clock, then looked back. His gaze softened. "Look, I'm sorry, I really am, but Pop Robinson sets the rules, not me. The grills take forever to cool down, so we do them at nine. Hate to tell ya this, but they're already clean as a whistle and shut down for the night. Now, I have to be somewhere at ten-thirty, but if you give me your drink or ice cream orders, I'll get them as fast as I can."

Katie started to rise, but Jack yanked her back down. "That would be great, Luke, just great. Bring six of your best chocolate shakes and six glasses of water, and we'll be on our way."

"But I don't want his stupid sha—"

"Hush, Katydid, I do, and if Luke here is nice enough to make them for us, everything is jake." He smiled again, all the while fondling a golden tress of Katie's smooth Dutch-Boy bob that curved against her jaw. "Besides, you need something in your stomach. I don't want you cranky on the way home." As if to underscore his romantic hopes, his hand absently caressed the long, pearl necklace that draped the front of her dress. His fingers lingered along her collarbone with a familiarity that deepened the already uncomfortable blush on her cheeks.

"Sure thing," Luke said, his eyes taking in the intimate gesture with cool disregard. His gaze met and held hers for several seconds, unnerving her with his apparent disapproval. He turned away.

Her ire soared. "Extra whipped cream and sprinkles," she said in a clipped tone.

He turned and nodded, full lips pressed tight. "You bet." He started toward the counter.

"And don't skimp on the cherries," she called after him.

He kept walking, but the stiff muscles cording his neck and back told her he'd more than heard. She forced a smile to deflect her embarrassment and took a deep breath. "Well, he's a sunny individual, isn't he? Night help must be hard to come by."

"At least he's nice to look at," Lilly said with a sigh.

"He's a two-bit soda jerk, Lil, with more attitude than brains." Roger Hampton glanced at the soda counter with disdain. "We oughta complain to Robinson."

"Humph . . . he's not that special," Katie said. Her eyes narrowed while she watched him scoop ice cream into the mixer.

"Come on, Katie, you're just miffed because you didn't get your hamburger. The man is a real sheik and you know it." Gen shot a look of longing across the room, then gloated with a grin. "But it is nice to know all men don't wrap around your finger as easily as Jack."

Jack honed in for a kiss. "Mmm . . . that's not all I'd like to be wrapped around," he said in a husky tone.

Katie squirmed and pushed him away. "Behave, Jack, or I'll make your life miserable."

He chuckled. "You already do, doll, but I love every minute."

Ignoring Jack's comment, Katie observed the soda jerk laboring over six chocolate shakes and wrinkled her nose. "Get your specs out, Gen," she said, her temper still inflamed, "he's more of a hick than a sheik from where I'm sitting. I mean, who has hair that color anyway? Blond straw, almost bleached white. Old men and hicks, that's who. And he doesn't even have the good sense or style to comb it back with Brilliantine, for pity's sake. I'll bet under that shirt, he's even got a farmer's tan. Let's face it—the man's a hayseed."

Lilly and Gen sighed as they watched Luke work behind the counter. "I believe I'd like a glimpse of that farmer's tan, wouldn't you, Gen?" Lilly whispered with a giggle.

The frown stayed on Katie's face until the soda jerk finally returned, toting a tray of milkshakes. "Six Robinson's specials." He deposited tall, frosty glasses to each at the table, along with six glasses of water. He set Katie's down last with a considerable thud. One maraschino from the mountain of cherries obscuring her milkshake rolled off, landing on the table with a plop. "Enjoy," he said with a stiff smile. "And let me know if you need more. I wouldn't want you to go hungry."

She swallowed hard, completely unsettled by his direct gaze. "I will. Thank you." He laid the ticket in front of Jack, then returned to the back to finish cleaning up. She stared at her shake and sighed, her appetite suddenly gone flat. With another frown puckering her brow, she pretended to sip, all the while watching Farm Boy wipe down the counter out of the corner of her eye. Okay, all right—she'd give him "good-looking," but she'd bet he was dumb as a post. Her eyes thinned as she took a token sip of her shake. And she would lay money on the table that good looks was the only box that character would fill on anyone's checklist.

Her mood darkened. He was probably just the type of man who was poison to women—strong, handsome, cocky . . . *controlling*. How many times had she seen it? A man like that, sweeping a woman off her feet only to pin her beneath his thumb for the rest of her life. Katie tore her gaze from the soda jerk to stare out the window, her jaw suddenly tight. A man like her father, whose iron rule dictated her every move.

Katie blinked to dispel her sudden onslaught of guilt. Not that she didn't love her father. No, Patrick O'Connor was the one man who Katie truly did respect and love, the one man whose approval she longed to win with every fiber of her being. A knot of hurt shifted in her throat. But it seemed her father's approval was something she'd never been able to achieve, no matter how she'd excelled in school. Total submission seemed to be all Patrick O'Connor wanted and the one thing Katie couldn't give, at least willingly. She sighed, his words haunting her as she stared out the window. *"You're a handful, Katie Rose, and God knows if I don't keep you in line now, some poor man will shoot me later."*

A handful. That's all she had ever been while her older sisters had always been "his girls." A distinction that had neatly separated her, not only from her father's approval, but from sisters almost seven to fourteen years older than she, sisters she'd never related to. Women who had sought—and found—a relationship like her parents—deep, loving, passionate. *And controlling.* Resolve furrowed her brow. Well, she loved her family, she did, but she wanted more than blind submission to a man. She wanted a career and independence. A chance to pry the thumb of male dominance off the heads of a generation of women who were finally coming into their own. Women who had won the right to vote, to have a career and enjoy equal standing in a world where, up until now, they'd only been second-class citizens.

"Hey, Katydid, wake up! You haven't even touched your shake."

She jolted back. The others were staring and half done. She gave him a feeble smile. "Sorry, Jack. Guess I'm not as hungry as I thought."

"That bozo didn't upset you, did he? Because if he did, I can tell Pop he needs new help."

"No, no, please. I'm fine, really." She watched as Farm Boy disappeared into the kitchen and ignored the warm shiver that traveled her spine. "Just a little tired, I guess."

Jack shot a glance at the empty counter and grinned. "Well, we got something that just might wake you up, don't we, boys?" He reached and tugged the menu card out of its glass holder on the wall and set it on top of his untouched glass of water, then gave her a wink. With a quick flick of his wrist, he reversed it on the table and slowly eased the card out from beneath the upside-down glass. The water sealed perfectly, a flood waiting to gush as soon as the "kid" picked it up.

Lilly and Gen gasped in unison. "Wow, how did you do that?" Gen sputtered. "Ol' Luke'll be madder than a wet hen when he cleans this table."

"Jack!" Katie's whisper was harsh. "Stop it . . . that's a juvenile thing to do—"

"Are you kidding? It's brilliant." Warren grinned and stretched over the seat to steal the menu card from the next booth. With a devious smile, he upended his own water glass while Jack kept watch.

"Stop it, Jack, now—I mean it." Katie's gaze shot to the counter, then back to Jack, Roger, and Warren. "I swear that sometimes you three act like children. I don't care how obnoxious that soda jerk was, nobody deserves a prank like this." She butted Jack out of the way in a huff and swung out of the booth. "Now, I'm going to the restroom for a towel to clean this mess up before he sees it, and so help me, if I find another upturned glass, Jack Worthington, you and I won't be on speaking terms."

She spun on her heel and marched toward the restroom, an odd mix of compassion and fury rising in her chest as her eyes flicked to the empty counter. Nobody deserved this humiliation and disrespect, no matter how bullheaded they were. Her lips flattened in a twinge of conscience. Even Farm Boy.

The thought took her back to Sister Cecilia's first-grade class, and the memory dampened her mood as thoroughly as Jack had dampened the surface of their table. How she wished she could forget the crotchety nun whose tight-lipped disapproval represented the first real pain Katie had ever encountered in her life. A time when she'd been torn from the warm acceptance of a home where she was her mother's cherished baby . . . to a cold, hateful classroom where she quickly became the outcast. The trauma of it all resulted in a pitiful little girl suddenly inflicted with red, scaly patches on her arms and legs. "Are you sure it's not leprosy?" the old nun had asked in front of the class, and the memory heated Katie's cheeks all over again.

It may as well have been. Overnight she'd become a leper, the "odd" little girl compelled to wear sweaters and knee socks during the warm weather while other girls wore ankle socks and short-sleeved shirts with their jumpers.

Katie absently rubbed her elbow where the psoriasis had once been, and her throat thickened at the cruelty of children—especially the boys. *Leper. Monster. Freak.* Her anger swelled at the names they'd called her, bullies who picked and prodded and pushed with their superior air. Moisture threatened beneath her closed lids, and she blinked to ward it off. Always the last to be picked on teams, always the butt of practical jokes, and always the target for comments so cruel, they'd left a lasting mark.

"Just so you know, freak, I only invited you for the present," Robert Shaw had announced when she'd arrived at his second-grade birthday party.

The pain had cut deep—separating her not only from the children who mocked her . . . but from a family whose affectionate teasing caused her to push them away.

Katie blinked in the restroom mirror, and her spine stiffened with the action. An unlikely deliverance had come in the form of a new school in the fifth grade, birthing a resolve so deep, it still ached in her chest. To prove to everyone—Sister Cecilia, the bullies, her father—that she was special. Somebody to be respected and loved. Somebody who would make a difference in the world. She'd made a promise to herself then that no amount of ridicule or bullying would stand in her way. With the fuel of her anger, she'd discarded sweaters and knee socks midway through that summer, embracing the warmth of the sun for the first time in years. And when school started in September and the psoriasis had mysteriously disappeared, Katie was left with the glow of new skin, a new start, and something even more astounding. She became popular . . . a feeling forever fused with a passion for those who were not.

"Katie!" Jack met her at the restroom door and plucked the towel from her hand. He tossed it on a nearby booth and tugged her toward the door where the others were waiting. "We don't have time for cleanup, doll—we gotta leave."

She skidded to a stop, her Mary Jane heels digging in. "Wait a minute, Jack—did you pay for the check?"

"Nope, let *Soda Jerk* pay for it," Jack said with a sneer that made it sound like a curse. "That'll teach him to be rude to my girl. Come on, guys, hurry." He opened the door and pulled her through, tripping over a scruffy-looking terrier sprawled across the side of the stoop.

The dog yelped, and Katie twisted free with a cry. "You big bully—you hurt the poor thing." She dropped to her knees and reached for his paw. "Hey, little guy, you okay?"

"Sorry, Katie," Jack said with a nervous glance at the counter, "didn't mean to step on the little mutt, but we gotta go—*now*!" Without waiting for her reply, he hoisted her up in his arms and sprinted to his Franklin Sports Coupe parked down the street.

"Jack Worthington, you stop this very instant!" Her voice rose to a shriek and her limbs flapped as she kicked and clawed to break his hold. Her irritation surged at the shock of Jack manhandling her. *Jack* . . . of all people! The man who catered to her every whim. In a wild lunge, she tried to gouge him, but he only clamped tighter, chuckling while he huffed to the car.

"Calm down, Katydid, we gotta get out of here."

Oh, she'd calm down all right—with a well-placed clip to his jaw! She gritted her teeth. As . . . soon . . . as . . . she . . . could . . . break . . . free. Her pulse pounded in her ears over the laughter of the group as they bolted for the Franklin and jumped in. Katie's temper boiled. Men were nothing but bullies—the whole sorry lot of them. Bloodthirsty for control over what they saw as the "weaker sex." Ignoring her screams, Jack opened the passenger door and tossed her in.

I'll show 'em weak. She landed with a bounce and scrambled back up. Jack blocked her with a broad grin. "Come on, doll, it's no big deal. We're just having a little fun. Look, I even got you a souvenir." He pulled her empty Coca-Cola glass out of his pocket.

Her jaw dropped. She snatched the glass and shook it in his face. "Jack Worthington, you are nothing more than a brazen thief, and I will not be a party to this! Now, I am marching back there right now and—"

"Jack, hurry!" Roger's voice held a warning.

Katie ignored them both and darted from the car, but Jack was too fast. He picked her up with a chuckle and silenced her with a sound kiss, tightening his grip when she started to kick. "Aw, come on, Katydid, don't be such a bearcat. Soda Jerk had it coming, and you know it. Now get in the car like a good girl—we gotta scram."

"How about you scram *after* you pay the bill?" An icy tone confirmed that Soda Jerk was in the vicinity. His voice, deadly calm from several yards away, packed as much heat as a whispered threat from the lips of Al Capone.

Katie froze in Jack's arms, which went as stiff as his pale face. With a slow turn, they faced an apron-clad Colossus of Rhodes, legs straddled and face chiseled in stone.

"*Put her down*," he whispered, his words as hard and tight as the muscle twitching in his face.

Jack lowered her to the ground with a scowl and eased Katie behind. "Says who?"

The soda jerk moved in close, towering over Jack by more than half a head. A rock-hard jaw, barely inches from Jack's, sported a full day's growth of blond bristle. His wide lips curved into a smile, but the blue eyes were pure slits of ice. "Says me, you little piker."

Jack leaned forward and jabbed a finger into the soda jerk's chest. "Piker? Who you calling a coward, Soda Jerk? I'm not paying for anything, especially shoddy service."

The wide smile broadened to a cocky grin. "My service may be shoddy, rich boy, but I guarantee my thrashing won't be. Trust me, your little girlfriend won't like it if I mess with your face, so I suggest you pay the bill . . ." He fisted Jack's pin-stripe shirt and jerked him up. *"Now."*

Genevieve screamed, and Warren and Roger jumped from the car. They circled Luke with fists raised. Suddenly it was Jack's turn to grin. "So, how's your confidence now, eh, big shot? Think you can handle three to one?"

Katie darted around to shove Jack hard in the chest. "Stop it now, or so help me—"

He pushed her aside. "Stay out of this, doll."

Warren eased in with a quick swipe, and the soda jerk dodged with the grace of an athlete. His wide grin gleamed white in the lamplight as he egged them on with a wave of his fingers. "Come on, boys, I've lived on the streets all my life, so have at it."

Roger lunged, and the soda jerk felled him like a tree with a right hook to his jaw. Out of nowhere, Warren rushed from behind, leg poised in a kick. *Big mistake.* Katie winced as the soda jerk latched onto his shoe and yanked him to the pavement with a sickening thud. She screeched in horror, then charged forward, only to be looped at the waist by Jack who tossed her back in the car, flailing and screaming. He turned with a loud roar and rammed his body straight for the soda jerk, head tucked like a raging bull. In a deft move of his foot, the soda jerk tripped him and sent him skidding into the street.

"Jack!" Katie jolted from the car and ran to his side. "Are you okay?" She helped him as he lumbered to his feet, the right trouser leg of his gray Oxford bags torn and streaked with dirt.

"Yeah, yeah, I'm okay. Just let me at that slimeball—"

"No!" She planted two petite hands on his chest and shoved him back with more force than her small size warranted. "You're done, Jack! Do you hear me? Or we're through."

He staggered back, a bloody hand to his head. "Come on, Katydid, don't talk like that—"

"I mean it, Jack, I swear." She whirled around, her eyes singeing all of them within an inch of their lives. "Warren, Roger—get in the car. *Now!*"

"Come on, Jack, are you gonna listen to her? We can take this guy."

She spun around, fury pumping in her veins. "So, what's it gonna be, Jack—them or me?"

He glanced from Katie to his friends and then back again, a nerve twittering in his cheek. His tone was tight as he exhaled his frustration. "Get in the car, we're leaving."

Muttered curses rumbled as the boys stumbled toward the coupe.

With a lightning thrust of her hand, Katie lifted Jack's wallet from the pocket of his trousers as neatly as a veteran pickpocket.

"Katydid, what are you doing—"

She ignored him and marched up to the soda jerk with fire in her eyes. At five foot two, she barely measured to the middle of his chest, but she didn't give a fig if he was seven foot five. No hayseed soda jerk was going to intimidate her! She glared up, annoyance surging at having to crane her neck. "How much do we owe, you roughhouse bully?"

He met her fierce look with cool confidence, sizing her up with that same probing gaze that had riled her before. "That'll be $2.48 total, *miss*. That's 15 cents for three Coca-Colas, $1.80 for six chocolate shakes—" A shadow of a smile edged the corners of his mouth. "Three cents for *extra* cherries—and 50 cents for the glass your boyfriend stole."

She peeled off two crisp dollar bills from Jack's stash and threw them at his feet, then spun around and snatched the glass from the seat of the car. With barely concealed fury, she shoved it hard against his rock-solid chest. "Here, keep the change. Not that you're worth it."

A massive palm locked onto her wrist before she could snatch it away. "Nice girls don't run with riffraff," he breathed.

The intensity of his gaze forced a lump to her throat. For a split second she barely drew air, their eyes fused while the heat of his hand throbbed against her arm. Then all at once, her pride resurged with a vengeance. "Nor care about the opinions of lowly soda jerks," she rasped, incensed at the shame that scalded her cheeks.

She jerked her hand free and slid into the car, refusing to give in to the tears that pricked at her eyes. She threw the wallet on the seat while Jack got in and slammed his door. He turned the ignition and shifted into gear. Humiliation and silence hung thick in the air as they jostled down the shadows of the cobblestone street.

"I'm sorry, Katydid," Jack whispered, and she nodded dumbly, blinking hard as she stared out the window. Her body shivered and she clutched at her sides, ashamed she'd lost her temper and belittled another human being. And it wasn't until the coupe rounded the corner and a solitary figure faded from view . . . that she allowed even a single tear to fall.

Privilege is wasted on the rich. Luke shook his head and watched as the taillights of the Franklin careened around the corner of the two-story Sears, Roebuck and Company, leaving a squeal of tires in its wake. He stooped to pick up the two dollar bills that the feisty rich girl had flung at him, and his lips quirked into a wry smile. She was a pretty little thing, even if she was spoiled rotten. A child of privilege and obviously used to getting her own way. He peered down the dim street lit only by the flicker of neon and squinted in the direction the coupe had disappeared. Humor tugged at the edges of his mouth. He'd give her one thing, though—she had more spunk and mettle in that tiny, little wrist he'd grasped than the whole carload of her rich friends put together. Luke's lips flattened into a hard line. Especially the pretty-boy lackey whom she obviously had on a short leash.

Nope, there weren't many fireballs like little ol' "Katydid," he thought with a grudging smile. At least not that he'd met anyway, which in the end was a good thing. He sure didn't have time to get involved with a woman right now, especially the in-your-face kind who seemed to have a knack for taking him down. Grazing his thumb against the edge of her glass, he ambled back to the diner, only to stop short at the door. He folded his arms and cocked a brow at the mangy mutt snoozin' between the potted urn and the red-brick stoop, legs limp in the air. "Okay, you little scamp, don't you have someplace else to sleep?"

The terrier's eyes slitted open and he yawned with a stretch of his hind legs. Luke crouched to his knees. "Sorry to disturb you, Sleeping Beauty, but this is a diner, not a hotel." He rubbed the dog's belly and frowned at the pronounced imprint of ribs beneath the smooth white skin. He sighed and rose to his feet. "Okay, I'm a sucker for the underdog—or the underfed dog—so I'll feed you. But just this once, and then you hightail it home, you got that?"

The terrier popped up and stretched his front paws with another yawn, wagging his perky, white tail. Luke laughed and opened the door, then closed it again with a noisy clang of bells. Two liquid-brown eyes followed him through the glass, the pup's head cocked in anticipation as black ears flopped over a curious black and white snout.

Luke shot a quick look at the clock and groaned. Ten-fifteen—Betty would be waiting. Sweet saints, he hated being late. He stashed the two dollars in the register, then ducked in the back to dig a half-eaten burger out of the trash, grateful he'd finished cleanup before the rich kids had left. He'd even washed the mixer after their shakes.

He sprinted to the front and grinned at the terrier, patiently parked in front of the glass. "Here ya go, you little beggar. Eat and go home, ya hear?" The terrier snatched the food from his hand and bolted away. Luke sighed and locked the door, sparing one last glance across the store.

A low groan rumbled in his throat. The booth the rich kids had occupied still needed to be cleaned. His shoulders drooped. Now he'd be late for sure. With a heavy sigh, he moved toward the table and stopped, shock flaring his eyes. His jaw tightened at the sight of six glasses of water, all upside down. Biting back a curse, he kicked at the booth and rattled the dishes. Man alive, what he wouldn't give to get his hands on those spoiled little brats again—he'd teach 'em a thing or two. He exhaled his frustration and strode into the kitchen to grab a couple of towels.

His anger suddenly tempered at the thought of one spoiled brat in particular. Hair like spun gold, eyes like blue fire, and an attitude way taller than she. Oh yeah, he'd like to get his hands on that one for sure. A grin twitched at the corners of his mouth. And he'd teach her, all right—a definite thing or two.

Katie bit her lip and eased the front door closed as deathly still as possible. She held her breath when the click of the lock echoed in the dark hall of her house, then released it again in one long, silent sigh of relief. Thank goodness the lights were out and her parents were in bed. Jack's watch had said almost midnight—long past her ten-thirty curfew—and tonight she wasn't in the mood for one of her father's "Katie Rose" lectures.

She leaned back against the heavy oak door and closed her eyes, her mood considerably dampened by the events of the night. Jack had insisted on taking everyone home first so she and he could be alone to talk. Her lips skewed into an off-center smile. Or at least, that's what *he* called it. Usually he pleaded and she forgave. He nuzzled and she reveled in the attention. Her jaw stiffened with annoyance. Except tonight. No, tonight, even Jack's kisses, which she usually enjoyed, had failed to stir her. And all because of some hayseed soda jerk.

"Nice girls don't run with riffraff."

Guilt assailed her, and her eyes popped open as she blew out a shaky breath. What in the world was the matter with her? Jack wasn't riffraff, he was the catch of the year and desperately in love with her. Looks, wealth, sense of humor, social standing, and intelligence—everything on her list and then some. A prospective lawyer, just like her, both slated for law school in the fall—Jack after graduating from college and she, gloriously enough, right out of high school!

She drew in a deep breath, hope winging at the thought of attending Boston's prestigious Portia Law School. Established exclusively for women in 1908, Portia's generous admission guidelines required only a high school degree, and the prospect of going to law school at the same time as Jack thrilled Katie to the bone. This was her chance—an era when women were flying high into their futures—literally—like Amelia Earhardt with her world record for female pilots. A shiver of anticipation raced through Katie. Well, she intended to set a record of her own—to be the first truly independent woman in her family. To pursue women's rights—first as a lawyer, then as a congresswoman someday. And Portia Law School was just the start. It was there where her plan would unfold to help women who couldn't help themselves, and there where she'd sow the seeds for her own financial freedom. And in Jack, she had the perfect complement—a man who not only shared her vision, but who enjoyed the distinct advantage of connections. Her lips slanted into a smile. Connections that included an attorney father who presided over one of the most prestigious law firms in the city, not to mention winning a senate seat last year.

Pride swelled in her chest as she made her way to the stairs. No, Jack was definitely not "riffraff." And furthermore—contrary to the warning of one truly obnoxious soda jerk—Jack Worthington was the man she intended to marry.

"*So* . . . what's the excuse this time, Katie Rose? A broken watch, a broken car . . . or just pure obstinance in flaunting your father's will?"

Katie jolted at the staircase, hand grafted to the newel post at the base of the oak banister. She groaned inwardly and turned, squinting into the dim parlor where the faint glow of a pipe could be seen. She sucked in a deep breath and wondered how she'd missed the sweet smell of tobacco in the air. Black Cavendish, with hints of maple and vanilla—Patrick O'Connor's trademark scent. She exhaled her nervousness. "Father, I'm sorry—we lost track of time."

"So, it's the broken-watch scenario then, is it, darlin'?" The bowl of the pipe smoldered, expelling a curl of smoke into the air.

"Uh, well, no, not exactly. I . . . forgot to wear my watch."

"I see. And I suppose Jack forgot his as well?"

Katie stood stiff in the door, stomach churning. "No . . . but you see, we stopped for a soda at Robinson's, after the picture show, you know . . ."

"Mmm . . . and they still close at ten, do they?"

She picked at her nails. "Um, yes, of course, but Jack took all the others home first . . ."

"Yes, I see your dilemma, then. A ten-thirty curfew—not near enough time for sodas and rides . . . or a friendly chat in the car."

Heat flooded her cheeks. "Father, really! We were only talking."

Her father tapped his pipe and then laid it aside. He shifted in the moonlight that spilled through the window. His handsome face was obscured by shadows, but she sensed his annoyance in the steely blade of his tone. "I may be fifty-one years old, Katie Rose, but I'm not ancient. I know exactly how much 'chatting' goes on in the front seat of a car." He released a weighty breath and patted the wide arm of his chair. "Come, sit a spell, darlin', will ya?"

Katie groaned and plodded in, quite certain this was one late-night "chat" she wanted to avoid. She took great pains to perch on the very edge of the chair, but her father's solid arm had a mind of its own and scooped her close to his side. She finally relented and leaned against his broad chest. The scent of musk soap and tobacco filled her senses with the warmth and safety of home. She sighed in reluctant surrender. "I'm sorry, Father. I'll try harder next time."

The rise and fall of his chest indicated a sigh followed by that low chuckle that always brought a smile to her lips. In a rush of love, she turned and clutched him tightly, the distress of the evening merging with her need to be held. As always, his arms did not disappoint. He gave her a fierce hug, and she closed her eyes to savor his husky laughter, warm against her ear.

"I forgive you, Katie Rose, and I love you more than I can say."

Relief rushed through her like an ocean swell. *Forgiven!* No stern lectures? No confinement to the house? No ridiculous curfews? She closed her eyes. *Thank goodness!*

"Which is why I'm compelled to do what I have to do."

Her eyelids flipped open.

"Apparently curfews and confinement don't carry the impact I hoped they would, young lady, so I've decided to lend them some assistance."

She jerked out of his embrace. "Assistance?" she said with a hoarse gasp. "You mean in *addition to* curfews and confinement?"

Patrick O'Connor struggled to maintain a serious demeanor. Which wasn't easy. The horrified look on his daughter's face begged to release the squirm of his lips to a full-fledged grin, but he tightened his jaw to fight the impulse. For what was surely the hundredth time in his life, Patrick wondered why the Almighty had chosen their most strong-willed child to be born last of all their six children, at a time when his and Marcy's energy was sorely depleted by age and exhaustion. The irony of it baffled him, forcing a tired breath through his lips. He was certain that Katie was responsible for more of the gray hair that glinted at his temples than his two sons and other three daughters put together. He thought of Charity, his second daughter whose stubborn streak rivaled his own. Yes, she had been difficult, no question. But it was Katie who'd been the true handful right out of the gate. He had a suspicion that Katie had been destined to be a difficult child—Marcy's horrendous morning sickness certainly confirmed that, as had Katie's arrival into the world a month and a half early. That event had prompted a constant vigil of prayer from sibling and parent alike that their listless infant would garner the will to live.

The will to live, he thought with a twist of his lips. *Mmm . . . and then some*. He released a weary sigh. Perhaps their prayers had been too diligent in those early months, for if Katie Rose had been blessed with anything, it was an iron will. A frown creased his brow. A will that had spent the last eighteen years butting heads with his own.

He inhaled a deep breath and slowly released it, lifting his chin to meet hers. "Yes, Katie Rose, *in addition to*. You and I both know you've never been good at following orders, and unless I want God to take me to task for not reining you in, I have a responsibility to teach you a valuable lesson."

With a lift of his fingers, he gently cupped her chin. "Your mother and I love you, darlin', but neither the world nor this family revolves around you, no matter how much you would like them to. There is a sequence of order and authority to be obeyed, beginning with God, the law, and then your parents. Consequently, your curfew will now be ten until you prove you are responsible enough to follow orders. In addition, your confinement begins tonight for the next two and a half months, and maybe the entire summer if you choose to defy me further. No dates with Jack, no gallivanting with friends, no shopping with your sisters. Nothing but church, family, and volunteer work."

"What?" The gasp from her colorless lips was little more than a hoarse shriek. Her face bleached as white as the expanse of her eyes. "You can't be serious. Jack will die!"

Patrick chuckled. "No, darlin', he won't. I guarantee he will survive, and hopefully be a little more inclined to get you home on time."

Her groan conveyed her life was over as she dropped her face in her hands. "But, I'll go crazy! What'll I do?"

He smiled and rubbed her shoulder. "That's where the volunteer work comes in."

Her head shot up, and her blue eyes circled in shock. "Volunteer work? You're joking."

He studied the look of scandalized panic on his daughter's face and knew he was doing the right thing. He had prayed long and hard for something that would save her from herself, a chance to curb that headstrong will of hers with a gentle dose of humility. He stared at the precious daughter before him, and a profound sense of satisfaction pervaded his soul, confirming to his spirit once and for all that *this* was it. "No, darlin', I'm not."

"But where? When?"

He avoided her eyes. "The Boston Children's Aid Society."

"An orphanage?"

"Yes, an orphanage, darlin', and more. The BCAS is an organization that reaches out to those not as fortunate as you. Tell me, Katie, when you're out slumming with friends, have you even noticed the children on the street? Those dressed in rags or sleeping in doorways? Well, they're there, and they need help." He sat up straighter in the chair and squared his jaw. "And *you're* going to give it to them. Both at the BCAS *and* its associate organizations, the Boston Society for the Care of Girls and the Massachusetts Infant Asylum."

"God, have mercy." Katie pressed a shaky hand to her chest, appearing about to faint.

"You'll actually be working in the main office most of the time," Patrick quickly reassured. "You know, paperwork, filing, typing, whatever they need." He hesitated. "You'll only work with the children when they need backup."

She groaned again, face buried in her hands. "How often and how long?" she whispered.

He shifted in the chair and stalled, suddenly wondering if he had gone too far. "Five days a week." His tone was barely audible.

She blasted from the chair as if her hair were on fire, and he wasn't all that sure that her eyes weren't—they cauterized him on the spot despite the dim lighting. "No!" she screamed, hands fisted at her sides. "I won't do it. You can't make me!"

Patrick rose to his feet, feeling the need to intimidate with his full six-foot-two height. He straightened his tense shoulders for the task at hand and narrowed his eyes. "I can, Katie Rose, and I will. That is, if you ever want to see Jack again."

A gasp sputtered from her lips. "You wouldn't!"

Patrick's jaw hardened. "Don't tempt me, darlin'. You may have designs on that boy, but they don't exactly match mine. He's hardly a good influence." He scanned the length of her, his lips tightening at the sight of rolled hose just below her short skirt and powdered knees. "Picture shows and sodas are one thing, Katie Rose, but as the father of a young woman not inclined to follow my lead, I worry about other things with a boy like Jack. Things like speakeasies and petting parties, for instance. So help me, if I ever catch wind of anything like that, you won't be seeing that boy—or any other—ever again."

"Mother will never agree to this—" Her voice was a threat.

"She already has, young lady. As the baby of the family, I know you think you have your mother wrapped around your little finger, but I assure you that in this case, we are in sound agreement. And quite frankly, both of us think you could do with some time apart from Jack."

Even in the moonlight, he spied color staining her cheeks. She jutted her chin, eyes glittering with defiance. "Don't force me to see him behind your back, Father."

He took a step forward, meeting her jaw to jaw. "And don't force me to withdraw all funds for law school, darlin'. That would be a real shame."

As if paralyzed on the spot, she stared, her shock evident in the glaze of her eyes and the bloodless pallor of her lips. Her voice trembled when she spoke. "Y-you w-wouldn't . . ."

The sight of her pain twisted his heart, and he reached to tug her close, ignoring the angry stiffness of her body. "I wouldn't want to, Katie, but I would have no choice." Patrick pulled back to look into her eyes. "I want to give you law school, darlin', I do—desperately. Certainly a woman with your keen mind and sense of purpose was meant for such a path, if ever a woman was. But I can't honor you with God's blessings if you choose to defy us, nor can I stand by and allow your disobedience to impede all future blessings he hopes to give. And it will, Katie Rose, make no mistake."

She started to cry and he handed her his handkerchief before tucking her against his chest. "Now, now, darlin', it's only a summer, not a lifetime, after all. My good friend Harris Stowe is on the board of directors, and he tells me it's the ideal opportunity for any young person aspiring to be a lawyer. So, try to think of it as preparation for law school, if you will, a kind of internship, eh? You'll be working with lawyers while you're there, what with adoptions and whatnot, so you may find you like it."

She sniffed and peered up, her tone nasal and waterlogged.

"If I don't die of embarrassment first." She blew her nose soundly, then swiped at her eyes. "I suppose I'll have to do it since you've left me no choice, but I have no idea what I'm getting myself into."

Patrick pulled her close and stroked her hair with the palm of his hand, his thoughts flitting to the Boston Children's Aid Society. A smile surfaced on his lips that he was glad she couldn't see. *No, you have no idea at all, my little mule of a daughter,* he thought to himself with a quiet sigh. *And heaven help them, neither do they.*

2

"Cluny McGee? Coming for dinner? Isn't he in prison?" Katie pulled a tray of dinner rolls from the oven and set it on the soapstone counter. The scent of fresh-baked bread filled her mother's spacious kitchen, watering her mouth and rumbling her stomach. Her lips kinked at the not-so-gentle reminder that she'd been too distracted to eat. At least, not since last night when Father had unveiled his diabolical plan to ruin her life. She flipped the oven door closed and turned, giving her family a wry smile. "Or is he out on parole?"

A chuckle parted from the lips of her older sister, Charity, whose twinkle in her blue eyes matched the glint of gold in her finger-waved bob. She awarded Katie with a cheeky grin that made her look more like ten years old than twenty-nine. "Ooooo . . . good one, Katie Rose. You never did like that little rascal, did you?"

Katie's lips squirmed to the right. "Nope. And 'little' is certainly the operative word. Little brat . . . big pest. Dear Lord, I hope he's changed."

"Hey, you two, go easy on the poor guy." Twenty-four-year-old Lizzie turned at the stove to focus on her sisters, her attention momentarily diverted. Pretty hairpins kept her short, chestnut curls off of her face as she mashed the potatoes. A fine sheen of steam misted her cheeks with a rosy glow. She bit her lip, as if warding off a grin, and then smoothed one hand over her pregnant stomach. "I'll have you know that not only is that 'little brat' now a lawyer, but he's anything but 'little' anymore."

Katie parked a hand on her hip, and the action puckered the low waist of her pale green shift. "A lawyer, huh? Well, good for him. Now he's legal *and* obnoxious."

"Goodness, what do you have against the poor kid anyway?" her oldest sister Faith asked. "Like Lizzie said, he's all grown up now, and from what I hear, you won't even recognize him." Bending to retrieve a bottle of milk from the icebox, she proceeded to pour six glasses, then pushed a loose strand of her short, auburn bob away from her green eyes. The youthful glow in her cheeks belied her true age of thirty-one. "Mother, are the kids eating out on the porch?"

Marcy O'Connor glanced over her shoulder while draining bacon grease from a skillet into a stone crock. Her new, stylish blond bob, coaxed by her daughters, was streaked with shimmers of silver that only heightened the blue of her eyes. "Yes, outside picnic-style, please. Might as well take advantage of the warm weather and spare my new cherrywood floor."

"Not to mention your back," Charity said with a quick squeeze to her mother's shoulders.

"Oh, amen to that," Lizzie muttered, arching with a groan and a stretch. Her hands pressed tightly to the small of her back. "Tell me, please. Does this backache *ever* go away?"

Charity grinned and began massaging her sister's neck. "Sure it does, honey. Mine left when the twins turned six."

"Oh, great," Lizzie moaned.

"Ignore her," Faith said with a crooked smile in Charity's direction. "My aches and pains left when each of my three girls were born." She reached for the dishrag to wipe up a dribble of spilled milk. "You should already know that after having Teddy. Once those babies are born, all the pain goes away."

Charity hefted a stack of dishes on the table and scrunched her honeyed brows. "Yeah, but what about that awful pain in your lower back? Remember, the one that gave you so many problems?"

Faith blinked. "What pain in my lower back?"

Charity dropped a piece of fried chicken onto each of six plates and licked her fingers with a lazy smile. "Oh, never mind. I forgot. That pain was much further south as I recall . . . and I think he's in the next room playing chess with my husband."

Faith grinned and threw the dishrag at her sister before hefting the pot of mashed potatoes from Lizzie's grasp. She returned to the kitchen table to plop steaming mounds on each of the plates. "Hey, Collin's not *that* bad. And I suppose Mitch isn't a pain in the posterior at times?"

Charity bobbled the dishrag in her hand while a wicked grin surfaced on her lips. "He's stubborn, he's Irish, and he's a man. What do you think?" She tossed it in the sink and joined Faith at the table to ladle gravy, pouring it on thick.

Faith's chuckle merged with her mother's. "So, Katie, you never did say what you have against poor Cluny. To be honest, I always felt sorry for the little guy. Goodness, abandoned by his mother, raised by a grandmother who wasn't much better, and then shipped off to New York to live with an aunt he barely knew. Other than his brief stay with Brady before Lizzie and Brady got married, he's had a life of sheer misery."

A grin curled on Katie's lips as she placed the rolls into a napkin-laden basket. "Which explains why he's so good at it—he made my life miserable." She sighed. "Okay, maybe he wasn't all *that* bad, I suppose, but the little beggar just had a way of getting under my skin."

"So does Collin, but you still love him," Faith said with a smile, never missing a beat as she swatted Charity's fingers from picking at the chicken.

Katie grinned at Charity's threatening gestures behind Faith's back. She toned it down to a smile and forced herself to focus. "But Collin is family—I *have* to love him. Cluny McGee was just so . . . *so* . . . annoyingly cocky." She pictured the puny street urchin that Brady had brought to dinner the Easter she was ten, and the memory of her instant dislike roiled in her stomach like indigestion. Despite his age of fourteen, he looked younger than her and yet he flaunted the same controlling air she'd seen in every bully she'd ever known. From the moment she'd met him, he teased her and baited her and pushed his way into her family and her life, winning the affection of everyone but her. A shiver traveled her spine. No, to her he was little more than a gnat, buzzing around every summer like those annoying fruit flies hovering over the bananas in her mother's kitchen. Tiny, taunting, and impossible to swat. Katie sighed, suddenly ashamed at how she had resented him so. "I don't know, the little twerp barely came to my shoulders, and yet he strutted around like he was ten feet tall, always trying to boss me around. I guess he just got on my nerves."

"Well, you will be civil to him tonight, won't you?" Lizzie asked in a pleading tone. "It is Brady's birthday, and you know how much that husband of mine has always loved Cluny."

Charity commenced spooning green beans on each of the children's plates. "Civil? Our Katie?" She chuckled. "She barely treats Jack civilly, and she actually likes him."

Lizzie tucked an arm around Katie's shoulders. "Katie, please. Give me your word. Tell me you will be nice to Cluny—just for tonight."

"Just for tonight?" Katie asked. She grinned. "Well, since the likelihood of ever seeing the little brat again is completely remote, yes, I promise you, Lizzie. I will be on my best behavior with Mr. Pain-in-the-Knickers McGee. Consider it my birthday gift to Brady."

"Mmm . . . Katie's 'best behavior.' Sounds a tad risky to me," Faith said, her tongue rolling inside her cheek.

Katie gaped. "Faith McGuire—I'm shocked! I expect that from Charity, but *you*?"

"What can I say—she's a bad influence," Faith said, licking potatoes from her finger.

The kitchen door flew open as Faith's husband strolled in, a tall, dark-haired man who made a beeline for the icebox. He stashed two tubs of ice cream next to the block of ice, then turned to press a kiss on the back of Faith's neck as he snatched a piece of chicken from the plate, all in one fluid motion. "Marcy, Cluny's here, so Brady said you can serve dinner anytime."

Faith slapped his hand and spun around. "Collin McGuire, you're going to lose an arm that way, mister."

His wife's annoyance prompted his trademark smile, along with a little-boy twinkle in his gray eyes. "But not the lips, eh, Little Bit? Wouldn't want to risk those, would we?" With a tug to her waist, he gave her a lingering kiss before heading for the door, drumstick in hand.

"Collin, wait!" Marcy crumbled the last of the bacon on top of the baked beans and grabbed two pot holders. She hurried to hand the casserole dish off to him at the door. "Here, you can pay for your thievery by taking this to the table. And would you mind herding everyone into the dining room, please? We'll be right in."

"Yesh, ma'am," Collin mumbled, drumstick lodged between his teeth.

"Charity, will you and Faith get the children settled outside while Lizzie and I carry food to the table? Katie Rose, you can pour the drinks—we have iced tea or lemonade." Marcy shoved two pewter pitchers into Katie's hands, then wisped a strand of silver-blond hair from her face. Her blue eyes sparkled with humor. "And for pity's sake, don't spill any on Cluny, you hear?"

Katie took the pitchers and gave her mother a thin smile. "Yes, ma'am, but don't blame me if he spills it on himself. I didn't call him Clumsy Cluny for nothing, you know."

"Katie . . ." Lizzie's voice brimmed with warning.

"*Just—kidding*," Katie replied in a singsong tone. She shot her sister a grin and pushed through the door with her backside, both pitchers anchored tightly in hand. Male voices rumbled in the dining room, and Katie zeroed in on Brady with a bright smile. "Happy Birthday, Bra—"

The smile died an ugly death as the pitchers slipped from her hands and crashed to the floor. Sticky puddles pooled at her feet, but all she could do was gape, drawing in little or no air despite the extended drop of her jaw.

Pandemonium erupted—Collin yelling for a towel and her mother rushing in, and everyone blotting and mopping and babbling words Katie couldn't comprehend. Instead, she stood like a statue, mounted to the sticky floor as surely as if lemonade and tea were glue. The heat of humiliation curdled her stomach, rose to her throat, and bled into her cheeks, confirming once again that Cluny McGee—aka "Soda Jerk"—possessed a true talent for misery.

His shock mirrored her own for the briefest of seconds before those wide lips eased into an annoying grin. Striking pale blue eyes crinkled in humor while he assessed her head to toe, finally settling on her face in painful perusal.

"Well, Katie Rose," he drawled in a teasing tone that hinted at a twang, "I see you still know how to make a splash."

Brady latched an arm around Cluny's shoulders. The man matched her brother-in-law's six-foot-three height, head to head. "You remember this little runt, don't ya, Katie? Cluny McGee? He's a big-shot lawyer now, but I remember how he used to pester the daylights out of you."

Cluny grinned, revealing a flash of white teeth against a deep tan. "I think it was the other way around, but I'm willing to let bygones be bygones if you are . . . *Katydid.*" He extended a muscled arm in a handshake truce. "No sense in crying over spilled milk . . . or milkshake, whatever the case may be. And by the way, the name has changed—I go by Luke now."

God help her, she wanted to whop him right upside that towhead of his! She gritted her teeth, completely incensed that he looked like a male model for *Vanity Fair*. The white thatch was now stylishly combed back with just the right touch of Brilliantine, and a double-breasted blue blazer slung casually over his arm, the perfect complement for tan linen slacks. His crisp, striped cotton shirt did little to hide his obviously muscular form, and Katie was appalled when more heat whooshed to her cheeks. She stared at the hand that had captured her wrist outside the diner last night and swallowed hard, contemplating slapping it away. But for Brady's sake, she reined in her temper and cautiously placed her hand in his. Upon contact, the heat of his palm unnerved her, and she jerked hers away, hoping the gummy remains of lemonade would cling to his skin.

"A lawyer?" she said weakly. "But . . . but . . . Robinson's . . ." The words seemed to adhere to her tongue, as sticky as the lemonade now coating her skin.

He winked. "I fill in sometimes . . . for a good friend of mine."

"Katie, we'll wait while you run upstairs and change," Marcy interrupted. "Goodness, I hope that dress isn't ruined. Cluny . . . sorry, *Luke*, it's so good to see you again . . ."

Her mother's words faded as Katie stood, fixed in a hard stare, still in a daze.

A gentle arm circled her waist. "I told you he changed," Lizzie whispered in her ear, "so be good, okay? And speaking of changing, you better hurry upstairs—Mother won't be able to keep Collin and Brady at bay forever, you know."

Katie blinked, then glanced down at the stains on the front of her dress. She nodded, still in shock that the soda jerk was conversing with her mother. The realization of what that could mean chilled her blood to the bone. As a boy, Cluny McGee had prided himself on besting her, taunting her at will, and clamoring for control. And today, the ghost of childhood past had returned to roost—harboring a secret that could chain Katie to the house forever.

Which meant one thing. Cold prickles of fear iced her spine as she mounted the stairs. Cluny McGee had won—*again*. Because no matter how much she wanted to smack that smirk off his handsome face, she couldn't. She was forced to be nice, hoping and praying it would seal his lips. Katie groaned and entered her room, thinking an ether-soaked gag would be more to her liking. She stared at her splattered dress in the mirror and scowled. Cluny McGee was indeed the "king" of misery. She grunted and hiked the dress over her head, sailing it across the room. *Humph! Long live the king—a royal pain in the neck. And may he have lockjaw forever.*

Despite almost seven years since he'd been here last, Luke had the strange sensation he'd never left. He bowed his head at the O'Connors' table, listening to the humble tone of Patrick saying grace, and a sense of gratitude seeped into his bones along with more than a bit of longing. This had been the type of family he had craved as a boy, and just being with them again made his heart race at the prospect of a family of his own. And one, hopefully, far different than what he'd known.

His thoughts drifted to the mother who'd abandoned him when he was thirteen, preferring the company of a drunken boyfriend to that of her illegitimate son. To her, he was an unfortunate mistake, while to his Gram, he was little more than a burden and the evidence of sin in her wayward daughter's life. His jaw stiffened. And to the families of the Southie neighborhood whose streets he roamed? Nothing but a bastard, unworthy of love.

He released a quiet sigh, joining the others in the sign of the cross as Patrick finished his prayer. It hadn't been until John Brady had taken him under his wing at the age of fourteen that he'd gotten his first real taste of being cared for, loved . . . his first true glimpse of family. And what he had seen, first with Brady and then the O'Connors, convinced him that family was worth everything he had to give . . . his love, his devotion . . . his life. A sense of longing rose within him so strong, it produced a sharp ache in his throat. He quickly reached for his folded napkin and shook it free, doing the same with the craving in his soul. He placed the napkin on his lap, laying it to rest along with his thoughts. A family of his own. Someday maybe, he reflected with a touch of melancholy, but certainly not for a long, long while.

"So, Luke . . . how long have you been back in Boston?" Patrick reached for the mashed potatoes and heaped a mound on his plate, then passed the bowl to his left. A gentle breeze stirred a renegade strand of Patrick's dark hair now glinted with silver at the temples. Damask window sheers fluttered behind him, infusing the room with the heady scent of lilacs and fresh-hewn mulch. Mottled sunlight flickered across a crisp, white tablecloth resplendent with a crystal vase of lilacs and the last of Marcy's creamy, white parrot tulips. The comforting sound of children's laughter drifted in the air, harmonizing with the chatter of birds and the yipping of neighborhood dogs.

A silent sigh of contentment escaped Luke's lips as he selected a crispy drumstick and a thigh from the plate of fried chicken Lizzie offered. He handed the platter off to Brady with a smile. "Thanks, Lizzie." He glanced up. "Not long, Mr. O'Connor. About a month. But I can tell you one thing—it sure feels good to be home."

Marcy smiled. "It's good to have you back, Clu—er, Luke—sorry. But if you don't mind me asking, Luke, why did they call you Cluny as a boy?"

Luke peered over his drumstick, the near-taste of Marcy's chicken watering his mouth. "My given name is Clarence Luke McGee, Mrs. O'Connor, but I was so puny that one of my mom's boyfriends started calling me Cluny instead of Clarence, and somehow, the name just stuck." He took a quick bite of his chicken, and the sheer flavor of it brought a smile to his lips. Taking a swig of his tea, he winked. "But, since I'm all grown up, I figured a lawyer needs a respectable name, so I go by Luke now."

"You've been gone a long time," Sean O'Connor said. Patrick's oldest reached for the pepper and bombarded his potatoes with a monumental dose.

Specks of the seasoning floated in the air like dust motes, causing Charity to snatch the napkin from her lap and stifle a sneeze. She sniffed and arched a brow. "Goodness, Sean, why don't you just take the cap off and pour the stuff on? You're as bad as Mitch. Now you won't even be able to taste Mother's food."

Sean's blue eyes twinkled as he grinned at his sister, and his blond hair gleamed in the sunlight. "Oh, I'll taste it, all right. That'll be the day when a bachelor who lives on his own doesn't enjoy his mother's food. And speaking of Mitch, where is he?" He glanced around. "And Steven?"

Charity snatched the pepper from Sean's hand and moved it far away. "The love of my life volunteered to eat outside with the kids."

"You mean *you* volunteered him to sit outside with the kids," Faith said with a chuckle. She glanced at her parents. "But where *is* Steven?"

Patrick reached for the salt and shook it unmercifully over his potatoes. A frown creased his lips. "Apparently your brother had a prior engagement. *Again*."

Marcy patted her husband's arm. "He's a young man in college, Patrick, and you know how independent young people are today. Goodness, sometimes I think you're way too hard on him." She smiled her apologies at Brady. "Steven promised he'd join us later."

"I doubt anyone here wants to stay up that late, darlin'," Patrick said with a droll smile.

Sean grinned, an ear of corn in hand. "So, how long's it been, Luke? Six, seven years?"

"Almost seven since I left Boston after Gram died. I turned

sixteen when I went to live with my aunt in New York, but I can tell you, it feels like a lifetime."

"Brady tells us you're a lawyer now. We're so proud of you, Luke." Marcy's forehead puckered. "You did get rolls, didn't you? They're not long for this world, you know, with Brady and Collin."

Collin looked up from buttering one of three rolls on his plate. "Hey, Sean's no lightweight, either."

Dimples deepened on either side of Sean's lazy grin. "Yeah, but I'm the good son, and Brady's the birthday boy, so that makes you the—"

"Pig-in-law?" Katie stood in the door in a fresh crimson-colored shift, arms crossed and brow cocked. Chuckles rounded the table while she sashayed into the room, flicking Collin on the head as she moseyed to her seat.

Luke rose while he waited for Katie to settle in, then sat back down with a grin.

"Watch it, Katie Rose," Collin quipped. "Don't get me started on your grace and poise with beverages."

Katie flipped her napkin open with a smirk and placed it on her lap. The lift of her chin defied the blush on her cheeks. She avoided Luke's gaze, obviously more interested in riling her brother-in-law than conversing with company.

Luke squinted hard, trying to see the pigtailed brat he'd once pestered within an inch of her sanity. Her manner seemed easy and casual as she volleyed insults with Collin, but he didn't miss the nervous flicker in her cheek or the death grip on the fork in her hand. The grin widened on his lips. She was older now, prettier and definitely more sophisticated, but underneath that head-turning facade, he sensed she was still the same little tyrant of a girl, armed with sharp quips and an aloof manner.

Patrick cleared his throat. "Luke, I think I speak for everyone when I say how proud we are of your incredible accomplishment. Brady told us how hard you've worked. A law degree for the most privileged of young men is impressive enough, but to attain such heights through the sweat of your brow, working a number of jobs along with your studies, well, that is truly a remarkable feat. I commend you. Have you nailed down a position with a law firm yet?"

Luke took a quick swallow of tea to wash down his food. "As a matter of fact I have, Mr. O'Connor, but not with a law firm. I've taken a job at the Boston Children's Aid Society."

A fine mist of lemonade sprayed across the table as Katie choked on her drink.

"Hey, Sweet Pea, you okay?" Sean patted while Katie wheezed.

Collin leaned forward with a glint in his eye. "Yeah, squirt, are you okay . . . or do we need to remove all liquids from the room?"

Faith elbowed her husband, then handed her water to Katie. "Maybe the pulp is giving you trouble. Here, take a drink of my water, but slowly."

Katie obeyed, her face as scarlet as her dress. She handed the glass back and took a deep breath, one hand to her heaving chest. "D-Did you say . . . the B-Boston Children's Aid Society?"

Luke blinked. "Yeah, I'm the new assistant director. Why, you know somebody who works there?"

A low, throaty chuckle rumbled from the far end of the table. "As a matter of fact, she does," Patrick said.

"Father!" Katie's voice was little more than a croak.

"Who?" Luke asked, his gaze scanning from Katie's horror to Patrick's amusement.

Color drained from Katie's cheeks as she leaned forward, a knife clenched in her hands. "Father, no! *Please* . . . you can't! This changes everything."

"Now, Katie, after our talk last night, you and I agreed that volunteering at the BCAS this summer would be a profitable experience for you."

Katie bounded to her feet. "I didn't agree—you coerced me! Mother, please . . . this is my last summer before law school. Can't you make him see that I need time to plan and prepare?"

A tiny wrinkle creased the bridge of Marcy's nose. Her gaze flitted from her daughter to her husband and back, reflecting her worry. "Darling, your father and I have discussed it at length, and I honestly think you'll love the BCAS—"

"No!" Katie slammed her fist on the table, upsetting her utensils. "I won't do it."

"Katie Rose—sit down this instant!" The edge in Patrick's tone shivered the air, cooling all smiles in the room. With a quiet pat of his wife's hand, he inhaled deeply, then released it slowly as his gaze returned to the daughter still rooted to the floor, her features as stiff as his. He lowered his voice to a level of warning. "Sit down, young lady, *now*. And-not-another-word."

In total fascination, Luke watched a battle being waged between the most stubborn girl he'd ever seen and the man from whom she'd obviously inherited it. Time seemed to still as Katie stared her father down, every muscle strained with resistance. He could hear her shallow breathing as her chest rose and fell in indignation, and the surge of her will appeared so strong that her body seemed to shimmer with intent, ready to explode, like a warm and shaken bottle of pop. And then painfully slow, as if all combustion had seeped out from her bottled anger, she lowered to her seat, the pout on her lips as flat as a week-old glass of Nehi.

Patrick released a heavy breath and speared a clump of green beans. He slid his wife a sideways glance and patted her hand, obviously noting the look of concern on her face. "Now, Marcy, we both know that this is exactly what Katie needs. She'll be working with lawyers and acquiring valuable experience before entering law school in the fall."

"Law school?" Luke stared at Patrick and then at Katie. His brow jagged high. "You're going to law school?"

Brady leaned close to Luke's ear, his voice a loaded whisper. "Easy . . ."

Katie's blue eyes narrowed, as if daring Luke to utter a single word. Her chin cocked up a fraction of an inch. "That's right. Women have minds too, you know."

Luke ignored Brady's subtle jab and planted both arms on the table. He leaned in, his lips twitching with tease. "Of course they do. And I for one am glad opportunities are opening up for women in a number of fields. I guess I just didn't peg you as someone who would be keen on a career. You just seem so much more suited to—"

"Marcy, dinner is delicious." Brady hooked a firm arm around Luke's shoulders and squeezed. "Thank you for the birthday celebration, and for inviting Luke too."

"Absolutely, Mrs. O'Connor, everything is wonderful," Luke agreed with a warm smile.

"More suited to what?" Katie said, her tone as serrated as the knife in her hand.

"Boy, these rolls melt in your mouth, don't they, Luke?" Brady sounded desperate.

"More-suited-to-what?" she repeated in a deadly whisper.

"They sure do, Mrs. O'Connor. Best I've ever had, as a matter of fact." Luke buttered another piece of a roll and popped it in his mouth, allowing his gaze to settle on Katie once again. He swallowed and grinned. "Oh, I don't know . . . marrying well?"

Katie gouged her chicken breast with a fork and slashed off a slice with her knife. Her eyes hardened and her smile was brittle. "For your information, I intend to do both, thank you."

"So, Luke," Lizzie said in a rush, "Brady says you've had offers from a number of law firms. Why the Boston Children's Aid Society?"

Luke glanced up at Lizzie and released a quiet breath. *Why?* His smile tempered at the memory of nights spent on the streets of New York, huddled with other homeless youth or "street arabs" as they were called. Lost kids who sought refuge in the alleys and doorways of Mulberry Street, otherwise known as "Death's Thoroughfare." The festering sore of New York slums, rife with sewage and rats. Foul. Rancid. Corrupt.

And home. At least until his aunt's current boyfriend would desert her once again. A lump shifted in Luke's throat. "Let's just say I owe a favor. The Children's Aid Society in New York offered me a hand when I needed it most. The pay isn't all that great, I know, but the payoff is. For me, it's rewarding to help get kids off the street."

Faith's eyes lit with excitement. She propped her elbows on the table. "Oh, Luke, I'm so proud of you! Tell me, do you get involved with the out-placement program, the one that sends orphans to the Midwest on trains? A friend of mine at church had a neighbor who died in the Spanish Flu epidemic about ten years ago. She was a war widow who left two little boys all alone. According to my friend, the Children's Aid Society sent the boys to Missouri on an orphan train. They were six and eight at the time, but both boys are doing well in Sedalia, Missouri, I understand."

Luke's heart swelled with pride. "Yeah, Faith, I do, although the train traffic is certainly dwindling. When Reverend Brace initiated what he called his 'family plan' in 1854, he wanted to see street orphans taken into a home and treated as part of a loving family. Since then, over 200,000 kids have been rescued from the streets and placed in foster families across the country. Some stay here in the East, but others get placed in the Midwest and even out West." He quickly gulped some tea to diffuse the tightness in his chest. "But the results weren't always positive, so attitudes are changing. Recently, state and local laws are focusing more on keeping families together, which is actually a pretty good thing. Especially when you realize that many of these kids are not orphans at all. Quite a few have one or two parents who are still alive, but due to neglect, abandonment, or just too many mouths to feed, the kids end up on the streets fending for themselves."

Luke shifted, suddenly aware his hand was fisted on the table. He slowly relaxed his fingers and took another drink of tea, then swallowed hard and managed a tight smile. "Like me, I guess. I won't lie to you—it's pretty tough seeing kids who have been discarded like trash, day in and day out. But the joy I get out of helping them . . . well, I wouldn't trade it for the world." His gaze veered to Katie and held. Mischief twitched at the corners of his lips. "Although to tell you the truth," he said with a hint of the Arkansas drawl he always reserved for a tease, "there are days when I'd rather be jerking sodas."

Katie shot to her feet. "Coffee, anyone?"

"And how about dessert too?" Faith said, rising with a smile. "Lizzie made birthday cake, and I brought brownies." She rounded the table to collect dirty dishes and stopped. A frown crimped her brow. "Katie, are you all right? You look flushed."

The bloom in Katie's cheeks blossomed into deep rose, bleeding into her face and neck. "I'm fine, Faith, it's just warm in here."

Lizzie snatched a napkin to fan her face. "Oh, thank you! I thought it was me."

"Yeah, Lizzie, I'd go easy on your husband's birthday candles this year," Collin said with a grin. He flicked Brady's head. "No sense in setting the place on fire."

Sean righted his coffee cup with a chuckle and a wink in Katie's direction. "No worries there—Sweet Pea can always put it out."

Katie shoved her chair in with a wry smile and snatched Sean's dirty plate, piling it on top of her own. "Not real smart, brother dear, mocking the person who'll be pouring your hot, *hot* coffee."

"Ouch . . . sounds dangerous," Luke said with a grin.

Her eyes seared him. "Depends. Having coffee, Luke?" she asked in a honeyed tone.

He lounged back in his chair and gave her a hooded smile. "Not on your life . . . *Katydid*."

With a press of her jaw, she spun on her heel and headed for the kitchen. She paused, one hand braced to the swinging door. "Everybody want coffee? Or should I bring in the tea too?"

Luke opened his mouth to retort, but shut it again when Katie shot him an icy look.

"No coffee for me, Katie. I need lemonade and lots of ice, but I'll get it." With a faint groan, Lizzie lumbered up, but Faith gently pushed her back in her seat. "Mother, Lizzie—stay put. Katie and I'll bring in drinks and dessert while Charity rounds up Mitch and the kids."

"Sweet saints, we have ice cream, I hope?" Patrick's voice reflected concern.

Marcy squeezed his hand and shot Luke a smile. "Yes, dear, Luke was nice enough to stop by Robinson's and bring Brady's favorites—butter pecan and vanilla."

"Oh, bless you!" Lizzie said with a grateful smile. She loosened the silk tie of her dress and commenced to fanning herself with a napkin. "If it's this hot in May, can you imagine how bad the rest of the summer will be? Bless you, Luke."

"Yeah, bud, thanks." Brady stretched and draped his arm across the back of Luke's chair while the others continued chatting around the table. "Ice cream's the perfect thing to cool us all off."

Luke gave him a sideways glance and arched a brow. His gaze shifted to the swinging door Katie had just barreled through. He lowered his voice to a whisper. "Oh, I don't know, seems pretty cool in here now."

Brady smiled and swiped a sip of his tea. "Don't worry about Katie. She'll warm up to you—eventually. You know she's always been a little touchy where you're concerned. But honestly, Patrick's right. Working with you at the BCAS will be the best thing for her."

"Yeah?" Luke let loose with a low chuckle and angled to face the man who had mentored him at the age of fourteen, the friend who had taught him about God. "Why?"

"Because other than Patrick, you're one of the few who stood up to her, challenged her."

"Drove her crazy?"

Brady grinned. "Yeah, that too. And trust me, Katie could use a little challenge right about now. I'm afraid the older Marcy gets, the more she coddles her. And her sisters are so busy with their own families that when they do spend time with her, they're more interested in getting along than butting heads. But you? No, not only are you someone who brings out the worst in her, but as her future boss . . ." Brady rolled his neck to work out the kinks. "You also have an opportunity to soften the worst in her." A lazy smile eased across Brady's face as he gave Luke's shoulder a friendly pat. "That is . . . if you can."

The door squealed open, unleashing a noisy barrage of children ushered in by Mitch and Charity, who each toted a tub of ice cream. Faith and Katie were hot on their heels, birthday cake aflame and steaming coffeepot in hand. Luke leveled his gaze on Katie, noting her stiff smile and the clamp of her jaw.

A soft chuckle reached his ears as Brady leaned forward and thumped his arm. "I have all the confidence in the world in you, Luke my boy, honestly I do. But if it's all the same to you . . . I'm hoping you're a praying man."

"Promise you'll talk to him, Mother, please? My life will be over if I have to spend the summer with Cluny McGee." Katie's voice was frayed as she washed and dried an ice cream dish and put it in the cupboard. With a labored sigh, she returned to the kitchen table where she commenced to flipping through the latest issue of *Vogue* magazine.

Marcy laid her granddaughter's forgotten doll on the table and squeezed Katie's shoulder. "He goes by Luke now, Katie, and of course I will, you know that. Although I do agree with your father that it could be a fun experience." With a not-so-reassuring smile, she patted Katie's cheek and moved toward the door. The resignation etched on her mother's face did not bode well for Katie's cause. Marcy turned, her eyes tender. "I promise I'll try, but you know your father once he's made up his mind."

Yes, she knew. She drew in a deep breath and blew it out with a blast of frustration, her stomach tightening at her mother's tentative tone. "It just isn't fair, Mother. Father's like a dictator with everything Steven and I do, and you know it."

Marcy's smile seemed tired. "Yes, your father is stubborn and certainly adamant about discipline, but he loves you and Steven with every breath in him, and although it may not seem like it at the time, he's only looking out for your own good. We both are."

"Good? Banishing me to some dreary office in the city where a cocky man can lord it all over me like Father does, day in and day out? No, thank you. This is exactly why I want to be a lawyer, Mother—to blaze the way for women who think they need a man to take care of them. Women like Mrs. Rhoades at church—everyone knows that tyrant she lives with beats her, but will she leave? Not on her life." Katie's jaw quivered with anger. "And in the end, it will probably cost her hers."

Her mother's tone was quiet. "Your father is nothing like Benjamin Rhoades, Katie Rose, and you know it."

"No, he isn't, and I love Father, I do, but he's just as controlling as every other man out there. Just look at Mitch and Charity—he refuses to let her work at her own store."

"She has children to care for, Katie—" Marcy began.

"Who are in school eight hours a day. I've heard Charity say she would love to work at the store with Emma, even for just a few hours, but will Mitch let her? Not on your life. And he bought the store for her when they got married, for pity's sake. Instead, he rules with an iron fist, just like Father. And

Collin? You and I both know the battles he waged over Faith's job before she got pregnant with the girls. No, Mother, you are not going to convince me that it's not a man's world out there, and I for one think it's time for a change. In the last decade, women have gotten the right to vote, taken charge of their own future in the workplace, and have broken free from Victorian dictates to forge their own morality—"

"You mean their own promiscuity," Marcy said with an edge to her tone. "The flapper lifestyle is hardly a lifestyle we condone, young lady, nor one that will make you happy."

Katie's shoulders slumped in defeat. "I know, and I don't embrace everything espoused today, really I don't. Alcohol and cigarettes and lewd behavior only cheapen the woman's cause, in my opinion, not to mention that it gives men what they want without any commitment." She blew her bangs from her face. "But a little more freedom would be nice, don't you think?"

Marcy chuckled. "You and I have all the freedom we need, young lady—your father provides us with a comfortable life, and we would do well to remember that."

"Mmm . . . ," Katie said with a fold of her arms. "I look forward to the day when I can provide my own comfortable life and do as I please." Her frustration escaped in a bluster of air. "Without the restraint of my father *or* my husband."

"Well, I have no doubt that if anyone can achieve that, Katie Rose, it will be you. But until then, there's a good chance you'll be working at the Boston Children's Aid Society this summer whether you and I like it or not."

Katie started to speak, but Marcy held up a hand. "And, yes, I will talk to your father, but I wouldn't get your hopes up. He seems to think that you'll thank him for this in the end." Her mother's face looked tired, but her tone had the slightest inflection of tease. "Of course, you could always pray about it, I suppose . . ." She blew her daughter a kiss at the door. "I'm heading up to bed now, so would you mind waiting up for Faith?" She nodded her head toward the smudged Kewpie doll she'd laid on the table. "Abby forgot her baby tonight, so Faith's on retrieval. Apparently it's Collin's turn to read the girls a story before bed. Good night, darling."

"Sure, Mother. Good night." Katie sighed as her mother departed the room, reflecting on her comment about prayer—the last thing on her list of solutions. She picked up Abby's Kewpie doll and pressed its two chubby palms together with a scrunch of her nose. Sometimes she wished prayer were as important to her as it seemed to be for the rest of her family. That would make life so easy—putting one's cares into the capable hands of a loving Father, as her sister, Faith, was so fond of saying. Katie tossed the doll back on the table. Well, if her heavenly Father was anywhere as stubborn as her earthly one, she wasn't too sure she wanted his help anyway. For the moment, it seemed far safer to put her faith in herself and her abilities rather than some long-distance God with a long list of rules.

"Sweet saints in heaven, it's like a steam bath out there." The screen door creaked as Faith hurried in, one fist flapping the front of her blouse to create a breeze. She shoved a limp strand of auburn hair away from tired green eyes and gave Katie a weary smile, her breathing winded. "Of course, it could have been the three blocks I ran to rescue Miss Kewpie, I suppose."

Katie jumped up with a smile. "Sit. How about a lemonade? You look like you could use one."

Hesitation flickered across Faith's features as she glanced at the clock, then relaxed into a smile when she dropped into a chair with a groan. "Actually that does sound pretty good, Katie, thanks. Mother in bed?"

"Yes, I think this heat wrings her out worse than it does Lizzie, and Father headed up a while ago. Something about a headache, I think." Katie poured a cool glass of lemonade for Faith, then one for herself before settling back in her chair.

Faith drained half her glass in one thirsty swallow. She clunked it down on the table with a grateful sigh. "Oh, that hit the spot—thanks. A headache, huh? Mmm . . . now that you mention it, Father did seem a touch cranky at dinner."

Katie's lips skewed to the right. "Oh, you noticed, did you? Can you believe he's making me spend my summer working for that annoying twit?"

"I thought Luke seemed rather nice." Faith's smile was gentle.

"Nice?" Katie's tone raised several octaves. "See, that's the problem with that pest—he always treated everyone nice but me. A regular Dr. Jekyll and Mr. Hyde. Charmed the socks off of my family, but treated me like dirt."

"I don't remember that," Faith said with a crinkle of her brows.

"You wouldn't—you never see the bad in anybody. But trust me, I didn't crown him King of Misery for nothing." She leaned forward with elbows on the table and squinted, the awful memories all flooding back. "Remember the baseball game at Lizzie and Brady's house when I gashed my knee?"

Faith nodded, her eyes suddenly solemn.

"The little beggar tripped me," Katie said with certainty. She hiked her leg up to tap a small, white scar on top of her knee. "Fifteen stitches, remember?"

"Come on, Katie, it was an accident."

Her gaze thinned. "So he said, but I know better. That twerp hoarded home plate like a vulture with an evil glint in his eye, and you're not going to tell me that it wasn't for one purpose and one purpose only—to send me flying."

A smile flickered at the edges of Faith's mouth, as if she were trying to stifle it. "He simply did what any great catcher would do, Katie, try to block the plate so you couldn't score. Besides, you know how important sports and winning always were to the poor little guy. God knows he didn't have much else going for him."

"Well, not friends, that's for sure, not with a nasty streak a mile long."

"Come on, you're going to have to do better than that. What else did he do to warrant your wrath?"

She jutted her chin. "In addition to pestering me when nobody was looking, you mean?"

Faith grinned. "Yeah, something where you can produce a witness."

"Okay." Katie leaned in with a retaliatory gleam in her eyes. "Once when I was playing hopscotch in the schoolyard with my classmates, that little pest rode by on Brady's bike and yelled, 'Hey, O'Connor, what's new in the dog world?' I was mortified."

A full-blown laugh escaped her sister, who promptly put a hand to her mouth. "Sorry, but to me, that sounds like a boy with a crush rather than one who hated you."

Katie gasped. "Bite your tongue!" She pressed a palm to her stomach. "I think I'm going to be sick."

Rising with a chuckle, Faith washed her empty glass in the sink and proceeded to dry it, casting a wary smile in Katie's direction. "Nope, Katie Rose, as a young woman who hopes to be a lawyer someday, I'd say you have no grounds for your case."

Katie studied her sister for several seconds, the smile on her face fading along with the tease in her tone. She drew in a deep breath, avoiding Faith's eyes as she idly traced the dimple of Miss Kewpie's knee. "You don't understand, Faith, he was . . . well, really hurtful to me." A sudden malaise settled and she buffed her arms out of nervous habit, fingers trailing down to the tip of her elbows where the lesions had once been. She swallowed hard, remembering with perfect clarity the hurt she had felt that day—the day Cluny McGee had stabbed her through the heart. Seconds passed before she was able to even utter the words, and when she did, she expelled them in a weak and wounded whisper. "He called me a leper, a freak of nature," she said, shocked that the very sound of those words still held the power to bring tears to her eyes.

Faith's smile sobered into soft concern. She reached to place a gentle hand on her sister's arm. "I'm sorry, Katie. That was a cruel thing for him to say, I know, especially after all the taunting you experienced in school. But he was just a boy at the time, and it was a long time ago. I'm sure he's changed."

Katie reflected on his harsh grip last night at the diner and suspected he hadn't. *Nice girls don't run with riffraff.* A chill skittered through her, and she quickly finished off the last of her lemonade. She thumped the glass on the table and faced her sister square on. "No, Faith, someone as ugly as he was to me doesn't change deep down. Other kids didn't know how much they hurt me with their barbs because I never showed them. But him—I actually opened up to him and told him how much it had hurt. For pity's sake, he was the one who talked me into taking off the sweaters and knee socks, telling me it didn't matter what others thought. I swear I never liked him from the get-go because he was a dead ringer for all those bullies who taunted me in school—always picking, pushing, doing everything in his power to try and control me. And then one day I finally let my guard down and confide in the little weasel, and what does he do? He turns around and wounds me with the most hateful words he can." Katie rose to take her glass to the sink, shaking her head. "Nope, I'm sorry, Faith—Cluny McGee is one bad memory I will never forget or forgive."

Faith's voice was quiet. "You need to, you know . . . or the hurt will never leave."

Katie peered over her shoulder at the sister whose faith in God was second to none, and wondered if she would ever experience the same calm and peace she saw in her. She returned to the task of washing her glass, then dried it and put it away. "Can we change the subject, please? Something is souring my stomach, and I don't think it's the lemonade."

"Okay . . ." her sister said slowly. "Then . . . what about Father—are you still mad at him too?"

Katie plopped into her chair with a huff, slapping through the pages of her *Vogue* without a clue of what she was looking for. "Of course—wouldn't you be? I mean, sweet saints, Faith, the man rules this house like a tyrant, always dictating what Steven and I can and cannot do." She glanced up, brows lifted in indignation. "And now he wants to rob me of my summer with Jack so I can bow and scrape to the one person I despise most in my life?" She shivered and continued rifling through her magazine. "I'm sorry, but in my book, that puts Father at the top of my mud list . . . right after Luke McGee."

Her sister didn't respond, and Katie heaved the magazine closed with a scowl. "Come on, Faith, even someone as God-fearing as you doesn't like to be pushed around. Have you forgotten how angry you were every time Collin tried to get you to quit your job at the *Herald* before you got pregnant with the girls?"

Faith sighed and propped her elbows on the table, hands clasped except for two tented fingers against her lips as she pondered Katie's question. "No . . . no, I haven't. I was furious each and every time, and you better believe Collin slept on the couch more than once on that very issue alone. But . . ." She glanced up, locking her gaze on Katie's. "I also know that our love wouldn't be as deep and strong as it is today if I had let my anger and hurt fester."

"You and Collin are married—that's different."

"Not really, Katie. Depth of love in any relationship blooms in the soil of respect, and bitterness will only poison any respect you hope to have. The bottom line is if we want God to bless our lives and our relationships, we have to do things *his* way. And he says we are to respect all authority he places over us." Faith released a weary sigh. "Which means you respecting Father or even me respecting my husband as the head of our home. We may not always agree with them, but we are called by God to respect them and their authority nonetheless. So basically, it's a matter of trust."

Katie's eyes spanned wide. "Trust? In a human being who wants to control my life?"

"No, Katie . . ." Faith said quietly. "In a God who wants to bless it."

She folded her arms with a grunt, her body suddenly stiff. "So let me get this straight—I'm supposed to kowtow to whatever Father wants me to do, even something as awful as slaving for someone I despise? And then God wants me to forgive them both in the process?" Her acute annoyance escaped in a noisy blast of air. "Impossible."

A hint of a smile curved at the edges of Faith's lips. "Difficult, yes, but not impossible, trust me. Not with God's help."

"Oh, and I suppose if Collin forced you to do something that completely went against every shred of common sense and emotion in your body—and I'm not talking something as insignificant as grousing about your job—that you would just lie down and surrender without a fight."

Faith sucked in a deep breath and released it slowly. "No, not without a fight, certainly . . . but the fight wouldn't be between Collin and me, hopefully." She looked up, capturing Katie's gaze with a silent plea. "It would be between my will and God's. And if I've learned anything from painful experience, Katie, it's that God's will is the path to my ultimate happiness . . . and yours."

Katie bristled at the awkwardness she always felt when her sister wandered into the realm of "God's will." She quickly covered with a forced smile. "Well, I have to hand it to you, Faith, you're a better woman than me."

"Not better . . ." Faith said with a quirk of a smile. "Let's just say a little more desperate for peace." She hesitated. "Would you . . . can we . . . pray about it?"

With a firm shake of her head, Katie slid Miss Kewpie across the table. "No, thanks, but I appreciate the offer. There's nothing to pray about, really."

Her sister expelled a gentle sigh. "Okay, Katie. Well, I better get back. Love you." With a quick squeeze of Katie's hand, she rose and snatched Abby's doll on her way to the door.

"Desperate for peace, huh?" Katie called after her, determined to end things on a much lighter note. She stood and rounded the table, following Faith to the door. "Well, come Monday morning, if that man so much as looks at me cross-eyed, you and he are going to have a lot in common." She gave her sister a quick kiss and then flashed her a crooked grin. "And trust me, sis, when I'm done with Luke McGee . . . 'desperate for peace' won't even begin to cover it."

3

"I mean, sweet saints, what are the odds?" Luke chuckled and shuffled a stack of applications into a neat pile before tossing them into a wire basket at the corner of his scarred wooden desk. Streaks of sunset filtered in through the second-story window of the Boston Children's Aid Society, lending a pinkish glow to the tiny office crammed with file cabinets, unpacked boxes, and well-worn furniture. A small antique mantel clock at the front of his desk chimed the six o'clock hour as he closed a folder sprawled open before him. With a flick of his wrist, he pitched the folder into another wire basket filled to the brim with client histories to be filed. He scribbled a quick note to himself, then shoved some final papers into a side drawer before rising to his feet, arms stretched high overhead. "Who would've guessed the little brat I had a crush on at fourteen would turn out to be the spoiled fireball who gave me trouble at Robinson's?" Lifting his navy suit coat off his chair, he flipped it over his shoulder and grinned at his two best friends. "I tell you, it's nothing short of sweet justice, because *now* she works for me."

"For us," Parker Riley corrected with an easy smile. He

leaned back in the chair in front of Luke's desk and braced his hands to the back of his neck. A twinkle lit brown eyes that regarded Luke with affection. "You're the assistant director and *I'm* the director, remember?"

Luke reached in his pocket and dug out a crumpled piece of paper. He sailed it across the desk to Parker with another grin. "A mere technicality, Parker, my boy. But since you insist on pulling rank, here's the name of the agent for the train to Texas. He's expecting your call."

Parker unwadded the note. "Come on, Luke, I can't read this. This is nothing but chicken scratch." He shook his head and handed it back. "Decipher, please."

"Here, give it to me." With a roll of her hazel eyes, Betty Galetti pushed a shock of russet hair away from her face before plucking the note from Parker's hand. "When are you going to learn, Parker? I'm the only one in this office who can read his writing . . ." She flattened the sheet out on the desk, then held it up to the fading light with a wry smile. "Or his mind, for that matter. Not that there's a lot to read, mind you." She squinted. "Alex Chrzanowski? McGee—are you sure this is right? Your spelling is atrocious."

Luke aimed a massive finger in her direction, but a grin softened his threatening stance, giving him dead away. "Hey, Galetti, you wouldn't have a job if it wasn't for me, so I suggest you treat both Parker and me with a *liiiiittle* more respect." He strolled around his desk to give her a playful squeeze on the neck. "And you can start with a home-cooked meal—it's bingo night, you know, and Mrs. Cox said we're on our own for dinner."

Betty giggled and scrunched her shoulders. She squirmed out of his reach and slapped his hand away. "Why am I always the one who has to cook when Mrs. Cox is out? Parker's a better cook than you and me put together."

Parker yawned and extended his arms in the air with a tired groan. "Sorry, but I'm the poor slob who has to put a budget together for the board tonight, so I'll be here for a while."

He rose from his chair and loosened his paisley tie, then shot her a boyish grin while rolling his sleeves. "But I'd love it if you could save me a plate, Bets," he said with a nod in Luke's direction, "*before* this guy eats it all."

Betty's smile shifted off-center as she stood, rising to her lithe, five-foot-ten height. She adjusted her knee-length pleated skirt, then patted the back of her chin-length auburn bob. "Believe me, Parker, I would love nothing more than making dinner for both you and Luke, but I promised Pop I'd close for him tonight."

"Again?" Luke frowned, coat draped over his shoulder and a hand parked on his thigh. "You told me you were only filling in at Robinson's once or twice, not on a regular basis."

"I know," Betty said with a sigh. "But Pop's had trouble finding reliable help, and honestly, I could use the money. After all, secretarial pay falls way short of what you two slave drivers make." She flashed a superior smile. "Though heaven knows I do most of the work."

"But I don't like you working nights," Luke said, his voice devoid of all humor. "And neither does Parker." He exhaled and softened his tone. "Come on, Bets, you can't keep this up—working here all day, then working nights too. Why don't you talk to Mrs. Cox about reducing your board? Maybe you can help in the kitchen or something, you know, to lower your rent. Or better yet, let Parker and me kick in a little extra."

Betty's eyes narrowed as she folded her arms to give him a cold stare, a pose Luke recognized all too well from their years in New York. Best friends from the start, they'd been two street orphans who'd forged an immediate bond.

"I can't ask Mrs. Cox for a reduction in board and you know it." Her jaw lifted the slightest degree. "And neither would you. That woman needs every dime she can get running a boardinghouse with two shiftless sons who refuse to work."

Parker pushed in his chair. "Then let Luke and me pitch in—"

"No!" The chin jutted further. "It's bad enough you had to talk the board into giving me this job, I will *not* take your charity too."

Luke took a step forward, lips compressed as flat as his mood. "You're as pigheaded as they come, you know that, Galetti?"

A hint of a blush colored her cheeks, but she stood her ground, meeting his scowl, nose to nose. "I doubt that's a true statement, McGee, at least as long as you're drawing air."

A soft chuckle parted from Parker's lips. "I'm afraid she's got you there, my friend."

Luke didn't budge. "Then I'm walking you home. I'll be there at ten-thirty sharp."

Betty sighed. "I'm a big girl, Luke, you're not responsible for me anymore." She hefted the box of files from his desk and headed for the door.

Luke caught up with her and tossed his suit coat over the box, then pried it from her grip. He forced a grim smile. "Somebody's got to look out for you, Galetti. Heaven knows you have no talent for it yourself."

Parker put an arm around Betty's shoulders. "Come on, Luke, give her some credit. She left the bum and moved to Boston with us, didn't she?" He gave her arm a squeeze. "Why don't you just walk her to work, and I'll walk her home, okay?"

"I don't need you two hovering over me all the time. I'll be fine, I promise."

Betty started to leave, but not before Luke blocked her way. "We'll do this our way, Bets, or not at all, is that clear?"

"You mean your way, don't you, Luke? It's not Parker obsessing over my safety."

Luke sucked in a deep breath and exhaled slowly. Painful memories tightened his gut—the guilt of their close friendship veering into something more before he'd finally broken it off. Pain he'd never meant to inflict, forcing her into the arms of a monster. Cold fury shivered him at the thought of how he'd found her that night, battered, bruised, a woman with whom he shared a bond closer than blood. And a friend he loved better than any sister. He released a weary breath. "I just care about you, Bets—is that a crime?"

Her defenses softened, and he saw a glimmer of the feelings she still harbored for him. "No, Luke, but you're going to have to let it go. It's not your fault. And it's in the past, where it belongs—leave it there. And for heaven's sake, stop looking back . . . please? For me?" The edge of her mouth lifted along with her brow. "You need to lighten up, kid, and embrace the moment."

He looked quickly away, moisture threatening his eyes. "I know, but we're family—Parker, you, and me. Neither of us are going to let anything happen to you ever again."

He heard her soft sigh and watched as she made her way to the door. She turned and smiled, and despite a faint shadow of sadness in her eyes, he was struck all over again at how beautiful she was. A nerve pulsed in his jaw. Especially to the wrong guys—guys that wanted a taste of her beauty, no matter the cost. Shame flooded through him.

Like I used to be.

"Thanks, guys. I'll file those histories on Monday." She turned to go.

Luke followed in her wake, his thoughts still muddled in the past. "G'night, Parker," he said absently. "Bets gets off at ten-thirty sharp, so don't be late or she'll leave without you."

"Hey, Luke—wait up. We need to talk about this new volunteer." Parker nudged the wire basket aside and sat on the corner of Luke's desk. "Given your history with this girl, I think it would be more professional if she answered to me rather than you."

Luke turned and shifted the box to one hip. "No, buddy, this one is mine."

"This one is *yours*?" Parker folded his arms and angled a brow.

Luke grinned. "Yeah, she's a spoiled brat who needs a firm hand, and we both know that's not you. I mean, look how you caved when I talked you into this job . . . *Boss*."

Parker sighed and tunneled his fingers through perfectly groomed sandy hair. "You and I both know there was no coercion involved, unless it was Father forcing me to be a lawyer instead of a priest like I wanted. And Father only gave me the directorship because I'm blood. He respects you a lot, sometimes more than me, I think."

"No, he gave you the directorship because you're the one with the brains and the calm and steady hand."

A ghost of a smile played at the edges of Parker's mouth. "All the more reason that the volunteer should answer to me and not you."

Luke squinted at his best friend. His smile faded as he tried to assess the truth of his feelings. Could he be fair and impartial? Memories of a ten-year-old spitfire sprang to mind, reminding him how easily she'd gotten under his skin. His thoughts shifted to the golden-haired beauty who needed to be reined in, and his pulse picked up. A slow smile eased across his lips as he adjusted the box on his hip. "No, Parker, our 'history' as you call it is all the more reason she should answer to me. According to Brady, this volunteer assignment was actually meted out by her father after she defied him one too many times. He hopes that working in the real world will teach her she can't always get her own way." His smile broke into a grin. "And I hate to tell you this, buddy-boy, but if she answered to you, that's a lesson she'd never learn."

Parker smiled and rose to his feet. "Okay, Luke, we'll do it your way. But don't think I won't be breathing down your neck if I see you abusing your power."

"Abusing my power?" Luke's brows sloped high, his voice wounded. "I'm a professional, Parker, I would *never* abuse my power." He boggled the box and strode for the door, but not before flashing a final gleam of white teeth. "Now Miss

O'Connor's 'power'? Oh, yeah—that's about to be abused, and you can take that to the bank of your choice."

With a lunch sack in her hand, Lizzie Brady paused at the window of McGuire & Brady Printing Company to peer inside, grateful for an opportunity to catch her breath. She tugged a handkerchief from her pocket and patted the grueling heat from her brow, wishing her pregnancy was during the winter rather than one of the city's hottest spells.

She smiled as she spied her husband's ink-splattered trousers beneath his favorite press. Despite the fact that his and Collin's business was making money and expanding all the time, John Brady still felt the need to crawl under every machine in the place, additional pressmen or no.

She squinted through the gold-lettered glass door that glowed in the sunlight and smiled. Thank heavens Brady's love affair was with machines and nothing else. Her hand gently caressed the mound jutting beneath her lavender percale maternity shift as she spied the Bible on the gnarled wood table in the back room. She grinned. That is, nothing else but family and God, she thought to herself with a thrill. She drew in a deep breath, heavily scented with gasoline, the smell of the sea, and a hint of mulch from the potted boxwoods she and Faith had talked them into. A soft prayer of thanks automatically sprang from her lips. It had been five and half years since she'd said "I do" to the man of her dreams, and somehow the dreams just kept getting better and better. She sighed and opened the door, unleashing a familiar tinkle of bells overhead.

Her brother-in-law, Collin, glanced up from the typewriter he was piddling with and broke into a wide smile, the welcome on his handsome face as warm as the day. "Lizzie! What are you doing here? You having sympathy pangs because we're slaving on Saturday?"

She stepped inside and closed the door, grateful for the slight gust of fans cooling the shop. Pushing at a loose curl that fluttered in the breeze, she tucked it behind her ear and hoisted the bag in her hand. "In a sense. Brady forgot his lunch again, so I'm taking pity on him."

Collin's smile eased into a grin. "Yeah, I know the feeling. I take pity on him all the time, but he never seems to notice. Hey, where's your little shadow?"

"Faith took him today," Lizzie said with a quick glance in the back. "Apparently it's time for my two-year-old son to experience his first official tea party, at least according to your Abby."

A tender smile merged with a gleam of pride in Collin's eyes, marking him as a doting father. "Yeah, that Abby's a bit on the bossy side, isn't she, though? I hope Teddy doesn't let her push him around just because she's a year older. Makes me wish I had a boy to show him the ropes."

"Well, I have a feeling Abby just may be your boy—a tomboy, that is. Faith said she fights her tooth and nail when she tries to curl her hair."

Collin leaned back in the chair and braced his arms behind his neck in a noisy stretch. His lips sported a faint smile, but there was a look of longing in his eyes. "Yeah, I think you may be right. But I'm hoping to have a real boy to carry on my name before all is said and done."

Lizzie grated her lip, her cheeks heating at the memory of Faith's words that her husband was "on a mission to have a son." She fanned her face with her handkerchief. "Boy, it's hot in here. I don't know how you stand it." Her glance darted once again to the back room. "Especially my husband, who I imagine spends a good part of his day under those hot machines."

Collin grinned and shot a look over his shoulder, where the whirring of additional fans kept Brady from hearing their conversation. "Yeah, I swear the man is addicted to gears and ink, which is a good thing, I suppose, since it means he deals with the presses instead of me." Collin stuck two fingers to his teeth and let fly with an ear-splitting whistle.

Lizzie winced at the sound, but smiled when her husband rolled out on a dolly, dappled with ink. He stood to his feet and grinned, then yanked a questionable towel from his pocket in an attempt to wipe ink from his hands. "Lizzie, what are you doing here, and where's Little Guy?"

Her heart did its customary flip when he brushed his lips against hers. "Faith offered to watch Teddy so I could bring your lunch. I'm not sure if your memory is that bad, John Brady, or if it's just my leftovers that you want to forget. But either way, you forgot your lunch . . . *again*."

He took the bag and gave her a crooked grin, which lifted a streak of ink on his chiseled face, a face that had turned her head from the age of thirteen. "Trust me, it's not the leftovers. You're the best cook in the family, after your mother."

Collin propped his feet on his desk and pulled a stack of invoices into his lap. He squinted at the paper on top and scratched the back of his head with a pen. "He's right, Lizzie, you know. But don't you dare tell Faith or I'll deny it flat out. Hey, Brady, didn't we already bill Mrs. Mullens for those party invitations last month?"

Brady opened the bag and unwrapped a wax-papered sandwich. He took a bite and moaned with pleasure. "Yeah, for the oldest daughter's birthday, but this one is for the younger daughter's. Can't believe I ran off and left this. You make the best meatloaf around."

Lizzie smiled at her husband, then cast a furtive peek in Collin's direction. "Uh, speaking of not telling Faith, Collin . . ." She swallowed hard. "Brady says you're still looking for a receptionist and that you interviewed a woman you used to . . . know."

Collin looked up in shock, pen frozen in hand. A wash of color flooded his neck and cheeks. He gave Brady a narrow look. "You told Lizzie?"

A thick knot bobbed in Brady's throat as he swallowed

a huge bite of meatloaf whole. His eyes glazed while he choked.

Lizzie pounded him on the back. "Goodness, Brady, are you okay?"

Her husband waved her off and cleared his throat, then leveled his gaze on his partner. Another lump bobbed, but this one wasn't from the meatloaf. "Yes, Collin, I did. She's my wife, and we pray about everything. You know that."

"But she's Faith's sister—are you crazy?"

Brady set the lunch bag on his desk and released a heavy sigh. He moved to position himself on the corner of Collin's desk and folded his arms, muscles corded tight. "No, Collin, I'm not. Just cautious. You know perfectly well how I feel about you interviewing a woman you've been involved with in the past. It's just not smart, and you know it."

Collin tossed the invoices away and jerked his feet from the desk. His eyes cooled to pewter. "For pity's sake, Brady, I love my wife. How can your brain even go in that direction? Evelyn is nothing more than a friend. One who needs a job pretty badly, not to mention that her qualifications are just what we need. She's personable, smart, has bookkeeping experience, and used to work for her uncle who was a printer. She's perfect for the job."

Lizzie saw the breath rise and fall in her husband's chest before he lowered his gaze to the crowded surface of Collin's desk, now littered with invoices.

"Were you . . . involved with her?" His voice was so low that Lizzie could barely hear it.

A shot of color bruised Collin's cheeks. His eyes darted to Lizzie before he jumped to his feet and slammed in his chair. "You're being ridiculous, and I've got deliveries to make."

Brady stood and gripped Collin's arm, his hand knuckle-white on the sleeve of his shirt. His eyes locked on his partner's with deadly calm. "I have to know, Collin. Were you?"

Collin flung Brady's hand away. "Yes! Are you satisfied?

But it was a long time ago, years before Faith. I swear to you, my intentions are purely professional."

"I know they are, but some of the most serious mistakes are paved with honorable intentions. The Bible admonishes us to 'be sober and vigilant because our adversary is like a roaring lion, seeking whom he may devour.'" Brady anchored two steady hands on Collin's shoulders, one on either side. The intensity of his brown eyes conveyed his concern. "I love you like a brother, Collin, and you're the best friend I've ever had, you know that. I trust you with my life. But I'm telling you right now from painful experience—we can't hire this woman."

Brady's words seemed to bleed the anger from his partner's body. Collin drew in a deep breath and then blew it out again in one long, agonizing sigh. He gouged the bridge of his nose with the heel of his hand. His voice was a whisper. "It's too late."

Brady dropped his arms. "What do you mean it's too late?"

Collin plunged his hands in his pockets and stared at the floor. "I hired her yesterday, while you were out on deliveries."

"What?" Brady took a step back. "Why?"

"Because she came in again, wanting to know if we'd made a decision." Collin flopped into his chair and put a hand to his eyes. "I swear I had no intention of hiring her, but she got to me. I practically haven't talked to the woman in almost twenty years, and suddenly here she is, telling me about her sick son, how hard it is for her and her mother to take care of him alone." Collin looked up, a glimpse of pain in his eyes. "She's a widow, you know. Her husband died six months ago, on the day their boy turned thirteen." Wetness glazed Collin's eyes. "That's younger than I was when my own father died." He blinked several times and looked away, his gaze trailing into a hard stare. "I know I shouldn't have done it," he whispered, "but I just wanted to help." He hesitated to draw in a deep breath. "She cried when I gave her the job, Brady. Said it was an answer to prayer."

Brady's ragged sigh filled the room as he eased back onto the desk. "Okay, Collin, I guess it's a done deal, then. We'll give her a chance. But I want your word on something."

Collin looked up, his eyes shadowed with fatigue. "What?"

Brady paused, studying his brother-in-law with gravity in his gaze. "I want you to promise that if that woman so much as bats an eye at you, you will let me know."

"For pity's sake, Brady, her husband just died—"

"I want your word, Collin, now. Or I will tell the woman myself that we can't hire her."

"I'm telling you, you're blowing this all out of proportion. She has no interest in me, and I certainly don't have any interest in her."

Brady leaned forward, eyes riveted to Collin's face. "Think about it, Collin. You're a magnet for women—always have been. Even now, I see how they look at you—"

Collin bludgeoned the desk with his fist, eyes as intense as Brady's. "Blast you, Brady, I love my wife—give me some credit, will you? Don't you think I know how some women look at me? But Faith is the best thing that has ever happened in my sorry life, and there is no way I will ever botch that up. For the love of Job, man, doesn't almost ten years of marriage prove anything?"

Lizzie watched as her husband slowly sat up, his spine steeled for battle. "It's not your marriage or your love for Faith that's in dispute here. Or even your ability to be faithful, although we both know that before Faith, that was sorely lacking. Ten years of women waltzing in here and flirting with you is one thing, ol' buddy. Working side by side with an attractive woman on a daily basis, especially one you used to be intimate with, well, I'm sorry—that's something else altogether." Brady stood to his feet, his tall frame towering over his partner like a threat. "Give me your word, Collin . . ."

Collin blinked, his look of disbelief settling into a tight press of his lips. He exhaled and looked away. His voice was a resigned whisper. "All right, I promise. But your imagination is running away with you. Nothing's going to happen."

Brady stood to his feet and rolled his neck, as if to dispel the tension in the room. "You got that right, ol' buddy, because I'm going to be tracking you every step of the way. This is not a smart thing we're doing here, Collin, and you know it. When does she start?"

"Monday. I'll give her my desk until next month when we take over the next store and knock out the wall. You and I can share your desk until after the remodel, okay?"

Brady sighed. "I guess that will work."

Lizzie blinked. "That's it, then? You're going to hire her?" Her words, laced with shock, spilled from her mouth before she could stop them.

Both Collin and Brady turned to stare, as if they'd forgotten she was even in the room.

She stepped up to her husband with one hand shielding her stomach and her eyes wide with astonishment. "I can't believe you're agreeing to this."

Brady rested his hands on her shoulders. "Look, Lizzie, this is between Collin and me." He gave her a quick peck on the cheek. "In fact, it might be best if you just head on home."

It was an order rather than a request, and Lizzie felt the prickles of resistance clear up her spine. She lurched away. "I will *not* 'just head on home,' and this is *not* just between you and Collin." She whirled around to give Collin the benefit of her ire. "And you! I suppose you weren't even going to tell Faith about this, were you?"

Collin lumbered up, his mood somber and his tone worn. "Come on, Lizzie, there's nothing to tell. We hired a receptionist and nothing more. And I know it's the pregnancy talking and not you—heaven knows how hormones can rile a woman when she's carrying a child."

"Don't you dare 'hormone' me, Collin McGuire—you should be ashamed of yourself!"

Brady shot him a look of warning, jerking a finger across his neck.

Collin ignored him. "Look, Lizzie, when Faith was pregnant, I can't count the times she was over the edge about the slightest little thing—"

The breath whooshed from her lungs. When her voice came out, it was barely a croak. "The slightest little thing?" she whispered.

"Now you've done it," Brady muttered. He clasped a strong hand on her arm. "Come on, Lizzie, I'm taking you home."

She jerked free of his grasp. Her voice rose to a dangerous level as she spit out each syllable with deadly emphasis. "*The-slightest-little-thing*, you say? Oh, and I suppose Faith would be pleased as punch to learn that the woman with whom her husband will be cozily working was once his—"

"Lizzie—that's enough." Brady stepped between them, ever to the rescue with his demeanor of calm. "Neither you nor I know Collin's past with this woman, and quite frankly, it's none of our business. Getting upset is not good for you, and it's not good for the baby."

"Or you, I suppose," she bit back with an angry heave.

He exhaled a weary sigh and tugged her firmly into his arms. For the briefest of moments, she struggled against him before collapsing in a tearful heap, limp against his chest. She felt the gentle stroke of his hand against her hair and closed her eyes with a shiver, thinking only of her sister.

"Lizzie, look, I'm sorry . . ." Collin's voice was low and heavy with regret.

She nodded, emitting a painful whimper.

Brady kissed the top of her head. "Come on, Lizzie. I'll walk you home."

Her body stiffened. "Not until Collin promises . . ."

She heard the soft intake of Collin's breath. "Promise what?"

"That you'll tell Faith."

"Lizzie, there's *nothing* to tell—"

Her eyes met his. "If it were Brady, Collin, I would want to know. So I could pray."

He swallowed hard and looked away. "Okay, Lizzie, I'll tell her—you have my word."

The weighty sigh that escaped her lungs suddenly left her depleted. She put a shaky hand to her chest and closed her eyes. Collin was probably right. She was overreacting, she was sure. Heaven knows that pregnancies had a way of wringing the fear from her faith. She opened her eyes and sucked in a deep breath, suddenly feeling foolish over her emotional outburst. She stood on tiptoe and gave Brady a shaky kiss. "Don't be late for dinner—we're having your favorite." She ducked her head and made a beeline for the door. "Have a good night, Collin," she called over her shoulder, then hoped they couldn't see the flush she felt on her face.

With a jangle of bells, the door shut firmly behind her while she released a quiet sigh, her hand limp on the knob. Heaven help her, she'd done it again—let her hormones get the best of her. She hurried down the sidewalk, quite certain that Collin was right. There was probably nothing to tell, but she'd pray about it all the same. She wasn't a woman to gamble, but when it came to the welfare of her sisters . . . she didn't mind hedging her bets.

Genevieve peeked out the kitchen window with a hint of worry in her voice. "I don't know, Katie, maybe we better go. What if your father comes home early?"

Katie removed a tray of hot cookies from the oven and plopped it on the table with two of her mother's pot holders. She pulled a spatula from the drawer and began sliding cookies onto a plate. "For pity's sake, Gen, he distinctly said

I couldn't go 'gallivanting with friends'—there was absolutely nothing about you and Lilly coming over."

Lilly swiped a hot cookie from the platter. "Or baking cookies," she said with a wink. "Yum—oatmeal—my favorite."

"My father's too. I'm hoping to reduce my sentence." Katie winked, reflecting on her list to coerce her father: 1) fix oatmeal cookies; 2) retrieve and sew favorite shirt from rag basket; 3) clean and polish chess pieces; 4) trim bushes he hadn't gotten to yet—

"Gosh, Katie, I still can't believe your punishment is to work the entire summer with a sheik of a lawyer." Lilly hopped up on the counter with a cookie wedged in her mouth and began swinging her legs as she munched. "You know, it's downright unfair how lucky you are."

Katie finished unloading the cookies and began scooping dollops of fresh cookie dough onto the sheet. She blew a strand of hair from her eyes and shot Lilly a pointed look. "Lucky? Are you crazy? Forced to slave the summer away working for a soda jerk, the adult version of my childhood nightmare? No, thank you, Lil. I'd rather be bound and gagged."

Lilly giggled. "From the sound of it, you may just get your wish. I have a feeling you'll have to mind both your tongue and your temper. He is your boss, after all."

Katie grunted and hoisted the cookie sheet into the oven. "He'll always be a soda jerk to me, nothing more than a hayseed with a law degree." She set the egg timer and heaved a sigh. "But you are right, Lil. He's just obnoxious enough to run to Father if I don't toe the line, so I have no choice. But I'll tell you one thing, this summer can't end soon enough to suit me."

"Or Jack," Genevieve said with an eye on the cookies. "He'll go crazy."

"Mmm . . . maybe not," Katie said.

"What do you mean, 'maybe not'?" Genevieve edged closer to the platter and took a reluctant sniff. With a defeated sigh, she moaned and snatched two cookies from the plate. "Thanks a lot, Katie—here goes my diet."

Katie quirked a brow. "You mean the one you break whenever you get around food? Look, Gen, how many times do I have to tell you to forget the diet—you look fine the way you are. Thin may be in, but we all know that men still like curves. Look at Theda Bara."

A pout formed on Genevieve's lips. "I know, but the styles all cater to the skinny minnies like you, and you know it. And you didn't answer me—what do you mean 'maybe not'?"

"I mean," Katie emphasized with a hike of her jaw, "that Father never said one word about the telephone, so I can talk to Jack almost every day."

"That is, when your father's not around." Lilly smirked, mouth full of cookie.

"Precisely." Katie notched her chin a degree. "And honestly, can I help it if Jack gets a whim to pay me a visit in the middle of the night by throwing a pebble at my window?"

Gen's eyes bulged as she choked. Katie poured a glass of milk, then patted her on the back as she gulped it down.

"You're going to sneak out?" Gen stammered, hand to her chest.

"No, just sit on the back porch. It's not like a date or anything. Besides, I told him no, but you know Jack—if he wants to see me, nothing will stop him."

"Nothing will stop who?" A baritone voice sounded behind her, and Katie gasped. She whirled around to glare at her brother Steven as he strolled into the kitchen. "You plotting trouble again, Katie Rose?" he asked with that slow, easy grin that melted many a girl's resolve. At twenty-one, her once shy and brooding brother had transformed into a confident and popular college man, traveling in circles that threatened her father's peace of mind even more, if possible, than she. He plucked several cookies off the platter and tweaked the edge of her bob on his way to the icebox. "I thought I smelled cookies in here. Bribery won't work, you know."

"Hello, Steven," Lilly whispered in a timid voice, hushed with reverence. All Gen could do was nod, her chipmunk cheeks bright red and chunky with cookie.

Steven poured a glass of milk and grinned at Katie's friends, his blue eyes revealing a twinkle. "Hi, Lilly, Gen. You part of this conspiracy too?"

"What conspiracy?" Katie demanded. She folded her arms.

Steven took a swig of milk and winked at Lilly. Color whooshed into Lilly's cheeks, making her and Gen a matched pair. "The one to defy Father and sneak out to see Jack."

"You're a fine one to talk about defying Father. At least I don't drink and carouse at speakeasies half the night."

Steven grinned and downed the rest of his milk. "Yeah, but you're not in college yet either, little girl." He sauntered toward the door, popping another cookie into his mouth before she could shoo him away. "And if Father catches you sneaking out to see Jack, you won't *ever* be." He turned, one muscled arm pressed against the swinging door as he swallowed the cookie whole. All at once the charm of his smile faded, and his blue eyes reflected the somber warning of an older brother. "Don't risk it, Katie. Father's used to me giving him trouble. But don't you risk your future by incurring his wrath. He deserves your respect."

"But not yours, is that it?" Her eyes challenged him.

Steven vented an almost inaudible sigh as he absently fanned a thick hand through dark, auburn hair. A hint of regret flickered briefly in his eyes, reminding her so much of the gentle brother of her past. But it didn't last long. A swaggering smile replaced his pensive air. "It's too late for me," he said with a final word of warning, "but not for you. Stay out of trouble, you hear?" He glanced at Gen and Lilly, reheating their cheeks with a pointed look. "And you two help her, okay?"

The door whooshed closed as Gen and Lilly sighed in unison. "Your brother is such a sheik." Lilly fanned her face with a pot holder. "Is he still dating what's-her-name?"

"Maggie Kennedy," Katie said with an edge in her tone. "And, yes, unfortunately. None of us like her, especially Father. He thinks she's a bad influence."

Gen chewed a cookie, her eyes lost in a dreamy stare. "Maybe, but I think Steven's the bad influence—the way he looks is pure danger for any girl."

"What I wouldn't give for danger like that." Another sigh parted from Lilly's lips.

"And speaking of danger," Gen said with a glint in her eyes. "Does Jack have any idea who you'll be spending your summer with?"

Katie scrunched her nose. "Trust me, Gen, the only 'danger' this summer will be if Farm Boy thinks he can push me around. But to answer your question, no, Jack has no idea. I figure there's no sense in stirring the pot, especially when the stove the pot is sitting on is stone cold."

Lilly glanced at Gen, then shot Katie a crooked grin. "I don't know, I'd keep that spoon handy if I were you. Gotta feeling that hayseed lawyer knows his way around a stove—and a girl." She wriggled her brows as she bit into a cookie. "And something tells me he has a knack for turning up the heat."

The egg timer beeped and Katie jumped. Her lips flattened into a tight line as she armed herself with pot holders. She removed the tray from the oven and placed it on the table. The warmth of the cookies steamed her cheeks along with a blush, forcing a stubborn bent to her jaw.

She gripped the spatula like a weapon, flipping a cookie too hard and breaking it in two. "Well, I'll tell you one thing, Lil," she said with a threat in her tone, "*if* by some freak of nature he *does* manage to 'turn up the heat' . . ." She popped the broken piece of cookie in her mouth and smirked. "It sure won't be me who gets burned."

4

The dreaded Boston Children's Aid Society. A silent moan wallowed in Katie's throat as she stood on its threshold, wishing she were anywhere but here. She smoothed her pleated skirt with sweaty hands while sneaking a nervous glance at the back of her legs to ensure her seams were straight. With a deep draw of air, she hiked her hem to readjust her rolled silk stockings, then allowed the navy material to flounce back to just below her knee. She straightened her shoulders, grateful for the two-inch heels of her new Mary Jane shoes, which helped somewhat in rising to the occasion of working with a pest from her past. She thought of Mr. Luke McGee at the age of fourteen—a little twerp who'd been almost a head shorter than she—and wished the little beggar had never grown an inch. She hiked her chin to summon her confidence. Even so, she'd lay good money on the table that her five foot two could take his six foot three any day of the week. *At least mentally.* Her lips squirmed into a devious smile.

Legal Department. The gold lettering on the bubbled glass door suddenly swam before her, and immediately she wanted to throw up—an effect Cluny McGee obviously had on her. But the die was cast, as her father liked to say, and she supposed there was no turning back now. She sucked in a bolstering swallow of air and put her hand to the knob, holding that very breath until the door squealed open.

She blinked twice, blinded by sunlight streaming in from a wall of imposing windows, each opened wide to the sounds of the city below. Somewhere outside, a jackhammer was grinding, merging with the wailing of a siren and the honk of a horn while an early-morning breeze ushered in the scent of the sea and the distinct smell of asphalt. Above it all rose the click-click of typewriter keys and the faint sound of men's voices punctuated by laughter.

The office itself, although quite large and rectangular, had a decidedly cozy feel, and Katie couldn't figure out why. Other than a few spindly potted plants by the windows and several framed city scenes interspersed on various dingy walls, the room was anything but warm. Certainly the dated gray file cabinets lining one side did nothing to help, nor did the three gargantuan wooden desks arranged in a row. Although a warm oak color, each was badly scarred and littered with papers, lending a disheveled air to the already shabby furnishings. To the far right of the room ran a span of three to four office doors, some closed, some beckoning with beams of hazy sunlight spilling forth, as if the glory of God resided within. Or someone cocky enough to *think* he was God, Katie thought with a shift of her jaw.

"May I help you, miss?"

Katie startled, suddenly aware she was gaping. She stared at the pretty woman who occupied the front desk, then straightened her shoulders and jutted her chin to deflect the heat in her cheeks. "Yes, thank you. My name is Katie O'Connor, your new volunteer for the summer."

The woman nodded and gave her a polite smile, but Katie thought she detected a glint of humor in her hazel eyes. She rose smoothly from her chair and moved effortlessly around the desk, extending a perfectly manicured hand. "Hello, Katie, we've been expecting you. My name is Betty Galetti, and I'm the secretary here."

Katie stared, totally aware that her jaw was sagging, but she was too stunned to care. Her eyes traveled from the top of the woman's shimmering auburn hair down to a sleek, shapely torso that flowed into two perfectly formed legs that went on forever. Katie extended a hand while her head tipped up in awe, feeling for all of her five foot two that she'd been stunted at birth. "Pleased to meet you, Betty," she said with a tone of respect. "And forgive me, please, but . . . would you mind if I asked how tall you are?"

The woman's full scarlet lips widened into a charming smile, despite the meticulous application of lipstick in the narrow Cupid's-bow style. There was no mistaking the twinkle in the hazel eyes now. "Only five foot ten," she said with a bold grin. "But the heels are two and a half inches." She cocked one perfectly shaped leg back, revealing a butter-cream pump with a high heel and a curved pointed toe, a near-perfect match for her pretty cream shift. She leaned close to Katie with a conspiratorial smile, then lowered her voice to a whisper. "Call me crazy, but I think the height helps when Luke—" a mischievous smile tugged at the corners of her full mouth—"I mean *Mr. McGee* . . . gets a mind to bully us around."

Katie awarded Betty with a genuine flash of teeth, almost giddy at the thought of moral support in her war against Luke McGee. "Trust me, if he's as cocky as he was at the age of fourteen when he barely came to my knees, I can't imagine what he must be like now. But so help me, I think I'm about to find out."

"No question about that," Betty said with a throaty laugh. "Come on, I'll show you where you're going to sit."

She led Katie to the third desk at the back of the room, right in front of a second-story window where she could see and feel the frenetic pace of the city below—clanging trolleys, darting autos, and an endless scurry of people and things. The energy of Boston, which, like the heat of the summer, seemed to ripple skyward in waves of exhilaration that triggered Katie's pulse. She closed her eyes and breathed in the promise of adventure and independence that came with a career in the city. She felt the coziness she'd sensed earlier slowly seep into her bones. *Mmm . . . maybe this will be fun after all*, she thought with relief.

"Good, you're finally here."

Katie's eyes opened a fraction, causing the contentment to sour on her lips. *Then again, maybe not*.

Luke glanced at his watch and forced a polite smile. "Good morning, Miss O'Connor, welcome to the Boston Children's Aid Society—we're glad you're here." He nodded toward a wooden time clock on the wall where the timepiece registered 9:10. His tone, as crisp and professional as the charcoal double-breasted suit he wore, matched the superior lift of his thick blond brows. A faint smile hovered on his lips. "But just for future reference, you may want to note we start work at eight sharp. Miss Galetti here will be happy to show you how to clock in."

His blue eyes lighted on Betty with hypnotic quality. "Betty, once you get her settled in, please bring her into Parker's office—we'll be going over agent applications." He turned to go.

"Uh, excuse me . . . Luke." Katie's tone attempted a show of humility.

The broad back froze before slowly wheeling halfway. The tight line of his chiseled jaw defied the faint smile on his lips. "Yes, Miss O'Connor? Oh, and just for propriety's sake, perhaps you better call me Mr. McGee."

The steel in her chin lifted to meet his. "I was just wondering . . . *Mr. McGee* . . . why do I need to clock in?"

He blinked. "Excuse me?"

Katie placed her purse on the desk and casually clasped her hands to her back, brows arched in innocence. "I mean, if this is volunteer work and I don't get paid, *sir*, why do I need to punch a payroll time card?"

The professional smile eased wide into battle as he turned to face her dead-on, arms casually crossed like an ad from *Vanity Fair*. As usual, those annoying blue eyes seemed to pierce right through her despite a glimmer of a twinkle. "Why, to keep track of your hours, of course, and to maintain both our professionalism *and* your commendable commitment to volunteer. After all, Miss O'Connor, this *is* a workplace."

She ground her jaw, incensed at the heat swarming her cheeks—a condition provoked only by the runt this man used to be. She propped hands on her hips and took a step forward, careful to enunciate each word slowly so it would sink into his hard, hard head. "But, *Mr. McGee* . . . I-don't-get-paid."

His exasperating calm remained intact, along with the patient curve of his lips. "Oh, but you do get paid, Miss O'Connor. I'm quite certain the reward of helping children will be more than payment enough." The smile tugged enough to indicate he was fighting a grin. "That and the promise of law school, *if* you should be fortunate enough to go." He glanced at his watch once again, then dismissed her with a dazzling smile. "Excuse me, but I'm late for a meeting."

For the second time since she arrived, Katie stood gaping, the click of his door a slap in her face. She felt the fire in her cheeks clear up to her eyes. "God, help me . . . I can't do this."

"Oh yes you can, sweetie." Betty placed a tapered hand on Katie's arm and steered her toward the time clock, a hint of soothing in her tone. She leaned close to whisper in her ear. "You just have to learn how to handle him."

Katie peered up, eyes squinted. "What, you have a manual on dealing with morons?"

Betty chuckled and pulled a time card from a slot, then nodded toward the closed door. "Nope, but I have some experience in dealing with *that* one. Here, just write your name on a card every week and punch it in this machine when you come or go." She handed the card to Katie with a secret smile. "Luke and I grew up together, you know, so I had to learn the hard way."

Katie snatched the card with a roll of her eyes. "As if there's an easy way with a clod like him."

The woman's smile shifted to the right. "Nope, nothing's easy with Luke, that's for sure." Her features softened for the briefest of moments as a touch of melancholy shadowed her smile. But then it was gone in a blink of her eyes. "Especially if you fall for him."

Katie froze, her hand glued to the time card she'd inserted halfway. "*Fall* for him?" she uttered in profound disbelief. She turned to stare, her jaw distended for the third time that morning. She snapped it shut, wondering why anything ever shocked her when it came to McGee.

Betty smiled and arched a brow. "Or so I've heard," she said in a smooth tone.

Katie rammed the card all the way in and jerked it out quickly, flinging it into an empty slot as if her fingers were on fire. "Well, the saints be praised, there's no danger there."

"The trick is to not let him rile you," Betty continued with a graceful flick of her hair. She moved toward Katie's desk with a mesmerizing sway of her hips. "It's kind of like a shark with the scent of blood in the water." She turned and smiled, trailing ruby-red nails along the back of Katie's chair. "If you let him get under your skin, you're lunch."

A moan erupted from Katie's throat. She plopped against the edge of her desk and folded her arms. "Oh, that's just great. I may as well stop breathing."

Betty's soft giggle floated up as she bent to open a drawer. "In these three drawers, you'll find everything you need for typing, filing, and general appeasement of both Lu—er, Mr. McGee, our assistant director, and Mr. Riley, the director."

"Well, at least he's not the top boss," Katie blurted in relief.

Sympathy radiated from Betty's patient smile. "Sorry. Parker Riley is Luke's best friend from school and a real softie with a heart of gold. Which means he usually lets Luke badger him into having his own way."

Katie groaned and put her face in her hands. "Maybe law school is not such a good idea."

"Oh, that's right. Mr. McGee mentioned you hoped to attend Portia Law School in the fall. How exciting!"

"Not if my father refuses to pay for it. Which, if he gets his way—" Katie jerked a thumb toward the closed door—"may just happen." She squinted up at Betty. "Do we really have to call him Mr. McGee?"

Betty blew on the keys of Katie's battered typewriter, and dust flew up in a cloud. She scrunched her nose. "Just for a while . . . at least till he loosens up. But believe it or not, he's just as nervous as you."

"He is?" Katie tried out the chair with a spin, then put her purse in the drawer. She peered up after opening and closing the drawers, making a mental list of questions to ask and things she needed to do. Her inner smile was devious. *Like annoy Luke McGee.*

"Yep. He says you're a handful."

"Humph . . . that's the pot calling the kettle black."

Betty grinned and reached for some papers off another desk and tossed them on Katie's. "Uh-huh, which is why I'm glad you're here. Bobbie Sue and I think this will be fun to watch. Come on, I'll teach you how to fill out these forms in a minute. But first, I need to show you something."

"Sure. Who's Bobbie Sue?"

Betty casually strolled the length of the room to the far front corner, motioning for Katie to follow. "Bobbie Sue Dulay. You might say she's our Southern contingent at the BCAS and a real ray of Georgia sunshine. She's kind of like a permanent paid volunteer who does whatever we need—typing, filing, babysitting."

"Babysitting?" Katie's incredulous tone took a turn toward sweet. "Oh . . . you mean for Mr. McGee."

Betty turned around with a chuckle and folded her arms.

"Oh my, Bobbie Sue's just gonna love you. No, she provides foster care when we need it. Has eight children living with her right now. That is, until we can place them in permanent homes. They're all in school, of course, which is why she's able to help us out during the day. Right now she's over at the BSCG, the Boston Society for the Care of Girls, which is an affiliation of the BCAS. Bobbie Sue fills in over there whenever Miss Lillian needs her."

"Miss Lillian?"

"The director for the BSCG. She's a little thing and every bit of seventy-five years old, but she's a real pistol who runs the orphanage as efficiently as a small army. She's worked at the BSCG for years, as far back as when it was called the Boston Female Asylum. Back then, it only took in orphaned and disadvantaged girls ages three through twelve. Now it takes in young women up to eighteen, providing schooling and skills they'll need on their own."

"Oh, that's wonderful!" Katie breathed. A surge of pride filled her chest that she would be working for an organization that bettered the lives of women. Her heart started to race. Maybe . . . just maybe . . . working at the BCAS would be a good thing after all.

"Bobbie Sue's over there today, filling in for one of the cooks who took sick."

A frown creased Katie's brow. "Goodness, not from the food, I hope?"

Betty grinned. "No, all of our cooks are great and pretty good at serving up just what our kids need." She stepped aside and waved her hand at the table behind her, which sported a brand-new dripolater coffeepot and several stacks of cups and saucers. Suddenly, in a flutter of sooty lashes, the sympathetic smile was back. "And speaking of 'serving,' your first task of the day will be to make coffee and take it in to Mr. McGee." Her lips twitched enough for Katie to notice. "He says it's to be your job while you're here."

Irritation bubbled inside of Katie's stomach like a pot of

vinegar about to boil over. "He wants me to make coffee *and* serve it to him?" she rasped, feeling the acrid steam in her eyes.

Betty chuckled and reached for the pot, then gave Katie a gentle pat. "Oh, you can do it, Katie," she whispered. She placed the pot in her hand with a wink. "Just think of it as poison."

"So, we're going with the retired pastor and his wife?" Parker glanced up from the application in hand, eyes pensive in thought. "Even though they're in their sixties and not the best subjects to travel?"

Luke paused for several seconds to rest his chin on his fist. He finally released a weary sigh and sat back, massaging the bridge of his nose. "Yeah, I think so, don't you? The younger couple could withstand the rigors of train travel with children far better, but their references are pretty scarce. I'm not sure we should take a chance. And the single man is out—he's not even from around here, so we have no idea of his history."

"So the Tuttles it is. I just wish we had a better selection of applicants," Parker said, staring aimlessly out the window.

Luke sighed. "Yeah, well, the pay is not exactly an incentive to beat down our door."

"No, I suppose not."

"Anyway, at least this is one of the last times we'll have to do this. In a few more months, no more orphan trains, no more traveling agents." Luke chucked the last application onto Parker's desk. He sank back in his gray padded chair and ran a thick finger along the inside of his collar, already feeling the heat of the day. Sweet saints, he'd give anything to loosen this tie and rip off this coat, which at the moment was only a few degrees shy of frying him to death. He glanced at Parker and frowned, envious of his rolled-up shirtsleeves and jacket draped over his chair.

Luke closed his eyes, hands braced to the back of his neck. "Where in the blazes is Betty?" he groused. "She was supposed to send in coffee a half hour ago."

"Since when does Betty 'send in' coffee?"

Luke's eyes remained closed. "Since the volunteer arrived."

The squeal of Parker's chair indicated he was getting comfortable, probably with feet propped up on the desk. "I see. And I suppose that's the reason for the brand-new jacket and tie? Which, I might add, won't seem so brand new after wearing it all day in this heat."

Luke cocked one eye half open. "What's your point?"

"Oh, I don't know. That maybe you're taking this volunteer thing a little too seriously . . . maybe even a bit opportunistically?"

Luke blew out a tight-lipped sigh. "I'm just trying to be professional. Is that a crime?"

"No, no, not a crime. But as both you and I learned in Old Man Flannery's criminal justice class, motivation is everything."

His eyelids lifted to assess the seriousness of Parker's manner. "Meaning?"

"Meaning that I'm just a tad curious—and maybe even a little concerned—about your motivation. You generally shed a suit coat and tie within minutes of crossing that threshold, and you wouldn't even wear one if you weren't worried about Harris Stowe waltzing in any minute, unannounced. And a volunteer bringing you coffee? Bobbie Sue would have you drawn and quartered if you pulled that on her. So, what gives?"

Luke exhaled loudly and sat up, arms flat on the chair and hands gripped on the edge. "Nothing gives. I just think we have a responsibility to be professional here. You know, make a good impression."

Easing his head back on his chair, Parker assessed him through dubious eyes. "You've never been concerned about making an impression in your life, McGee. You wouldn't even own a suit if I hadn't insisted on you taking my old ones for this job." He paused, studying Luke with a degree of fascination. "It's this new volunteer, isn't it? You're shining up your image for her, changing who you are to impress her, aren't you?"

A scowl tainted Luke's lips. He slashed his hand through his hair, wreaking havoc with the Brilliantine. "You're out of your mind, Riley. I'm not changing who I am for anybody, especially some spoiled rich kid with her nose in the air."

"Oh, really? And how much did that suit set you back, Luke?"

Luke bolted up from the chair, the heat from the blasted suit bleeding into his face. "You looking for a fight, Riley? 'Cause if you are, just give me the word."

"Well, that would be one way to get you to take the stupid coat off, I suppose."

Luke ripped it off and tossed it over the back of the chair. "There, does that make you happy? All comfy-cozy now?"

Parker scrunched his face and scratched the back of his neck. "Not really. As long as I've known you, you've always thumbed your nose in high society's face. For pity's sake, I practically had to put a gun to your head to get you to wear a tie to your first interview. Now you're not only trussed up with one that looks like it costs a week's salary, but it's choking you to boot. That's not like you and you know it. I want to know—what's going on?"

Luke glared at his best friend and felt his eyes burning all the way to the back of his head. His sarcastic comeback got as far as his teeth when the truth of Parker's words struck like a blow to the gut. With a faint groan, he doubled over and exhaled, finally sagging into the chair with a hand to his eyes. "Is it that obvious?"

There was a hint of a smile in Parker's gentle tone. "Well, not to someone who doesn't know you, but to Betty and me? Uh, we're thinking that maybe you hit your head on the tub."

A chuckle erupted from Luke's throat. He cuffed the back of his neck, hoping to deflect the embarrassment he felt. "Yeah, well, it must have knocked me out cold, I guess, because sweet mother of Job, I didn't know I was such an idiot."

"Sometimes. But mostly you're a great lawyer with a big heart who cares more about the kids on the street than the money in your pocket or the suit on your back. Which brings me to my original question—what gives?"

Luke mauled his face with his hands, then dropped them flat on the arms of the chair. He looked Parker straight in the eyes. "I don't know, Parker. Blame it on Katie O'Connor, I guess, dredging up memories from my past."

"What kind of memories?" Parker shifted to get comfortable, eyes sharp with concern.

Luke jumped up and moved to the window. He shoved his hands deep in his pockets. "Painful ones, I'm afraid. You see, I met her and her family at a vulnerable time. My mother had just run off with another worthless boyfriend, which in the end was a good thing because that meant I'd have less bruises at night. And my gram, well, she raised me pretty much out of duty only, when she wasn't traipsin' off to her sister's in Arkansas. That's when Brady—Katie's brother-in-law—took me under his wing. That man taught me what it felt like to be loved, respected." Luke stared out the window, grateful Parker couldn't see the moisture in his eyes. He blinked to sidetrack his tears with a bitter laugh. "And believe me, I didn't get a lot of respect back then. I was fourteen going on fifteen but looked all of ten. And on the streets of the Southie neighborhood, poor, spindly, snot-nosed kids didn't fare all that well . . ." His jaw tightened. "At least not if your mother was a whore. Which meant," he said with a definite edge in his tone, "that I was a bastard, an outcast, somebody to be trampled underfoot . . . lower than street trash." He closed his eyes, remembering Katie's words on the porch swing that day.

"And why would anyone like a street rat like you?"

"What d'ya call me, O'Connor?" he'd asked, shock leeching the blood from his face.

Her blue eyes had been as hard as he'd ever seen, fury glinting in their watery depths. "Street rat!" she screamed again, bolting to her feet with hurt in her face. "Nobody would ever like a street rat like you."

He blinked in shock. What had he done? All he'd said was that Esther Mullen had a crush on him and he thought she was pretty.

Katie shoved him hard. "Go on, get out of here and leave me alone. I don't want trash like you for a friend."

Trash. The violence of that one word had split his heart wide open. With a rage he hadn't known he possessed, he'd bludgeoned her with the only weapon he had. "Yeah? Well, I don't want a leper for a friend, either. You're not just ugly, Katie O'Connor, you're a deformed freak of nature." Her face had been a mask that said she didn't care, but the pain in her eyes had made him sick to his stomach. And then she had hauled off and whopped him so hard, he could still hear his ears ring.

Luke turned and gave Parker a melancholy smile. "Trust me, nobody had a truer talent for trampling than Katie O'Connor. As warm and inclusive as Brady and the O'Connors were, Katie was as condescending and obnoxious." Luke sighed. "Unfortunately, I liked the little brat, and I'm not sure why. I never met a ten-year-old with a sharper tongue. But I'll tell you—from that perky little nose stuck in the air to the constant roll of those blue, blue eyes—what can I say? I was a mass of raging hormones in an underdeveloped body. I was fascinated by her, wanted to best her, wanted to prove I was somebody she could respect."

"We're talking about a ten-year-old here, Luke. She's a woman now. Don't you think it's time to cut her some slack?"

Luke grinned and strolled back to his chair, opting to follow Parker's lead and prop his feet on the desk. "She may look like a woman on the outside, Parker, but trust me—inside she's still that sharp little thorn in my side, telling me I'll never be more than dirt beneath her dainty, upper-crust feet. If you could have seen the contempt on her face when she thought I was a soda jerk the night I filled in for Betty, you'd understand. Now that she knows who I am—the riffraff from her past—I just think it's best to nip it in the bud. Besides, that's the whole reason she's here in the first place—as a punishment meted out by her father to teach the little brat some humility." Luke loosened his tie and rolled up his sleeves, flashing another gleam of teeth. "And who better to teach her than me—the bane of her existence?"

Parker studied him for a moment with brows furrowed in thought. "So, why not best her again? Teach her what kind of man you've become—treat her with respect."

The grin on Luke's lips faded to a scowl. "I'll treat her with respect when she earns it."

Parker nodded and folded his hands on his chest. "Oh, I see. You mean like the ten-year-old did with you?"

Luke's eyes narrowed. "What'd you have for breakfast? It's giving me indigestion." He plucked a half-eaten roll of Life Savers out of his pocket and pelted one to the back of his throat before offering one to Parker.

Parker shook his head, a faint smile curving the edges of his mouth. "Yeah, well, trust me, it's not as bad as the nausea you get when your best friend loses sight of what's important for childish revenge."

"Why are you gunning for me this morning, Riley?"

Parker exhaled a noisy sigh. "Because I hate to pull rank on you, Luke, but if you continue with this vendetta against that poor volunteer—"

Luke shot to his feet. "*Poor* volunteer? She's the spoiled daughter of one of the top newspaper editors on the Eastern seaboard. The woman probably spends her days painting her nails and her nights painting the town."

"You know what I mean. No matter who she is or what

she's done in the past, the woman doesn't deserve the grief you're planning to give. You're a professional and an extension of the BCAS, for pity's sake. And most importantly, you're my best friend and a man I respect and admire. Who," he emphasized with a lift of his brows, "committed his life to God, as I recall."

Parker's words sucked the venom right out of Luke's well-planned revenge. He thought of the promise he'd made to Brady, both as a kid and then a few years back, when his life had been on the skids in New York. Brady had bailed him out both times—first with a place to live at the age of fourteen when his gram left, and then with college and law school when Luke's future had been nothing but bleak. Thanks to Brady's support and prayers, Luke had walked away from the street gang that had been his life, determined to make a difference and do the right thing—for himself, for Brady, and for God. He dropped in the chair, suddenly depleted. "You should've been a criminal lawyer, you know that? You really know how to nail a guy to the wall."

"Naw, I can only do it when I really care about something—like a friend who's more of a brother. Otherwise I'm a marshmallow, and you know it."

Luke sucked in a deep breath and slowly released it. "Thanks, Parker. I guess I got a little off-track this time."

"Well, you usually right yourself fairly quickly, Luke, but since the BCAS is involved, I figured I'd exercise some of the authority I so seldom get to use."

Luke smiled. "You use it more than you know, and I'm glad. As Brady is fond of saying, I need to be reined in every now and then. Although once you meet our new volunteer, you're going to have a whole new appreciation for my talent to be civil."

"She can't be that bad, McGee. I haven't seen a woman yet you couldn't turn around."

"Yeah? Well, you're about to see your first."

Parker chuckled. "Good, I'm looking forward to it. And by

the way, have you had a chance to go over the new histories that came in last week?" Deep ridges dug into Parker's brow, suddenly altering his good mood. "Bobbie Sue knows one of the kids, apparently. Says he's been living in an alleyway on Pernod since his grandma died of pneumonia last month."

Luke felt his stomach constrict, and his expression sobered along with Parker's. "God, please . . . don't let this be another one on his way to Deer Island."

"No, Bobbie Sue says this one's not ready for the juvenile reformatory just yet—he's a good kid, apparently."

"Yeah," Luke said with a twist of his lips. "They all are until they live on the streets awhile, then it's all downhill."

Concern shaded Parker's features. "Look, maybe I need to be the one at municipal criminal court every morning instead of you, Luke. I think serving as a bondsman for juveniles placed on probation is starting to wear on you. Like maybe it's too personal, you know?"

"No, I'll be fine, Parker, but it never ends, does it?" He sighed and put a hand to his eyes. "Sorry, but I've been too wrapped up processing adoption papers the last few days to go over the histories you asked about, but I will today, I promise. That is," he said as he lumbered to his feet, "once I pump some hot, strong coffee into these veins."

Parker arched a brow and angled his chin, engaging some of the authority he so rarely enjoyed. "Which, as usual, you'll get for yourself, right?"

Luke grinned. "If you were any kind of friend, you'd let her serve me just once . . ."

"Nope, I'm afraid you'd like it too much, and then it'd become a hab—"

"Excuse me, Mr. McGee? I knocked, but I guess you didn't hear me. I have your coffee, sir." Katie poked her head in the door.

Both men jumped to their feet. Parker hurried to take the tray and carefully set it on his desk. He extended his hand. "Welcome to the BCAS, Katie. We're glad to have you aboard.

I'm the director, Parker Riley, and I understand you already know my assistant, Luke McGee."

Katie rewarded Parker with a warm smile and a handshake before giving Luke the perfunctory nod. "Yes, Mr. Riley, Mr. McGee and I are old acquaintances."

"Please call me Parker, Katie. We don't stand on formality here. And as far as getting us coffee, well, Luke and I are pretty used to getting our own."

With a lift of her pencil-thin brows, she gave Luke a pointed look. "Well, then, I'm pleased to be able to serve you at least this once," she said in a sweet tone. With polite efficiency, she handed one of the cups to Parker. "Cream and sugar, I believe?"

"Perfect, Katie, thank you."

"You're welcome. And here you go . . . *Luke* . . . just as you like it."

Luke reached for the cup, unable to contain a grin. "Thanks, Katie. This is a real treat."

"No problem . . . *sir*. Can I get either of you anything else?"

Luke lifted the cup to his mouth, poised for a jolt of caffeine. "No thanks, this is just perfect . . ." A spray of coffee spewed from his mouth. "Sweet mother of Job, what is this?" he croaked.

Katie turned with surprise on her face. "Why, coffee black, lots of sugar."

With a horrified look, Luke swiped his mouth with a handkerchief and swallowed fiercely to clear the taste from his throat. "I hate sugar in my coffee," he rasped.

"Oh dear," Katie said with a pucker in her brow. "Betty must have said 'hold' on the sugar, and I thought she said 'a whole lot of sugar.' Here, I'll get you another cup."

"No!" Luke fended her off with a hand in the air. "Like Parker said, we usually get our own." His smile was strained. "But, thank you."

She bit her lip and scrunched her nose. "Goodness, I'm

sorry, Mr. McGee, but undoubtedly that might be the safest course of action." She smiled at Parker. "Is your coffee all right, Mr. Riley?"

"Perfect, Katie. And it's Parker, remember?"

"Yes, sir." She reached to gingerly place Luke's cup and saucer back on the tray. Avoiding his gaze, she backed out of the office with tray in hand. "If you'll excuse me, I'll just empty this." She hurried out, leaving them in silence with the click of the door.

Luke leaned back in the chair and folded his arms, eyeing Parker with tight lips and an "I told you so" jag of his brow. "Now you see what I mean?"

Parker took a sip of his coffee while watching him over the rim of his cup. "Come on, Luke. It could have been an honest mistake."

Luke plopped both arms on the desk and gaped, his jaw swagging in disbelief. "Are you kidding? The only thing honest about that woman is her utter disdain for me. And as far as being a mistake?" He stood and snatched his coat from the chair, pinning his friend with a warning gaze. "Gotta feeling, Parker ol' buddy, that her being here is only the first of many."

5

Wonders never ceased—she actually liked it here! The thought sent little ripples of shock skittering through Katie's body as she typed at her desk—just as it had when the realization struck over a month ago after only two days on the job.

She supposed it could be the comfortable friendship she'd forged with both Betty and Bobbie Sue, not to mention various other volunteers who came and went throughout the week. Or maybe it was just the intense satisfaction of helping women in need—from unfortunate young girls at the Boston Society for the Care of Girls, to the pink-cheeked babies at the Massachusetts Infant Asylum. Whatever the reason, just knowing she played a part in lifting them up brought a sheen of pride to her eyes. Not only at the realization she was working on behalf of underprivileged girls at the BCAS, but that someday soon as a lawyer, she'd work on behalf of all women to secure their rights in a generation that was forging ahead.

Katie sighed and reached for her coffee. And, of course, there was Parker Riley. Sweet saints above, what a wonderful man! Hands down one of the nicest human beings Katie had ever met and a director more inclined to serve than be served. For the first time, Katie understood the cozy feeling she'd encountered her first day—a feeling not tied to ambiance or furniture, but to people themselves, a cohesion of personalities that felt so much like family.

The pungent scent of her typewriter ribbon rose to her nostrils, mingling pleasantly with the smells of the city and the aroma of her coffee as she sipped from her cup. She set it down and continued to plunk on the keys of her Remington, incredibly grateful—for the very first time—that Sister Mary Clare had been relentless with practices in high school typing class. Katie pushed the return lever with a focused glint in her eyes, rolling her lower lip with her teeth while entering information on the last of the adoption forms. With a sigh of satisfaction, she jerked the paper from the platen and placed it neatly on the pile, all ready for Luke.

Her rose-colored lips squirmed to the right. *Luke.* Or *Mister McGee*, as she insisted on calling him. Mmm . . . another story altogether. Although as much as she hated to admit it, he wasn't as bad as she'd feared. He mostly kept his distance, she noticed, at least when it came to her—polite and professional, just like the first day on the job, only this time without the smirk. Maybe Parker Riley had more clout than Betty knew, Katie thought with a triumphant smile, because something had certainly taken the starch out of Mr. Luke McGee's shorts.

"Now there's a devious smile with a plot in the making, wouldn't you say, Bobbie Sue?"

Katie jolted from her reverie to see Betty grinning at her as if she were privy to her thoughts about a certain someone's undershorts. A blast of heat broiled Katie's cheeks, and as habits were hard to break, she silently blasphemed Luke McGee. Ignoring her obvious discomfort, she pursed her lips and narrowed her eyes, hoping to intimidate the two grinning troublemakers and salvage her pride. Her chin jutted high. "Well, if you two have extra time on your hands to watch a poor, defenseless volunteer, then perhaps, *ladies*, the next pile of adoption forms should be yours."

"Well, butter my biscuits, would you look at that color on our sassy girl's face," Bobbie Sue said, her generous Southern drawl as thick as molasses. "I do declare, it's pert near the batter of my red velvet cake!" Mossy green eyes twinkled with tease in a round face edged with silver waves crowded with freckles despite a heavy dose of powder and rouge. She splayed sausage-like fingers against the ample bodice of her bright green dress and rolled her eyes. "And 'poor'? Honey chile, if I had glad rags like you, I'd mosey myself down to Harper's Beez-Arr and get me a real paying job." Her hearty laughter boomed through the office like a rolling clap of thunder, complemented by the squeaking of her chair as she shook with hilarity.

The sound was nothing but contagious, and when coupled with the sight of the fifty-year-old woman's ample body quivering in the chair like so much lime Jell-O, Katie had no choice. She grinned and aimed a Gem clip at her friend, narrowly missing the side of her short silver bob.

Bobbie Sue hooted and ducked. "And, honey chile, don't get me started on 'defenseless,' cause I shore ain't got all day."

Betty crossed her shapely legs and leaned back in her chair, nibbling on one of the cookies Katie had baked for Bobbie Sue's birthday. She arched a shapely brow with a grin as affectionate as Bobbie Sue's. "She is a little on the feisty side, but she sure can bake. Although she has been somewhat of a disappointment in the cooking department. I thought by now she'd cook up a little trouble to add some spice to our life." She winked at Katie. "And Mr. McGee's."

Another swell of heat invaded Katie's cheeks, and she launched a cocky grin along with a second Gem clip in Betty's direction. "Can I help it if the little twerp has grown up and acquired some manners? If I didn't know better, I'd swear he drank all that sugar I gave him the first day. Something sure has sweetened his meanness."

"Our Luke,'mean'?" Betty chuckled. "Come on, Katie, he's a pussycat once you get to know him, isn't he, Bobbie Sue?"

"Mr. Priss?" With tongue in cheek, Bobbie Sue swiped a clean sheet of paper off her desk and shoved it into her typewriter. "Sure is, unless you're typing his letters or playing Pinochle. I do declare, when it comes to grammar or games—that man is downright diabolical because he sure hates to lose."

Katie lifted the stack of forms from her desk and rose, cradling them to her chest. "Diabolical. Mmm . . . now there's an appropriate word. And speaking of the devil," she said with a smirk, "I have forms to deliver."

"Why don't you deliver another cup of coffee?" Betty suggested sweetly. She tugged a sheet of paper from her typewriter and held out the letter she'd just typed while she patted her mouth in a fake yawn. "I could use a little excitement. Have him sign this, will you?"

Katie snatched the letter from her hand as she breezed by her desk. "Oooo, hot coffee . . . good idea! And if he doesn't drink it, I can always scald his leg."

Bobbie Sue chuckled and proceeded to bang the keys of her typewriter, the tap-tapping as sharp and merciless as a gangster's gunfire. "Bless your pea-pickin' heart, sassy girl, you're almost as nasty as me."

"Not yet," Katie quipped with a firm knock on Luke's door, "but I'm working on it." At the sound of Luke's answer, she shot a sassy smile over her shoulder and entered his domain, leaving the door ajar.

He waved her in as he spoke on the phone, then absently indicated she sit, which she did, but she had the distinct feeling he'd already forgotten she was there. His troubled eyes said he was a million miles away, engaged in a conversation that put a ridge in his brow. The coat was off and the tie was loosened as he sprawled back in his chair, feet on his desk and one hand cocked behind his head. A roll of peppermint Life Savers lay half open on his desk, and she was tempted to take one. Instead, she glanced at his tan, muscled arms beneath shirtsleeves rolled up and bit her lip. Her gaze wandered to the bulge of a bicep beneath his striped cotton shirt, and she felt a blush heat her cheeks. She took a calming breath and looked away.

A heavy sigh erupted from his lips, and the hand propped behind his head suddenly shifted to shield his eyes. "When did you see her last?" he asked.

Katie took advantage of his oblivion to study him—this enigma from her past—something she seldom allowed herself to do. From her memories of the man, he was prone to being cocky and way too sure of himself. There was no way she'd wanted to reinforce that by giving him the time of day. But assessing him now, she was reluctant to admit that the annoying little twit had managed to become a fine-looking man. The loathsome freckles she had once despised were now lost in a summer tan that Betty swore survived nearly all year long. Apparently the grown-up version of Cluny McGee still roamed the streets with the ruffians, spending weekends, nights, and even some lunch hours playing with the kids. Kickball, basketball, football, whatever and whenever—day or night, rain or shine. The man was obsessed with kids and sports, according to Betty, who claimed Luke McGee had a following on the streets that rivaled the Pied Piper.

A groan left his lips, and Katie's attention shifted from the span of long trousers on the desk, to the wide, sensuous mouth pressed tight in a frown. His eyes were closed and brows crimped, as if he were drained by the voice on the other end, and for the first time in her life, a sliver of sympathy eked forth for Luke McGee.

"I'm on my way," he said and then slammed the phone down with a touch of temper. His eyes suddenly registered on her face with a flicker of annoyance. "What do you want, Katie?"

She blinked, her sympathy burning out faster than a quarter-inch fuse. She stood to her feet and tossed the forms and letter on his desk. "Your adoption forms, *sir*, and a letter Betty needs you to sign. You can give it to her yourself." She turned to go.

"Katie, wait."

She paused, still facing the door.

"Can you sit down again—please?" His voice was contrite.

She sucked in a deep breath and returned to her seat, hands folded on her lap and face stiff ahead, refusing to look him in the eyes.

He didn't speak right away, but when he did, it trailed on the heels of a soft chuckle. "You are such a mule, Katie Rose."

Her head snapped up, jaw tight and eyes waging battle.

He gave her a boyish smile. "Look, I'm sorry, okay? About snapping at you, I mean." He reached for Betty's letter and signed it with a flourish before disarming her with a teasing grin. "Not about the mule part, though. We both know it's the truth." He pushed the letter toward her, then began unrolling his sleeves, finally lifting his coat from the back of his chair and putting it on. His eyes suddenly sobered. "I gotta go find a lost kid, but I have more forms, if you don't mind." He retrieved folders from his desk and held them out with a conciliatory smile.

"Sure," she said in a clipped manner. His gentle tone eased some of the tightness in her jaw, but she avoided his eyes nonetheless, snatching the files and heading for the door.

"By the way," he said before she could escape, "everybody agrees—you're doing a wonderful job. I'm sure your father will be glad to hear that."

She stopped, not daring to turn around for the dreaded blush rising in her cheeks. She swallowed hard, her voice strained. "Thank you, Mr. McGee."

"Katie." He spoke it gently, barely above a whisper, and the sound caused her stomach to flutter.

She froze, hand on the knob. "Yes, Mr. McGee?"

"Call me Luke . . . okay?"

She took a deep breath and shot a nervous glance over her shoulder. The look in his eyes made her mouth go dry. "Yes, sir, Luke," she said stupidly, appalled at the rush of warmth whooshing through her body.

His phone rang again, and he turned to answer it. She closed the door and pressed the files to her chest, her heart pounding faster than Bobbie Sue's fingers on her Remington keyboard. Neither woman looked up from their tasks, and Katie had never been happier to be ignored. She was sure her face was on fire and her pride all in flames. And the last thing she needed from either of them was any more heat.

She laid the letter on Betty's desk and hurried back to her own, relieved to have something to occupy her thoughts—to focus on anything other than the roiling confusion in her mind. What in the world just happened? Her stomach was quivering and her pulse was racing, and all because of a compliment from Cluny McGee? Never in all of her life had she believed she'd miss the annoying little beggar—so arrogant, so irritating, and so easy to hate. Sweet saints, where was he now when her knees were knocking and her mind turned to mush? She picked up a file with quivering hands and slammed it back down, palm pressed tight to obliterate the shaking. *No! This can't be happening—I am not attracted to that, that . . . puny little pest!*

The "pest" suddenly strode from his office like a man on a mission, lips clamped tight in a face of chiseled granite. Katie's heart stopped, only to reengage after he barreled into Parker's office and slammed the door. She swallowed hard at the sight of his daunting six-foot-three frame that clearly defied any credence to the term "puny."

Katie blinked and put a hand to her queasy stomach, feeling the need to powder her nose. She yanked her purse from her drawer and told Betty she'd be right back, then bolted from the room. Running down the hall, she knocked on the ladies' restroom and entered, careful to lock the door behind. She sagged against the sink with labored breathing, then finally allowed herself to face the woman in the mirror—the one who had just experienced her worst nightmare.

God, help me . . . I'm attracted to Cluny McGee!

A faint, pitiful groan issued forth as she wavered, still reeling from the shock of the encounter. Dear Lord, how could this have happened? When had prickles of annoyance turned to prickles of heat? Katie put a hand to her stomach and sucked in a deep breath, painfully aware that no man had ever made her feel this way. She thought of Jack with his easy manner and hungry kisses, and knew they'd never made her feel like she did right now. Her knees all but buckled at the thought.

No! Jack was everything she wanted—the culmination of a perfectly planned list and the husband of her dreams—smart, handsome, rich, and politically connected. Together they could climb to social strata she'd only dreamed about, allowing unprecedented advantage in her quest for women's rights. Her resolve tightened, along with her stomach. And no penniless, streetwise lawyer was going to get in her way.

Her lips leveled in defiance. She bent over the sink to wash her hands and scrubbed hard, hoping to sanitize her mind from further thoughts of Luke McGee. It would be easy, she vowed, avoiding him as much as he seemed to avoid her. She could do this—less than two months remained.

She reached for the towel and dried her hands, grateful her pulse was returning to normal once again. The thought suddenly occurred that she hadn't seen Jack in over a month, and a surge of relief washed over her. Of course—that was it! She missed Jack, that's all. Missed his humor, his kisses, his affectionate doting. Her mouth trembled into a shaky smile as she tossed the towel back on the rack. Maybe a midnight rendezvous was in order after all, despite her brother's warning. Her heart began to race. Yes, Jack's heated kisses were just what she needed to clear the fog from her mind. She jerked the door open, quite certain she had a workable plan—

To get back in the arms of the man of her dreams . . . and out of the arms of danger.

Head throbbing, Luke closed his director's door and flopped into a chair.

Parker looked up from his work and glanced at his watch. "Ready?"

"Nope." Luke massaged his temples with the span of his hand. "Sorry, Parker, gotta ditch the meeting. Gabe's on the lam."

Parker sagged back into his chair, disbelief dropping his jaw. "Again? Dear Lord, how can one little girl get in so much trouble?"

Thoughts of Katie O'Connor as a pigtailed brat came to Luke's mind, and he attempted a smile that hurt. "A lot, apparently. Only this time it involves stolen money."

"What?" Parker tossed his pen on the desk in frustration.

"Yep. Mrs. Merkle complained to Harris Stowe who complained to Carmichael, who complained to me, not ten minutes ago. Claims Gabe stole money from Mrs. Merkle's cookie jar and took a hike. They've been looking for her all day with no luck. Carmichael wants me to go smooth things over with Mrs. Merkle and then hunt down the little thief."

Parker pinched the bridge of his nose, looking as if he had suddenly developed a headache of his own. "What are we going to do with her, Luke? The kid's a full-time job." He glanced up, peering between his fingers. "Was Carmichael mad?"

Luke's smile was more of a scowl. "Uh, slightly. Says the next time she pulls a stunt like this, she's on the next train to Podunk." His lips pulled into a dry smile. "Along with me." He sighed and rose to his feet. "Blast it, Parker, why can't families be happily ever after?"

Parker stood, slipped his coat off his chair, and put it on. "I don't know, Luke, but if they were, we'd be out of a job.

Which, come to think of it, would be a pretty good thing. I'd probably be a priest in some cushy confessional, and you'd be only who knows what."

Luke exhaled. "Yeah. You got any aspirin? I feel a killer headache coming on."

Parker bent and pulled a bottle from his drawer. He handed it to Luke, then glanced at his watch. "Gotta go. Carmichael's expecting me at four-thirty. I hate these late meetings—I think he does it just to get on our nerves. I guess he knows you're not coming?"

"Yeah, he knows." Luke emptied two pills in his hand and shot them to the back of his throat. He swallowed like it was candy. "I have a couple of headaches I gotta deal with. First the one in my skull, then the one on the streets."

Parker grimaced. "How do you do that without water, anyway?"

Luke tossed the bottle on the desk and headed for the door. "Practice, Parker," he said with a pained smile over his shoulder. "Compliments of a little girl who thinks she's tougher than me." He opened the door and strode into the main office area with Parker close behind. Betty jumped up to follow, notebook in hand.

Luke stopped dead in his tracks, peering at Betty. "Where are you going?"

She blinked. "To the board meeting upstairs. Carmichael wants me to take notes."

"But I need her here, Parker, in case Gabe shows up. It's just a preliminary meeting, right, so we don't embarrass him in the real thing next week? Why does he need Betty?"

Parker moved on past, beating Luke to the door. "Because he likes to look at her legs, McGee, and we both know it." He looked over his shoulder, hand on the knob and brow cocked high. "You gonna be the one to tell the senior partner and supervisor no?"

Luke mumbled under his breath and glanced at Bobbie Sue with hope in his eyes.

"Oh-oh, Boss, don't look at me." She reached for her purse in the lowest drawer and then lumbered to her feet, slamming it closed again with the toe of her shoe. "I'm already late, and there's no tellin' what shape that poor ol' house of mine'll be in." She tucked her purse under her arm and sidled past Luke with a sheepish grin. "Sorry, but my darlin's are bakin' me a cake tonight, and I sure ain't lookin' to have my kitchen burn down. See y'all Monday, ya hear?"

"Make 'em do the dishes," Parker called, watching Bobbie Sue hurry down the hall.

With a faint smile on her lips, Betty gracefully scooted around Luke, allowing a sympathetic pat on his shoulder as she passed. "Don't worry, Luke. Katie will be here till five, and then I'll be back as soon as the meeting ends, okay?"

"I can stay till Betty returns," Katie offered from the back of the office.

Relief eased the stress in Luke's face. He turned to give Katie a near-painless grin. "Bless you, Katie, you're an angel. You sure you don't mind?"

Katie's mouth quirked into a smile. "Goodness, that may well be the first time I've ever been called that, but yes, I can stay as late as you like. Due to my father's warped sense of discipline, I have no other plans this weekend, if you recall."

He smiled. "Thanks. If these two are still in the meeting, then I should be back no later than six. And if a bossy, obnoxious runaway shows up and tries to push you around, hogtie her in a chair and gag her if you have to, but don't let her go, okay?"

Katie slanted a sheet of paper into her typewriter and gave the platen a spin. "You bet. Thanks to you, I have a wealth of experience in dealing with both bossy and obnoxious, not to mention enough adoption forms to keep me busy until the middle of next week . . . *sir*."

A second grin surfaced on Luke's lips in spite of the nagging headache. "Glad I could be of service, Miss O'Connor. Her name is Gabriella Dawn Smith, but she goes by Gabe—don't let her buffalo you." He turned and pinched Betty on the cheek with a wink, then followed them both out the door. He gave Betty a hard stare. "And you—don't sit on Carmichael's side of the table, you hear?"

Katie smiled and released a pent-up breath as soon as she heard the door click. She spun her chair around to peek out the window, scooting back a smidge when Luke appeared on the street below. The heat of the day obviously was taking its toll despite his best intentions, because she saw him shed the jacket and sling it over his shoulder before rolling up his sleeves. He rounded the corner, and Katie slouched back in her chair with a frown. He really was a decent sort, she supposed, but it galled her all the same. It just wasn't fair that such a little weasel had become such an annoyingly handsome man.

With an abrupt shove against the windowsill, she spun around and adjusted the form in her typewriter before opening the first file at her side. She squinted to make out the scrawl of Luke's notes, then poised her fingers over the keys, suddenly seeing his face in her mind's eye. She took a deep breath. She could handle this. It was just a bothersome complication and nothing more. One that required a little more finesse on her part, to be sure, but not impossible. She would simply keep her distance and rein in these irksome feelings at the same time. She sharpened her focus and began to type, forcing her mind to dwell only on the facts she needed to record.

An hour later, she was halfway through the stack and totally absorbed when she heard a quiet squeak at the door. Out of the corner of her eye, she saw a blur of navy blue shoot into Luke's office. Katie caught her breath and slowly rose to make her way to his door, careful to close it again after she stepped inside. She scanned the crowded office, past the antiquated file cabinets hugging the wall and over to the other side of the room where a coat rack loomed, bedecked by some battered-looking boxing gloves. Next to it stood a table stacked high with boxes above and below, some filled with files, others bulging with footballs, basketballs, baseballs, gloves, and bats. Her gaze returned to the large oak desk in front of the windows, its heavy wooden base the perfect place for an orphan to hide. Katie strolled over to Luke's chair and settled in, crossing her legs and folding her arms. She fought a smile and peered under the desk, suddenly eye-to-eye with a grimy ragamuffin all balled up in a frown.

Katie arched a brow. "Excuse me, but do you have an appointment?"

The frown deepened into a scowl. "Ain't you got nothin' better to do than spy?"

Katie pursed her lips and narrowed her gaze. "Nope, it's what I get paid to do." Her mouth crooked up. "That is, if I get paid."

"I ain't comin' out," the ragamuffin threatened, eyes squinted even harder than Katie's.

"Suit yourself," Katie said with nonchalance. She rose and strode out the door, returning a few moments later with a half-eaten platter of Bobbie Sue's birthday cookies and two coffee cups. She set everything on the desk and selected a nice, fat cookie. With a contented sigh, she leaned back and took a bite, closing her eyes while emitting a soft moan. "Sweet saints in heaven . . . if I say so myself, these are some of the best I've ever made. Just the right touch of vanilla, you know? And chocolate-fudge icing that literally melts on your tongue." She popped the rest of the cookie in her mouth and sucked the chocolate off her finger.

"You tryin' to bribe me, lady?" The tone was hard and brittle, unlike Katie's cookies, which were soft and moist.

With a satisfying swipe of her tongue, Katie licked a touch of frosting from her lips. "Nope, I can see you're quite comfortable under that desk, knees bunched to your chin."

Dark, almond-shaped eyes glared back, half lidded and glinting with ire.

Katie casually reached into the bottom drawer of Luke's

desk and pulled out one of the Nehis he kept in his stash, along with a bottle opener. She popped the lid off, took a long swig, and then wiped her mouth with the side of her hand. "Ah . . . now that hits the spot on a hot day."

Long pause. "Is that grape?"

"Uh-huh. My favorite."

Longer pause. "Luke's too."

Katie cocked her head. "Really? I thought he liked orange." She took another drink.

"Sometimes, but mostly grape. Like me."

Katie's brows inched up in surprise. "No kidding, you too? Grape Nehi has been my favorite since I was knee-high to the nuns, no pun intended. I used to close my eyes and pray that the water fountain at school would be grape Nehi." Katie frowned. "Regrettably, it never was." She put the bottle to her lips, ready for another glug.

"You gonna drink that whole blasted bottle?"

Katie hesitated, the bottle propped against her lower lip. "You shouldn't talk like that."

A thick crop of freckles bunched up in a scowl. "Well, are ya?"

"Maybe. Maybe not. Depends."

"On what?"

"Whether you want to join me, sitting in a chair like a human being."

The brown eyes squinted again. "Is this a trick?"

Katie sat back in the chair and put a hand to her chest, eyebrows dipped in obvious offense. She flattened her lips to ward off a smile. "No, I'd rather be typing forms like I've been doing for the last eight hours, how 'bout you?"

Seconds passed before the ball of limbs and freckles began to move, disentangling beneath the desk in calculated and cautious movement. Katie scooted back and stood while a slip of a little girl unfolded to barely three foot high, revealing spindly legs skinned and scarred. She couldn't be more than five years old, and her patched navy blue jumper was wrinkled and bunched. Katie's heart squeezed at the tight-lipped look of suspicion on her sweet little face, a face that sported traces of soot and more freckles than the law allowed. Tresses of dark brown hair framed her heart-shaped face, both of which were badly in need of a wash.

The little tyke eyed Katie up and down. "You ain't very tall."

Katie squared her shoulders and stood up straight, thinking this was one tough, little orphan for only five years old. She folded her arms, going for intimidation. "I'm taller than you."

The half-pint strolled to the side and studied her, folding her arms like a junior version of Katie. "Not by much. Who the devil are you, anyway?"

"You shouldn't talk like that."

"I can talk any way I want—you ain't my mama. And it's a good thing too, 'cause if you was, I'd be punier than I am."

Katie snatched the plate of cookies from the desk with a lift of her chin. She draped her hand over the back of Luke's chair. "I may not be your mama, young lady, but I am the one holding the cookies, so I suggest you set your little carcass in this chair and watch your tongue."

"You're mean!" the little brat said, lips ground tight.

"So are you," Katie replied, taking a bite of a cookie. "So what's it going to be?" She chewed and the little brat glared, but the moment Katie tipped another swig of Nehi, the battle was won. The ragamuffin plopped in the chair with her nastiest look yet. Katie held out the plate with a smug smile. "Mark my words, Gabriella Smith, these are the best cookies you'll ever eat."

Gabe grunted and filched a big one. "Shore better be, for all the trouble they cost. How'd you know my name, anyway? From Luke?"

"Yep." Katie bent to pull a new Nehi out of Luke's drawer. Her teeth scraped her bottom lip. "Uh-oh, the last grape."

A devious smile sprouted on her lips. "Somebody won't be happy."

Gabe smiled for the very first time. "Luke ain't never happy, least when it comes to me. He thinks I'm a bother."

Katie popped the lid off with the opener. "Well, aren't you?" She poured half of it in a cup and handed it to Gabe with a lift of her brow before taking another sip of her own.

Gabe grabbed it and guzzled, a full-fledged grin on her face as she wiped her mouth with her sleeve. "Yep. Only way I can get him to notice me. We're gonna get married."

Grape Nehi spewed from Katie's mouth, spraying Gabe with a fine mist of pop.

"Lucifer's nightgown!" Gabe croaked, jumping out of the chair. "You just spit all over me."

Katie gaped and snatched the cookie from Gabe's hand. "I don't think I want my cookies going into a trash heap like your mouth, young lady. Apologize!"

Gabe gummed her lips in defiance.

With lightning speed, Katie seized the girl's cup. "No apology, no Nehi, it's that simple."

"You're a bully!" Gabe shouted.

"Takes one to know one," Katie countered with a sneer. They stood nose to nose, locked in silent seething for several seconds until Katie won out. Gabe flopped into the chair, arms crossed and lower lip protruding. "Sorry," she whispered, barely audible.

"I can't hear you . . . ," Katie said in a singsong voice.

"Sorry!" she screamed, wildfire burning in her eyes.

Katie stifled a smile and held out the Nehi and cookie. "Now, one more time, and I'll bind and gag you like Luke suggested."

Gabe glanced up through slitted eyes. "He said that?"

"Yep. Says you're bossy and obnoxious." Katie parked herself on the corner of the desk and upended more Nehi.

Gabe popped the rest of the cookie in her mouth and

snitched another two, a grudging hint of respect in her tone. "Humph. Bet he says the same about you."

"Yes he does, as a matter of fact. So you see, we have a lot in common."

"Why, you wanna marry him too?" Gabe eyed her with suspicion, chewing her cookie.

Katie choked again, but this time she kept the spray to herself. She pressed a hand to her mouth. "Good heavens, no. He's not my type."

That seemed to relax the little spitfire as she sank deeper into the chair. An elfin grin puckered on her little lips. "Well, he sure is mine. I think he's gor-geous."

Katie scrunched her nose and chewed. "You think?"

"Heck yeah, don't you?" The brown eyes suddenly widened with the wonder of a child.

"I suppose," Katie said with a squint. "If you like the tall, arrogant, magnetic type."

"What's mag-net-tick mean?"

Katie jumped up, quite sure her face was flame red from the sudden surge of heat she felt in her cheeks. She pulled a chair around the desk next to Gabe's, hoping the little smart aleck wouldn't notice. "It means to draw people like a magnet."

A surprisingly low chuckle rolled from the little girl's mouth. "Booooy-oh-boy, that's for dead sure. Why, half the ladies at the society are loopy over him and most of us kids too. Not to mention the teachers."

"The society?" Katie nibbled on the edge of her cookie.

"Yeah, the Boston So-ci-e-ty for the Care of Girls. Sounds real snooty, don't it? But it's nothing but an orphanage, although it's better than most. Lots of gals just like me who nobody wants. And I can tell ya right now, that every last one of 'em thinks Luke is the cat's meow." A smug smile tipped Gabe's mouth as she reached for another cookie and shimmied back in her chair. "But he likes me the best, which is why we're gonna get married someday." She paused and wheeled the chair back several inches, wrinkling her nose as she spied Katie's blush. "Hey, you ain't gonna spit again, are ya? Your face is red like you're gonna puke."

Katie narrowed her eyes. The little squirt suddenly reminded her of Cluny McGee. She nursed her pride with a deep breath of air, then exhaled. "So, why'd you run away?"

Gabe gulped her Nehi while eyeing Katie over the rim. "You ever meet Mrs. Merkle?"

Katie shook her head and took a final bite of her cookie.

"Well, she's old and whiney and smells like VapoRub." A faint shiver rippled through the little girl. "I can't stand VapoRub. And the old coot she's married to who coughs up spit? Passes wind like it was a fine talent." She scrunched her nose as if the smell suddenly permeated the room. "You ever live in a crackerbox that reeks with Vapo and gas? Trust me. It ain't a feast for the senses, if you know what I mean."

Katie did, and slowly gulped the last of her cookie, her appetite suddenly gone with the wind. "The Merkles—are they your foster parents?"

"Shoot, no—" Her eyes darted to Katie's face as she slowly scooted away, obviously concerned about her slip of the tongue. "Sorry, I forgot. Anyways, they're too old, but I guess Luke's desperate. Carmichael don't like me, ya see, 'cause I stir up things at the pokey—"

Katie blinked. "The pokey?"

"The so-ci-e-ty," Gabe said with pained enunciation. "Keep up with me, will ya? Anyways, I've been in eight foster homes inside of six months," she said with a gleam of pride in her eyes. "So, it's just a matter of time before I get to live with him."

"With Luke?" Katie latched a hand on Gabe's chair, jerking her close.

"Well, not Luke exactly, at least not right away, me being a girl and him being a boy. But I'm bankin' on living with that tall drink of water he lives with 'cause that way I can stay nice and close until we get married, ya know?"

A squint furrowed Katie's brow. "The tall drink of water?"

"The giant redhead . . . *Gull-let-tee*." The name came out like a sneer. "Shoot, I hate big women, 'specially when they slink around all hotsy-totsy like her. I think Luke used to be sweet on her, you know, back in New York, but now they're just friends." Gabe's skinny legs did a little shuffle as her chair scooted even closer to Katie's. Gossip gleamed bright in her eyes. "Although it don't take a genius to see she wishes it were more."

Feeling very "ungenius" and just a little stupid, Katie bent close, knee to knobby knee. "You mean to tell me that Betty and Luke were—"

The freckles bobbed up and down. "Stuck on each other in a big way, tighter than tar paper."

Katie swallowed hard, for once unconcerned about the heat in her cheeks. She could barely get the next words out. "And now they . . . live together?"

"Yep, all three of 'em—Luke, Parker, and the broad."

The blood drained from Katie's cheeks. "Sweet mother of Job."

Gabe stared, then broke into a grin that curved from ear to ear, obviously thinking Katie was short on brains as well as height. "Not together in the same room, you goose, in the same house, at Mrs. Cox's Boarding House."

"Oh!" The blood returned to her cheeks . . . this time with reinforcements.

"Anyways, whenever I run away, Luke usually lets me stay with Galetti for a night or two 'cause he feels guilty about shipping me back to the pokey." She winked. "But the way I see it, it's just a matter of time before I get to live with her—and Luke—all the time. I turn eight next month, you know, and Luke promised he'd find me a family before then."

It was Katie's turn to stare, her brain desperately trying to process all of this information. She suddenly blinked in shock, hand to her chest. "Eight? You're almost eight?"

The almond eyes thinned considerably, as did the tight press of her rosebud lips. "You ain't no prize in the height department, either, ya know. At least I'll have a chance to grow." A smirk lifted the corners of her mouth. "You're as good as done."

"Ahem."

Both Katie and Gabe jerked in their chairs, wide-eyed as they turned toward the door. Luke stood, arms folded and shoulder cocked against the doorframe, the tight smile on his face anything but friendly as his eyes honed in on Gabe with a menacing glare.

Which had absolutely no effect as Gabe shot to her feet. "Luke!" she cried, bubbly enough to put a Nehi to shame.

"Don't you 'Luke' me, you little troublemaker. I've been searching for you for the last hour." He strolled in with a testy look on his face and tossed his coat on his desk. His eyes took in the two empty bottles of grape Nehi and narrowed considerably. "What's this, a tea party? With *my* Nehis?"

Gabe hiked a thumb in Katie's direction. "It was the runt's idea, not mine," she said with a cherubic smile, distancing herself from Katie several feet. She leaned forward and lowered her voice to a whisper, hand to her mouth. "She tried to bribe me."

Katie folded her arms and gave Gabe the evil eye. "*Runt*? You wolf down three of my cookies and call me a runt?"

Luke strode around the desk, clamped a muscled arm to Gabe's skinny one, and pushed her into the chair with not-so-gentle force. He butted back on the edge of his desk and folded his arms, his eyes as steely as the night at Robinson's. "So help me, Gabe, this has got to stop. You're burning bridges faster than I can put the fires out. Carmichael's gunning to put you on the next train to the Midwest, and I'm not all that sure I won't let him."

For the first time, Katie saw fear in Gabe's eyes, which were glazed with a sudden sheen of tears. She jumped up and thrust herself into Luke's arms with a sob, softening the hard line of his jaw. "Luke, no! Please don't make me leave. I want to live with you, you know that."

Arms stiff at his sides, he seemed paralyzed for several painful seconds and then with a low groan, he swallowed the little girl whole in a ferocious hug. He tucked his head against hers, but not before Katie saw the pain in his eyes. "Gabe, you know you can't live with me—we've been over this again and again. You need a family to love you, a mother and father who will raise you the way you deserve."

Heart-wrenching sobs shook her small frame. The sound was muffled against Luke's chest but still pierced the air . . . *and* Katie's heart. "But I d-don't want a f-family—I love you!"

He pulled away and cradled her little chin in his massive hands. "And I love you too, kiddo, you know that. Which is why I want the best for you—a mother who's there for you day and night to get you through these formative years. Not an unmarried man who's never home."

Her little fists knuckled white as she clutched his wrists with all of her might. "Then l-let me live with G-Galetti, please! At least th-then I c-can be close to you."

He squatted low and put his hands on her shoulders, his voice raspy with regret. "Gabe, you need a mother who's home all the time, to be there for you, to take care of you. Betty works hours as long as mine. Besides, you know as well as I do that Mrs. Cox doesn't allow kids."

Gabe sniffed and jutted her lower lip. "She would if you asked her, the old b-battle-ax."

A hint of a smile pulled at his mouth. He fished a handkerchief from his pocket and pinched it to her nose. "She has two worthless sons that she doesn't trust around kids, so she's only looking out for you." His face softened with concern. "As am I. Blow."

She blew hard and released a quivering sigh. "You sending me back to the Merkles?"

His jaw shifted as he wiped a stray tear from her mottled face. "Nope, that bridge has been effectively burned to the ground, you little squirt."

"Good. They smell."

Luke exhaled a heavy blast of air and stood to his feet. He propped his hands low on his hips and studied her through half-lidded eyes. "Mrs. Merkle said you stole money. Did you?"

The heat of his stare caused her to squirm. She dropped into Luke's chair with a grunt. "Shoot, Luke, it was just a nickel for a hot dog. I gotta eat, don't I?"

"Not if you have to steal. And don't give me the sad act, you little beggar. Mrs. Merkle may smell, but I know good and well she fed you."

Gabe bit her lip and peeked up through soggy lashes. A touch of regret actually shadowed her eyes. "I'm sorry, Luke. I won't do it again, I promise."

He sucked in a deep swallow of air and huffed it out again. A ghost of a smile hovered on his lips. "See to it you don't. I'm doing everything in my power to find you a good home, Gabe, but you're not making this easy." He glanced up at Katie with tired eyes. "Thanks for staying, Katie. I hope this little monkey didn't give you too much trouble."

Katie smiled and tweaked the back of Gabe's neck, prompting a giggle from the little girl's throat. "Nothing a few cookies and Nehis couldn't handle."

"Good." He took Gabe's hand and pulled her to her feet. "Come on, kiddo, I'll take you back."

She jerked free from his grasp with panic in her eyes. "To the Merkles'?"

"Nope. Back to Miss Lillian."

A lump bobbed in her throat. "Luke?"

He paused, giving her a sideways glance. "What?"

Katie's heart pulled in her chest. Gabe seemed so small and forlorn, her tiny hand swallowed in his—a lost little girl with no family of her own.

"Do you think . . . I mean, could I, maybe . . ." Gabe worried her lip, eyes wide with hope.

Luke ran a hand over his face and blew out a sigh, silent for several seconds. His shoulders finally slumped in defeat, but his voice was edged with warning. "All right, okay. But only if Betty will have you, and *only* for tonight." He aimed a threatening finger for obvious effect, the sternness all but compromised by the tenderness in his eyes. "You have to do whatever Betty says without any lip, and if Mrs. Cox so much as hears one peep out of you, I swear I'll drag your little carcass to the BSCG so fast, your head will spin. Understood?"

She squealed and clutched him about the waist. "And can we play Pinochle too? Please?"

His lips curved into a lopsided smile. "You're lucky I have a weakness for pushy women, little girl, or I'd send your sassy attitude home to Miss Lillian tonight, *without* Pinochle." Luke winked at Katie, which immediately triggered another heat wave in Katie's cheeks.

With a thick swallow of air, Katie hurried toward the door. "Well, have fun, you two. Nice to meet you, Gabe." She screeched to a halt, nearly colliding with Parker and Betty.

"Whoa, what's your rush, Katie?" Parker leaned against the jamb and crossed his arms as he peered in at Luke. "I see you found her. So what's the excuse this time?"

Luke's lips skewed into a wry smile. "Mrs. Merkle smells, apparently."

"Like VapoRub," Gabe said. "And Mr. Merkle—"

"Has an intestinal problem," Katie said in a rush.

"So I can't go back there," Gabe explained.

Betty strolled into the office and dropped several sheets of paper on Luke's desk, then shot a secret smile in Gabe's direction on the way to the door. "Makes perfect sense to me." She glanced at Luke over her shoulder. "By the way, Carmichael had me take notes for you, and there's a couple things he wants first thing Monday morning."

"Sure, thanks. Uh, Bets?" Luke's voice was hesitant.

Betty turned at the door, a single brow cocked in question.

"I was wondering if Gabe could bunk with you tonight.

I sort of promised we'd play Pinochle. That is, if it's okay with you." Luke gave Betty a pitiful smile.

Betty's eyes softened as she studied him, her lips pursed tight in thought. Her gaze shifted from Luke to Gabe, and the softness seemed to harden into a silent threat. "She'll do whatever I ask? Brush her teeth, take a bath, and go to bed when I say, no backtalk?"

Luke gave her a boyish smile. "You're the boss, Bets. If the little baggage doesn't do what you say, I'll cart her back to Miss Lillian tonight, no questions asked."

A reluctant smile softened the lines of her lips. "You're deadly, Luke McGee, you know that? Worse than a thimble-rigger on Ann Street, you are." Her eyes zeroed in on Gabe. "And you—you're as good at conning him as he is at conning me. Come on, you little vagabond."

Gabe reached for Luke's hand. "That's okay, Luke'll bring me."

Luke ruffled the top of her head. "Sorry, Gabe, but you heard Bets—I've got some work to do before I go, so she and Parker will take you home. I'll be along in an hour or so, okay?"

Parker extended a hand. "Come on, kiddo, if you're good, you can look at my comics."

Gabe shuffled toward the door, shooting Luke a pleading look. "Don't take too long, okay?" She glanced at Katie. "Thanks for the cookies and Nehi. You're not so bad for a runt."

Katie grinned. "Thanks, neither are you."

Parker ushered Gabe and Betty from the office while Luke dropped into his chair with a groan. He began to read Betty's notes, apparently oblivious that Katie was still in the room.

She backed out the door, feeling a prick of sympathy at the exhaustion on his face. "Good night, Luke. Don't stay too late," she whispered.

He looked up with a touch of surprise in his eyes. "Sorry,

Katie, I didn't realize you were still here. Thanks for staying—I really appreciate it. Have a good weekend, okay?" He returned to his reading with a hand to his eyes, and somehow she felt lost as she quietly closed his door.

Moving slowly, she made her way to the time clock to punch out and then went to collect her purse from the drawer. Her mood was a little blue, and she wasn't sure why. Outside the window, she spied Betty and Parker holding Gabe's hand and swinging her high every few feet or so. Their laughter floated up, taunting her on a breeze. She sagged against the sill, wishing more than anything she were playing Pinochle tonight. She clutched her purse to her chest, suddenly missing them all.

With acute frustration, she threw back her shoulders and stood up straight, desperate to shake this unsettled feeling. "What's the matter with me?" she muttered under her breath, completely baffled by her melancholy mood. Could it be the weekend, she wondered, the fact that all of her friends would be out while she was confined? And yet, thoughts of Jack and the gang left her surprisingly cold. With a deep sigh, she pressed her forehead to the window screen and closed her eyes, reluctant to leave and go home. And then it came to her, as light and firm as the screen against her skin. She was lonely, she suddenly realized. Lonely for the closeness that Betty and Parker and Luke all shared, lonely for their friendship, for the sense of family they created . . . lonely for . . . *Luke*?

She sucked in a harsh breath, the thought seizing her with a cold wave of fear. *No!* She listed against the windowsill, her mind glazed with shock. *Not him, please, no* . . . It was just attraction and nothing more.

Isn't it?

She closed her eyes and put her face in her hand, seeing beyond the handsome face and heart-melting grin. In one short month, the bane of her past had become the haunt of her present, drawing her to him like he drew everyone else. A magnet of a man who was warm and kind and giving . . . and, she swallowed hard . . . *incredibly poor*.

Her purse slipped to the floor, but Katie could only stand with her hand to her mouth while panic struck deep in the pit of her stomach. She bit her lip hard. She would not do this, she vowed. She would *not* fall in love with a man who was not part of her plan. She needed Jack—a man with ambition and political connections, someone who not only supported her dream of championing women's causes, but whose wealth and family could help her achieve it. She put a shaky hand to her eyes and expelled a jagged breath, quite certain that would never be Luke—a man shackled to the streets and content to stay there.

"Katie, are you okay?" Luke loosened his tie and stared, concern creasing his brow as he watched her, her body slumped at the window with a hand to her eyes. She didn't move, and the tightness in his gut increased. He approached quietly, afraid he would startle her. "Katie?"

"Oh!" She whirled around, staggering against the sill with a hand to her chest.

He clutched her arm to steady her, and the color drained from her cheeks. Softening his hold, he absently grazed her skin with his thumb, then ducked his head and smiled, eyes tender as he studied her. "Sorry, I didn't mean to frighten you. Are you all right?"

She nodded stiffly, her gaze glued to the massive hand on her arm.

Worry wrinkled the bridge of his nose and he braced both palms on her shoulders, convinced something was wrong. Her face was white and her breathing labored, and he could swear he felt a hint of a tremble. "No, I can feel it. Something's bothering you." He pressed his hand to her forehead. "Are you sick?"

She jerked back from his hold and butted up against the window, arms crossed and hugging her waist. "No!" she said too quickly to suit him, clearly avoiding his eyes. "I mean maybe a little dizzy, but nothing serious. I just need to go home . . ."

He shifted, suddenly concerned it had to do with him. He plunged his hands in his pockets and softened his tone. "Katie . . . is it me? Did I say or do something to upset you?"

She shook her head, gaze bonded to the floor. "No, Luke, really, please, I just need to—"

He nudged her chin up with his thumb, and her lips parted with a sharp intake of breath. And then he saw it. The gentle rise and fall of her chest, the soft rose in her cheeks, the skittish look in her eyes, flitting to his lips and then quickly away. Comprehension suddenly oozed through him like heated honey purling through his veins. Could it be? Was it possible that cold, callous Katie O'Connor was beginning to warm up? To him, of all people—Cluny McGee, the pest from her past? The thought sent warm ripples of shock through his body, thinning the air in his lungs. His gaze gentled, taking in the vulnerability in her eyes, the fear in her face, and all he wanted to do was hold her, reassure her.

As if under a spell, his gaze was drawn to her lips, parted and full, and the sound of her shallow breathing filled him with a fierce longing. "Oh, Katie," he whispered, no power over the pull he was suddenly feeling. In slow motion, he bent toward her, closing his eyes to caress her mouth with his own. A weak gasp escaped her as she stiffened, but he couldn't relent. The taste of her lips was far more than he bargained for, and he drew her close with a raspy groan. With a fierce hold, he cupped the back of her neck and kissed her deeply, gently, possessive in his touch. His fingers twined in her hair, desperate to explore.

And then all at once, beyond all understanding, her body melded to his with an answering groan, and he was shocked when her mouth rivaled his with equal demand. Desire licked through him, searing his body and then his conscience. With a heated shudder, he gripped her arms and pushed her back, his breathing ragged as he held her at bay.

"We can't do this," he whispered. He dropped his hold and exhaled, gouging shaky fingers through disheveled hair.

His gaze returned, capturing hers and riddled with regret. "Believe me, Katie, as much as I want to, I've learned the hard way to take things slow. I should have never started this, and I'm sorry. Will you forgive me?"

Forgive him? She stared at him through glazed eyes, her pulse still pumping in her veins at a ridiculous rate. She never wanted this, couldn't stand the sight of him, and now here she was, tingling from his touch and desperate for more. Addicted to the "King of Misery." The very thought inflamed both fury and desire at the same time, muddling her mind. She was torn between welding her lips to his or slapping him silly. With a tight press of her mouth, she opted for the second and smacked him clean across the face.

His jaw dropped a full inch, complemented nicely by a slash of red across his cheek.

Her chest was heaving, but at least it wasn't from his touch. She narrowed her eyes and clutched her fists at her side, not all that sure she wouldn't slap him again. "So help me, if you ever touch me again, you will be the sorriest person alive."

He slowly rubbed his cheek with the side of his hand, exercising his jaw as if to make sure it still worked. His eyes glinted like blue glass, sharp and deadly. Even so, the swaggering smile of old eased across his face. He bent forward, his tall frame looming over her like a bad omen, and his voice held that cocky drawl so reminiscent of his past. "What's the matter, Katie Rose," he whispered, "does my *touch* make you nervous?"

The heat in her cheeks went straight to her temper. She iced him with a cool gaze. "Nervous? Around you? Hardly. You can dress up in a suit all you like, Luke McGee, but to me you'll always be the same cocky street brat with a twang in your voice and grime on your face."

She knew her words hit their mark when a red blotch crawled up the back of his neck like a rash gone awry. A nerve pulsed in his temple, but his smile never wavered despite the steel edge of his jaw. One blond brow jagged high in challenge. "Is that a fact? Well then, how about a little experiment? Kind of like when you were eleven and I bet you couldn't be nice?" He leaned close, his voice as hard as his eyes. "What d'ya bet I can make you nervous now?"

She tried to shove him out of the way. "I'm going home."

"Not yet," he whispered, blocking her in with a push to the wall. His voice, like the dominance of his hold, was a force to be reckoned with. "You always packed a wallop for a little girl, *Katydid*, but this time you picked the wrong street brat. You can turn your nose up at me all you want, but we both know that slap wasn't so much about an innocent kiss . . ." He bent close, his eyes on fire and the scent of peppermint hot against her face. "As how it made you feel."

His words seemed to vibrate through her, low and thick in the air. She shuddered, and the force of his savage look trapped all protest in her throat.

"To you I'll always be riffraff, something vulgar and crude. Well, welcome to my world, *Miss* O'Connor. And, please, let me show you how we do it on the 'streets.' Because if I'm going to take a beating, you can bet your bottom dollar on two things for sure. One—I'm going to get my money's worth." A dangerous smile surfaced as his gaze focused on her lips. "And two . . ." His mouth hovered just above hers while his voice trailed to a whisper. "I'm gonna make you *real* nervous in the process."

In a catch of her breath, he took her mouth by force, his late-day beard rough against her skin. A faint moan escaped her lips and all resistance fled, burned away by the heat of his touch, leaving her weak and wanting. His mouth roamed at will, no longer gentle as he devoured her, ravenous against the smooth curve of her throat, the soft flesh of her ear. With a guttural groan, he jerked her close with powerful arms, consuming her mouth with a kiss surely driven by the sheer will to ravage.

And then in a frantic beat of her heart, he shoved her away.

She gasped, numb as she thudded against the wall. His chest was heaving and his eyes were hard, focused on her with cool disregard. "There. Now that makes two of the sorriest people alive." He grabbed her purse from the floor and threw it on her desk, then rubbed his mouth with the side of his hand. "Better run home, *Katydid*. Heaven knows the riffraff that roam the street this time of night."

He turned and walked into his office, slamming the door hard.

She stared, her body still quivering from his rage. Closing her eyes, she sagged against the wall, too stunned to move and too shaken to care. She pressed a trembling hand to her mouth, her lips swollen from the taste of him. She was doomed, she realized, and the thought shivered through her like a cold chill. She wanted a man she didn't really want, and the very notion weakened her at the knees. He had called her one of the sorriest people alive. She grappled for her purse and put a hand to her eyes.

And God help her, she was.

6

Luke closed the heavy oak door of his second-story bedroom at Mrs. Cox's Boarding House and sagged against it, wishing he could sleep for days. Bone-tired, mind-numbing sleep, enough to take him far away from the painful realization that he had just made a royal fool of himself tonight—with a girl who had always branded him as such.

He kneaded the pad of his thumb against his temple, desperate to alleviate the headache that had been throbbing all night—the one that reached its peak earlier in the evening when he'd slammed the door on Katie. Starting at the age of ten, she apparently had a knack for giving him headaches, when she'd mocked him about his small size, his shabby clothes, and the Arkansas twang in his speech—anything to remind him he was little more than dirt beneath her feet.

His jaw hardened. But dirt beneath her feet or no, that hadn't stopped her body from responding to his, not that she would ever admit it. She may not be attracted to him as a person, but as a man, the passion in her kiss told him all he needed to know. The memory suddenly surged through him like the sticky June heat outside his window, stifling his air. A silent curse hissed from his lips as he hurled his suit jacket across the room. Either way, she had made a fool of him. *Again.*

He plopped on the bed and took off his shoes, throwing them against the wall one at a time to vent his anger. The sound ricocheted in the cozy room he called home. He fumbled with the top two buttons of his shirt and then impatiently jerked it over his head. With a tight grimace, he aimed it at his shoes in a well-crumpled ball. The effect of clothes strewn wildly across his orderly room seemed to appease him somewhat, giving outlet to the acute frustration bottled inside. He typically took great pains to keep his room tidy—bed made, clothes neatly hung up—keenly aware that this humble abode was more of a home than those in his past. Mrs. Cox's Boarding House was far from luxurious, but the worn look of the spacious room was comfortable enough. The single bed with its faded quilt suited him just fine, as did the grey, striped wallpaper adorned with various oil paintings, each painted by Mrs. Cox herself. A tall, oak wardrobe had seen better days, as had the cherry-wood desk in front of the chintz-curtained window, but to him this room was an oasis, a respite . . . and certainly better than any he'd known before.

He slumped on the bed and put his head in his hands, not moving a twitch at the sound of a knock on his door. "What?" he called, his voice muffled by the hands still covering his face.

Parker peeked in apparently, then pushed the door wide. "Are you okay?"

"Fine," Luke muttered. He reached down to yank his socks off, then pitched them across the room to keep company with the shoes. He pushed himself up from the bed and ripped off his sleeveless undershirt. He flung it away and gave Parker a wary eye. "Why, don't I seem okay?"

Parker slacked a hip against the door and folded his arms, his gaze taking in the various clothing items littered across the floor. "Well, no, now that you mention it. You were awfully quiet at Pinochle tonight, no gloating visible at all despite winning every game. So unlike you."

Luke ignored him and unfastened his belt. He dropped his trousers to the floor and stepped out of them, then sent them sailing with a jab of his foot. They landed on the suit coat in an unsightly heap.

Parker scratched his head. "And then there's the memory problem."

"What memory problem?" Luke paused, pajama bottoms in hand.

Parker rubbed his jaw and straddled the arm of Luke's overstuffed chair, flicking a black sock off the edge, one with a hole in its heel. "You know, forgetting where your closet is?"

Luke put on his pajama bottoms and traipsed to the window to open it all the way. He returned to his bed and pulled the sheet back. "What do you want, Parker? I'm tired."

The humor faded from Parker's voice, but just for an instant. "What's eating you, Luke? I don't see you like this very often—distant, quiet . . . humble. Not to mention a total slob."

The barb didn't even coax a faint smile. Luke dropped on the bed with a squeal of springs and braced his arms behind his neck, eyes closed. A faint breeze ruffled the scant blond hairs on his nearly smooth chest, helping to cool the moist warmth of his skin. "Let it go, Parker, I'm fine. I just need to get some sleep."

Luke's jaw tightened as Parker remained silent. He could almost hear the gears turning in his friend's head, thinking of ways he could dissect Luke's sour mood. Parker Riley was a good friend who obviously missed his calling as a priest, no thanks to his father who had pushed him into law. The man was obsessed with purging one's soul—both his and Luke's—of all the sinister things that could keep it from peace. Luke's stomach muscles tightened as he waited for Parker to express his concern—a concern sure to be as relentless as the throb in Luke's head.

"That's good, Luke. I'm glad to hear that you're fine, because we all thought you seemed a little distracted and subdued." He paused for effect. "Especially Gabe. She thought it was her."

Guilt squeezed in Luke's chest, and he muttered under his breath, regretting that he'd allowed his anger to ruin his evening and ultimately Gabe's. His eyes slitted open. "You told her it wasn't her, didn't you? That I had a horrible headache?"

Parker nodded and folded his arms with wary concern in his eyes. "Yeah, I told her, and so did Betty, but you know how stubborn she is. At any rate, I think Betty calmed her down with one of your Nehis from the pantry after you left."

Luke expelled a sigh. "Good. I'll make it up next week, maybe take her to Robinson's."

"Yeah, she'd like that. You mean the world to her." He hesitated, as if to take great care in choosing his words. "Betty and I, well, she likes us well enough, I suppose, but you—it's like you two are cut from the same cloth, like you're blood, you know? She seems to thrive just having you around." Parker stood to his feet. "Well, I'll let you get some sleep. Good night."

A silent groan rattled through Luke's chest. He didn't know how Parker did it, but somehow he always wheedled in. Suddenly Luke felt like unloading all the frustration throbbing inside. No, not *felt*, he thought with a hoarse catch of his breath . . . *needed*. He sat up abruptly, his eyes piercing the back of Parker's head. He paused to draw in a deep breath while Parker opened the door.

"I kissed her," he said, his voice little more than a rasp of shame.

Parker froze at the door, hand stiff on the knob. "What?" He whirled around, shock glazing his eyes. "Who?" he breathed, although the look on his face said he already knew.

Luke swung his legs off the bed and sat on the edge, hands braced on his mattress with head bent. "Katie," he whispered. The mere sound of her name stabbed him anew.

Out of the corner of his eye, he saw Parker visibly sag, body listing against the door. Suddenly he slammed it closed with a harsh flick of his wrist. "For the love of heaven . . . Luke, why? You can have any woman you want. Why risk the integrity of the office to satisfy a juvenile crush?"

Luke swabbed his face and then shielded his eyes with a shaky hand. "I don't know, Parker. I swear I never had any intention of going there. But she seemed depressed after everyone left, and I was concerned about her and then . . ." He swallowed the lump in his throat and looked up. "It just happened."

Parker dropped to the arm of the chair. He slashed blunt fingers through meticulous sandy hair and then glanced up, brown eyes dark with distress. "And how did she respond?"

A sense of satisfaction seeped in, causing Luke's lips to thin into a tight line. "She liked it—a lot." He sucked in a deep breath and slowly released it again, peering up at Parker with a sheepish smile. "And then she hauled off and slapped me so hard I thought she broke my jaw."

Parker stared in disbelief and then grinned from ear to ear. "Thank God! I hope that teaches you to keep your hands off the help."

Luke rubbed the back of his neck, his brief satisfaction giving way to shame. He stared at his bare feet, avoiding Parker's eyes. "Well, it does now. But it sure didn't then."

"What do you mean?" Parker whispered, his voice far from steady.

Luke sighed. "It means I lost my temper."

"And what does *that* mean . . ." Parker asked again, suddenly sounding like Luke's director rather than his friend.

Luke gave him a sideways glance and a grimace of a smile. "It means I pushed her to the wall and kissed the daylights out of her." He exhaled a shaky breath. "Or at least the meanness, I hope."

Parker groaned and jumped to his feet. He started pacing. "For the love of all that is decent and good, McGee, what were you thinking? I'll tell you what—you weren't, at least not with your brain. If Harris Stowe catches wind of this, your butt will be in a sling, and I'll help him put it there."

Heat snaked up the back of Luke's neck. "It won't happen again, Parker. I was way out of line, and I realize that now."

Parker halted mid-stride, a stormy look in his eyes. "You can bet your bottom dollar it won't happen again, because so help me, if it does, I'll kick your sorry butt myself. She's a volunteer, for pity's sake, hand placed by Harris himself." He jabbed a finger toward Luke, the warning in his tone as clear as the anger in his eyes. "You stay far away from that girl, McGee, do you hear? From now on, all of her assignments come through me. I want nothing more out of you except a short apology and then hello and goodbye, is that clear?"

Luke nodded.

"Good." All at once, the fury faded from Parker's face. He sank his hands deep in his pockets and stared at his shoes, no longer Luke's superior, but now his friend. His voice deepened with concern. "She's no good for you, you know. I've never seen a woman affect you like this one, Luke. Too much power from your past, too much for you to prove. You can have any woman you want. But I'm telling you as a friend, please—leave this one alone."

The gravity in Parker's tone drew Luke's gaze to his. "Don't worry, Parker, I have no intention of going near Katie O'Connor ever again. But just for the record—she doesn't affect me like you think."

One of Parker's shaggy brows jutted high. "No? Well, I don't know where the old Luke went, but take my word for it—I haven't seen him since the day that girl crossed our threshold."

Luke squinted up at Parker, an edge of confidence hardening his tone. "Yeah? Well, you can bet your sweet mother that I affect her as much as she affects me."

Parker strolled to the door and grasped the knob, stopping long enough to cast a worried look over his shoulder. His tone held a hint of humor, but there wasn't a trace of a smile to be found on his face. He grunted and opened the door. "Yeah, that's what I'm afraid of."

Grinding her lip, Katie glanced up at the clock on her nightstand. Two minutes to midnight. Shaky air shuddered from her lips as she closed her tattered copy of *Anne of Green Gables* with a nervous thud. Her gaze slid to her closed bedroom door, hoping her parents were finally asleep. She swung her legs out from her bed to the floor, and her limbs felt as wobbly as if she were tiptoeing on her mattress rather than hardwood floor. Pausing, she cocked her head and closed her eyes to listen for the sound of her parents' voices—that is, if she could even hear them over the pulse thrumming in her ears. They had talked forever it seemed, their muffled conversation seeping through her bedroom wall for well over an hour. But all had been quiet for the last thirty minutes or so, thank heavens, and Katie finally exhaled the breath she'd been holding.

She reached for her robe at the foot of the bed and then stopped, the image of her sheer nightgown in the mirror infusing a rush of heat to her cheeks. She hadn't seen Jack in over a month and a half, and the thought occurred that a robe and nightgown might not be the wisest choice of attire. A lump bobbed in her throat. She had enough problems keeping him in line in the front seat of his car after every date; a midnight rendezvous on the back porch in her robe and nightgown would not be a smart move. Especially if Father happened to catch her.

She dressed quickly, then inched her bedroom door open, and quietly slipped down the hall, heart thudding wildly as she tread lightly past her parents' room. Guilt stabbed within, but she quickly forced it away, determined to focus on her primary concern at the moment—meeting Jack on the back porch without her parents' knowledge. With the tiniest twinge of regret at defying her father, she eased the kitchen door open with nary a squeak, completely convinced she needed to see Jack tonight. She didn't want to flout her father's will, but what choice did she have? There was no way she could allow an attraction to Luke McGee to continue, not with her future at stake. Her jaw hardened as she nudged the screen door open and stepped out on the porch. No, there was no question about it—Luke McGee's kisses were pure poison . . . and Jack was the only cure.

His shadow rose from the swing at the end of the porch, and she sensed his excitement before she ever saw the look of longing on his moonlit face. He moved forward with a tender smile and swept her up in his arms, devouring her with a kiss that took her breath away.

"Gosh, doll, I've been crazy without you," he whispered.

A soft giggle bubbled in her chest and she kissed him back, reveling in the look of love in his eyes. "I've missed you too, Jack."

He carried her to the swing and settled in with her on his lap, giving her a fierce hug before nuzzling her neck. "You have my word, Katydid—I will never miss your curfew again." His mouth wandered back to hers and with a low groan, he eased her back on the swing with another hungry kiss.

With a palm to his chest, she chuckled and squirmed free from his lap, choosing to snuggle beside him while his arm tucked her close. Jack's kisses were nice, but it was the way he made her feel inside that sent warmth swirling through her—his love, his doting, his undying *approval*. She breathed in the heady bouquet of her mother's cottage roses mingled with the faint scent of Jack's lavender cologne and sighed with contentment, grateful for the noisy trill of tree frogs and locusts that would obscure any noise. With a squeeze of his hand, she rested her head against his broad shoulder, always amazed at how secure and accepted she felt in his arms.

"So tell me," she said in a breathless tone, "how was lunch with your father's professor friend at Harvard?"

Jack's laughter rumbled low and rich in her ear, and the return press of his hand indicated his excitement for the topic. "Gosh, Katydid, we are going to *love* law school—especially you." He deposited a kiss on her head and hunkered down in the swing. The enthusiasm in his voice vibrated in the air along with the crickets. "Professor Morris talked about everything we could expect—you know, how hard it is the first year, reading case studies until your eyes sink into their sockets. And then it's like learning a whole new language as far as terminology and logic is concerned. But man alive, the cases we'll study—things right out of the headlines like the Scopes 'Monkey' Trial four years ago or *Meyer v. Nebraska* a few years back, which Professor Morris claims is a landmark case for parents' rights."

He leaned forward and grinned. "Not to mention the famous Persons Case going on in Canada right now, over whether a woman should be considered a person or not—can you believe it, Katie? Think of it—women's rights—that's right down your alley. I tell you, doll, I get goose bumps just thinking about it—how the path we've chosen will affect people's lives for the better." He squeezed her again, emitting a low chuckle. "Then, of course, there's also the money we'll make doing it."

Katie swiveled to face him, fervor burning in her eyes. "Oh, Jack, I've never wanted anything as much as I want this—the chance to really do something with my life and help others in the process." With a tiny squeal of joy, she lunged into his arms, rewarding him with a kiss that made him moan. She pulled away, her voice quivering with emotion. "Just think of what we'll be able to do together," she whispered. With a stroke of his cheek, she blinked to clear the sudden wetness from her eyes. "Thank you, Jack Worthington, for sharing my passion."

He cradled her face in his hands, and the stark love and admiration she saw in his eyes was a balm to her aching soul. "Gosh, Katie, I can't help myself. I've never met another girl like you, doll—so strong, so smart, so sure of herself. With most girls, it's only the latest fashion or social function that interests them, but you—you have so much drive, so much passion . . ."

His eyes settled on her lips with the same starry-eyed look he always wore when she was around, and somewhere deep down inside an empty hole filled up, brimming over with his approval. She closed her eyes with a wavering sigh. Approval she seldom received from anyone else.

Especially her father.

"I love you, doll," he whispered, and she felt the gentle touch of his lips graze against her skin.

With a rush of gratitude, she twined her arms around his neck, savoring the way he made her feel—loved, admired, respected.

Special.

He deepened the kiss, and she relented this time, allowing him to tug her back onto his lap without protest. With a gentle brace of her shoulders, he dipped her back in his arms, tingling her throat with the caress of his mouth.

"Oh, Jack . . ." she whispered, knowing full well she should stop, but too needy to care . . .

Somewhere through the haze in her mind, she heard the clearing of a throat, and with a sharp catch of her breath, she launched from Jack's arms like a tadpole on hot pavement. Her breathing was as labored as Jack's as she splayed a palm to her chest and gaped at her brother.

"Sean! What on earth are you doing here?" she rasped, the heat in her face conflicting with the coolness in his.

With his typical casual air, Sean slowly mounted the porch steps and deposited a bag at the base of the back door. He rose to his full height, and suddenly she noticed a basketball under his arm and sweat stains on his shirt. Beads of perspiration glistened on his face as he allowed a faint smile, but his usual gentle humor couldn't mask the disappointment in his eyes. "I guess I could ask you the same thing, Katie Rose," he said quietly, then cocked a hip to the wall. "I promised Father I'd drop off a part he needs in the morning, and I thought I'd do it on my way home after a game of one-on-one with Pete." His smile faded away. "But I didn't realize you'd be in the midst of some one-on-one of your own—"

"We were just talking," Katie said in a rush, the heat in her cheeks belying the truth of her statement.

Her brother's lips curved just a hair as he assessed them through dubious eyes, his voice gentled by a trace of humor. "Some conversation, Katie Rose." His gaze shifted to the man beside her. "Evening, Jack."

Her whisper softened into a plea. "Sean, please—you're not going to tell Father, are you? I haven't seen Jack in almost a month and a half, and we were mostly talking, I promise . . ." She swallowed hard, desperation choking her words.

Jack slipped an arm around Katie's shoulders to pull her close, his tone contrite. "Look, Sean, I love your sister, and nothing happened."

Sean rubbed the back of his neck. "Go home, Jack. Now."

"You're not going to tell Father, are you?" Her voice was as tight as the nerves in her neck.

With a weary sigh, Sean fisted the screen door handle and glanced up through lidded eyes, leveling a serious gaze in Katie's direction. His gentle disapproval flamed her cheeks with shame as only this brother could. "Not if you promise never to do this again," he said calmly, "and if Jack hightails it home right now."

Relief flooded, and she nodded. Spinning on her heel, she gave Jack a quick hug and a nervous smile. "Go home, Jack. I'll see you at the end of summer, all right?"

He shot her brother a hard gaze before cupping Katie's face in his hands. He brushed her lips with his own. "I love you, Katydid, and you can count on it. You're worth the wait, doll." He squeezed her hand and shuffled past Sean, ignoring him as he lumbered down the steps.

Katie watched until he disappeared around the house, then sucked in a deep swallow of air before facing her brother. The look on his face made her heart sink. "You're not mad at me, are you?"

The screen door barely squealed as he opened it. He held it for her, studying her through tired eyes. He tugged on her hair and gave her a quiet smile. "No, Katie, I'm not mad . . . just a little disappointed, that's all." He waited until she moved past him into the house, and then quietly closed the screen door behind her. His eyes were gentle with compassion, but his words pierced her to the core. "You're better than this, Katie Rose," he whispered. He turned and descended the steps, his voice following behind. "Good night, Sweet Pea. Be sure and lock the door."

She blinked, moisture blurring her eyes as he faded into the night, leaving her with an awful ache in her chest. Swallowing the shame in her throat, she slowly closed the door and flipped the lock with trembling fingers.

"You're better than this, Katie Rose."

Hand to her eyes, she slumped against the wood while her shoulders sagged in remorse.

No, she wasn't.

At least . . . not to anyone but Jack.

"Well, it's your lucky night, Little Bit. The girls want *you* to read them a story." Collin wrapped his arms around Faith's waist from behind and bent to nuzzle her neck. Her shoulders scrunched in ticklish protest, which only made him squeeze all the tighter. "Don't try to fight me, Mrs. McGuire," he breathed in her ear, "it's a balmy summer evening, and I want time alone with you on the porch." He chuckled and plucked the dishtowel off her shoulder and slung it over his own. "And we both know I always get what I want . . . and so do you, apparently," he said with a wry smile. He butted her out of the way. "You read, and I'll finish the dishes."

Faith eyed the scalloped-potato casserole dish thick with baked-on crust. "Are you sure? The potatoes were in the oven way too long, and I'm afraid that dish may be crustier than you at the end of a busy day."

His gray eyes narrowed as he rolled up his sleeves, giving her that slow smile that spelled nothing but trouble. He flicked her with the towel while his voice became a husky threat. "You best get those girls in bed and fast asleep, Little Bit, because there's a full moon outside, plenty of stars, and the crickets are crooning." He assaulted the casserole dish with the same intensity she heard in his voice, pausing to shoot her a look of warning. "I'll be up shortly to kiss them good night, but then I want to sit on the swing . . . *alone* with my wife. Or I'll be showing you 'crusty.'"

She was still smiling when she ascended the stairs and entered the girls' pink gingham room, their giggles and squeals not boding well for sleep. Propped against the doorframe with arms folded and a smile on her face, she watched her stepping-stone daughters—ages five, four, and three—with pride in her eyes as they tumbled on the bed. She was grateful they were so close, although it meant they insisted on sharing the same room. A fact which, Faith noted, usually kept their high-energy personalities more keyed up than not.

"What d'ya say we read our books in my room so we can play a trick on Daddy?" she announced, mischief curling the edges of her mouth.

Squeals bounced off the walls as the girls bounced off the bed with a riot of curls, frilly nightgowns, and giggles that melted her heart.

"Ooooo . . . what kind of trick, Mama?" Isabelle asked. Her eldest daughter grinned with an imp of a face framed by long auburn curls.

Faith snatched the chosen book from the nightstand, then

grabbed two more for good measure and gave them a perky grin. She hefted her youngest in her arms and planted a wet kiss on her rosy cheek. "We're gonna make Daddy growl like a bear, right, Abby?"

"Will he be mad like a bear?" four-year-old Delaney asked. Her freckled cheeks bunched with concern as she trailed her mother down the hall, toting a Raggedy Ann doll close behind.

Faith tucked her to her side with a chuckle and then ushered them into her room. "No, Laney, Daddy will just be pretending, but it will be fun to watch, won't it?"

She plopped three-year-old Abby onto the bed, then crawled in beside her, bracing herself as Bella and Laney charged in on top. She settled them down and reached for Bella's book, and then led them in good-night prayers so they'd be all ready for bed. She'd gone through all three of the books when she finally heard Collin coming down the hall. Her stomach fluttered. "Shhh . . . under the covers," she whispered. She tucked Abby close to one side while Bella and Laney cuddled on the other. "Remember, not a peep." She flashed Collin a grin as he entered the room.

"What are you doing in here—" Collin appeared in the door with a pucker in the ridge of his brow. His gaze lighted on the squirming bulk beneath the covers, and he shook his head, the frown melting into a smile as he ambled into the room with his hands on his hips. "You know, Little Bit, if you keep putting on weight like this, your nickname won't fit any more than your clothes." He gave her lumpy thigh a squeeze, prompting a peal of laughter from beneath the covers. Collin grinned and leaned to give Faith a quick kiss before plopping down beside her on the bed. "My, but we're ticklish tonight, aren't we, though?" He explored the extra padding, tickling as he went while the blanket bubbled with wild movement and little-girl giggles.

Laney popped up out of the covers with a delighted grin. "Daddy, it's us!"

"Oh, thank goodness," Collin bellowed. He jerked the cover back, exposing three grinning little girls, all dressed in pink. "I thought your mother was just getting fat!"

Bella flung her arms around his neck. "Can I have a piggyback ride back to our room?"

"Only if you promise to stay there and go to sleep," Collin said with a wink in Faith's direction. He lifted Bella high in the air and positioned her on his back, then scooped both Laney and Abby up into his arms with a determined grunt. They squirmed and giggled against his chest, a picture of love in motion that brought a smile to Faith's lips. Collin paused at the door to give her a half-lidded look obviously meant as a threat. "And you," he warned, "head to the back porch *now* . . . or else." He disappeared down the hall, along with the squeals and laughter.

Faith grinned and jumped up from the bed, humming to herself as she made her way downstairs to the kitchen. On the way to the back door, she eyed the basket of lemons on the counter and had a sudden urge to make lemonade. The perfect thing for a moonlight swing with her husband, she thought with a quick glance down the hall. She pulled out her cutting board and had one lemon half squeezed when Collin appeared in the door, his look as sour as the fruit in her hand. He rolled up his sleeves and walked to where she stood at the counter, then plucked the lemon from her hand and placed it on the cutting board.

"This is *not* the back porch, Little Bit," he said with a swerve of his lips, then promptly steered her toward the door.

"But doesn't a cold lemonade sound good?" she asked, licking her lips at the thought.

"Not as good as having you all to myself on the back porch the one night we aren't exhausted." Collin dropped onto their wooden porch swing and pulled her close, not missing the opportunity to feather the lobe of her ear with his mouth.

A familiar warmth surged as she leaned into his embrace,

seduced by both her husband's lips and the beauty of the summer night. She closed her eyes and snuggled close. "Oh, this is nice," she whispered, trying to remember the last time they had taken a few moments to just sit and cuddle like this. Lately it seemed like all Collin did was work late at the shop while she tended to the girls, each too spent to allow more than a token kiss before collapsing into bed.

"It is," he whispered. The warmth of his sigh caressed her cheek. "When did life get so complicated, Faith? It seems like it's been forever since I really held you in my arms . . ."

She stroked his cheek with the tips of her fingers, mesmerized by the firm line of his jaw, now bristled with dark stubble. "It's been hard with your schedule lately, Collin, I know, and the girls really miss you. So it's no surprise they've been finding excuses to sleep in our bed. But Laney's cold is much better, so she shouldn't be bothering us tonight, and Abby hasn't had a nightmare since last week, so we should be safe there." Her eyes softened as she glanced up to stare into his. "Nor am I likely to fall asleep on you, my love. That's more your habit lately than mine."

Collin released a heavy sigh and leaned back in the swing, his contrition apparent in the squeeze of her hand. "I know, but things should get better with the new hire starting next week."

She sat up, excitement bubbling her tone. "So you finally hired someone? That's wonderful! Who? The retired gentleman who had his own shop or the one with the accounting experience?"

Collin drew her back to his chest, his voice an octave lower—and quieter—as it rumbled against her ear. "Neither. Brady and I went with the last person to interview for the job."

She felt the touch of his lips against her temple as his fingers idly toyed with the *V* collar of her blouse. Somewhere an owl hooted, merging with Collin's soft moan as his mouth wandered to the lobe of her ear. He shifted her close, and the scent of musk teased her senses while his lips strayed to tease the edge of her mouth.

Wriggling from his grasp, she smiled. "Don't keep me in suspense—who did you hire?"

His hand stilled on her waist while silence hung in the air, thick as the summer night.

"Collin?" She scooted back, searching his eyes in the moonlight. "Now you've got me curious. Which man did you hire?"

A knot dipped in his throat. "Neither. We hired a woman. A widow, actually."

She frowned. "Does she have the experience you need?"

A weary sigh escaped his mouth as he rubbed the side of her arm. "Enough. She worked at my father's shop years ago for a time and then at several small print shops, in bookkeeping."

"So you know her, then? Is she an old family friend?"

He hesitated. "Yes, but it's been years since I've seen her. And actually, I—well, Brady and I—felt kind of sorry for her because she's been through a lot in her life. Her husband died recently, leaving her with a sick boy and sparse savings, and she has no income whatsoever." He released a weighty sigh and sagged back in the swing, fingers pinching his forehead. "She's more than qualified, mind you, but she will require some training. I don't suppose it was the smartest move we've ever made, but I—well, we—just wanted to help."

Faith leaned to press a kiss to his cheek, the feel of his late-day beard prickly against her lips. "I think that's sweet—helping a widow in need. You're a good man, Collin McGuire."

He didn't smile. His gaze dropped to the long sailor tie of her middy blouse as he fondled it with his fingers. "Not always, but my heart's in the right place." He swallowed hard and looked up, stroking her cheek with solemn eyes. "I love you, Faith, more than anything in this world."

She leaned back on the swing and smiled, drawing lazy

circles on the smooth plain of his arm. "I believe I'd like to see how much," she whispered.

With a wrenching groan, he pulled her close and clutched her tightly to his chest. He buried his head in the crook of her neck. "You are the best thing that has ever happened to me, Little Bit, and I would be lost without you."

She squeezed him back, a prickle of concern surfacing. "Me too, Collin. Are you . . . sure you're all right?"

His chest quivered as a heavy sigh blew warm against her neck. "More than all right," he said, his lips intent on exploring her throat. Her pulse was racing when his mouth finally found hers, teasing her with a gentle tug of his teeth. "Now," he whispered, "where were we?"

7

Who wants lemonade?" Katie stood at the door of the back porch, pitcher in hand.

"Oh, bless you!" Her mother said while her sisters and Charity's best friend Emma looked up from the picnic table her father had built for the grandchildren. Marcy backhanded a limp strand of hair from her moist forehead. "This heat is relentless," she muttered, pushing aside sewing materials strewn across the table. "And we need a break from these costumes. Goodness, I don't remember the Fourth of July parade being this much work before. But then I suppose with six grandchildren riding on a float, it's bound to take some time to outfit them all."

Charity jumped up and relieved Katie of the stack of tumblers tucked under her arm and started passing them out. "You're a genius, Katie. I'm hot just watching the sweat roll off Mother and Lizzie." She sat back down and plunked the last glass on the table with a look of longing at the children as they darted and squealed through the sprinkler. She absently ran a hand along the damp neckline of her polka-dot sundress, then measured the air with index finger and thumb.

"I swear I'm this close to making a fool of myself with a romp through the sprinkler."

Katie's lips skewed into a lopsided smile. "But you're *so* good at it, sis, so why stop now?" She gave Charity's shoulder an affectionate squeeze as she poured her lemonade.

A soft giggle floated from Emma's lips, lifting a faint mottled scar on one side of her mouth. "It does seem to be a talent of hers," she said softly. She butted her shoulder against Charity's in an affectionate tease, her gentle grin making her disfigured face seem almost beautiful.

Charity gave Emma a sideways glance, lips pursed in a playful scowl. "I don't need degradation from you, Emma, I have sisters for that." Her eyes narrowed. "And a son."

Katie chuckled and plopped down on the bench, pouring the last of the lemonade into her own glass. "Sorry, sis, but as Emma says, you're just so talented at making a fool of yourself, for which I'm forever grateful. In the past, it always helped keep Father's focus off of me."

Almond-shaped eyes narrowed over the rim of her glass as Charity took another drink. She swiped her mouth with her hand and lifted a perfectly manicured brow. "Well, I mustn't be too good at it anymore because you and Steven seem to be the only ones incurring his wrath these days. Speaking of which," she said in a suspicious drawl. "How's the 'punishment' going?" She rested arms on the table and gave Katie a devilish grin. "Is Cluny McGee still making your life miserable, I hope?"

The summer heat chose that moment to converge in Katie's cheeks, and a silent groan lodged in her throat.

Lizzie's eyes lit up as she leaned in, as close to the table as she could get with a neat, little mound beneath her lavender sleeveless shift. "Ooooh, yes, we want the full scoop on that good-looking boy. Brady sees him at the gym but never breathes a word about Luke's life. So ... are you warming up to him now?"

Faith chuckled and took a swig of lemonade, a definite

twinkle in her green eyes. "Mmm . . . I'd say so, judging from that glaring shade of red on her face." She lounged back on the bench and gave her sister a mischievous smile. "Come on, Katie Rose, spill. Is something other than the summer heat putting that warmth in your cheeks?"

"Faith McGuire!" Katie choked on her lemonade. "You're as bad as Charity."

"Hey," Charity said in a hurt tone. "She's not the saint you think she is, right, Mother?"

Marcy smiled and fanned her face with a sewing pattern. "Mercy me, I don't think any of us are ready for canonization just yet." Her smile shifted to the right in a rare display of sarcasm. "Especially your father." She took a drink of lemonade and shot Katie a sympathetic smile. "I still think he was too harsh on you, with volunteer work *and* confinement for the summer." With a roll of her eyes, she gave a soft grunt. "And he says *I'm* the one going through the change."

Faith rubbed her mother's back with the ball of her hand, causing Marcy to close her eyes and moan. "He is a man, Mother. You know how stubborn they can be."

"No, tell me, please—I have no idea," Charity said with a matching roll of eyes. "Mitch is king. He was supposed to take Henry fishing today, but instead he's at work." She peered at Marcy. "With your husband, I might add. Father's the editor, for pity's sake, Mother—the boss. Explain to me why he and his assistant editor have to work the weekend?"

Marcy rotated her neck as Faith massaged her back. "Your father claims Mr. Hennessey called a mandatory meeting." She moaned softly. "Oh, lower, Faith—yes, right there . . ."

Charity sat up sharply, her gaze riveted to the backyard. "Henry! Put that sprinkler down right now or so help me, I'll come out there and give you a wet, sloppy kiss." She sighed and slumped back on the bench. "Men! God, please—give me the grace to deal with my son, my husband, and now, apparently, the owner of the *Boston Herald*."

"A kiss? You threaten him with a kiss?" Lizzie gawked, a smile of disbelief on her face.

Charity's lips shifted. "Yeah, the kiss of death, apparently. Seems my son would rather brave a spanking from his father than a kiss from his mother, the little dickens. Be grateful for girls, Faith. I have a feeling that boy is destined to make me old before my time."

"What goes around comes around," Faith said with a wiggle of brows.

An impish grin surfaced on Charity's lips as she nodded at Katie. "Well then, we should be in for quite a show when this one starts having babies."

Thoughts of Luke and babies suddenly collided in Katie's brain, and she choked on her lemonade again, certain that the color in her cheeks had reached heatstroke proportions.

"Ooooo . . . it's not often we see you embarrassed, Katie," Charity said, rubbing her hands together in anticipation. She plopped her arms on the table and leaned in with a wicked smile. "Can't be babies that has you all heated up . . . unless, uh, it's tied to thoughts of Luke McGee?"

Katie shot up from the table, almost tumbling her drink. "More lemonade, anyone?"

Charity clamped a firm hand to her arm and pulled her back down. "Oh, no you don't, kiddo. I may have a talent for making a fool of myself, but I've also been blessed with a sixth sense when it comes to romance. There's something brewing in that brain of yours regarding Luke McGee, and I for one want to know what it is."

"Oh, do you like him?" Lizzie breathed, ever the advocate for romance.

With a loud groan, Katie pressed her palms to her face, feeling the heat of her skin through her fingers. "No, I don't like him!"

"Then why are you seven shades of red?" Charity asked, more than a little smug.

"Because he still makes me miserable," Katie said in an acidic tone.

"Is he still obnoxious to you?" Faith asked. There was a hint of concern in her voice.

A flashback of him pressing her to the wall and kissing her soundly popped in Katie's mind, and the heat of the thought invaded more than her cheeks. "No! Yes! Oh, I don't know."

"What do you mean you don't know? Is he nice to you or not?" Charity demanded.

Katie snatched a sewing pattern and began to fan her face. "Most of the time."

"And the rest of the time?" Charity asked, "badgering" also high on her list of talents.

"He's nice all of the time, all right?"

"So you do like him. Oh, Katie, that's so exciting!" Lizzie said with a glow in her cheeks.

"No, Lizzie, I don't, I promise." Katie grabbed a scrap of material and began to swab the sweat from her neck. "He's turned into a nice man, and that's all I can say."

"A nice and attractive man . . . ," Charity said with a dance of her brows.

"Yes."

"But you don't like him," Faith said.

Katie shot Faith a definitive glance. "No."

Charity cocked her head, eyes squinted in thought. "Are you attracted to him at least?"

"Oh, for pity's sakes, Charity, is that all you have on your mind? Yes, I'll admit the little brat has grown into a very handsome man, who even manages to be civil most of the time. But I can tell you right now that I have my sights set on Jack, not a street rat named Cluny McGee."

"Luke McGee," Emma said quietly, watching the whole scene through gentle eyes.

Katie sighed and slumped in her seat. "Yes, Luke McGee. And I didn't mean to call him a street rat because he's actually turned out to be . . . ," she swallowed hard, "a pretty decent guy." She glanced around the table with pleading eyes. "Look, I like working at the BCAS, I do, and all of the people there—including Luke—are really great. But it's still work and a punishment that's cut me off from Jack, so if it's all the same to you, can we please change the subject?"

Faith squeezed Katie's arm. "Sure, Katie." Her gaze lighted on Lizzie. "So . . . what do you think of our husbands hiring a poor widow? A pretty sweet thing to do, wouldn't you say?"

Lizzie blinked, eyes wide. "You think it's 'sweet'?"

"Of course I do, don't you?" Faith cocked her head and reached for the Betsy Ross costume she'd been working on.

"Well, I have to admit, 'sweet' is not the first word that came to mind."

"Why? They could have hired any of the several men who applied, but they chose to help a poor old widow instead." Faith stuck a needle in her mouth and adjusted the hem on the costume.

"'Old'?" Lizzie croaked, her fingers numb against the silky white material for the Statue of Liberty. "He told you she was old?"

Faith glanced up, confusion wedging her brow. "He said she was an old family friend."

Lizzie gulped and Charity honed in, her interest in the Uncle Sam costume in her lap suddenly gone awry. "You mean she's not? Old, I mean?"

All eyes focused on Lizzie, whose face now felt like Katie's had looked earlier. She swallowed her discomfort, aware that this time, her warmth had nothing to do with pregnancy.

"Lizzie?" Faith lowered the Betsy Ross hoop skirt in her lap. "She's not old?"

A chestnut strand of hair bobbed against Lizzie's damp brow as she shook her head.

"Have you seen her?" Faith asked.

Lizzie nodded, and the stray strand quivered in response.

An edge crept into Faith's tone as she leaned forward, her green eyes narrowing a touch. "Really. Then how old *is* she, exactly?"

True to her form, Lizzie hesitated with a pregnant pause. "Collin's age or younger," she finally said with a shift in her throat, her gaze stuck on the needle in her hand.

No one said a word as Faith quietly laid her costume aside and inched to the edge of her seat, her manner calm enough, but her voice slow and menacing. "Well, *then* . . . is she pretty?"

Lizzie looked up, gnawing at her lip. She nodded again.

Charity slammed her hand on the table. "Sweet saints, what is wrong with those two, hiring a beautiful woman to work in the office with a bunch of men—are they crazy?"

"I didn't say she was beautiful," Lizzie began.

"Young and beautiful, young and pretty—same difference to me." Charity huffed. "Either way, Brady and Collin should know better. Widow or not, she needs to go."

Faith took a deep breath and eased back onto the bench. She pulled her sewing into her lap. "No, Charity, we're being silly here. The woman needs a job, and Brady and Collin were kind enough to give her one. And I'm sure part of the reason Collin agreed is because he wanted to help out an old family friend. Besides, she's qualified—he told me she's worked in several print shops including his father's, so the woman has experience."

Lizzie touched Faith's arm, her eyes contrite. "More than you know," she whispered.

The color faded from Faith's cheeks. Her gaze fused to Lizzie's. "What do you mean?"

Lizzie scraped her teeth against her lip before continuing, her voice low. "I mean he was supposed to tell you, Faith—Collin promised he would tell you . . ."

"Tell me what?"

Lizzie drew in a fortifying breath. "That, yes, Evelyn does

have experience at Collin's father's shop because she worked there the summer before his father died." Lizzie paused to catch her breath. "Collin's junior year in high school . . . when Collin was . . . involved with her."

"Involved with her?" Faith repeated, her voice barely audible.

She blinked, and Lizzie saw comprehension flicker across her sister's face, her memories of Collin's sordid past flashing through her mind, no doubt.

Faith closed her eyes. "How do you know?" she whispered.

"Mama, can we have something to drink? We're thirsty." Laney shook Faith's arm, jolting her and everyone at the table.

Emma immediately rose and gripped the pitcher in her hand. "I'll get it. Laney, go tell the others to stay where they are—we don't want you kids traipsing water into the kitchen or getting your costumes wet, all right, sweetheart?"

"Okay, Emma." Laney bounded off to rejoin her cousins in the sprinkler.

With a tender look in Faith's direction, Emma disappeared into the kitchen.

"How do you know?" Faith asked again, her words barely audible.

"Because Brady and I confronted him the day after he told us he hired her. He admitted to being involved with her back then."

"So it was Collin's decision?"

Lizzie sighed. "Yes, but Brady made Collin promise that if this woman gave him any indication whatsoever that she had the slightest interest in Collin, he would let her go."

Faith stood to her feet. "I see."

"What are you going to do?" Lizzie whispered.

"Help Emma with the lemonade," Faith said, her voice painfully quiet.

"Faith, please—you need to talk to Collin," Marcy said.

She rose and put an arm around her daughter's shoulder. "Tell him how much this upsets you."

Faith attempted to smile and patted her mother's hand. "I will, Mother, I promise."

"Men," Charity muttered under her breath. "Sometimes they are so blind to the obvious."

Faith paused, appearing to struggle to maintain a calm demeanor. "Charity, I know you're all upset for me, but don't be, please. I am perfectly fine. I trust my husband, and I will talk to him about this, I promise. Now if you will excuse me, I'll go see what I can do to help Emma."

Emma heard the screen door squeal open and glanced over her shoulder, a nearly squeezed lemon lodged in her hand. She took one look at Faith standing inside the door with a hand to her eyes and quickly put the lemon down. She took a step forward. "Faith, are you all right?"

A deep breath rose and fell in Faith's chest as she opened her eyes, valiant in her attempt to conjure a smile. "I'm fine, Emma. Just a little dizzy from the heat." She walked to the cupboard to pull six tumblers off the shelf. "This heat wave is something else, isn't it? It's a brutal day."

Emma tucked an arm to Faith's waist, her voice soft and low. "They're not like us, you know, the men that God brings into our lives—they're as different as the night is from the day."

The tenderness of her tone seemed to unravel Faith, causing her to list against the counter with a broken heave.

Emma wrapped her in a gentle hug, her head resting against Faith's. "They don't see things the way we do, Faith—the temptations, the dangers. But I truly believe that once you explain to Collin how you feel, he will understand your concerns. I can feel it in the depth of my soul that he only wanted to help this woman."

A faint shiver traveled Faith's body, and Emma tried to absorb it by tightening her hold. "You know, Faith, you and

Collin or even you and I can talk about this all we want, but in the end, the only thing that will resolve your fears will be the God who delivers us from them all." She paused to stroke a comforting hand against Faith's hair. "Would you like to pray about it?"

Faith nodded, pulling away with a tearful heave. She sniffed and wiped the wetness from her eyes with the side of her hand. "Thanks, Emma, I would like that." She dug a handkerchief from her pocket and dabbed her nose with a shaky smile. "I'm not used to being on this end of the prayers, I'm afraid. I don't know how to thank you."

"You can thank me by not letting the devil deceive you into thinking God's not in control of this situation, because he is. He'll show you and Collin what to do." Emma took Faith's hand in hers and bowed her head, eyes closed. "Heavenly Father, we ask you to be in the midst of this situation between Faith and Collin. Give them both wisdom and clarity of mind to do what you would have them do, and we pray for your outcome. Your Word says you give peace in the midst of a storm. Please, Lord, give Faith peace now in the midst of this short storm in her life, and unleash your blessings on her marriage to this man that she loves with all of her heart. Thank you, Lord, and amen."

Faith squeezed her hand and cocked her head. "Where did you learn to pray like that?"

Emma smiled. "When I moved back with Charity from Dublin, I used to go to Brady's Bible studies with both her and Lizzie for a while."

A grin creased Faith's lips, and a twinkle returned to her eyes. "He's good, isn't he?"

Emma's soft chuckle floated in the air as she nodded. "That he is."

"Man, it's hot out there." Faith's brother Sean pushed into the kitchen through the dining-room swinging door, his cheeks ruddy from the heat of the day. He wiped his brow with the rolled sleeve of his once crisp white shirt, flicking away a limp strand of light, sandy hair. "Hi, Emma, Faith, what are you doing here?" Inquisitive eyes, the same sky-blue as his mother's, lit up when he spied the lemon rinds on the counter. "Is that fresh lemonade?" he asked, making a beeline for the pitcher.

Faith pulled a tray from the cupboard. "Fresh squeezed by Emma Malloy herself."

"Bless you, Emma." He reached for the tallest glass he could find in his mother's cabinet. "Want me to chip some ice?"

"Nope, already done. Just need to finish here and then pour some for you and the kids."

"The kids are here?" Sean strolled over to the kitchen window to squint outside, ducking his six-foot-two frame to allow full view. "What's going on, a picnic?"

Emma finished pouring six small tumblers of lemonade, and Faith placed them on her tray, hoisted the drinks with two hands, and headed for the door. "No, we're helping Mother sew costumes for the Fourth of July parade." She paused, her hip butted against the screen door. "Hey, why aren't you at the store? I thought you worked on Saturdays."

Sean's lips tightened almost imperceptibly, diminishing the wide smile on his handsome face. "I do, but I had to get out of there today." And then, as quickly as it had faded, the warm smile returned, complemented by a wink. "Just one of the many fringe benefits of being manager of my own store, you know."

Faith grinned. "Impressive. Well, the kids will be thrilled to see Uncle Sean, I'm sure, but I'd suggest changing out of those good clothes into some of Steven's or Father's old ones before you come out—we have a bit of mud going on out here." Her gaze shifted to Emma with a grateful smile. "Thanks again for the lemonade, Emma, *and* for the prayer."

"You're welcome, Faith," Emma called over her shoulder while she poured a glass for Sean. "It will all work out, you'll see."

"What will?" Sean asked as the screen door slammed behind his sister. He leaned back against the counter and folded his arms with a quizzical look, long legs crossed at the ankles.

Emma nibbled on the side of her lip, reluctant to divulge the private matter between Faith and Collin. But then a thought struck. She handed him his glass as she assessed him with curious eyes. From the moment she'd met Sean O'Connor almost nine years ago, she knew him to be a sensitive man. Warm, unassuming, and always a quip on his lips and a twinkle in his eye. The first time he had laid eyes on her, the compassion in his face had touched her, his shock evident when he'd learned the husband she'd fled in Dublin had scarred her features with hot grease. Although Sean had never spoken of the incident since, Emma knew that it had jolted him. A kind and gentle man to all he met, Sean was particularly so with her, and the gift of his friendship was a treasure for which she was truly grateful. She cocked her head with a hint of a smile, watching as he all but drained the glass in his hand.

He was not Collin McGuire with his moody good looks nor Mitch Dennehy with his gruff, handsome appeal, or even John Brady with his quiet depth of passion for God and family. But Emma had sensed from the start that Sean O'Connor held his own charm for women who frequently sought him out, although she knew few ever met with success. Charity had mentioned once that the horror of WWI seemed to change him somehow, almost as if it had soured him on women. Not that he'd dated all that much before he'd been drafted, she said, but once he'd come home again, he seemed to steer clear of any of his sister's attempts at matchmaking. And Charity couldn't help but worry, quite certain that some French girl had obviously broken his heart. But Sean would only laugh and sidestep her queries with a grin, apparently determined to ignore her incessant badgering on the subject.

A confirmed bachelor in the truest sense of the word,

Charity's brother seemed more than content with his life, too busy with work, friends, and sports to devote time to a woman. At the age of thirty-three, he was a tall, strapping man, lean and muscled from an endless array of sports. Be it basketball, football, or baseball, the "love of his life" was clearly the game, and Sean O'Connor played it better than most. Whether butting heads on the field or court, or coaching boys on St. Stephen's team, Sean had learned to master the perfect defense against the game of romance.

He drained the rest of the lemonade and grinned, rubbing his nose with the side of his hand. "What? Do I have pulp on my face? You're staring at me like you're up to something, Mrs. Malloy." He cocked a brow. "Maybe deciding if I'm worth a second glass of lemonade?"

She laughed and tugged the empty glass from his hand. "Well, I think you're worth it, make no mistake about that. But I *would* like a payment of sorts." She poured more lemonade and handed it back, her head cocked in shy question. "Your opinion, actually . . . as a man."

Surprise lighted in his blue eyes for the briefest of seconds before the generous smile stretched across his face. He relaxed and cocked a hip against the counter, eyes playful. "My opinion, huh? If you weren't already married, Emma Malloy, I'd think you were sweet on somebody and looking for a man's view as to how to make him notice."

She caught her breath, well aware that her cheeks were flaming. The memory of the abusive husband she'd left back in Ireland pricked at her conscience. She lowered her gaze and swallowed, desperate to fight the embarrassment of Sean's comment. As if she could turn the head of any man with scars on her face. She whirled around to clean up the counter. "No, of course not. It's a question that pertains to men and women working together."

He set his glass down with a chuckle. "Okay, shoot."

Her lashes lifted slowly, eyes tentative as she met his. "If you were a happily married man, do you think working with an attractive young woman would pose a problem . . ." She looked away, lashes lowering to shield her discomfort. "You know, possibly incite . . ."

"Temptation?"

She nodded, her gaze meeting his once again. "Yes. Do you?"

He frowned. "Depends."

"On what?"

The ridge of his brow wrinkled in thought. "Well, whether there were a lot of other people around, I suppose, or whether this man and woman worked closely together alone." A frown suddenly shadowed his features and he blew out a breath that seemed to hold a tinge of frustration. "Or whether the woman had designs on the man."

"What if he was involved with her a long time ago?"

The blue eyes narrowed as they studied her face. "I wouldn't think that would be a good thing, would you?"

Emma drew in a shaky breath and shook her head. "No, no I wouldn't."

He hesitated, his voice protective. "Emma, I don't want to pry . . . but what's this all about? Is . . . everything all right?"

She smiled. "Yes, everything's fine. And thank you for answering my question. It's just something I was curious about, but also something private that relates to a friend."

Sean heaved a sigh and leaned back against the counter, muscled arms folded across his chest. His tone deepened to a more serious level. "Well, speaking of temptation," he began with a slight catch in his throat, "perhaps you could give me the benefit of your opinion as well." The tight press of his mouth indicated a subject matter not to his liking. His lips quirked into a faint smile as his eyes met hers. "As a woman, that is."

"Of course."

He paused and exhaled loudly, as if the subject matter had robbed him of his good mood. "That's why I'm home early today . . . because of a situation at work that I'm not really sure how to handle." He peered at Emma, his look painfully serious, completely devoid of the gentle humor that usually resided there. "I wouldn't trouble you with this, Emma, but I'm not sure who else to ask. I don't want to ask my mother or sisters, because heaven help me if they ever caught wind of this." He swabbed a calloused palm across his face with a faint groan. "Sweet saints, they're so desperate to see me married that they would probably pester me to death." He released a huff of frustration and looked up, his gaze pinned to hers. "I'm happy with my life, Emma. I don't need anything to complicate that, which is why I'm not looking to get involved with a woman. But there's a young lady at the store—" his lips slanted into a wry smile, "and I use the term loosely, given today's flapper mentality—who has, well, made it pretty clear she'd like to be on 'friendlier' terms."

Emma's eyes widened. "A customer?"

"No, not a customer . . . ," Sean began.

"Oh my goodness, not an employee, is it? You're the manager, Sean—I certainly would put this young woman in her place, gently but firmly."

Sean grimaced and scratched the back of his neck. "Well, she doesn't exactly work for me, either." He blinked at her, clearly perplexed. "You see, she's the owner's daughter."

Emma's lips circled into a soft "oh" before the words even left her mouth. "Oh, my."

"So you see, it's a rather awkward position."

"Oh my, yes," Emma whispered. She listed against the counter and propped a palm to her mouth. She took a deep breath. "Well then, you'll just have to do your best to avoid her."

The corner of his lips swagged into an off-center smile as his eyelids lowered enough to indicate skepticism. "Yeah, well, that's hard to do when one is cornered in the supply room."

A soft gasp popped from Emma's lips as heat skimmed into her cheeks. "No!"

"Afraid so. Turned around with a clipboard in my hand,

and the woman had me in a lip-lock so fast, I forgot which one of us was taking inventory."

Emma bit her lip, attempting to ward off a smile. "Oh, Sean, I'm so sorry."

"Me too. I knew she was interested—I'd be deaf, dumb, and blind not to notice her visits and obvious flirting—but I had no idea she'd be so brazen. What's with women today, anyway?"

Emma shook her head, a hand to her mouth to hide a smile.

"Well, now I'm forced to deal with it, and I don't know what to do. I have to discourage her, not only because I don't want a woman in my life, but because her father wants her to marry some high-profile New York dandy she's been seeing. And to make matters worse, Rose—that's her name—has 'Daddy' wrapped around her little finger. I've worked eleven long years at Kelly's Hardware to get where I am now, and Rose is just the type of woman who could steal it all away." He sighed and reached for the pitcher to pour himself another glass. "Unfortunately, she tends to hold a grudge." He held the pitcher out, brow raised. "Want some?"

"No, thank you."

He set it down and leaned back against the counter, glass in hand. "If I don't handle this just right, it could jeopardize my whole future." He took a deep swig of lemonade and then made a sour face. "But that's not the worst part," he said with a quiet sigh.

Emma cocked her head, brows knit in question. "What is?"

He glanced up, his blue eyes candid and more than a little nervous. "I liked it. And I can't afford to. Feelings like that only weaken a man, line him up in some woman's sights so she can go in for the kill." He shuddered. "No, thank you. So you see, I need some sound advice."

"Yes, I would say you do," Emma said in a breathy tone. She looked up, squinting her eyes. "Maybe you could tell her you're interested in someone else. Of course, you can't lie, so is there any other woman who appeals to you more? You know, if you were looking to date?"

Sean's brow jagged up in humor. "You mean more than Rose? After that kiss?" He inhaled deeply and gave her a quirk of a smile. "Not without it being a bald-faced lie."

"Oh." Emma nibbled on the edge of her lip.

"There must be something I can do," Sean said slowly, his face screwed in thought. Suddenly a boyish smile broke through. "I know, I can tell her I'm seeing someone."

A crease puckered between Emma's brows. "But that would be a lie because you're not."

He grinned and buffed the sides of her arms like a big brother. "Don't be so modest, Mrs. Malloy. Of course I am. I'm 'seeing' you right now, aren't I? That cute, little face crinkled in confusion and that glint of moral determination in those serious gray eyes? And I'll see you next week too, and the week after that, depending on what family function we've got going, right?"

"Well, I don't know—"

He laughed and twirled her high in the air. "No, don't say another word—this is perfect, and you know it. Next time Rose Kelly gets too close, I'll just tell her I'm sorry but I'm 'seeing someone.'" He set her down again, steadying her with a firm grip when she wobbled back on her feet. He gave her nose a playful tap. "I just don't have to tell her it's a very good friend."

With a glance at his watch, he shot her a grin, then gave her a wink over his shoulder as he strode to the door. "Thanks, Emma—you're one in a million. Gotta go change."

The door swished closed, leaving Emma gaping as it squealed on its hinges. She shook her head, unable to fight the smile that tugged at her lips. "Yes, you go change, Sean O'Connor," she whispered to herself with a soft chuckle, "but not too much, you hear? Some lucky woman is going to want you just the way you are."

8

Done! Katie jerked a sheet from her typewriter cylinder and released a silent groan, placing the last page from Parker's board-meeting notes on a neat pile. Who would have thought twelve men could be so chatty? Twelve women at a tea party, maybe, but not men discussing the progress of the BCAS in the last six months.

Betty glanced over her shoulder with a sympathetic smile. "All finished?"

"Yes," Katie said with a noisy exhale. She checked it off her to-do list and sagged back in her chair. "Who knew that sweet, quiet Parker could be so painstakingly verbose? Would you believe I've typed twenty-four pages?"

"What?" Bobbie Sue huffed and reeled more paper into her platen. "Girl, get on your knees and thank the good Lord above. I still ain't finished with Prissy Boy's notes yet, and I'm nigh near forty-five."

"*Pages?*" Katie shrieked. "He gave you more than forty-five pages of notes to type?"

Bobbie Sue rolled the back of her neck, emitting a low groan as she stretched. "Yes, ma'am, he did, and that's in addition to our Miss Betty here typing up the minutes. But do you think our boys could use her neatly typed notes that go to the board members? No, siree, Bob. They gotta have their own private notes just the way they want, with every *q* and *p* laid out just so." She glanced over her shoulder at Katie with a sideways smirk. "Especially our Mr. Priss."

Katie grinned and propped her chin in her hand. "Why do you call Luke 'Mr. Priss'?"

One thick, silver brow jerked high as Bobbie Sue seared her with a look. "You ever type any of his letters, missy? The man is as smart as a whip, but sweet mother of pearl, he can't spell to save his soul. But he's a master at grammar and punctuation, sure enough, so he puts you through the paces there, with indentations and commas just so, and heaven help you if your margins aren't pretty. You miss a comma or two with Mr. Parker or the words ain't centered perfect, and life is still good. But Mr. Luke? Mercy . . . even the angels can't help you." She hitched a thumb in Betty's direction. "Which is why I let this girl handle most of his work. I swear the woman's got a gift with that boy."

Betty hunched her shoulders and pulled her purse from the drawer. "What can I say, the 'boy' and I are close. I learned to handle him when he was no more than a thug on the streets."

A twinge of jealousy prickled under Katie's skin. She spied a stray page she'd forgotten to type and moaned, snatching it up from the floor. "No! I can't believe I missed a page."

Betty stood to her feet and stretched, and even her yawn looked graceful. "Do it Monday," she said. "Parker doesn't need it tonight—he's tied up in another meeting with Carmichael that will probably last till six." She tucked her clutch under her arm and strolled to the time clock to punch out. "Go home, Katie. You too, Bobbie Sue."

Bobbie Sue was up like a shot, purse in hand. "Don't have to tell me twice," she muttered. "I got hungry kids to feed." She winked at Katie. "And it's bingo night at St. Raphael's."

Katie glanced at Betty. "But it's only after four. Why are we leaving before five?"

Betty smiled. "I promised Luke I'd make dinner tonight if he let me go home early." She knocked on Luke's closed door, then popped her head in. "I'm heading out. Spaghetti or meat loaf?" she asked, then chuckled at his answer. She turned to wink at Bobbie Sue and Katie before glancing back in. "Mind if I send the girls home too? Parker's in a meeting till late."

She closed his door with a smug smile. "See, I told you we were close. Have a good weekend." She halted. "Ooops, sorry, Katie. You're still under house arrest, aren't you?" She scrunched her nose. "Do you really have to go the whole summer like this?"

Katie sighed. "I hope not. Luke gave Brady a good report to pass on to Father, so I'm hoping he'll lighten up on the confinement."

"Land sakes, girl, your daddy is a regular Simon Legree! Doesn't he know young girls can't be all cooped up?"

Katie's lips zagged into a devious smile. "Apparently not, Mizzzz Dulay." She wriggled her brows. "Would you care to enlighten him for me?"

"You did ask him about my birthday dinner next week, didn't you?" Betty said.

"No, but I will—this weekend, I promise."

She arched a brow. "Tell him your attendance is mandatory, a team meeting with food."

Katie smiled. "Okay, now scoot. Mr. Priss will probably be a bear when he gets home after the stack of new files I saw Parker put on his desk."

"Yeah, lucky me, huh? You coming, Bobbie Sue?"

"Comin'!" She hurried to clock out and then shot Katie a toothy grin. "Tootle-oo, sassy girl. And don't you be stayin' late, you hear?"

"I'm right behind you, I promise." She waved them out the door and slumped back into her chair with a faint smile.

Suddenly the office seemed like a morgue without them, and Katie sighed. Too quiet. And too lonely.

Her gaze darted to Luke's closed door, and her heart felt a twinge. "Yeah, lucky Betty," she muttered under her breath, wondering what it would be like to be that close with Luke McGee. Living with him, cooking for him. She blew out her frustration and started battering the keys, stopping occasionally to squint at Parker's scrawl. When she finished the sheet, she jerked it free and placed it on the pile, then slashed a diagonal line through her list for the day. She suddenly frowned, devoid of the usual satisfaction of tasks checked off a list. Her eyes flicked up to Luke McGee's closed door, and she scowled. It was a sad day, indeed, when completion of her beloved lists did not bring her joy. Her eyes narrowed. And all because of *him*.

She heard Luke's laughter and knew he was talking on the phone. She closed her eyes and listened intently, then heard it again. Her thoughts suddenly strayed to the night one week ago when he had kissed her not once, but twice. She opened her eyes to stare at the wall where he had pinned her, and the memory unleashed a flood of heat. With a catch of her breath, she jumped up. "I'm going home," she whispered, more to convince herself than the will to go. Truth be told, she didn't want to leave. At least not yet. She was desperate to clear the air with Luke.

Not that he hadn't made his own sad attempts at easing the tension between them. No, he had apologized on Monday first thing, strong-armed by Parker, no doubt. Called her in his office right after she'd arrived and asked her to close the door. His manner had been distant and cool, and as flat and professional as those prissy letters Bobbie Sue complained about typing. He told her he'd been out of line and it wouldn't happen again. And to make sure, she'd report solely to Parker. He'd avoided looking at her throughout the whole awkward conversation until the very end, when he'd stared her straight in the eyes. It was then that she saw his regret and his shame.

She had been heated up until that point, ready to rip a piece of his heart out and stomp on it for good measure. But something about the humility in his eyes disarmed her, stealing her thunder and leaving the ache behind. The ache to be in his arms again. To feel his lips on hers. To be a part of his life. In the end, she'd simply nodded and walked out of his office, numbed by the shock of her feelings. The week had progressed with no contact or communication whatsoever, as if cold, hard glass had been erected between them. He was the same Luke, laughing, teasing, joking—just not with her, casually avoiding her gaze and keeping his distance whenever they were in the same room. And for pity's sake, she was Katie O'Connor—when it came to friends, she wasn't used to being on the outside looking in . . . at least, not anymore.

A chill shivered her arms, and she rubbed them with her palms, gaze lighting on his door. She couldn't bear another week of this, shut out as if she didn't even exist. She rose and moved toward his office, desperate for a truce. With sweaty hands, she knocked.

"Come in."

She opened it a crack and peeked in.

"Hold on." He paused, hand over the phone and his smile polite. "You heading out?"

She shook her head and eased inside the door.

He stared, the whites of his eyes widening enough for her to notice. "Do you need something, Katie?"

She worried her lip and nodded. "I need to talk to you."

A muscle worked in his throat. "It can't wait till Monday?"

She shook her head, and a loose strand from her Dutch boy bob quivered against her cheek. She shoved it behind her ear and took a step forward, her eyes conciliatory. "Please?"

His gaze never left her face as he put the phone to his ear. "Look, something's come up. Can I call you later?" He glanced away and grinned. "Yeah, yeah, I'll call this time, I promise," he said in a husky voice he'd obviously intended as a whisper.

Jealousy stabbed within, and Katie turned to study an array of sports awards and plaques adorning his wall. A click of the phone in the cradle signaled he was through, and she looked back. "Do you mind if I sit down?"

He straightened and nodded, rolling away, as if to distance himself.

Sucking in a deep breath, she slipped into a chair and tucked her arms to her waist, gaze pinned to the antique clock that sat front center on his desk. "Thank you," she whispered.

"What's this all about, Katie?"

She looked up then, and the guarded look in his eyes bolstered her intent. "Luke, you apologized to me about last week, but I . . ." She swallowed hard, pride clogging her throat. "Well, I didn't get the chance to do the same, so I'd like to apologize now."

He blinked and said nothing, the blue eyes as remote as they'd been all week.

She squared her back and clasped her hands in her lap. "I said some things that were really unkind and . . . provoked you, I know." Her gaze diverted to the window, unable to bear the coolness of his manner. "But you took me by surprise, you see, and I reacted badly. Both in my words and in my . . . well, my response to your—"

He shot to his feet. "Katie, it's over and done. We've both apologized, so let it go. It's time to go home."

She rose to her feet and leaned forward, palms pressed to the front of his desk. "No, it's not over and done, Luke. You treat me like a leper around here."

He cuffed the back of his neck and exhaled. "What do you want from me, Katie?"

"I want you to talk to me and not through me, I want you to joke with me like you joke with the others, and I want you to treat me like you treat Parker and Betty—as a friend."

He slacked a hip and crossed his arms. "No."

"No?" She straightened, disbelief arching her brows. "I can't be a friend?"

"That's right." He shifted, and a muscle twittered along the hard line of his jaw.

"But, why?"

He leaned palms on the desk like she had, rolled sleeves revealing two muscled arms corded with strain. "Because it's no good, Katie. Too much butting heads, too much bad history." He rose to his full height and sucked in a deep breath, releasing it slowly. His eyes burned into hers as his voice lowered to a whisper. "Too much chemistry."

She swallowed hard. "We can be friends, Luke. I have no designs on you, I promise. For pity's sake, I'm practically engaged to Jack. He's the man I have every intention of marrying."

He gave her a thin look, sarcasm curling his lip. "Yeah, I can see he was on your mind last week."

Heat stung her cheeks. "I missed him, all right? I hadn't seen him in over a month."

He snatched a stack of papers from his desk and shoved them in a drawer, then slammed it hard. "Well, cheer up, Katydid, you only have a month and a half to go."

She clutched her arms to her sides, avoiding his eyes. "A month and a half that I refuse to be ignored by someone that I—" She hesitated, shocked at the words hovering on her tongue.

"Someone you what?" he asked in a clipped tone.

Her eyes lifted to his in the first honest show of sincerity she had ever given Cluny McGee. She sucked in a deep breath. "Have come to . . . respect and admire," she finished quietly, the whispered admission a startling revelation in her brain.

The words seemed to dismantle the barriers he'd erected, and she felt the slow breath he released as if it were her own. Something glinted in those remarkably clear, blue eyes, but she couldn't discern if it was shock or some deeper emotion buried deep down inside. Either way, it prompted the barest of smiles at the edges of his lips. "Thank you, Katie," he whispered, head bowed as he stared at the floor. "You have no idea what that means to me."

She released a slow breath of her own. "So we can be friends?"

He looked up beneath hooded eyes and gave her a smile that caused her stomach to flutter. "I don't know, Katie Rose. Sounds like a risky proposition to me."

Her grin was shaky. "That's the problem with you, Luke McGee. No adventure. What's the matter? Afraid of being bested by a girl?"

His grin challenged hers. "Nope, I'm game." He lifted his jacket off the back of the chair and slung it over his shoulder, his eyes searing hers with both warning and tease. "That is, as long as it isn't a contact sport."

She quickly held out her hand to deflect the heat in her cheeks. "No contact whatsoever, except a handshake to seal the deal, okay?"

He paused, then slowly reached across to put his hand in hers. "Okay, but I can tell you right now that Parker's not gonna like us being on friendly terms."

They shook, and the warmth of his palm swallowed her hand whole. She pulled away, ignoring the butterflies in her stomach. "Since when does Parker affect what you say or do?"

He strolled toward the door and opened it, waiting for her to go ahead before he flipped the light switch. A cocky grin tilted the corners of his mouth as he ambled toward the time clock. He gave her his customary smirk. "Good point."

Heaven help her, her stomach hadn't rolled like this since she'd been pregnant with Abby. Faith paused on the sidewalk of Tremont Street to press a shaky hand to her queasy abdomen, wishing that the source of her nausea were due to pregnancy. But she knew better.

She clutched the sack lunch tighter in her hands and straightened her shoulders, her eyes honing in on a small blue and white sign at the end of the block where her husband was working a rare Saturday. Her jaw tightened at the same time that her stomach did another flip, and she forged on, determined to get a good look at the new trainee.

From the moment Lizzie had dropped the bomb last week, Faith had been in a fog. Too angry at Collin to confront him, too angry at herself for not trusting him. She'd promised her mother she'd talk to him, and she would. Just not yet. Too many emotions had kept her roiling in indecision for a week, fearful of making a fool of herself if she were wrong . . . fearful of losing her temper if she were not. And so she had prayed, over and over, determined to be rational and clear-thinking in this whole situation. Cool and calm to avoid going off half-cocked.

Until this morning. The man had bolted out the door as if his feet were on fire, leaving his lunch behind—something Collin McGuire would *never* do. Her stomach did another roll and her lips flattened as she marched down the street. She slowed as she neared the shop window and then eased to the side to peek in. Her heart caught in her throat . . . and then in a whoosh of hot air, it drop-kicked back into her chest with a blast of fury. She fisted the knob of the door and heaved it open with an angry clash of bells, slamming it hard against the wall.

So much for calm.

Her husband lunged from the woman in his arms as if he'd been shot. He gaped at Faith, blood leeching from his face. "Faith! What are you doing here?"

She hurled the door closed again with a shriek of bells and a shudder of the wall. Her eyes singed him with green fire, and then shifted to char the woman beside him, whose face was as white as Collin's. "You forgot your lunch," she said in an icy tone as she strode toward his desk. She held the sack in the air and then dropped it in his in-basket with a noisy splat. "But I guess you weren't hungry." She crossed her arms and cauterized him with a look that pronounced him guilty on the spot. Her eyes flitted to the pretty woman beside him, back pressed to the counter and hand to her chest, then flitted back. She cocked her head. "At least not for food."

Blood gorged his cheeks, and she had never seen Collin McGuire flush that shade of scarlet before. He took a dangerous step forward with hands fisted tight, and the gray of his eyes could have been frosted pewter. He latched a steel grip to her arm with a tone as low and deadly as a whispered curse. "How dare you accuse me or that woman of anything sordid. It was nothing more than a simple hug, and we'll talk about this at home."

She flung his hand away, her eyes blazing. "No, we'll talk about it here!"

"Collin, I think it's best if I leave . . ." The woman's voice fairly wavered with fear as she snatched her purse from behind the counter, but Faith didn't care. She stared her down, all the more incensed that the woman's green eyes and auburn hair matched hers to a T. *Obviously my husband's coloring of choice*, she thought with renewed fury.

"No, Evelyn!" he ordered. "You stay. My wife and I can discuss this in the back room."

He clamped a tight hand to her wrist in a near-death grip and all but dragged her through the door, slamming it hard. He flung her hand away and then clenched his fists at his sides, the thick muscles of his arms ridged with tension. In all of their ten years of marriage, she had never seen him display such anger, and the very thought served to temper hers. His face was still flushed and his lips clamped white, silent for several seconds as if not trusting himself to speak. She sensed he teetered on the edge, his glare hard and unblinking. His muscular body stood stiff, no movement but the rise and fall of his chest and a tic at the base of his temple.

She swallowed hard, her anger giving way to his. "I'm sorry for losing my temper, but you have no idea how that looked . . ."

He stared her down, his words little more than a hiss delivered through clenched teeth. "It was a simple hug, Faith. To thank me for the job, and nothing more."

She folded her arms and jutted her chin to fight the tremble in her lips. "You should have told me, Collin, told me that you knew her before."

"I did." He bit out the words.

Her anger resurfaced. "You led me to believe she was an old family friend." She took a step forward and jabbed a finger in the air, aimed at the door. "That woman in there is anything but old!" Fury burned in her eyes. "And from what Lizzie says . . . *and* your base inclinations before we were married, I'm betting she was way more than a friend."

A rare curse hissed from his lips and he gouged the back of his neck in obvious frustration. "Blast your sister," he muttered. "For pity's sake, why did she tell you?"

Faith blinked, completely stunned. She clutched her arms to her waist to stop from slapping his face. Her upper body thrust forward in anger. "Because my husband didn't bother!" she shouted, unconcerned with the woman in the next room.

"And for precisely this reason!" he yelled back, his noise level matching hers. "Look at you—ready to condemn me and that woman for something that isn't true."

She shivered and fixed her gaze to the floor. "Lizzie says you were . . . involved with her." Her eyes flicked to his face. "Is that true?"

The air seemed to heave still in his throat, her question obviously stealing his wind. He looked away. "Yes," he said, sucking in a deep breath, "but that was almost twenty years ago, Faith, and we were both kids. For pity's sake, she's a widow with a thirteen-year-old son."

She paused, fear trapped in her throat, and for a brief

second, her eyelids flickered as she tried to form the words on her tongue. "Did you . . . sleep with her, Collin?"

His face bleached white. He slashed shaky fingers through his dark hair, refusing to meet her gaze. She tensed, watching the muscles in his throat work hard.

It was only seconds before he answered, but it seemed eons until he lowered his head to stare at the floor. "Yes."

She listed to the side, shock and jealousy warring within. She'd always known the kind of man he'd been before God, well aware of his reputation with women. But she wasn't prepared for the pain of it now, so close and so personal. She lifted her chin. "More than once?"

His head jerked up and his eyes seemed to plead, sorrow and shame evident in their depths. "Yes," he whispered, "but why dredge it up, Faith? It's only hurtful to the both of us, and it doesn't matter now—"

"It matters," she rasped, her voice thick with pain. "It's the difference between a night of indifference and a relationship in which you gave this woman a piece of your soul." She looked up, her eyes locked on his. "How long, Collin?"

He exhaled slowly, the fight leaving his body. "Over a year," he whispered, his voice resigned. "We were young and stupid, Faith, barely sixteen." He put a hand to his eyes. "We had dreams of getting married one day."

She staggered back, bracing herself with a hand to the table. She knew his past, but the reality of that woman in his bed cut through her like a shard of glass. She closed her eyes and pressed a hand to her mouth, rivulets of tears seeping through her fingers.

Within one silent heave, he was at her side, seizing her in his arms with fierce possession. He buried his face in her neck, his words and kisses repentant in the folds of her hair. "Faith, I'm sorry, I was stupid. I should have told you, I know, but I didn't want to hurt you." He pulled back to stare at her, palms caressing the sides of her face. Moisture glimmered in his eyes. "I love you, Faith, more than life itself, and I would never hurt you for the world."

She sagged into his arms, her body heaving. "Why, Collin? Why would you hire her?"

She felt his hand in her hair, stroking her, comforting her. His voice was low and thick with emotion. "I can't explain it, Faith, but I . . . had to. I swear I had no intention of hiring Evelyn, ever. But when I found out she just lost her husband to a debilitating disease, watched him die a slow, hard death, I . . ." She felt his shiver all the way to her bones. "I couldn't help but think, what if that was you or me, if one of us were to . . ." His voice broke, and she clutched him tightly, pressing in to become one in his pain.

He drew in a deep breath and exhaled slowly, bundling her closer. "Forgive me, Faith, please. I should have told you."

She pulled back to stroke his cheek, the shadow of dark stubble rough beneath her hand. Her eyes softened as she stared up at her husband. "I love you, Collin McGuire, because of your sensitive heart and sometimes in spite of it. But you and I both know . . . this woman can't stay."

Sorrow reflected in his eyes. "I know it's painful for you, Faith, having her here. And it's painful for me, truly. But I can't let her go. She has a sick boy to support."

"She'll find another job."

His fingers traced the curve of her jaw, eyes gentle but firm. "No, Faith, she won't. She hasn't worked in years, and her schedule is . . . sporadic at best."

Faith cocked her head. "Then why—"

His hand glazed across her lips, caressing her mouth, stilling her words. His voice was quiet, but it pulsed with feeling, reflecting the man she was privileged to love. "Because she needs the money, Faith. She needs to get by, just until her son . . ." He looked away, and she could see the tears well in his eyes. He swallowed his emotion in one painful gulp. "He's very sick, in and out of the hospital at various times. Evelyn's mother will stay with him while she works, but there are days when she . . . she won't be able to be here. No other employer would agree to that, Faith." His eyes returned to hers. "Trust me on this, please. I can't let Evelyn go."

She stared at her husband, moved by the intensity in his eyes, the passion in his face. The passion that had once driven him as a lost young man prone to dark moods and a hunger for love. The same passion that now cherished and protected her and the girls every day of their lives. He was a man gifted with a wellspring of love. How could she stop the flow of his heart?

She released her surrender in one frail breath. "All right, Collin. I trust you."

He crushed her to him in a desperate hug, his broken words muffled in her hair. "I love you, Faith, with every fiber of my being. No other woman has ever captured me like you, possessed me so completely. You and the girls . . . you're my reason to live, the reason I rise in the morning and the breath in my lungs."

Hot tears sprang to her eyes and she clutched him with violent devotion. "I love you, Collin, with all of my heart, and I trust you. God has used you to pour abundant blessings into my life." She closed her eyes and allowed her trust to rest in both God and her husband. "And Evelyn's, apparently," she whispered against his chest.

And at the sound of her own words, peace lighted upon her soul.

9

We're going to *Kearney's*?" Katie asked in a shocked whisper. She stared up at one of Boston's most notorious pubs with a look of awe.

Betty gave her a sideways glance and grinned. "It's my birthday, so it's my choice. And this is where I wanted to go."

Katie's tone was almost reverent. "But I've heard rumors it's a speakeasy, and I've never been in one before. Jack promised to take me, but Father's threats always kept me away."

Betty glanced back at Parker and Luke, deep in conversation a few paces behind. "Don't worry, we won't be tipping booze if I know those two." She looped her arm through Katie's and stared wistfully at the charming glass-pane-and-brick storefront with its red potted geraniums and a green awning emblazoned with "Kearney's Café." "We'll be sitting up front in the café, not in the speakeasy in the basement," she said with sigh. "Although I'd give my mother's eyeteeth for a frosty Guinness along with a hamburger right about now."

Katie tugged on the brass handle of the ornate cherry-wood door, and instantly her mouth watered at the rush of tempting smells that escaped the noisy pub. The sound of a jazz piano rag set her legs twitching while the aroma of frying fish and chips and grilled meat rumbled her stomach. She held the door for Betty. "Maybe Luke will buy you a beer for your birthday."

Betty laughed as she sailed inside, tugging Katie along while Luke propped the door for more patrons behind them. She leaned close to Katie's ear. "Maybe the Luke I used to know, but not this one. He's gone all chaste on me, like Parker. Heaven forbid either of them should break the law."

"Chaste? Luke?" Katie halted on the spot, grateful for the barrage of music, laughter, and off-key singing that covered her shock. The memory of Luke's ravaging kiss against the wall suddenly heated her more than the sticky closeness of the crowded room, making it hard for her to breathe. Her eyes drifted closed for a moment and she swallowed hard, irritated by the heat that pulsed in her cheeks. She'd been far from successful in forgetting what happened that night. And she knew as sure as the flutter in her stomach, Luke McGee's lips, his hands, his intent had been anything but "chaste."

"Oh, look, those people in the back are leaving—come on!" Betty literally dragged her through the crowd to the back of the pub in the direction of a rounded booth in the corner, not quite vacated. Betty smiled and waited patiently as the party gathered their things and departed. With a smug look, she slid into the booth and pulled Katie in alongside, her lips close to Katie's ear. "Trust me—complete bluenoses, both he and Parker." Her eyes followed Luke and Parker as they made their way through the crowd to the booth. "But Luke wasn't always like that, I can tell you that. Back in New York, our boy had quite the reputation with the ladies."

"You mean . . . ?"

Betty gave her a pointed look. "And then some."

Katie gulped. "Oh."

For the briefest of moments, a hint of melancholy shadowed Betty's face. "Yeah, but then he got religion," she said with a slant of her brow, "and now he and Parker are a matched set." Her voice softened as she watched their approach. "But you know what? Sometimes I really, really miss the old Luke."

"What's your rush, Galetti? You act like they're giving away free beer or something." Luke jerked his tie loose and shed his jacket, placing it neatly folded between Katie and him before dropping into the booth. "Man, it's hot in here." He rolled his sleeves and gave Betty a grin. "Are you sure you don't want to eat somewhere we can sit outside?"

Betty pursed her lips. "Nope, it's my birthday, and you and Parker promised me dinner anywhere I want." She folded her hands on the table. "So I suggest you stop grousing, McGee. I could have just as easily chosen Frankie & Johnnie's and set you both back a pretty penny."

"She's right, you know," Parker said, tie still intact but jacket discarded on the seat. He sifted a hand through sandy brown hair as he scanned the café. "Anybody see a waitress?"

Luke leaned back against the cherry-wood booth with arms folded and eyes closed. "Yeah, Shirl knows we're here—she waved when we came in."

"You mean when *you* came in," Betty said. "Come on, McGee, wake up! This is a party."

One of Luke's blue eyes edged open. "Can't help it—the heat's putting me to sleep."

"I'll bet a nice, frosty Guinness would wake you up," Betty said with a wiggle of brows.

The slitted eye closed once again. "How 'bout a nice, frosty Bevo instead?"

"Come on, Luke—make me a happy woman just once—embrace the moment. I want to celebrate my birthday with alcohol, not near beer." The pout was evident in Betty's voice.

"Bevo has alcohol, Bets," Parker said with a patient smile. "One-half of one percent in the finest malt beverage Anheuser-Busch makes."

"You guys are hopeless," Betty muttered. She gave Katie a look. "See what I mean?"

"You spinning tales about your superiors to this innocent young woman, Galetti?" Luke's eyes opened to reveal a hint of a tease.

"Humph, nothing to spin. You guys make the Hardy Boys look like Capone's thugs."

"Sorry for the wait." A perky brunette with unusual green eyes plopped four menus on the table. She scanned the booth with a bright smile. "It's good to see you again, it's been too long . . . Parker, Betty . . . *Luke*."

It was obvious from the look in the waitress's eyes that it was particularly good to see him again. Katie frowned, taking an immediate dislike to the woman.

A heart-melting grin lit Luke's face as he crossed muscled arms on the table. "Hi, Shirl. Yeah, it's been brutal at work lately. No rest for the wicked, I guess."

Miss Perky pressed her order pad to her ample chest and smiled. "You? Wicked? Now why do I find that so easy to believe, Luke McGee?"

"Because you're a Dumb Dora," Betty whispered to Katie behind her menu.

Katie giggled, and Luke shot them a look of warning before inflicting further charms on the waitress. "Well, 'wicked's' not on the agenda tonight, Shirl, so just bring Parker, Betty, and me a round of Bevos while we look over the menu." He glanced at Katie. "What'll you have?"

"Well, since a Guinness is out of the question . . . I guess I'll have a Bevo too."

He turned back to Shirl. "Bevo all around, then."

"Sure thing," she said with a sultry smile. She stacked the few dirty plates left on the table, then leaned to wipe it clean with a wide stretch that Katie felt sure was for Luke's benefit.

"So, when's Bobbie Sue coming?" Parker asked after Shirl left, his attention focused on the menu.

Betty glanced at her watch. "As soon as she gets the kids fed and watered, I suppose."

"I hope she doesn't take too long—I'm starved." Katie flipped her menu on the table and glanced at Betty. "I just may order two hamburgers."

Luke glanced up. "Settle down, Katie Rose, this isn't Jack you're stiffing with the bill, you know. Just two impoverished lawyers."

"You can fit two hamburgers into that tiny body?" Betty asked, mouth gaping.

Katie nodded. "And a chocolate milkshake, if I'm really hungry." She tilted her head and gave Luke a smirk. "Like tonight."

Luke glanced at Parker with a groan. "I don't have enough cash. Did you bring enough?"

"For the girls, but not for us to eat too," Parker said with a serious face.

Katie placed a hand on Luke's arm, her face the picture of innocence. "Don't worry, McGee, something tells me ol' Shirl will take something other than cash."

His gaze flitted to the hand on his arm before it rose to settle on her face with a lazy smile. "You think?" he asked in a husky tone.

Blood rushed to her cheeks. She jerked her hand away and placed it in her lap. "I meant washing dishes, McGee. Get your mind out of the gutter."

He grinned and leaned back against the booth. "Can't. It's where I was born, remember?"

"So, what's it going to be?" Shirl reappeared, suddenly smelling a whole lot more like gardenias than chicken-fried steak. She unloaded their drinks on the table, took their orders, and then disappeared again with a final smile in Luke's direction.

Katie cradled the icy mug in her hands and allowed her thoughts to drift as Betty, Luke, and Parker bantered over the strengths and weaknesses of the Red Sox vs. Yankees. She took a sip of near beer and felt contentment in her bones, as if she belonged here, an integral part of these people she'd come to love and admire. Not like with Jack and the gang, where her sharp tongue and driving ambition always set her apart, elevating her to a point where she felt removed. True, she liked the control she seemed to have over her old group, but this—this was different. A caring, a depth that she couldn't quite put her finger on. Relationships that were less surface and more substance, providing a connection that was so new to her. She released a quiet sigh as she settled back in the booth, smiling as Betty took a potshot at Luke.

And speaking of "new," she thought with a sideways glance, her feelings for the man beside her were totally unprecedented. Even Jack couldn't flutter her stomach with a look or a word like Luke McGee, and she was very careful to admit that the thought still scared her silly. But true to his word, since the night they had sealed their friendship with a handshake, Luke had treated her with the same unassuming warmth and camaraderie he enjoyed with Parker and Betty. And Katie had reveled in it. A loner by nature, suddenly she didn't feel so alone anymore.

Of course, initially Parker hadn't been happy about her and Luke's newfound friendship, just as Luke had predicted, and Katie wasn't really sure why. She took another sip of her drink and studied him now, this strong, silent man who was Luke McGee's best friend. He'd begun to open up with her over the course of her term at the BCAS, and Katie knew without a doubt that Parker Riley was both a high-caliber man and the true definition of a friend. He was the quietest of the three, but somehow Katie sensed he was also the strongest, possessing a fierce allegiance to Luke and a protective kinship with Betty. A silent support, who unlike Luke with his charismatic personality or Betty with her dry wit, was more than content to fade into the background while his two best friends took center stage.

"Oh, no, you two aren't going to start talking shop on

my birthday!" Betty's threat disrupted Katie's train of thought.

Luke reached for Betty's hand, stroking it with his thumb. "Come on, Bets, this is Gabe we're talking about here. I haven't had a chance to talk to Parker since his meeting with Carmichael."

Betty's lower lip jutted, prompting a smile and a plea from Luke.

"Just a few minutes more, I promise," he said with a boyish grin, "then I'll kiss your feet for the rest of the night."

Betty's lips pulled into a faint smile. "Throw in a back rub, and you have a deal." She leaned close to Katie as Luke turned to Parker. "Royal suckers for a woman's pout, both of 'em."

"No, he can't do that!" Luke's outburst recaptured their attention. "We can barely keep tabs on her here in Boston—it's sheer suicide to send Gabe on a train to the Midwest by herself."

"She won't be by herself, she'll be with ten other orphans and the Tuttles, remember?"

Luke groaned. "I forgot about the Tuttles—Gabe will eat them alive! No, Parker, we can't let Carmichael do this to her—or to them."

"We don't have a choice, Luke, Carmichael's made up his mind." Parker's eyes reflected the same pain as his friend's. "Unless you can find an iron-clad arrangement for Gabe before the end of the month, she'll be on that orphan train to the Midwest whether we like it or not."

A faint hiss of a swear word parted from Luke's lips. "It'll kill her," he whispered, "not to mention what it'll do to me."

"Maybe not," Parker said quietly. "As long as she's in Boston, Gabe has her heart set on living with you, which we both know is impossible. The Midwest might be just what she needs."

Luke stared, his face a study in anguish. "God knows how I wish I could adopt her."

"You know better than that. For one, Carmichael wouldn't allow it, and two, Gabe needs a solid home with both a mother and father."

"I know," he whispered, his gaze lost in the murky depths of his near beer.

Betty reached over to tug at his hand. "Come on, Luke, cheer up. You're always harping on me to pray about every little thing. So pray for Gabe—that God finds her the perfect home. Then trust him to do it—isn't that what you always tell me?"

His gaze shifted to Betty. "You mean you actually listen when I spout off? I always thought you were just humoring me."

She patted his hand with a sympathetic smile, then took a sip of her drink as she eyed him over the rim. "I am, honey, but you seem to eat that stuff up, so I thought I'd give it a try."

"Move over, people, the party is here!" Bobbie Sue blew in with all the bluster of a Georgia hurricane. She sidled in next to Luke, promptly butting him into Katie who elbowed Betty to move over. "Sweet Robert E. Lee, y'all look like somebody died." She sniffed at Luke's half-empty Bevo and wrinkled her nose. "No wonder. Too cheap for the real stuff downstairs, eh, boss men?"

Parker smiled and nursed his drink. "We don't need alcohol to have fun, Mrs. Dulay, at least not with you here. And yes, we are too cheap. Not to mention it's against the law."

"Tsk, tsk. Well, I figured as much, so I came prepared." She winked at Betty and lifted her skirt to reveal a hidden flask tucked into the garter on her leg.

"Come on, Bobbie Sue, this is a dry party." Luke tried to grab the flask, but she held it away.

"It may be dry for you and the boss, Mr. Priss, but this here birthday girl and I are going to celebrate the way the good Lord intended." She leaned to toss the flask into Betty's lap. "When the Good Book bans liquor from its pages, I suspect I will too. But till then, Miss Betty and I plan to have a proper toast on her birthday."

"Bless you," Betty said with a chuckle and poured a touch of the flask into her half-empty Bevo, ignoring both Luke and Parker's looks of disapproval.

"You're a big girl, Galetti," Luke said. "If this place gets raided, I'm not bailing you out."

She grinned and quickly slipped a hefty pour of the flask into Katie's drink before Luke could object. "If this place gets raided, McGee, you'll be in the cell next to mine. Only you'll be stone-cold sober while I'll be warm and gloriously tipsy."

"With a glorious headache in the morning, no doubt," Parker said with a wry smile.

Luke reached for Katie's glass, but Katie jerked it away, clutching it to her chest like it was the nectar of the gods. "Oh no you don't, McGee, I'm a big girl too, remember?"

His eyes narrowed. "Eighteen doesn't qualify as 'big girl' to me, Katie Rose, and besides, while you're with me, I have a responsibility to your father. Give me your glass—now."

"You're not my father."

"No, but I'm the man who has his ear *and* your employer. Hand it over."

"Come on, Luke, don't be such a fuddy-duddy. It's my birthday, and I want Katie to have a toast." Betty shifted closer to Parker, inching Katie along with her.

Ignoring Betty's plea, Luke trained his eyes on Katie. "Give me the drink, or so help me, I'll be forced to tell your father."

"You wouldn't . . . ," she whispered.

The blue eyes never blinked. "Try me."

Heat blistered her cheeks and suddenly all she could see was Cluny McGee, besting her once again. With a quick flick of her wrist, she downed half a spiked beer in three horrendous gulps before Luke could jerk the glass from her hand. Betty chuckled and slapped her on the back while Bobbie Sue whooped loudly, both ignoring the fire in Luke's eyes.

Katie choked, the alcohol burning her throat in a delayed reaction, and Luke shoved his near beer into her hands. She took a long gulp and handed it back, chest heaving.

He seared her with a look. "You're a brat, Katie Rose, and two and a half months confinement is not near long enough."

"Well, I'm quite sure you'll remedy that," she said with a defiant tilt of her chin and suddenly realized she could care less. A relaxing warmth oozed through her that made her feel almost giddy. Whenever Jack had tried to get her to drink alcohol, she'd adamantly refused, determined that no man or substance would ever control her. But now, when Luke had ordered her to turn over her drink, she found herself less concerned with the substance than the man. It was bad enough her father had license to order her around; the last thing she needed was for Luke McGee to think he could do the same. A shiver traveled Katie's spine. Sweet saints, deliver her from a husband like that! Thank heavens for Jack, because no man—other than her father—was going to order her around. *Especially* Luke McGee.

Betty tossed the flask back to Bobbie Sue. "Don't be such a killjoy, Luke, it's my birthday. Besides, you and Parker could do with a nip or two yourselves, you know." She shot him a grin. "Especially you, *Mr. Priss*. You were a whole lot more fun when you drank."

Luke scowled. "And what's with the 'Mr. Priss' stuff? It's Parker who wears the starched shirts and aftershave that makes him smell like some rich-boy pantywaist."

Parker appeared wounded. "Hey, McGee, I'm not the one attacking you here, remember?" He lifted his Bevo with a crooked smile. "Besides, my family may have money, but I'm a working stiff just like you. And since when does good grooming qualify as prissy? Let's face it—you've earned the name fair and square with your obnoxious clerical demands on these lovely ladies."

"Hear, hear," Bobbie Sue bellowed with a tip of her newly

spiked beer. "You preach it, Mr. Parker. This boy here's given me more headaches than my eight kids put together."

"I'm particular, so sue me," Luke muttered in a hurt tone. He glanced past Bobbie Sue at Shirl, who was headed their way with a tray heaped high with dinner. "Good—now you people can chew on something other than my hide."

Shirl plopped the hefty platter on the table and started unloading plates all around. She set Luke's down with a wink. "Double bacon cheeseburger, extra bacon, just how you like it."

"Thanks, Shirl," he said with a ready smile, "and we have one more order, if you don't mind, along with another round of Bevo. Tell her what you want, Bobbie Sue."

Bobbie Sue glanced at Luke's food and opted for the same, sending Shirl on her way with another over-the-shoulder smile at the man of her dreams.

Katie's gaze flitted from the thick stack of bacon on Luke's burger to the two measly pieces on each of hers. She frowned. And his pile of fried potatoes was downright obscene too. "You must have a pound of bacon on that burger. For pity's sake, what'd you do, bribe her?"

He pulled several pieces of bacon off and handed them to Bobbie Sue. "This'll tide you over till your food comes." His eyes shifted to Katie's plate. "Unless Miss-Eyes-Bigger-Than-Her-Stomach can part with one of her burgers till Shirl delivers yours."

Katie pushed her plate toward Bobbie Sue, who grinned and took a sandwich. "Why, thank you, sassy girl, much obliged."

Luke lifted the mammoth burger to his lips, pausing to give Katie a weighted gaze. "Bribe her? No, *Katydid*, because unlike you, some women actually enjoy doing what I ask."

"Ask maybe, but force? Do they enjoy that?"

He bit into his sandwich and chewed slowly, a smile surfacing at the edges of his lips. "Sometimes," he said, heating her with a shuttered look while he took a slow swig of his drink.

Katie's cheeks flamed hot, and she itched to slap that smug smile off his handsome face. Instead, she turned to Betty while nibbling a scrawny piece of bacon. "So, how are the ribs?"

With a swipe of her tongue, Betty licked the remains of barbecue sauce from the corner of her mouth. "De-lish," she said with a dreamy smile, "and well worth the money, especially since Luke and Parker are paying the bill."

Katie grinned and popped a pickle in her mouth. Whether from Bobbie Sue's vodka, Luke's presence, or the company of good friends, a warm glow spread through her as the evening continued. Shirl kept them supplied with plenty of Bevos while Luke, Betty, and Bobbie Sue supplied them with plenty of laughter. With a contented sigh, Katie pushed her empty dessert plate away and sneaked a reluctant peek at her watch. *No!* She leaned back in the booth and closed her eyes, her friends' laughter filling her with longing. It was eight o'clock, she thought with a wave of frustration, and Father had warned her to be home early. A silent groan lodged in her throat.

"Betty?"

Katie's eyes jolted open as a tall brunette strolled over to their booth, scarlet lips agape and a glazed look in her eyes. The scent of alcohol clung to her like a cheap perfume as she waved on a group of lady friends who were heading toward the door. "What in the world are you doing here?" the woman asked, her bloodshot eyes narrowing. "And where's Leo?"

Betty's face leeched to the color of the napkin still pressed to her lips. Her fingers shook as she lowered it to her lap. "I'm j-just in town for the weekend, to visit friends." She swallowed hard. "Leo had to work."

The woman's eyes shifted to Luke, and a sneer lifted the corners of her mouth. "With him? Does Leo know?"

Luke half rose to extend his hand with a forced smile. "Imagine running into you here, Roberta. Small world."

She ignored him and returned her gaze to Betty, whose face looked as pale as if she had just thrown up. Or was about to. "Since I moved to Boston a while back, I don't get to see Leo all that often. A pity, really." Her black eyes glittered with scorn. "But maybe I'll just have to give him a call soon . . . you know, to reconnect."

Betty sat up higher, shoulders squaring and chin lifting despite the pallor of her skin. "You do that, Roberta. And I'll be sure to tell him on Monday that I saw you."

"Please do," she said with a cold smile. Her eyes scanned the table with obvious disdain before she turned on her three-inch heels and traipsed toward the door to join her friends.

Betty sagged back into the booth with tears rimming her eyes.

Luke tapped Bobbie Sue on the shoulder. "Let me out." Bobbie Sue complied and Luke edged out of the booth with suit coat in hand. He reached into his pocket and pulled out a twenty-dollar bill and tossed it on the table. "Pay the bill when Shirl comes, will ya, Parker? I'll meet you outside."

"What are you going to do?" Betty rose up in the booth, palms pressed tight to the table.

Luke slung his jacket over his shoulder with that annoying air of confidence that had once gotten on Katie's nerves. "Gonna make a few amends, Galetti, that's all." He winked and shot her a wayward smile that wreaked havoc with Katie's pulse. "I can't abide it when a woman holds a grudge."

"Leave it alone, will you, Luke? It won't do any good—she hates you. Besides, it's too late. Leo will know where I am by morning."

A nerve twitched in his cheek despite the wide smile on his lips. "No, he won't, Bets. Not when I get done schmoozing his cousin." And with another smile that spelled trouble, he turned and strode toward the door.

Parker rose and scanned the bar. "I'll go hunt Shirl down for our bill."

"What was that all about?" Katie placed a gentle hand

on Betty's arm. "And are you okay? Who was that woman anyway, and what's Luke going to do?"

Betty sighed and sipped more of her spiked beer, her eyes glassy over the rim of her mug. "My ex-boyfriend's cousin. Used to have a thing for Luke before he gave her the brush. I guess he's gonna *smooth* things over."

"But, why?"

Betty blinked, as if to diffuse the tears in her eyes. She upended her drink and squinted at Bobbie Sue. "Got any more of that hootch, Miz Dulay? I could use a stiff one about now."

"Sure thing, honey, here you go." Bobbie Sue shoved the flask across the table, and Betty snatched it up, along with Luke's unfinished glass of Bevo. She dumped half of his near beer into her glass and poured the rest into Katie's, topping both off with a hefty dose of vodka. "Here, Katie, we might as well salvage this party. Things won't look so bad once we finish these." She tossed the flask back to Bobbie Sue who promptly strapped it back on her thigh.

The whites of Katie's eyes expanded as Betty chugged her drink, and then with a bob of her throat, she stared at the glass in her own hand. She knew she shouldn't drink it because she was already a little tipsy. And Luke would be livid if he found out, not to mention her father. She gnawed on her lip, craving more of the glorious warmth she was feeling at the moment. After all, it had only relaxed her, not made her drunk. And relaxation was a good thing, right? She released a silent sigh. Especially with Luke sitting too close for comfort. She sucked in a deep breath and cast caution to the wind, finally bolting a hefty swallow as she sank back against the booth. The taste burned her tongue, and she wrinkled her nose. "But why does Luke have to smooth things over?"

"To seal her lips," Betty said with a wry smile. "And trust me, nobody's better at sealing lips than our Mr. McGee."

Katie winced, Betty's comment burning as much as the vodka glazing her throat. "But why? Seal her lips from what?"

Betty and Bobbie Sue exchanged glances before Betty downed another gulp. "From telling my ex-boyfriend where I am. He tends to get slap-happy, you see, especially when his punching bag disappears from New York."

A second sip of vodka pooled in Katie's mouth while her eyes flared in shock. She swallowed hard. "You mean he hit you?"

One edge of Betty's mouth curled in disgust. "That's putting it mildly. You might say I was his own personal boxing gym."

"No," Katie whispered. She took another quick gulp of her drink, and then another. A thick, languid warmth began to creep through her veins. "Will he come after you?"

"Not if Luke has anything to say about it. Seems he's appointed himself chief bodyguard and friend." She finished off her drink with a stiff tilt of her glass just as Parker returned.

"The bill has been paid and Shirl amply compensated," Parker said. "Although she was disappointed that Luke's flown the coop. Let's go." He lifted his coat from the seat and helped Betty from the booth. His eyes flicked in Katie's direction. "You coming back to the house with us, Katie? We play a pretty mean game of Pinochle."

Katie upended the rest of her drink and tried to stand, but her legs felt as limp as the soggy potatoes at the pit of her stomach. She blinked several times to clear her eyes, but Parker seemed to be swaying. "'Fraid not, Parker. Father said dinner only, then straight home. I'm to be back before he and Mother get home from a wedding." She put a hand to her forehead, suddenly feeling woozy. She squinted at her watch. "What time izz it, anyway?"

Bobbie Sue laughed and tucked an arm around Katie's waist, helping her out of the booth. "Eight-thirty, sassy girl, and way too early to go home drunk."

"Drunk?" Parker grabbed her shoulders. "Katie, look at me!"

Her head bobbed up. "Mmm?"

He groaned. "Tell me you're not drunk, please."

A silly smile eased across her face. "Okay. I'm not." She hiccupped.

His gaze darted from Bobbie Sue to Betty. "Tell me you didn't give her more to drink."

Betty wrapped an arm around Parker's shoulders. "Come on, Parker, it's a party. We hardly gave her anything—she's just a lightweight."

Katie nodded slowly. Her eyelids fluttered closed as warmth seeped through her body.

He groaned. "So help me, Galetti, I have a good mind to fire you. She's only eighteen, for pity's sake, and her father's as tight with Harris Stowe as this noose you're trying to put around my neck. Luke is going to cinch me up."

"No, he won't. You're the boss. Besides, Luke is all bluff when it comes to you, and you know it. Relax—it's my birthday. What you need is a swig of Bobbie Sue's flask."

"No, thank you," he said in a clipped tone. He leveled an arm around Katie's waist. "Come on, Katie, we'll take you back to the boardinghouse. You need some strong coffee."

Katie's eyes popped open. "Uh-oh, can't, Parker. Gotta go straight home. Or I'll never see Jack again."

He sighed and rubbed his forehead, which was pinched in a frown. "What time will your parents be home from the wedding?"

She blinked several times. The warmth purling through her body suddenly ran cold. "Soon," she muttered, "so I haf ta-go—*now*." She started forward, weaving on her feet.

Bobbie Sue and Betty shored her up on either side, looping their arms through hers. "Come on, Sass, we'll take you home," Betty said with a chuckle. "Although you're going to miss the fireworks between Luke and Parker."

"Oh, drat," she muttered, "I loooove fireworks."

Betty and Bobbie Sue dragged her through the noisy pub and out the front door. She was met with a glorious blast of cooler air, which restored her good humor. Euphoria swelled in her chest as she stared up at the sky. "Oh my, look at that moon, will ya?" She giggled and broke free from Bobbie Sue and Betty, extending her arms in a joyous twirl. "Makes me wanna fly!"

"Whoa, girl," Betty said with a chuckle as Katie teetered on the cobblestones. She snatched her at the waist. "You're already flying pretty high, honey."

Katie giggled. "Whoops, thank ya, Bets, but ya hafta admit, it's a beauooootiful night!"

"It won't be so beautiful if we don't get you home before your parents," Parker grumbled. He cinched an arm to her waist and scoured the street. "Where the devil is Luke?"

Betty motioned her head toward a nearby alley. "Over there, in the shadows. With *her*."

Katie looked up, and suddenly her elation fizzled faster than foam on a warm Bevo. Heat stung her cheeks as she stared, stomach clutching at the sight of Luke McGee's broad back bent over a shadowed woman butted against the alley wall. It wasn't difficult to see that she was locked in his arms, and Katie felt a sharp jab of jealousy.

Parker handed her over to Betty while his gaze shot to the alley. "Bets, you need to duck out of here before that dame sees you again, and Katie needs to get home. Because if Luke sees her like this, your birthday's not going to be so happy. We'll meet you back at the house."

"You got it, Boss," Betty said with a chuckle. "But what if her daddy's home?"

"Then you have no choice but to take her to Robinson's for as many stiff cups of coffee as it takes to sober her up. But whatever you do, do *not* let her father see her this way, understand?"

Betty planted a kiss on Parker's cheek. "Sorry for all the trouble, but isn't this fun?"

"Loads," he said in a droll tone. "Now, get her out of here—fast."

"Yes, sir. Tell Lover Boy he can drop the act. It's making me nauseous." Betty latched on to Katie's arm and hauled her down the street.

Bobbie Sue hustled to keep up. "Hold on . . . this ol' body has a few years on it, you know."

Katie jerked her arm free and dug in her heels, swaying on her feet. She glowered at Betty, hands balled into fists at her side. "Was Luke necking with that . . . that bimbo?"

Betty's lips pressed tight. "All in the service of a friend," she muttered.

"But that's diz-gusting! And sick!"

"Not as sick as you're going to be if that giggle water takes a turn in your stomach, sassy girl," Bobbie Sue said between heavy breaths.

"Or if Luke or your daddy catches you drunk," Betty added with a lift of her brow. She clamped a firm arm around Katie's waist. "We need to get you home before it's too late."

"Katie, wait up!"

"Uh-oh," Betty said with a quick glance over her shoulder. "We got trouble." She pressed her lips to Katie's ear. "Let me do the talking, you hear?" She slid her arm from Katie's waist to hook it around her elbow instead.

Luke huffed to a stop, hands on his knees while Parker trailed behind with a grim look in his eyes. "Bets, Bobbie Sue—Parker's going to walk you back to the house while I take Katie home. I need to speak with her father."

Betty and Parker exchanged glances. Betty pursed her lips and tightened her hold on Katie's arm. "He's at a wedding tonight, so no need. And Katie wants to show me something at her house, so we'll walk her home." She perched a hand on her hip and gave him an off-center smile, obviously to divert his attention. "So, you engaged or what?"

He grinned and wiped his mouth with the side of his hand. "Pert near. What took you so long, anyway? My lips are chapped raw."

"So, did it work?"

Luke tucked an arm around her shoulder and pulled her close to deposit a kiss on her forehead. "Like a charm. Silence—bought and paid for with a promise to call when I'm in town again." He grinned. "Consider it a birthday present, Miss Galetti, although I wasn't planning on spending *that* much." He patted her cheek and pushed her back, then tugged on Katie's arm. "Come on, Katie Rose. I promised your father I'd get you home safe and sound."

Katie stumbled against him, nose flat against his rock-hard chest. The faint smell of musk and peppermint and Luke teased her senses, forcing the blood to warm beneath her skin. She closed her eyes and emitted a soft, little moan, wishing she could stay there forever.

He clutched her with a low chuckle. "The near beer set you on your ear, Katie Rose?"

"Luke, I told you, Bobbie Sue and I can walk her home." Betty made an attempt to peel her from Luke's chest, but Katie only released a languid sigh and curled her arms around his waist.

Instantly, his muscles tensed beneath her hold. "Katie?"

She slowly lifted her head and blinked, lost in the hard chiseled line of his jaw, that dangerous cleft in his chin, and those incredibly blue eyes that always pierced right through her.

Like now.

He held her at arm's length, scanning her face with fatal accuracy. His eyes darkened to pewter in the lamplight. "Are you drunk?"

"She's just feeling the effects of that first drink," Betty said quickly. She tugged her out of Luke's hold, causing Katie to wobble on her heels. "I'm taking her home, *now*."

Luke yanked her back with a hard grip. "Get your hands off her. I want to see her walk."

He let go of her arm, and Katie swore that the group of them were running in circles. She closed her eyes, but the spinning only got worse, forcing the food in her stomach to begin to rise.

"Katie!" Her eyes popped open at Luke's command. "Walk to me—*now*!"

She stared, incensed at his order and wishing he'd just stand still, for pity's sake. Her chin jutted in indignation as she propped her hands on her hips, ignoring the fact she was swaying as much as he was. "I don like your attitude, McGee. Why don you jus walk ta me?"

Bobbie Sue snorted.

Luke's jaw hardened, defying his gentle tone. "Katie, will you *please* walk over here?"

"Musch better," she said with satisfaction and proceeded to sashay to where he stood, focusing hard on each step she took. A smile sprouted on her lips as she approached . . . until a ridiculous cobblestone tripped her up and sent her flying into his arms. Inhaling deeply, she was intoxicated by the scent of him and looked up with a silly grin. "They really need to fix that."

Suddenly she was airborne, swooped up in his arms with cheek pressed hard against his chest. She sighed and let her head drop back in contentment. "Mmm . . . this is nice."

A swear word sizzled the air.

"So help me, somebody's going to pay for this." Luke seared Betty with a glare. "Did you give her more booze?"

Betty hunched her shoulders. "Not all that much, honest. She's just a lightweight."

He swore again. "She's eighteen, Galetti, and *my* responsibility. Blast it all, she can barely walk." He shot Parker a look of fury. "And you? You let them do this to her?"

Parker shoved his hands in his pockets, the slump of his shoulders clear evidence of his guilt. "I wasn't there, Luke, because I left to pay the bill. But the bottom line is she did it to herself. Nobody forced her to drink it, unless it was you with all your bullying." He sighed. "You should know by now you can't tell Katie what to do."

"Nope." A soft giggle bubbled from Katie's throat, followed by a hiccup.

Luke hoisted her roughly to his chest, blistering all of them with a look that signaled his good humor was long since spent. "You better start praying right now, Parker, that I beat her parents home, or you and I, ol' buddy, will be licking Carmichael's boots for a long time to come. That is, if he doesn't give us the boot first." He spun on his heel and started to jog toward Donovan Street, grateful he was in shape from the gym. He glanced down at Katie with her eyes closed and a dreamy smile on her lips, and he was tempted to dump her sorry little carcass on the front porch where her father would find her. Confinement for the next three years—that's what the little brat needed.

"Luke, we're sorry!" Betty called after him, but he ignored her, too furious at himself for talking Patrick O'Connor into even allowing Katie to come along tonight. The man had clearly been hesitant, unwilling to break with his daughter's confinement, but Luke had convinced him she had earned it. He swore under his breath. He had no one to blame but himself.

A wobbly giggle floated up and he glanced down, his heart softening at the look of innocence on her face as she bounced in his arms. And suddenly, he couldn't help it—a smile pulled at his lips when she spoke, her words disrupted by every stride he took. "Ar-re . . . y-you . . . swe-aring . . . un-der . . . y-your . . . bre-ath, . . . Lu-ke Mc-Gee?"

"You bet I am. You seem to have that effect on me," he said, breathing hard and fast.

Her sweet face bunched in a frown. "O-oh, . . . tha-at's . . . n-not . . . g-good, . . . is it?"

He grinned. "No, ma'am, it's not." He slowed as he rounded the corner of Donovan Street, squinting hard to see if Patrick O'Connor's Model T was parked against the curb.

Thank you, God! The street was empty in front of their house, and all was dark except for their porch light. He reached their front walk, huffing like he'd just run the Boston Marathon, then butted Katie up with his knee while he opened the gate. Her soft giggle rose like a caress to his face. He glanced down and her eyes met his with a gentle smile.

"Thanks, Luke," she whispered, drawing his gaze to her mouth.

He swallowed hard, suddenly painfully aware of her body in his arms. With a nervous exhale, he propped her next to the front door.

Get her inside, McGee, and into her bed.

The thought took his mind in the wrong direction, unleashing a throb of heat so strong, shame crawled up the back of his neck. "Do you have a key?" His voice was a croak.

She tilted her head and gave him a shy smile. "Iz op-pen."

He turned the knob, and pushed the door ajar. A small lamp in the hall cast a dim glow in the shadowed foyer. He tugged Katie from the wall and guided her in, reluctant to even enter the house. She stood there, a faint slant in her stance and a half-lidded glance that made his pulse trip. He steadied her with a hand to her arm, and then quickly fished a roll of peppermint Life Savers out of his pocket. He put the roll in her palm and closed her fingers over it.

"Katie, listen to me. You need to go upstairs right now and go to bed. But first, I want you to brush your teeth and suck on these mints as soon as you can. Do you understand? If your parents come home, just pretend you're sleeping, all right? Because if your father sees you like this, you and I are both going to be in a lot of hot water."

Her head bobbed slowly. "'Kay," she whispered, and her smile made his mouth go dry.

He shot a nervous glance out the door. "Can you make it up the stairs?"

She nodded again and just stood there, swaying on her feet with arms limp at her sides. A yawn interrupted her smile as her eyes flickered closed, and the roll of Life Savers dropped to the floor with a thud. Luke groaned and snatched them up. He flicked the front door closed with his foot and swept her up in his arms like she was one of the toddlers at the orphanage.

"Come on, Katie Rose," he muttered under his breath, "I'm putting you to bed." He took the stairs two at a time, then stopped at the upper landing and looked both right and left. "Which way?"

Her eyes fluttered open and she waved an arm before it dropped to her side like dead weight. "Las' door on right."

He ducked in the bathroom on the way and helped her brush her teeth before he carted her to her bedroom, where hazy moonlight spilled through lace-curtained windows. The scent of her was more potent here—Pears soap and a hint of roses—lingering in the air to tease his senses. Not unlike the woman in his arms. He sucked in a deep breath and set her on the bed, gripping her shoulders when she started to topple.

"Katie!" He shook her firmly, his voice tense. "Wake up! Where's your nightgown?"

Her eyes flipped open and she smiled, wagging a finger in the direction of the closet. "On th' door." Her arm flopped back to her side.

He snatched a long, silky gown off the back of the closet door, then tossed it into her lap. "Look, Katie, I'm leaving now, so you need to get dressed for bed, okay?"

"'Kay." She started to fumble with the buttons of her blouse, and Luke couldn't get out of there fast enough. He stopped, hand on the knob and head cocked to the side. "When your parents come home, you have to pretend to be asleep, do you understand?"

No answer.

"Katie! Do you understand?"

A soft, little snort was the only reply.

He turned and groaned. The little brat was flat on her back, eyes closed and nightgown puddled on her chest.

Gritting his teeth, he tugged her up and to the edge of

the bed before squatting before her, desperate to ignore the lacy camisole peeking out of her half-buttoned blouse. He swallowed hard and shook her. "Katie—you gonna put that nightgown on, or you gonna make me do it?"

She jerked awake, eyes spanning wide.

He dangled the gown under her nose. "It's a simple question, Katie Rose. You gonna take your clothes off, or am I?"

Even in the moonlight, he could see the color rise in her cheeks, and the horror on her face made him grin.

"I'll do it!" she said with a hoarse croak, clutching the nightgown as if she were stark naked.

"Good, then get busy." Tugging at her shoes, he tossed them on the floor, then reached beneath the hem of her skirt to remove her stockings.

She slapped his hand with an amazing amount of force for someone so inebriated. "Are you crazy? Whad'ya doing?" She sat up ramrod straight, fury apparently the only thing that could break through her vodka stupor.

He rose to his feet and stared her down, hands cocked on his hips. He managed to wipe the smile off his face. "Saving your neck, you little brat. Now if you don't get that nightgown on and get under those covers right now, I'll do it for you."

"Turn around!" she hissed. The rosy glow from Bobbie Sue's vodka was apparently fading fast.

He rotated slowly while a smile creased his lips. Her stockings flew by, one by one, landing in a heap to the right of him before a skirt pelted at his back, obviously with a bit of temper. He grinned until lacy unmentionables sailed by and landed at his feet. Suddenly his mouth went dry.

The sheets rustled, followed by a sulky "I want my Life Savers."

He fished the candy from his pocket and turned, bobbling the roll in his palm with a tight smile on his lips. She lay there looking like an angel, golden hair splayed across her pillow and the glow of moonlight in her cheeks. But he knew better. Her eyelids were heavy, but she still managed to sear him with a look that snapped him into the past. All of a sudden she was eleven again, and the memory of their first Life Savers encounter thickened in his throat. He crouched next to her bed and opened the roll, taking his time as he popped one in his mouth. He held another in the air, taunting her. "Mmmm . . . minty."

She blinked, jaws clamped tight, but he didn't miss the faint twitch of a smile. With a smug lift of his brow, he rotated the little, white circle an inch from her nose while sucking his own mint slowly, his gaze fused to hers.

"Here you go, Katie Rose," he whispered in a husky voice, "just like when you were eleven." He gently prodded the candy . . . slowly, deliberately . . . into her mouth. Her breathing became shallow when the pad of his thumb lingered like a caress, and he felt his own heart hammer in response. The scent of peppermint drifted in the air like a heady perfume, enticing him to taste more than the candy in his mouth. He released a halting breath, thumb still tracing the contour of her lips while a dangerous heat radiated beneath his skin. She watched him with shuttered eyes and a faint smile, and then in a jagged beat of his heart, she snapped her teeth so hard, they grazed his thumb with a sharp click.

He jerked back with a hoarse rasp, all air suspended.

The superior smile was vintage Katie O'Connor. "A bit twitchy, are we?"

He rose to his feet, nursing his thumb like she'd bitten clean through. His lips twisted. "No more than usual when you're around, Katie Rose."

She closed her eyes and sank back into the pillow with a contented smile, sleep settling on her features as she slowly sucked on her mint. Picking up her shoes and clothes, he tossed them in the closet, then waited for her to finish, observing the gentle shifting of those soft, full lips. Until they stilled.

"Katie . . . are you done with the mint?"

Her chest rose and fell with the rhythm of sleep. Luke

leaned close and squinted. He sighed. Sleep was good. But not with a Life Saver lodged in her throat. "Katie," he whispered, "did you finish the candy?"

"Mmmm . . ." Her eyelids fluttered open before closing once again.

With a weary release of breath, he bent to pry a finger into her mouth and swiped her tongue. Reaching for his handkerchief, he pocketed the half-dissolved disk of candy that adhered to his finger, then leaned to press a gentle kiss to her cheek.

At his touch, her lips tilted into a dreamy smile. "Mmm . . . I love you, Luke McGee," she whispered, and then rolled to her side with a soft, little snort.

He rose to his feet and stared, his heart comatose in his chest. Drawing in a deep breath, he bent to tuck the sheet tightly to her chin, finally exhaling shaky air. What he wouldn't give to make it so. But he knew better. His lips tightened. Alcohol had a way of distorting the truth.

He bent to graze her cheek with his fingers one last time, then slowly lumbered to his feet. "I love you too, Katie Rose," he whispered.

And he was stone-cold sober.

10

So . . . did our Mr. Priss scream all the way home?" Betty slid Katie a sideways glance, hazel eyes sparkling.

Katie shifted the box of files in her arms and shouldered past a mailman as she and Betty hurried down Boylston Street en route to the Boston Society for the Care of Girls. Businessmen in three-piece suits swarmed around them while young women in pleated skirts and dropped-waist dresses powdered their noses or patted bobbed hair in a rush to get to work. The shrill whistle of a traffic cop and the bleating of taxi horns mingled with the puttering of autos and the laughter of little girls as they skittered alongside mothers on an outing in the city. Katie hugged the box to her chest and quickly sidestepped a young boy toting a wagonful of newspapers. The corner of her mouth shifted up. "Surprisingly, no. He was actually pretty civil, if you can believe that."

Betty grinned and adjusted the long silk scarf draped over her left shoulder. "Or maybe you were too sloshed to notice," she said with a wink.

"I was *not* drunk," Katie insisted, chin notching up several degrees. Her lips pursed tight while they waited at the corner for traffic to stop. "Maybe a little tipsy, yes, but that's all, I assure you."

A uniformed officer blew his whistle and waved them on, and Betty chuckled, gripping a manicured hand to Katie's arm to steer her across Tremont Street. "Tipsy enough that our boy had steam rising from that towhead of his, either from his Irish temper or just plain tuckered out from carrying you home."

Katie cocked her head and readjusted the box in her hands, practically running to keep up with Betty's long-legged stride. "Luke has a temper?" she asked in surprise. "Funny, I've never seen it before." Unfortunately, as soon as the words left her lips, heat steamed her face at the memory of his savage kiss against the wall at BCAS, a kiss surely provoked by "temper."

Betty's throaty chuckle floated through the air as she shot a grin her way, and Katie desperately hoped the warmth of the summer day would explain the blush she felt in her cheeks. "Oh, he's much better now at keeping it under wraps than he used to be, thanks to both Parker and Brady's influence. But when he and I were kids on the streets of New York? I'll tell you what, that boy was nothing but a short fuse looking for a hot fire."

With a tug of her arm, Betty eased past a herd of elderly ladies on a shopping spree, then took off at a fast clip, causing Katie to gasp for air. "Hey, Galetti—my legs aren't as long as yours, you know, and at this pace, *you* may have to carry me."

"Sorry," Betty said with a flash of teeth. She plucked the box from Katie's hands and continued to maneuver through the rush-hour crowd. "I forget what a runt you are."

She slowed her gait, and Katie tried to catch her breath as she squinted up at her friend. "So, how did you and Luke meet, anyway? You've never told me."

Betty's pace tapered off as she gave Katie a soft smile. "Oh, McGee and I go way back. He lived with his aunt in the same building as ours when I was fourteen and he was sixteen. He was a runt back then, but he sure was a wiry little thing." A wistful look settled on her features as she stared straight ahead, seemingly oblivious to the throng of passersby milling about. "No question about it—the boy was meant to be a lawyer. He had a true gift for defending me." The wistful look fled with a thrust of her jaw. "Or at least he tried."

"Defend you? From what?"

"From other street arabs like us—homeless orphans—not to mention drunken bums or gangs who taunted the rest of us for sport." A veneer hardened her tone. "And, of course, my stepfather, who had a nasty habit of slapping me around when Mom was down for the count."

The muscles tightened in Katie's throat. She halted Betty's stride with a hand to her arm. "No, he beat you? And your mother too?" Her breathing shallowed as she tried to imagine Patrick O'Connor laying a cruel hand on his wife or children. A cold shudder traveled her body at the thought, and then a rush of gratitude squeezed in her chest. *Why had she been so lucky . . . and poor Betty had not?* She swallowed hard, her tone thick with emotion. "And nobody stopped him?"

"Nobody could stop him," she said with acid in her tone. She continued walking. "Although heaven knows, Luke tried. Do you know that little runt actually attempted to negotiate with him? Promised to steal liquor for him if he would leave me alone."

Katie gasped. "Did it work?"

"Naw. Seems the man was mean, sober or drunk." Betty's eyes scanned a five-story building looming overhead that dominated the entire block. She gave Katie a hard smile. "So naturally when my mom died, I became his primary pastime."

Katie spun around, disbelief dropping her jaw. "No! Your mother died? Oh, Betty. And you were left with a monster like that?"

Tragedy shadowed Betty's features, making her seem much

older than her twenty-one years. She yanked on the steel handle of the beveled glass door of the Boston Society for the Care of Girls and held it open till Katie hurried through. "Yeah, it about killed me, which is why McGee and I left to live on the streets." Her features softened at the mention of Luke. "Nobody ever loved me like Luke before, took care of me and defended me like that." Her full bottom lip revealed the barest of quivers. "We're family, Luke and me. I'd lay down my life for the man . . . and he would do the same."

She perused the cramped lobby until her gaze lighted on a middle-aged woman slumped over a desk in the corner, eyes trained on a typewriter. Her fingers flew over the keyboard in a blur while the rapid-fire clicking of the keys ricocheted throughout the marble lobby.

Betty strolled over and dropped the box on the desk with a loud thump, causing the woman to jerk up in her chair. "Now that's what I call being focused, Vera," Betty said with a lazy grin. "You jump higher than Luke when I sneak up on him."

The woman gaped, palm to her chest and dark eyes wide with shock. "Goodness, Miss Betty, I never even heard you come in!"

"Apparently," Betty said with a one-sided smile. She peeked at the letter in Vera's typewriter. "So, Miss Lillian has you beating the bushes for more donations, does she?"

Vera pushed a shock of black hair away from her eyes. "Yeah, well, it seems the budget has fallen short again this year, and Mr. Carmichael is none too happy. Which, of course, puts poor Miss Lillian in a dither. Apparently she feels that—and I quote—'those blasted Feds are cooling off the market.' Swears the higher interest rates and stricter terms for borrowing will be the death of us yet." Vera blew a strand of bangs from her eyes. "Of course, it's all Greek to me, but she's convinced the skyrocketing market has investors skittish. You know, afraid the bubble's going to burst, so they're tightening the purse strings."

"But Margaret gave you the donor list for the BCAS, didn't she?" Betty asked with a squint of her brows.

"Yes, but Carmichael's on the warpath over there too, placing the same demands on Margaret as he is on Miss Lillian. Believe me, I've spent hours looking behind every bush and under every rock for more possible donors, but to no avail." Her brows quirked up as she gave Betty a skewed smile. "It seems these days, donors are as scarce as Carmichael's good moods."

"I can get you a list of new donors," Katie said with a step forward. She extended her hand to Vera, who shook it with confusion in her eyes. "Nice to meet you, Vera—I'm Katie O'Connor, Betty's summer volunteer."

"A new list of donors? St. Peter's gate, how?" Vera's voice conveyed true respect.

Sympathy edged Katie's smile. "My father is the editor for the *Boston Herald*, and he just *happens* to be the co-chair for this year's auction for the Fogg Museum."

The awe on Vera's face made Katie grin.

"Well, mercy me, I do believe the heavens just opened up and fell into my lap, Miss O'Connor." Vera shook Katie's hand with all the enthusiasm of a thirsty soul jerking a rusty water pump. "Do you really think you can get me a list?"

"If anybody can, Vera, it's Katie. And when you're done typing it up, it might be a good idea to send a copy to Margaret too, and then you two can share the credit for recruiting more donors. I don't want Carmichael chewing her ear off, either."

Vera tugged a handkerchief from her sleeve and mopped her brow. "Will do, Miss Betty, and bless you, Miss O'Connor—you just saved me weeks of work."

"It's the least I can do for another working girl, Vera. And call me Katie, please. We're all on the same team, you know."

"Amen to that," Betty said with a flick of her scarf. "Vera, here are the files for next month's placements, all ready to go. Is Miss Lillian in her office? Katie's here to fill in today for Emily, but I want to introduce her to Lillian first."

"No, she's in the kitchen with Virginia and Alli because Mrs. Okes is running late."

Betty headed for a set of wooden doors with windowpanes foggy with grime. "As if that woman doesn't have enough to do," she muttered, "now she has to cook too?"

"You know Miss Lillian," Vera called from behind. "Nice to meet you, Katie."

Betty gave Vera a backhanded wave. "Yeah, I know Miss Lillian. Thanks, Vera."

"I'll get that list to you within a couple of days," Katie called as Betty tugged her through the door. It slammed behind them, and Katie found herself racing to catch up while Betty marched down the glossy wooden hall, high heels clunking like a small army. Sunlight streamed in through a tall window at the far end where the sound of children's laughter lilted in the air.

"Miss Betty!" A flock of little girls bombarded Betty as she passed an open door, squeals and hugs and high-pitched voices clamoring for her attention. She hefted a brown-eyed moppet with blond ringlets high in the air and gave her a noisy kiss. "Ruthy! Looks like somebody's eating their spinach—you've gotten so big! Popeye would be proud."

Ruthy giggled, pink cheeks aglow with Betty's praise. "Gabe gives me all her vegetables," she announced with pride, "and now I'm almost as tall as her!"

"Are not!" Gabriella Dawn Smith folded her arms and narrowed her eyes. "You're only five, and a puny five at that."

Betty gave her the eye. "Better watch it, Gabe, or Ruthy will pass you up if you don't eat your vegetables." She nodded in Katie's direction. "You want to end up like her?"

Gabe squinted up at Katie, smile twitching and a gleam of trouble in her eyes. "Shoot, no. She's a twerp, but I shore don't want to be no Amazon like you. At least being a runt is better than going around with your head in the clouds."

"Gee, thanks, Gabe," Katie said with a tweak of the girl's braid. "I feel so loved."

Betty grinned. "Girls, this is my summer volunteer, Katie O'Connor. She used to be friends with Luke when she was about your age."

That got their attention. Five little girls suddenly focused on Katie with new respect.

"Hey, you didn't tell me you used to be friends with Luke. Were you his girlfriend?" Gabe asked with a suspicious fold of her arms.

"Uh, nobody was his girlfriend back then," Katie said with a crook of a smile. "I was ten and he was fourteen, and he barely came to my chest. Not to mention he was obnoxious." The smile died on Katie's lips as she studied the faces of the little girls before her. She may as well have been on trial for heresy—five sets of eyes condemned her on the spot. "Uh, but now Luke and I are good friends and I think he's the bee's knees."

The girls giggled and Betty leaned close. "Nice footwork." She put Ruthy down and ruffled her hair, shooting a peek into the classroom. "Where's Miss Trudy?"

"In the bathroom," a freckle-faced girl said with a giggle. "Gabe made her laugh, and she snorted coffee all over her blouse."

Betty and Katie exchanged grins. "Well, go on, then," Betty said, shooing the girls back into the room. "I'll stop by after my meeting with Miss Lillian, okay?"

The girls' chatter faded as Katie followed Betty down the hall to the last door on the right. With great ceremony, Betty flung the door open to reveal an enormous kitchen with massive windows lining the side wall, sashes open wide to the sounds and smells of the city outside. Autos rumbled by while pedestrians bustled to and fro, infusing the airy kitchen with a hum of activity that matched that of the women preparing lunch for the day. The room appeared clean, although the black and white linoleum was long since yellowed with age.

A bank of white cast-iron sinks shared a wall with several black gas stoves where deep pots bubbled with steam. Two young girls chatted and peeled vegetables at the sink while a tiny, elderly woman with dyed black hair stood before a huge wooden chopping block. Barely five foot tall, the frail-looking dynamo slapped and pummeled bread dough with a ferocity that indicated she was anything but frail. The mouthwatering aroma of stew drifted in the air, winning out over the hint of fresh asphalt being poured across the street by a crew of grimy workers. Katie's mouth began to water as she followed Betty into the room.

"Now why do I suspect Carmichael's on your mind right about now, Miss Lillian?" Betty strolled over to the woman and gave her shoulders a quick squeeze.

Miss Lillian stabbed the dough with renewed fervor as she gave Betty a crooked smile that transformed her delicate face into that of a weathered imp with twinkling blue eyes. "Mind your tongue, Miss Galetti. We only speak of Mr. Carmichael in the most reverent of tones."

Betty snitched an oatmeal cookie from a plate on a nearby table and tossed it to Katie, then filched another with a devious grin. "'Speak,' yes, but our thoughts? Mmm . . . good thing they can't 'speak' our mind."

A hoarse chuckle tripped from Miss Lillian's lips as she gave the dough a final deadly thrust. "Amen to that," she said with a swipe of her brow. She lifted a silver watch pinned to the lapel of her white blouse. "You're early for our meeting. I have cobbler to make."

A pretty brunette turned at the sink to give Miss Lillian a patient smile. "We can handle it, Miss Lillian, at least until Mrs. Okes gets here. Why don't you go to your meeting?"

The ball of fire ignored the soft-spoken girl to heft a crate of peaches off the counter. She plopped them on the worn wooden table with a tight press of her lips and then foraged for a stainless steel bowl from a white cupboard. "My meeting can wait, Virginia, but I'm afraid that hoard of hungry ruffians cannot." She scrounged in a drawer for a knife and marched back to the table while skinning a peach with a scowl on her face.

"Now I *know* you're thinking of Carmichael, Lil, because we both know the man's a real peach." Betty dug in the drawer for a knife of her own, then handed one to Katie with a grin.

Miss Lillian shot a quick glance at the girls at the sink, then fought the squirm of a smile. "Hush, young lady, this is a Christian environment here, and well you know it." Pitch-black eyebrows drawn on in a crooked line lifted as she nodded at Katie. "And who's this—reinforcements, I hope?"

Betty hooked an arm around Katie's shoulders and grinned. "As a matter of fact, yes. Parker sent Katie to fill in for Emily because Bobbie Sue is sick."

Miss Lillian squinted, forcing paper-thin crinkles to fan at the sides of her eyes. "Oh? Nothing serious, I hope?"

"Nope, just a nasty cold, I think, but Parker told her to stay away." Betty tossed a peach to Katie, who caught it midair. "This is Katie O'Connor, our summer volunteer. Katie, this is the heart and soul of the Boston Society for the Care of Girls, Miss Lillian Radake."

In her heels, Katie towered over the petite woman by at least four inches, but the glint of steel in the shrewd blue eyes garnered more respect than if Miss Lillian had been ten feet tall. Katie extended a shaky hand, her admiration for the woman before her thickening the air in her throat. "Oh goodness, Miss Lillian, I can't tell you what an honor it is to meet you! Everyone at the BCAS speaks so highly of you and the work you do here, that I feel like I almost know you."

"Thank you, Katie. I wouldn't believe everything they say, you know." A twinkle lit her eyes. "Especially Mr. McGee—he tends toward the blarney at times."

"Katie plans to enter law school this fall," Betty said. She dropped into one of the chairs at the table, eyes trained on the peach in her hand as she peeled a long, fuzzy curl. "She wants to champion women's rights."

The twinkle in Miss Lillian's eyes glinted with respect. "Well, good for you, young lady. Women have certainly made great strides this decade, but as Alice always says, 'When you put your hand to the plow, you can't put it down until you get to the end of the row.'"

Awe stilled Katie's tone to a mere hush. "Alice? *Alice Paul?* The founder of the National Women's Party? You know her?"

A hoarse chuckle rattled from the old woman's lips. "I had the privilege of meeting Miss Paul in Seneca Falls in 1923 for the celebration of the seventy-fifth anniversary of the Woman's Rights Convention. That's when she introduced the Lucretia Mott Amendment, you know."

Katie could barely breathe. "You were there? When she introduced the Equal Rights Amendment?" She gaped at Miss Lillian, hand splayed to her chest.

A healthy grin that may have been porcelain dentures flashed across Miss Lillian's face. "Yes, my dear, a historical day for women everywhere, you can be sure. Alice Paul is a bright woman with a fire in her belly to help downtrodden women." Miss Lillian patted Katie's arm and lowered herself into the chair next to Betty. "Who, I might add, had the same fire in her eyes that I now see in yours."

Katie sank into the chair next to Miss Lillian's and started peeling her peach, her eyes misty with hope. "Oh, yes, Miss Lillian, I plan to study the law, but my real dream is to advocate women's rights in Congress like Jeannette Pickering Rankin." Katie sighed. "Imagine . . . the first woman in the legislature! What great strides she's made on behalf of women everywhere."

"Indeed," Miss Lillian said with a nod. Her eyes flitted to the two girls chatting at the sink, and for the first time, Katie noticed the steel leg braces beneath the skirt of the shorter one. "But regrettably, I fear the strides will not keep pace with the hardships."

Betty's eyes followed Miss Lillian's, and her voice lowered to a whisper. "No luck finding Alli a position yet?"

"No, but I'm not giving up." A tenuous puff of air drifted from the pinched lips of the older woman. "The good Lord is not adverse to hounding, apparently, given the example of the persistent widow who badgered the unjust judge in the Bible, so I am hoping for a positive resolution. We have three months until Alli turns eighteen, to place her in a family or a position that will afford her a living."

"What happens if you don't?" Katie's voice was quiet.

Miss Lillian sighed again. "At the age of eighteen, our young women, whether serving an apprenticeship in a family or living here as Alli does now, must move on. Some marry, others continue their associations with families they've apprenticed with, and many others utilize the skills they've learned here to earn a living and fend for themselves." Miss Lillian focused on the fruit in her hand, but not before Katie saw a glimmer of moisture in her eyes. "But with Alli," she whispered, "there's not only the ravages of polio that hinder her ability to work, but . . ." A knot shifted in the old woman's throat as her eyes lighted on the back of the girl with soft, brown curls edging her shoulders. "She was also recently diagnosed with epilepsy, which manifested itself along with a speech impediment."

"Seizures?"

Unbidden tears sprang to Katie's eyes at the quiver of Miss Lillian's chin, which now elevated as she reached for another peach. "Yes, from the age of sixteen. Alli has struggled with slow speech and a terrible stutter ever since, especially when she gets nervous. That, along with the stigma of epilepsy, has made it difficult to place her, I'm afraid, whether in an apprenticeship like most of the older girls . . . or in a job. People think she's slow, but as anyone here will tell you, Alli's speech and mobility may be impaired, but the size of her intellect is not . . . nor her heart. She's excellent at numbers."

Katie blinked to diffuse the tears in her eyes while her hand stilled on the peach. "What will happen to her?" she whispered. "She won't be alone, will she? Or out on the streets?"

"Oh, no, no, we won't let that happen." Miss Lillian swiped the side of her eye with the sleeve of her blouse and managed a smile. "If the board won't allow Alli to stay on here, we'll simply find a home for her elsewhere, even if it's with an old, crabby woman like me."

The pretty brunette named Virginia turned and wiped her hands on a towel. "Miss Lillian, I need to run downstairs for more vegetables, but Alli said she'd finish the cobbler, if you like." Virginia smiled and disappeared through a door at the back of the kitchen while Alli hobbled toward their table.

"Miss Lillian, please . . . may I do the peaches?"

Katie's heart squeezed in her chest. The handicapped girl looked all of fourteen and as petite and delicate as Miss Lillian herself. There was nothing particularly eye-catching about her, eyes and hair a nondescript brown and a tiny pug nose that seemed out of place in her narrow face. But there was something strong in her gentle manner despite a frail frame as wispy as a butterfly's wing and a voice as soft as a whisper. She wasn't pretty . . . until she smiled. Katie's breath caught as the girl's face took on the glow of an angel. Hope seemed to shine forth like a beam from heaven, transforming not only the homely girl before them, but all those graced by her presence. "I j-just l-love p-peaches," she said with a lilt in her tone, eyes lighting on Katie with a sweetness that caused Katie's throat to ache. "D-don't you?"

Katie nodded, overcome with such a rush of emotion that she found it difficult to speak. She extended a shaky hand. "I most certainly do, Alli. My name is Katie, and I'll be working with you and Virginia today."

The brown eyes blinked, and then if possible, outshone her beautiful smile. She took Katie's hand and shook it slowly, the slightest hint of mischief lighting on her lips. She attempted a wink, which came off comical due to the faint pull of a palsy on the right side of her face. She leaned in close. "Hi ya, K-Katie. Who knows? After Miss B-Betty and Miss Lillian leave for their m-meeting, m-maybe some of the p-peaches won't make it into the b-bowl."

Miss Lillian chuckled and rose to her feet. "A small price to pay for cobbler that melts in your mouth. Do you know how to bake, Katie?"

"Cookies, yes. Cobbler? Uh, no. But I'm willing to learn."

"Good." Miss Lillian rose to her feet with a small grunt and swiveled her neck, obviously working out some kinks. "Alli can teach you. She's a wonder with cobbler." She patted Alli's cheek with a weathered hand that lingered in a tender caress. "As long as she doesn't eat all the peaches, that is. Nice to meet you, Katie. Come, Miss Galetti . . . I believe we have placements to discuss."

Betty turned and wriggled her brows as she followed Miss Lillian to the door. "Hey, Alli, after you teach her to make cobbler, can ya teach her to be sweet and gentle like you?"

Katie grinned. "Sweet and gentle, eh? Wouldn't that throw our Mr. Priss for a curve?"

"Not just Mr. Priss," Betty said with a chuckle, giving a jaunty wave as she left.

Katie rubbed her hands together. "Okay, Alli, I'm hungry. Let's start peeling."

A grin as bright as the summer sun transformed the mousy girl into a radiant being, prompting another threat of tears in Katie's eyes. "P-peaches are my favorite," Alli said with an innocent smile that made her almost beautiful. "How 'b-bout you?"

"Yeah," Katie said with a catch in her throat. She plopped into the chair with a silly grin and picked up a piece of fruit. "They are now."

Everything was perfect! With a skitter of excitement, Marcy glanced at the clock on the parlor mantel. It chimed ten, and her gaze flicked to the face of her husband as he lounged in his favorite chair with a newspaper in his lap. Katie had gone to bed early, and Steven was in his room, affording Patrick and her a rare evening to themselves. Marcy gnawed on her lip and secretly observed him for clues to his mood. He was relaxed, she knew, because his feet were propped up on the ottoman, shoes off and legs casually crossed. A late-summer breeze fluttered the window sheers, bringing cool relief to a sticky day. His handsome face was smooth and free from the worry lines so often etched in his brow after a trying day at the *Herald*, and his short dark hair—salted liberally with silver at the temples—rested against a small corduroy pillow tucked neatly behind his neck.

Marcy set her sewing aside and rose to her feet, careful to temper the smile that tugged at her lips. Yes, tonight was the perfect night to broach the subject, she concluded with anticipation bubbling in her chest. She had fixed his favorite dinner—chicken and dumplings topped off with coconut cream pie—winning her a warm smile and a kiss of gratitude. She had even taken the time to dab a touch of perfume to her neck, an effort that had paid off handsomely with a second lingering kiss. Marcy bit back a grin and moved toward his chair. No, Patrick O'Connor was definitely ripe for the picking tonight, and somehow she didn't feel the least bit guilty. This was far too important, and she wanted it far too badly.

Easing down on the arm of his chair, she leaned in to press a kiss to his temple, the heady scent of his musk aftershave warming her senses. "Patrick?"

"Mmm?" He glanced up from his paper, and suddenly his distracted look melted into a smile. He hooked an arm to her waist and tugged her close. His breath was warm against her neck as his mouth wandered in to a kiss. "You smell good tonight, darlin'," he whispered. A low chuckle vibrated against her cheek. "That's dangerous, you know, if you're looking to sleep."

Marcy turned to face him, her breath quivering with elation. She clutched his hand between hers. "Oh, Patrick, I couldn't possibly sleep—at least not until we talk . . ."

He squinted and gave her a curious smile. One brow slanted up. "About what?"

She felt like a little girl at Christmas, flushed with excitement. "Patrick, you know how much I love being a mother, and how awful it's been for me since, well, since the change of life—"

"Marcy, you'll always be a mother—"

She placed a palm to his face. "I know, but I won't always have children to raise."

He shifted, his smile diminishing somewhat. "You have grandchildren—"

"But they aren't mine to keep. And I can't nurture them day in and day out."

"For pity's sake, you have Katie and Steven to nurture, and they sorely need it."

Marcy released an anxious breath and gripped his arms, her eyes pleading with his. "But in a few short years, they'll be gone, and I'll be alone."

"We have each other," he whispered, a shade of hurt in his tone.

She quickly pressed her mouth to his in gentle coercion, deepening her kiss before pulling away. "I know, Patrick, and I love you with everything in me." She searched his eyes with her own. "But please believe me—I'm not ready to stop being a mother."

He stroked her cheek slowly, his eyes pools of sympathy steeped in love. "Darlin', your periods have ceased—you know there can be no more babies."

"Not babies, Patrick, *children*! I can still have children."

He blinked while confusion furrowed his brow. "What are you saying?"

She clutched his shirt with her fingers, desperate to convey the desire of her heart. "Foster parents, Patrick, for children who have no family of their own. Lost children who have no one to love them, to nurture them. I can do that—I *have* to do that!"

His shock was apparent in the drop of his jaw. Marcy wasted no time in driving her cause home. "Katie told me about a seven-year-old girl named Gabriella Dawn Smith, almost eight, a sprite of a girl whose parents abandoned her as an infant."

He pushed her away and jolted to his feet. "No, absolutely not—"

She jumped up, her heart hammering in her chest as she seized his vest with bloodless fingers. "Please, Patrick, I've never begged you for anything before, but I'm begging you now." Tears streamed down her face as she pressed on. "She lives at the Boston Society for the Care of Girls, but Katie says the director wants to send her away on one of those dreadful orphan trains—"

"She's trouble, Marcy, I guarantee you—and that's why they're shipping her out—"

"Patrick—*please*! I need this girl, and this girl needs us, if only for a season." Her voice cracked on a sob, and she knew the shock in his eyes had stolen his tongue. She forged on. "Katie says she has no place to go, except on a train to the Midwest with total strangers. And there's no assurance she'll arrive safely as she's known to run away."

Patrick remained silent, a hand to his eyes. His shoulders slumped as she hurried on, not sparing a chance to refute.

"She's Luke's charge, Patrick, and he's worried sick about her, and Katie and she are friends . . ." Her voice quavered into a soft heave. "Please . . ."

She heard his heavy sigh, and hope flickered in her heart like a dying flame awaiting a gentle breeze. His hand dropped to his side as he stared at her through weary eyes, tempering his gaze with caution. "I will pray about it, Marcy—"

She circled his waist with her arms and peered up, tears of hope glimmering in her eyes. Her tone was a fragile plea. "I've already prayed about it, my love, from the moment

Katie told me about this little girl, and I know it's the right thing to do. Please, Patrick—whatever you ask, I will do. Only don't deny me this."

She watched as he stared, his face a painful study of a man in love with his wife—tenderness and hope, mingling with worry and fear. The questions were there in his eyes. Should he go against his gut just to keep peace with his wife? Was this the right thing for this woman he loved? Seconds passed like hours while she imagined him pondering the thoughts that pulled at his mind.

He finally drew her close with a loud exhale of air. "All right, Marcy," he said quietly, "since this is so all-fire important to you, we'll do this your way . . . for now. But—" he wagged a threatening finger in her face—"at the first sign of trouble, Miss Gabriella Dawn Smith goes, do you hear? And you *will* back me in my discipline, do you understand?"

She lunged into his arms with a joyful cry, almost toppling them both into the chair. "Oh, Patrick, I love you so much! And I mean it—anything, I'll do anything."

He chuckled and planted a kiss in her hair, steadying her with a firm grip to her arms. "Don't think I won't be taking you up on that, darlin'." His eyes twinkled as he cupped a hand to her waist. "In fact, I've a mind to collect right no—"

The clomp of heavy footsteps clambered down the stairs, drawing their gazes to the foyer. Marcy froze at the sight of Steven heading for the front door. *Lord, no, not now!*

Patrick dropped his hold on her waist and strode toward the hall, shooting a quick glance at the clock on the mantel. "And where do you think you're going?"

Steven turned, brows arched and a stiff smile on his lips. "Out. With Maggie."

"At this late hour?" Patrick's tone hardened considerably.

Steven strolled to where Marcy stood. He kissed her cheek and gave her a quick hug. "Good night, Mother."

"Steven, please don't be too late," she whispered against

his neck, her stomach in knots at what this could do to Patrick's good mood.

Steven gave her a gentle smile, the only reminder of the shy and introspective boy he used to be. Her heart squeezed with love for this once small and gangly son, who'd possessed a gentle heart and quiet manner. He stood before her now, a handsome young man who had discovered the wild ways of an unfettered generation, craving adventure along with a college education.

He turned to Patrick, his stance as steely as his father's. "Yes, at this late hour. And I won't be home till late. Good night, Father." He opened the door.

Patrick grabbed his arm and spun him around, matching his son's towering height inch for inch. "You will *not* be crawling home at all hours of the morning, out gallivanting with that woman, do you hear? If you aren't home by midnight, the bolts will be locked."

A nerve twitched in Steven's chiseled jaw as he eyed his father with cool indifference. "Then I'll sleep elsewhere," he said with icy calm.

Marcy hurried to her husband's side and placed a gentle hand on his arm. "Patrick, he's a grown man in college, twenty-one years old," she whispered.

"And living under my roof, Marcy, enjoying the benefit of an education that *I* provide."

Steven stepped through the door without looking back, ushering in a gust of warm air that chilled Marcy to the bone. "Good night, Mother." The door slammed behind him, clipping his words even more than the coolness of his tone.

She slipped her arms around Patrick and laid her head against his chest. His heart was racing and his muscles were stiff. "Let it go, my love," she said quietly. "He's not a little boy anymore, he's a man. We have to allow him some freedom."

His rib cage expanded with a heavy sigh. "Freedom to thwart us at every turn."

She pulled away and touched a palm to his face. "We have

good children who sometimes go through difficult times. Look at Charity—she's settled down and hasn't been trouble since."

His lips quirked. "That's because Mitch has to contend with her now."

Marcy smiled. "Even so, Steven and Katie will both be fine too, you'll see."

He released a weary breath and lifted her chin with the tip of his finger. "And you want more children," he said with a jag of his brow. He bent to brush a light kiss to her lips, his tone thick with sarcasm and more than a little tease. "I swear, you're killing me, woman."

She grinned and kissed him back. "I hope not. I can't raise them alone."

With a tug of her hand, he ushered her to the staircase, pulling her close to bury his lips in the crook of her neck. "Mmm . . . I suggest you head up and get ready for bed, Marceline, while I lock the doors and turn out the lights. I believe the fine print said 'whatever I ask.'"

She smiled and started up the steps, then whirled around to hug his neck. "Oh, Patrick, I love you so much—more than I can ever express."

The edges of his mouth tilted into a dangerous smile while he assessed her through gentle eyes. "Yes, well, I suggest you keep that in mind, darlin'," he said in a husky tone. He planted a kiss on the tip of her nose, then headed to the parlor with a purposeful stride. "Especially when I come to collect."

11

A boulder in his gut. That's what it felt like as Luke stared out his office window in a daze, oblivious to the blare of horns and the shriek of police whistles that always accompanied Friday-night rush hour. He leaned back in the chair and put a hand to his eyes, legs crossed on the sill and his heart as heavy as the ton of rocks Carmichael unloaded this week.

Come Monday morning, Gabe would be gone—and there was not a blasted thing he could do about it. Luke squeezed his eyes shut, and the very thought forced moisture to well beneath his lids. He swabbed them with the sleeve of his arm, then massaged his temples to ease the onset of the headache that was sure to follow.

It wasn't fair, he railed to himself. She deserved so much more. More than a ticket on a train bound for the Midwest, more than total strangers to depend on, and certainly more than leaving the only home she'd ever known. He released a halting breath. She deserved what Brady had given him—a chance to get off the streets and learn that not all people were bad. A chance to make something of herself and prove she was more than riffraff. He opened his eyes, allowing them to trail into a dead stare as a knot shifted in his throat. A chance to know there was a God in heaven who actually cared for every matted hair on her stubborn little head.

I will not leave you orphans . . .

Luke thought of the Scripture Brady had given him so long ago, and he gouged his eyes with the pads of his fingers. Oh, what he wouldn't give to take her himself. Raise her, love her, teach her what Brady had taught him. But neither he nor Carmichael could allow that. Gabe needed a home that was solid and stable, two parents that would give her the love she deserved. And this was a chance for that—a home, a family that could change her life forever.

If she didn't run away first.

No! He bolted up, beads of sweat blistering the back of his neck and his breathing harsh and fast. But somehow he knew she would. He gripped the arms of his chair until his knuckles pinched white. She'd run away and be lost forever, alone and vulnerable. The very thought caused fear to feather his spine.

Let not your heart be troubled, neither let it fear.

His breathing slowed and his gaze jerked up, scanning the heavens. "You said you would never leave us nor forsake us, Lord, but where are you in all of this? Gabe needs you, and I need you. I've prayed for months for a good home for her, you know that, and yet there's been nothing." He sucked in a deep breath and sagged back into his chair, releasing the air in his lungs as thoroughly as he knew he had to release Gabe . . . into God's hands. "Forgive me, Lord, because I do trust you. You've never failed me, not once since I've given my life to you. So I believe you have Gabe in the palm of your hand because you've proven yourself faithful to me over and over. And one way or the other, you *always* answer my prayers."

A knock sounded, and he spun around, spying Katie at the door. His lips quirked into a half smile. *Well, almost always*, he thought as her blue eyes peeked in.

"I'm leaving now, Luke. Is there anything you need before I go?"

Yeah, Katie, a hug would be nice.

Heat singed the back of his neck and he coughed, clearing his throat. "No, I'm good. Have fun this weekend." His brows pinched in a frown. "Oh, sorry—are you still on confinement?"

She grinned and sidled past the door, closing it carefully behind her with a pretty blush on her cheeks. "Yes, until tomorrow night, that is, when I have my first date with Jack in over two and a half months."

Luke forced a smile to cover the scowl in his mind. "Lucky Jack," he said with a tease in his tone, but truer words had never crossed his lips, and suddenly the thought blackened his mood further. Over the summer, he'd made the startling discovery that Katie O'Connor was everything he wanted in a woman, and somehow he'd known it from the age of fourteen. With little or no effort on her part, she had won his affection—from a cold shoulder at the age of ten, to a teasing smile at the age of eighteen—and Luke would give anything to be more than just friends. But they had a deal, and she had a boyfriend, and Luke was a man of his word. The scowl finally won out as he looked away, intent on shoving papers into a drawer.

She hesitated. "Are you sure you don't need anything before I go? You look . . . tense."

Tense? Because two people he loved were leaving his life forever? He blew out a sigh of frustration and wheeled in his chair to stare out the window. "No, Katie, go home. I'm just down about Gabe, that's all. Go on, get out of here and have fun this weekend."

Go home to Jack, Katie Rose.

His stomach tightened at the sudden click of her heels, and shock expanded his eyes when she perched herself on the edge of his window. She crossed silky legs and leaned forward, palms flat on the sill and blue eyes sparkling with excitement. Her mouth twitched with a smile, as if a secret hovered behind those full, sensuous lips, and the tease of her proximity triggered his pulse till he thought he couldn't breathe. A gentle breeze from the window rustled her silk dress, and the scent of roses drifted in the air, warming his blood.

"What's on your mind, Katie?" he asked, heat crawling up his neck at the realization of what was on his.

"The same thing that's on yours, apparently," she said with a mysterious smile. "Gabe."

His pulse slowed. "Gabe? What about her?"

Katie bit her lip and then grinned outright. "I have a foster family for her."

He sat up straight in the chair, fingers gripped white on the arm. "W-What? W-Where?" His words tripped over his tongue, moving faster than the hammering of his heart.

Her laughter floated in the air like the sound of hope. "A wonderful family, really—large, well-to-do, and so full of love that Gabe will think she died and went to heaven."

He couldn't help it—tears stung his eyes. "Who?" he whispered.

Her gaze was tender as she studied him, the wetness in her eyes matching his own. "The O'Connors of Boston," she said softly, then put a hand to her chest and blinked back her tears. "Goodness, you think she'll mind sharing a room?"

He stared, disbelief stealing the air from his lungs. And then in a jolt of comprehension, it whooshed back in, flooding his body with such joy and emotion, he thought he would faint. In one frantic clip of his heart, he swallowed Katie up in his arms and squeezed as if he would never let go, his deep laughter rumbling against her hair. "Woman, I could just kiss you," he shouted, and then all at once his breathing stilled as he set her back down, suddenly aware of her body pressed against his, the burn of his hand on the small of her back.

Their gazes met, and heat traveled his bloodstream like alcohol, drowning all inhibition he may have felt. He saw the vulnerability in those wide blue eyes, heard the tremulous breathing drifting from those soft, parted lips, and all reason fled from his brain, disarming all good intent. In slow and careful motion, his hands cupped the sides of her face like a caress, his gaze fixed on her mouth before shifting to lose himself in her eyes. He feathered her lips with the pad of his thumb. "Thank you, Katie Rose," he whispered, "for giving me so much joy."

He wanted to fight it, knew it should only be a kiss on the cheek, but his body seemed drugged with her. His eyelids weighted closed as he moved near like a man in a trance, compelled to graze his lips against hers. Upon touch, their shallow breathing became one as he nuzzled her mouth with his own. And then, in a ragged beat of his heart, she melted into him with a familiarity that destroyed all restraint. He clutched her body to his, deepening the kiss that just cost him a promise he'd made. "God help me, Katie, I want you—"

Somewhere in the recesses of their minds they heard it, that gruff clearing of a throat that seemed so very far away. And then harsh reality struck, and Katie jerked violently from his arms as if he had thrust her away.

"I knocked, but I guess you didn't hear it." Parker stood with arms crossed in the open door, voice rock hard and jaw even worse.

An unnatural shade of red bled up Katie's neck and face like a thermometer registering a fever of 105. "P-Parker . . . Mr. Riley . . . it's not what it seems. L-Luke was just thanking me . . ."

The hard line of Parker's mouth twisted as his eyes flicked to Luke with a penetrating look. "A simple 'thank you' wouldn't have been enough?"

Luke grinned and looped an arm around Katie's shoulders, ignoring both the heat at the back of his neck and Parker's incriminating stare. "Not for this, old buddy. This amazing woman here just found our Gabe a home with an incredible family."

The anger on Parker's face fused into shock, and then blossomed into a reluctant grin. "No kidding? Who?"

Luke scooped Katie close and planted a kiss on her head. "Katie's parents have agreed to take Gabe in, so that should shed some light on the level of gratitude I might have had."

Parker ambled into the room and plopped into one of the chairs at the front of Luke's desk, his lips flattened in a near smile. "Nope, but you and I will talk about that later. For now, I think we better let Katie go home."

Katie slipped from Luke's grasp with another rush of pink in her cheeks. "I'm on my way," she said, sounding breathless as she hurried toward the door. She turned, hand on the knob. "Oh, and Luke, Father said to bring the papers by anytime tomorrow. Then you can fill them in on all the details before Gabe moves in on Monday."

He stared at the woman who had just made him the happiest man in the world. And, if God answered his prayer—could very well do it again. "Thanks, Katie, for everything."

"My pleasure," she said, and then flushed again before she quickly closed the door.

Parker's eyes met his in the inevitable showdown. "I'm happy about Gabe, you know that, but what the devil do you think you're doing, McGee?"

Luke turned to stare out the window, the smile fading from his face as he steeled himself for his superior's wrath. He felt the joy seep out of him as he sighed, hands pressed to the sill and shoulders slumped in defeat. "I'm in love with her, Parker."

The words all but echoed in the room, and Parker's silence confirmed their impact. Luke rotated to face him, then crouched on the sill where Katie had sat just moments before. "I'm through with just friends. I want more."

Parker hesitated, lips clamped in silent disapproval. "Does she?" he finally asked, watching Luke through veiled eyes.

Luke sifted his fingers through his hair and exhaled. He

looked up with a sheepish smile. "Her body does, there's no question about that. But her heart?" The smile disappeared as Luke's gaze trailed to the floor. "I don't know."

"What about this Jack character—I thought she was in love with him?"

Luke massaged his hairline with the palm of his hand. "I don't know."

With a jut of his brow, Parker leaned back in his chair and plunked his feet on Luke's desk. "You don't know a whole lot for somebody about to make a fool of himself."

Luke looked up, rewarding Parker with a half-lidded glare. "I know if she's kissing me like that, she can't be in love with any high-society milksop."

"Milksop? That's a little harsh, isn't it?"

Disgust wormed its way into Luke's smile. "Not on your life—the man's a wimp. She's got him wrapped so tightly around her baby finger, he could be a yo-yo."

Parker smiled. "You mean like she has you?"

"Funny, Riley, real funny." Luke plucked his suit coat off the back of his chair, dismissing Parker's comment with a cocky smile. "I'm only laying low until I have her wrapped around mine, then we'll just see who runs the show. Besides, with Gabe living there, I'll have the chance to see Katie as much as I want, Jack or no Jack. And if Rich Boy wants to give me a fight, I may just rough him up. Either way, I plan to date Katie no matter what Jack—" Luke gave Parker a pointed look, "or you—think about it. Come on, let's get out of here—Bets is cooking tonight."

"I sure hope you're not biting off more than you can chew, McGee." Parker rose with a loud exhale, resignation clear in his tone. "But I will admit—this is an interesting turn of events. Changes the color and complexion of everything. Gabe living with the O'Connors—who would have thought?" He shook his head. "That Katie is really something—taking a complicated and messy problem and parsing it down to one basic solution that makes everyone happy. I'm partial to simple black and white, so this is pure genius. It's enough to make me want to kiss her myself."

Luke cuffed an arm to his best friend's shoulder and gave him a threatening grin. "I'd suggest not, Parker ol' buddy," he said as he walked him to the door. "Unless, of course, you're partial to simple black and blue as well."

Faith glanced at the clock over the stove for what seemed like the hundredth time, berating herself for being so stupid. Nine o'clock and still no Collin. With renewed vigor, she scrubbed the last remains of spaghetti sauce from the cream enamel of her kitchen stove, certain the dishrag would wear straight through to the cast iron beneath. She blew a strand of hair from her eyes with enough frustration to cause a stiff breeze, then looked at the clock again. A man should be at home with his wife and children on a Friday night, not hobnobbing with some other woman and her son while his wife kept his dinner warm in the oven.

If hobnobbing were accurate at all.

Heat that had nothing to do with the oven rolled into her cheeks, bringing shame along with it. She sucked in a deep swallow of air and discharged it, hopefully along with her guilt. She closed her eyes as her hand stilled on the stove, as limp as the dishrag in her hand. "Forgive me, Lord, for thinking such thoughts," she whispered, conviction from this morning's Scripture flooding her mind.

Finally, brethren, whatsoever things are true, whatsoever things are honest, whatsoever things are just, whatsoever things are pure, whatsoever things are lovely . . . think on these things.

"I *will* think on what is true, honest, and lovely," she said in a bold voice. The sound echoed loudly in her cozy cream and wood kitchen, suddenly reminding her that her children were in bed and she was all alone.

Again.

Whatever is true. She forced herself to focus as she swabbed down her heavy oak table, wiping away perilous thoughts along with the cold spaghetti. What *was* true was that Collin McGuire was an incredible husband and father, working hard to ensure his family came first.

Most of the time.

She grated her lip. No, that wasn't fair. His family always came first and would have tonight if she hadn't said yes . . .

"Evelyn's son wants to meet Brady and me," he'd said with hesitation. His gray eyes had scanned her face carefully, watching, waiting . . .

She had flashed her most reassuring smile. "I think that sounds nice. When?"

Relief eased across his features. "Friday night, after work. I shouldn't be late."

"Of course, take your time."

Faith rinsed the dishrag and stole another peek at the clock. 9:30. She dried her hands and reached for the teakettle, squaring her jaw. *Of course, I hadn't meant literally.*

No! She could do this, she could. *Whatever is honest.* She filled the teapot with water and set it to boil, remembering the time Collin had confessed to an unexpected afternoon of stickball with street urchins outside the back of the shop. That was the Saturday she'd asked him to watch the children so she could run an errand, but he had to work, he'd said, a rush job to get out the door. A smile softened the edges of her mouth. Later that night, the man had spilled the guilty truth, obsessive about honesty and totally uncomfortable with guilt burning a hole in his gut. Tightness in her chest eased as she spooned sugar into her favorite mug. The whistle of the kettle sang in the air, and she sighed with relief, anxious to warm the chill in her fingers. She poured the boiling water into her cup and steeped her tea with a slow, easy motion.

Whatever is pure. She sank back into her chair and closed her eyes to take a sip. The comfort of Earl Gray steamed her face and coated her throat, warming her with thoughts of Collin. Before they were married, he'd been a man of base appetite, indulging in the pleasures of the flesh at every whim of his will. But God had won out, and Collin's passion for lust had changed, becoming a passion for purity that had won him the true love he craved.

Whatever is lovely. She warmed her hands on the sides of her cup and felt a shiver of heat that tingled all the way to her toes. Certainly the easiest "whatever" of the lot, for if Collin McGuire was anything, it was "lovely," Faith thought with a languid sigh. She closed her eyes and envisioned the man who had fathered her children, and tears readily pricked her eyes. *Thank you, God, for giving me the desire of my heart!* In her mind's eye she saw his smoldering good looks and his teasing ways, and warmth rushed through her body that had little to do with the tea in her hands. At thirty-four years of age, Collin seemed to be a man who only improved with time, and whenever he walked through her door, he never failed to trigger her pulse.

And Evelyn's?

Her eyes popped open and she sucked in a harsh breath, fisting the mug. "No! I trust my husband, I do!" Without hesitation, she began to pray, desperate to ward off any such thoughts.

She glanced up as a key in the door sounded just as the clock in the parlor chimed ten. With unsteady hands, she set the mug on the table and rose, smoothing her skirt with far too sweaty palms. She heard his footsteps in the hall and waited, then darted to the sink to wash her empty cup, desperate to appear nonchalant.

She never turned around, but she heard his approach all the same, and her stomach fluttered at the press of his lips against her neck. "You waited up. I'm glad," he whispered, arms twined around her waist. "I missed you, Faith."

He eased her around and scanned her face, eyes sober with apology. "I'm sorry I'm late."

A hoarse chuckle caught in her throat as she pulled away. She hurried to the oven to retrieve his dinner. "You must be starved."

"Actually, no. Evelyn's mother insisted I eat."

She stared, pot holders adhered to her hands as she held his plate of spaghetti, now as dry as the roof of her mouth. "Oh."

"You're upset."

"No, no, I'm not. I just wish you'd called."

He took a step forward and gently removed the plate from her hands. "I did. Bella said you were giving Abby a bath, so I asked her to tell you not to save dinner." Taking her hand in his, he led her to the table. "I can eat. Will you sit with me?"

She swallowed hard and nodded, careful to keep her mood light as she chattered about her evening with the girls and fetched him a glass of milk. Placing it on the table, she retrieved utensils and a napkin before slipping into the chair next to his, giving him a ready smile. "So . . . what's Evelyn's son like?" she asked. "Other than being a typical thirteen-year-old boy?"

Collin twirled his fork in the spaghetti and took a bite, studying her as he chewed. He drank some milk and then set it down with a heavy sigh. "I'm afraid there's nothing typical about Tommy. He's confined to bed most of the time, not able to play with other kids or even get outside for a little fresh air." He bent to shovel more noodles in his mouth, but not before Faith saw a glimmer of moisture in his eyes. He quickly chewed and swallowed. "The poor guy is little more than skin and bones, but he has a mind and a wit sharper than any kid I've ever seen."

With a catch in her throat, Faith placed a hand on his arm. "I'll bet it meant the world for you and Brady to visit."

He gulped more milk, eyeing her as it glugged down his throat. He swiped his mouth with the side of his sleeve despite the napkin in his lap. "It did, you could tell. I guess he's starved for male attention because he lit up when Brady and I walked in." Collin averted his gaze to focus on his dinner, his voice slow and measured. "So when Brady had to leave after an hour, I don't know, I just felt like I needed to stay for a while, you know?" He rolled more spaghetti on his fork and popped it in his mouth. He looked up with a faint smile. "Did I tell you he's a master at chess? *Which* is why I'm late tonight, as a matter of fact. Actually, it's pretty embarrassing. The kid gave me a thrashing that would make your father proud."

Faith grinned, relief ebbing through her at the sullen tease on her husband's face. "Mmm . . . I'll bet that information will come in handy if I ever need leverage. I'm sure both Mitch and Father would have a heyday with that bit of news."

He looked at her then, his eyes as soft and intense as his daughters' when they whispered their prayers to God. Without warning, he suddenly dropped his fork with a clatter and hauled her onto his lap. She heard his sharp intake of breath as he cocooned her in his arms with a tight squeeze, burying his head in the crook of her neck. His voice was low and gruff and so thick with emotion, tears stung her eyes. "You don't need leverage with me, Mrs. McGuire," he whispered, "I need it with you. I love you more with every waking moment, Faith, and I can't help but wonder—how in God's name did I ever find a woman like you?"

Her heart swelled till she thought she would burst, and her eyes welled at the moisture she felt on her neck. "In God's name, Collin," she repeated softly, "where the desires of one's heart always rest." She pressed a gentle kiss to the edge of his bristly jaw as a wellspring of gratitude dampened her cheeks. "The desires of our heart, my love. Both yours," she whispered, "and mine."

"Jack, I *have* to go in! You want another two and a half months between dates? Besides, I'm cold." Katie pushed him away, a smile quirking her lips at the moonstruck glaze in his eyes.

He made a valiant attempt to reel her back to his side of the car in spite of two palms flat against his argyle vest. In a deft move, he bypassed her barrier with a lift at the waist to deposit her on his lap, disarming her with a hungry kiss before she could object. "I'll keep you warm, doll." His whisper faded to a groan. "Oh, do you have any idea how much I missed you?"

Yes, she did.

He'd shown it all night. From the five-pound box of chocolates and two dozen long-stemmed red roses, to the lavish dinner at Boston's finest restaurant and endless kisses in the car. Without question, Jack Worthington was everything she'd ever wanted in a man—rich, handsome, ambitious, well-connected . . . and eating out of her hand.

She held her wristwatch up to the light of the streetlamp that filtered in through his side of the car. "It's five minutes before ten, Jack, and if I don't rattle that doorknob at the exact stroke of the hour, you're going to learn what missing me is really all about." She unlatched the driver's door and wiggled off his lap to hop onto the running board before landing on the street.

He swung out of the car and grabbed her hand, tugging her back into his arms. His eyes were intense in the shadowed light. "Katydid, wait! I need to tell you something,"

And then before she could stop her jaw from sagging, John Henry Worthington dropped to one knee, right there on the leaf-littered cobblestones of Donovan Street. "Katie Rose O'Connor, I want more from you than two and a half months between dates and ten o'clock curfews." He held up a diamond ring that sparkled in the lamplight like the hope in his eyes. "I want to see you every day and sleep with you every night. I want to hold you and kiss you and love you whenever I want. So what do you say, Katydid—will you marry me?"

She stared, jaw still extended, and then slowly took the ring with a quivering hand and placed it on her finger. She held it up to the light. "Oh, Jack, are you absolutely sure?"

He rose to his feet while his deep chuckle echoed in the still night air. He lifted her up in his arms to give her a kiss that more than confirmed his mind was made up. "I love you, doll. Always have . . . always will." He hooked an arm around her shoulders and ushered her toward the front door. "Come on, let's go tell your parents."

She glanced up, slowing her gait. "Let's tell them tomorrow, Jack, please? I want to enjoy this moment all by myself, just for tonight *and* think how to prepare them for all of this. But come to church with us tomorrow and stay for lunch, and we'll take it from there, okay?"

He kissed the top of her head and led her up the front-porch steps with a lovesick grin. "Okay, Katydid—anything you say. Good night, doll."

She turned the front knob, and after a final lingering kiss, he sauntered back to the car, hands in his pockets and a whistle on his lips.

Katie closed the door and gently fingered the ring before slipping it in her pocket with a warm sigh. She sloped back against the carved wood of the front door in contentment, hands cupped firmly on the steel knob. She sighed again and then smiled. *Good job, Katie Rose—you're right on track for the future of your dreams!*

"Katie? Is that you?"

Her father's voice drifted from the parlor, and Katie made a futile attempt to smooth her hair and straighten her teal jersey dress that suddenly felt too snug. Worrying her lip, she glanced back at her stockings to make sure her seams were straight, then touched a nervous hand to her mouth and prayed her lipstick wasn't too smeared. She squared her shoulders and sailed into the room. "Yes, it's me—right on ti—"

Blood drained from her cheeks. There, as cozy as the candles glowing on the warm maple mantel, sat Luke McGee—in *her* house, playing chess with *her* father. *Sweet angels in heaven, what's he doing here?* She stared in shock, remembering their kiss in his office yesterday, and the blood rushed right back, warmer this time and clear up to the roots of her hair.

He rose to his feet—all strapping six foot three of him—further unsettling her with a half-mast look that traveled from the top of her disheveled hair down to the short hem of her dress that was obviously askew. His eyes roamed up again to fix on her face with a knowing gaze. He gave her a thin smile. "Hello, *Katydid*. Did you have a good time?"

If possible, more heat flooded her cheeks, and her chin angled high, incensed at both his implication and the fact he had invaded her territory. This was *her* home, and Jack was *her* fiancé—she had no reason to be embarrassed by the likes of Luke McGee and his condescending notions. And he had no reason to be here, piercing her with that smug look that always made her feel so guilty. She gave him a tight smile. "Hello, Luke, what are you doing here?"

One blond brow jagged up. "Gabe," he said in a clipped tone, his smile looking as if it might crack. "I suppose with all the excitement of seeing *Jack* again, it must have slipped your mind that I was coming by."

Gabe! The paperwork, of course. Her breath thickened in her throat. She'd just assumed Luke had come by this afternoon while she'd been out shopping with her friends. Embarrassment bloodied her cheeks once again, further singeing her temper.

"You look flushed, Katie, are you feeling all right?" Marcy put her knitting needles aside and rose, bustling over to her daughter with motherly concern.

Katie absently wiped moist palms down the side of her skirt before adjusting it further. "Yes, of course," she said with a quick kiss to her mother's cheek. She drew in a fortifying breath and gave her father a bright smile. "Hello, Father. I hope you've managed to impart some humility to our Mr. McGee here. I'm told when it comes to games, he tends to be a bit smug."

"I'm afraid that's a lesson for another day, Katie Rose. This young man has served up a generous piece of humble pie, and I don't mind saying it wasn't to my taste." He rose and extended his hand. "Thank you for making my wife a very happy woman, Luke," he said with a dry smile. "Although I can't say the same for me, at least when it comes to chess. We're looking forward to welcoming Gabe to our family on Monday, but if you don't mind, I think I'll just go up to bed and nurse my wounds."

Luke laughed, and shook his hand. "I think the prospect of another mouth to feed may have you a little distracted tonight, Mr. O'Connor. And as far as my skills at chess, the man you really want to play is my director at the BCAS, Parker Riley. He was our resident champion in law school, so trust me, I've had lots of practice."

A hint of challenge sparkled in Patrick's tired eyes as he headed for the door and draped an arm around Marcy's shoulders. "Good, then we'll have you both over for dinner soon so I can salvage my pride. Thanks again, Luke." He leaned to buss his daughter's forehead. "Good night, Katie Rose. Will you turn out the lights and lock the doors?"

Marcy paused to touch the side of Katie's face. "Did you have a good time with Jack tonight, darling?"

With a hike of her chin, Katie avoided Luke's eyes and focused on her mother. "Wonderful, Mother. I didn't know how badly I missed him until I opened that door tonight."

"Good," Marcy said. "And if he keeps getting you home on time, I made your father promise to extend your curfew, so be sure to tell him that."

Katie leaned to kiss her mother's cheek, then her father's. "I will. Sleep well, you two."

Her parents ascended the stairs, and Katie turned her attention to Luke with arms folded and clutched to her waist. She gave him a nervous smile, her stomach as skittery as if she'd missed curfew. "So, it's all settled then? Gabe's coming home on Monday?"

He unrolled his shirtsleeves and buttoned the cuffs, then reached for his briefcase on the sofa. "Yep, it's a done deal. Gabe is one lucky little girl, thanks to you. I told her this afternoon, and I haven't seen her this excited since I bought her buttered popcorn and three grape Nehis at the Regal last year." He moved toward the foyer, then turned to face her just inside the parlor. His eyes softened. "I don't know how to thank you, Katie. You saved her life—and mine."

She blushed and hurried to douse the various lamps in the room, almost out of breath as she rejoined him in the foyer. "She's saving mine too, you know. With Gabe in the house, Father's attention will be diverted away from me." She smiled and rubbed her arms, her hands sweaty against the clingy material of her thin sleeves. "Who knows? I may actually be the good daughter for once."

With a slow lift of his hand, he feathered a finger down the side of her jaw. "You are the good daughter," he whispered, "just a bit headstrong."

Her pulse accelerated, and she took a step back. "Can I . . . get you anything before you go? A drink of cider, water . . ." Her eyes scanned the hall, suddenly lighting on the box of candy. She rushed to uncover the lid of the heart-shaped box. "A chocolate with cream center?"

His eyes narrowed at the heart box flanked by an obscene spray of red roses. A thin veneer coated his tone. "I guess ol' Jack was pretty glad to see you. No, I doubt he'd want his confections wasted on a soda jerk. But a cold drink of water would sure hit the spot."

"No problem," she said, hurrying toward the kitchen with a wave of her hand. "You wait here, and I'll be right back." She bludgeoned through the swinging door as if she were running for her life. And in a way, she felt as if she were. The man in the next room made her downright uncomfortable, especially with Jack's diamond ring burning a hole in her pocket. She slumped against the counter and pressed a hand to her eyes.

All she wanted to do was to get through her last week at the BCAS and stay as far away from Luke McGee as humanly possible. She couldn't trust herself around him—that much was clear. Every kiss the man had given her had certainly proven that, and although he could melt her resolve with the touch of his lips, she refused to allow him to destroy her dream. She flipped open the cabinet door and jerked out a glass, holding it beneath the tap with a shaky hand. Nothing was going to stop her now. She *would be* Mrs. Katie Worthington, one of the finest legal minds in the city. And with Jack's money and political connections, she'd be well on her way to a seat in the Congress someday, hopefully to make a difference on behalf of women everywhere. Her lips thinned into a grim line. And no heated kisses were going to stand in her way.

The kitchen door creaked open and she whirled around, causing water from the glass to slosh onto the floor.

He folded his arms and slacked a hip against the door while that annoying smile curved to the edges of his mouth. "A little twitchy, are we?"

She grappled for the dishrag and suddenly laughed, the motion helping to dispel her anxiety somewhat. Glass in one hand, she stooped to wipe up the water with the other, managing to give him a crooked smile. "No more than usual when you're around, Cluny McGee." She stood to her feet and tossed the rag in the sink. "Do you want ice?"

His approach was achingly slow as he strolled toward her. With a casual air, he took the glass from her hand and set it on the counter while his warm gaze welded to hers. He moved in close, wedging her against the sink by just the mere threat of his presence. She swallowed hard and craned her neck up, wishing her voice hadn't fused to her throat.

Massive palms slowly grazed the side of her arms, as if he thought she might be chilled, but the heat they generated made her feel anything but. In fluid motion, they moved to her waist, the gentle caress of his thumbs all but stealing her air. His blue eyes deepened in intensity as he leaned in, and his husky voice made her mouth go dry. "Let's face it, Katie Rose," he whispered, "I don't want ice, I don't want water, and I definitely don't want chocolate."

She caught her breath when his words melted warm in her ear.

"I want you . . ."

And before the air could return to her lungs, his mouth dominated hers with such gentle force, it coaxed a breathless moan from her lips, heating the blood in her veins by several degrees. "Say it, Katie Rose . . . say that you want me as much as I want you."

She could barely speak for the racing of her pulse, and her breathing was as rapid as his. Powerful arms refused to relent, drawing her close as his lips trailed her throat with an urgency that made her dizzy. "Say it," he whispered again, "tell me you care for me too."

"Luke, I—I . . . I do," she breathed, too disarmed to deny it.

His mouth took hers like a man possessed, deepening the kiss until she was putty in his hands. And then all at once, he pulled away to cup her face with his palms, his eyes so full of love, it took her breath away. "That's all I needed to know, Katie. And I promise from now on, I'll be taking it slow. I don't want to rush this."

She blinked, her pulse thudding to a stop. "Rush what?"

He bent to give her a warm, unhurried kiss. "Us," he whispered against her mouth. "I'm in love with you, Katie Rose."

She pushed him away, the shock of his words breaking his spell. "Luke, no, you can't!"

Two puckers crimped the bridge of his nose as he fanned a gentle hand through her hair. "It's too late, Katie, I already am. And I thought you had feelings for me too."

The edge of the counter bit into her back as she tried to distance herself with a hand to his chest. Her voice was a pained whisper. "I do have feelings for you, Luke, but I'm . . . afraid only as a friend and nothing more." She looked away, unable to bear the hurt in his eyes. "I'm sorry if these . . . encounters . . . led you to believe there could be anything between us, but as you said, it's too late." She swallowed and forged on, fumbling for the ring in her pocket. She avoided his eyes while she put it on. "You see, Jack asked me to marry him tonight, and, well . . . I said yes."

Silence pounded in her ears as she waited, and when seconds passed, she finally looked up to gauge his response. And in one halting breath, she was face-to-face with Cluny McGee once again. Years melted away as she stared at the little boy with the swaggering confidence that never quite masked the hurt in his eyes. Even now, the wide lips curled into that cocky air that told her she didn't matter, that he didn't care what she thought of him. Only she knew better. For some reason she could never ascertain, she had always mattered to Cluny McGee, and somehow the knowledge had always strengthened her. She watched him now as his hurt hardened to anger, and the breath seized in her throat when he gripped her by the arms.

"A friend and nothing more, and yet you kiss me like that? You're lying, Katie."

"I'm attracted to you, Luke, it's true, but nothing more, I swear."

"So you're in love with Jack, are you?" He jerked her close and kissed her hard, driving any thoughts of Jack completely from her mind. When he released her, she sagged against the counter, knees weak and chest heaving. His voice was as sharp and cold as the stainless steel edging that cut into her back. "Tell me, *Katydid*, does he know how readily you can fall into another man's arms?"

Shame broiled her cheeks and anger rose to her defense. Her hand flew back to slap his face, but he locked her wrist midair with a painful hold. "Is that all this was between us then? A little fun while your rich boyfriend was off-limits?"

She wrenched her hand free. "I never started any of this, and you know it. It was you."

His fingers dug into her arms as he pressed her to the counter. "No, but you sure finished it, didn't you? Selling yourself to a man you don't love just to satisfy a driving ambition that will never make you happy. Oh yeah, Betty told me—your jaded dreams to marry Jack and his money, use his family to rise to the top." He leaned in, his breath hot against her face. "So ol' Jack is everything on your all-important checklist, is he? And that's what you want? A rich-boy pantywaist who will kiss your feet and do whatever you say? Well, bully for him. But he isn't the one who races your pulse, is he, Katie?" The pressure of his fingers increased and he pulled her close, making her wince. "My kisses are good enough, but my life isn't, is that it?"

"Let go, you're hurting me!"

His abrupt release jolted her against the counter as surely as if he had shoved her away. "No, Katie," he whispered through clenched teeth, "you're hurting yourself, and I guarantee it's a pain that will last a lot longer than a few seconds." He looked away, his anger evident in the heave of his chest and the clench of his jaw, and then with a sharp hiss of a curse, he turned and strode to the door.

"Luke!" Her heart lurched forward.

He paused, hand on the door and his back as rigid as the wood beneath his palm.

"Please believe me, I never meant to lead you on. I've planned to marry Jack all along, and you knew that."

He glanced over his shoulder, muscled arm poised against the door. His voice was cold. "Don't worry about it, I wouldn't want to interfere with your *plan*." He spat the word as if it were an obscenity, then slammed his fist against the door and spun around. "You know, Katie, you've always been a cold and callous little thing, but I actually believed it was just a front. You know, a thin coat of steel to protect your fragile little heart? But I was wrong. Seems that steel is as thick as that stubborn head of yours when it comes to making life decisions. Despite the heat and fire in every kiss we've shared, you're a cold, cold woman, Katie O'Connor. The kind that chooses a marriage as cooly as you choose a bank to store your money. Your 'plan' is your god, and God help anybody who gets in your way." He turned to go.

Nausea curdled in the pit of her stomach. "Luke, forgive me, please. I'm sorry . . ."

He halted halfway through the door. She watched as he drew in a deep breath and suddenly that broad back straightened, tall and strong like the man he'd become. And when he finally spoke, the anger seemed tempered somewhat and laced with regret. "I know, Katie," he said, head cocked to reveal a profile resigned to a fate he didn't choose. "You're sorry, and so am I. But I'll get over it, don't worry about me. But you?" A hoarse laugh spewed from his throat, devoid of all humor. "I hope I'm wrong, truly I do. But something deep inside tells me your 'sorry' has only just begun. My best to you and Jack."

And with a cool swish of air, he was gone, leaving her with nothing but an eerie creak as the door groaned on its hinges . . . and a cold prickle of fear that he may just be right.

Luke stormed down Donovan Street in a vile mood, profanity poisoning his tongue with a foulness he hadn't tasted in a long, long time. It should have been the perfect evening—moist and warm with the hint of a cool breeze, fragrant with the scent of fresh-mown grass and the promise of rain. But cozy three-decker homes, bathed in the haze of the full moon overhead, seemed to mock him instead, lamplight twinkling and taunting from lace-curtained windows.

A stray cardboard box from a neighbor's trash heap littered the sidewalk, and he bludgeoned it with his foot, thinking he should be kicking himself instead. Somewhere he heard the haunting strains of jazz, filtering from one of several open windows along the cobblestone street, each spilling light onto perfectly manicured lawns. Through fluttering sheers he saw families in silhouette—a mother rocking a child, a husband kissing a wife—and his anger flared at the painful reminder that he was once again on the outside looking in. A street orphan with no home of his own—shut out because he wasn't good enough. The bastard of a whore who lived his life in the streets, just like the trash put out at the curb. He shoved his hands in his pockets and muttered a curse, the harsh sound lingering in the thick, humid air as it defiled both his thoughts and the still of the steamy summer night.

She'd done it again—made a fool of him—something that came as naturally to Katie O'Connor as breathing. Sweat beaded the back of his neck—half from the heat of the late-August evening, half from the fear of how he would cope—cope with being in love with a woman who would never love him back, never want him. Correction: she wanted him, but only his body and not his soul. Irony curled his lips as he kicked a rock from his path. At one time, that would have been the perfect scenario—a woman who wanted him with no strings attached. But not now. Not with her.

"She's no good for you, you know. I've never seen a woman affect you like this one, Luke. Too much power from your past, too much for you to prove."

He sucked in a harsh breath and slashed shaky fingers through his hair, knowing full well that Parker had been right. Katie was no good for him. As children, they had battled for power, but in his need for her approval, she had always won. Sure and strong and driven, she was a little girl and now a woman who knew exactly what she wanted. And with a stab of pain in his chest, he realized it would never be him. Because the same drive and determination that drew him to her—caused him to love her—now drove her away from ever returning that love. He put a hand to his eyes, the truth as stark and glaring as the buzzing streetlight overhead. Attraction or no, he would never be more to Katie O'Connor than merely a friend who could race her pulse.

Like Betty was to me.

Air seized in his throat as his heart thudded to a stop. *Betty!*

He started to sprint toward Robinson's, shame thick in his throat and his heart pumping faster than his legs. Dear God, how could he have forgotten? He lifted his arm to glance at his watch and then groaned, upping his pace when he saw he was thirty minutes late. The one night he was supposed to walk her home, and he'd let her down. His chest heaved with regret as he skidded around the corner, huffing to a stop when he saw lights in the diner window. He sucked in a deep breath and leaned over, hands on his knees. *Thank you, God—she's still here.*

Breathing hard, he jogged up to the door and tested the knob, glancing at the crooked "Closed" sign displayed in the window. *Good girl*, he thought when the lock wouldn't budge, then quickly loped around the corner to the back of the diner.

A merge of shadows and moonlight cast an eerie glow throughout the alley, distorting trashcans heaped high with refuse. Suddenly he saw that the back door was ajar, and fear coiled in his stomach like a snake about to strike. He eased it open.

"Bets? Are you here?" Scanning the dimly lit kitchen, his gaze darted from the polished steel refrigerators to the sink piled high with a shift's worth of dishes. His heart hammered in his chest, and he raised his voice, as sharp and edgy as the stainless steel knives Pop kept in the drawer. "Bets! Are you here?"

"Back here . . ." Muffled words drifted from the storage room.

He bolted to Pop's pantry and froze, his stomach constricting at the sight of Betty huddled in the corner, head bent and arms wound around her knees. He rushed to kneel beside her and touched her hair, his voice steady, but his palm shaking. "Bets, what happened? Are you all right?"

She started to cry and he slid to the floor and pulled her into his arms. "Tell me what happened," he whispered.

A shiver rippled through her, and she clutched him tightly as her heaves shuddered against his chest. "L-Leo w-was here."

His blood slowed to a crawl. "When?"

"R-right b-before cl-osing. He wants me b-back."

Luke closed his eyes while prickles of ice shivered his skin. Blast it all, if only he hadn't been late! "Did he hurt you?" he whispered, his voice ready to crack.

She answered with a heave, and he gripped her at arm's length. Bile rose in his throat. Her cheekbone was swollen from hairline to jaw, mottled with a bruise that was just turning blue. Remnants of scarlet lipstick smeared the side of her mouth where a tiny split in her lip oozed the same color blood. He swallowed his rage and cupped her good cheek in his hand, determined to keep the moisture from welling in his eyes.

"Did he hurt you anywhere else?"

She shook her head and looked away, her fingers fluttering to the collar of her once crisp, white blouse, now soiled with grease from the grill and chocolate stains from the fountain.

She started to rise, and he helped her up with a steady hand, assessing her from head to toe. His gaze lighted on a gap in her blouse where she'd misbuttoned her shirt, and his stomach tightened when he noticed the top button was missing. He clutched her arms and forced her to face him.

"Tell me the truth, Bets—did he do anything else?"

She tried to push him away. "No, Luke, a couple of slaps for old time's sake, and nothing more, I promise. His calling card, you know," she said with a harsh whisper.

"Then why is your blouse gaping open and missing a button?"

A faint wash of color stained her pale cheeks as she looked down before she turned away to rebutton her shirt. Her voice forced a hint of humor, sounding more like the friend he knew and loved. “I’m a slob, you know that about me, Luke. I spilled chocolate and took my blouse off to try and wash it out, that’s all, and I lost a button in the process.”

He stared at her back, unconvinced as his eyes took in dirt stains that ran the length of her shirt and rumpled skirt.

When he didn’t answer, she glanced over her shoulder with a hitch of her brow. “*Before* the lowlife showed up.” She tucked her blouse firmly into her waistband and adjusted her skirt, then moved to the sink to fill both washtubs with water, obviously making an effort to convince him she was all right. “But I am glad you’re here. You can dry the dishes.”

He ambled over to retrieve a towel from a drawer and slung it over his shoulder. “How did he find you?” His voice was as measured as the soap she poured into the water, swishing until bubbles puffed high. “How does Roberta know where you live or work?”

She attempted a chuckle that came out too brittle. “Unfortunately, Leo’s smart. He found out I lived in Boston and remembered the only family I ever mentioned was a second cousin by the name of Robinson.” She piled a stack of dishes into the water and shot him a glance along with a hard smile. “Who just happened to own a diner.”

Luke blasted out a sigh that was more of a growl. “So much for influence over Roberta.”

Betty actually smiled. She patted his cheek with a deposit of soap bubbles along the scruffy line of his jaw. “Don’t worry, McGee, your influence is still intact, so don’t think you’ve lost your charm. It was Roberta’s friend, Dot, who gave me away.” Betty grunted as she scrubbed dried catsup off a plate. “The little floozy actually invited him down for the weekend.”

She handed him a dripping plate, and he took it and grasped her hand with a gentle hold. His voice was low. “I’m asking you again, Bets, and I want the truth. Did that scumbag try anything else? Because if he did, I'll kill him."

A bitter laugh tripped from her lips as she pulled her hand away. She mauled another plate with the dishrag, obviously avoiding his eyes. "I already told you, Luke, he just got fresh and a little rough, that's all, so there's no need for murder tonight." She glanced up with a tight smile. "Would you mind wiping down the booths and balancing the register while I finish the dishes? I didn't get much done with him here."

He exhaled a long, weary breath. "First, I want to know what he said."

She vented with a sigh and closed her eyes, her hands perfectly still in the water. "Says he misses me and wants me back. Plans to move here. He's looking for a place this weekend."

"What'd you say?"

She laughed again, the sound of it hollow. "I told him no, of course. And then he hauled off and hit me."

Luke's jaw was so tight, he thought it would crack. "Is he staying with Roberta?"

"No!" she said quickly and then doused a soapy plate in the rinse. She handed it to him with a patient smile. "With Dot."

He tossed the towel on the sink and pulled a clean dishrag from the drawer. He drowned it in the rinse, then squeezed till it was bone dry. *Like Leo's neck*. "You're not going back with him, you know."

She closed her eyes and swallowed hard. "I know."

"We'll get through this, Bets, I promise."

A faint smile trembled at the corners of her mouth as she nodded. "I know, Luke." She pushed an auburn strand of hair from her eyes and then turned, lips pursed into a tired smile. "Now, get busy. I don't want to be here all night."

"I want a cut of your pay, Galetti," he said over his shoulder. His tone was full of tease, but his stomach was full of knots.

"Sure thing, McGee," she called from the kitchen, "just as soon as I get a cut of yours for the meals I cooked this week."

He swiped the surface of a booth with a faint smile, raising his voice. "That's extortion, Bets, and you know it. And blackmail doesn't pay."

But then neither does assault and battery, he thought with a grunt, envisioning his fist in Leo's bloody face. His jaw hardened to rock.

Too bad. He could use the money.

12

Luke calmly shut the door of Betty's room and then wheeled around like a madman, almost leveling Parker in the process.

"Hey, hold on, buddy, don't run me down—I'll get out of your way."

Luke ignored him and charged to his room, heaving the door open with an angry thrust that sent it banging against the wall. He stalked to his closet and began rummaging through his suits, hunting for the trousers he had on the night they were at Kearney's.

Parker followed and quietly shut the door. "Getting angry won't solve this, you know."

"No, but getting even will. That bucket of scum has had my fist coming for a long time."

"It's not what she wants, Luke, and you know it."

He shoved through the suits hanging on the rack, his voice hard. "Which is why I've left it alone, Parker, even when that lowlife laid his filthy hands on her again and again. But not now, not here." He jerked a pair of trousers off a hanger and rammed a hand into the pocket, unearthing a folded scrap of paper. He hurled the slacks aside and tore the paper open. His eyes burned like acid as he stared Parker down, jabbing a thumb against his chest. "This is my territory, and my friend, and I'm going to make sure he never comes near her again."

"If you won't listen to Betty, then listen to me. Your temper can't handle it, Luke, and we all know it. You're cool and calm most of the time, but for some reason when it comes to Betty, you've got this blind spot, this pin in a grenade that makes you blow. I've seen you in fights before. For pity's sake, you almost killed a man over her, and you were barely nineteen at the time. Don't do this, Luke, I'm begging you. One pass and a slap isn't worth it. He isn't worth it—you could injure or kill him in the state of mind you're in. Why risk your life and your career, not to mention your friendship with Betty?"

Luke stared, fury pumping in his chest. "A pass and a slap? Is that all you think happened?"

"According to Betty—"

"She's lying, Parker!"

"You don't know that."

Luke leaned in, the piece of paper clenched hot in his fist. A swear word hissed from his lips. "Her blouse was gaping open and there was a button missing. And from the looks of the back of her skirt, he sure wasn't there for a chat." He shoved the paper in his pocket and ripped open the bottom drawer of his bureau.

Parker took a step forward. "What are you doing?"

Luke didn't answer. He tore through the drawer, hurling clothing onto the floor. He finally stood and bobbled four welded steel rings in his palm. His smile was as hard and cold as the metal in his hand. "Just a little souvenir from the streets of New York."

The whites of Parker's eyes expanded in shock. "Brass knuckles? You'll kill the man! For pity's sake, McGee, you're not in a gang anymore, running with thugs from the Lower

East Side, you're a respectable lawyer." Parker moved to the door, the hard line of his jaw matching Luke's, edge to edge. He folded his arms and stood his ground. "I can't let you do this."

Luke pocketed the knuckles and gave Parker a grim look. "And I can't let you stop me. Once and for all, I'm going to make sure that scum never bothers Betty again."

"You don't even know where to find him," Parker said, his voice almost a plea.

Luke retrieved the paper from his pocket and held it up. "Nope, but I know where to find Roberta. Fourteen A Humphrey Street—where blood will spill and justice will be served."

Parker butted up against the door, fingers flexed at his sides. "You're wrong. He's at Dot's, not Roberta's."

Cool rage twitched beneath his skin as Luke moved toward the door, his gaze pinned to Parker in silent threat. When he spoke, he ground out each word, his tone tight with tension. "Who-lives-in-the-same-building-as-Roberta. Get-out-of-my-way, Riley."

A nerve flickered in Parker's jaw. "Sorry, Luke. You'll have to go through me first."

Every muscle in Luke's body tensed. "Have it your way, my friend." He delivered a solid punch that doubled Parker over at the waist. Luke jerked the door open, and Parker bulldozed it closed with his body, rebounding with a jab of his foot.

Luke's grin was almost predatory. "You fight like a girl, anybody ever tell you that?"

His chest was heaving as he gave Luke a lidded stare. "Yeah, well, my education was in law school, McGee, not on the streets." He charged forward, head to chest, toppling Luke on the bed in a squeal of springs.

With a lightning thrust of his arms, Luke vaulted him onto the floor with a hard thud, depositing him against the bureau in a dazed and crumpled heap. He wiped his mouth with the side of his hand and strode toward the door, then turned, his fist white on the knob. "I love you like a brother, Parker, but if you ever get in my way again—or tell Betty about this—you won't walk for a week." His hand shook as he eased the door closed, fighting the urge to slam it off the hinges. He glanced down to the end of the hall, where light bled beneath Betty's door, and fresh rage flooded his veins. So help him, he would kill that bucket of scum or die trying.

Jerking the front door open, he locked and closed it again before flying down the steps of the boardinghouse. A stab of regret tightened his gut, but he never broke stride. Parker would be stiff in the morning, but it couldn't be helped. He glanced at his watch in the glow of the lamplight, then plunged his hands in his pockets and headed north. It was half past midnight, and Humphrey Street was over thirty minutes away, but Leo would be at the bars for a while, he was sure. Luke's lips flattened into a hard line. Celebrating his manhood, no doubt, over the fact that he could beat up a woman.

His fingers curled through the steel rings in his pocket, their cool touch causing a once-familiar adrenaline to course through his veins. It had been years since he had been in a real fight, at least since Brady had taken him off the streets with his talk of God and a chance for a new life. More guilt slinked in, and Luke picked up his pace, unwilling to let thoughts of Brady or Parker or Betty diminish his rage.

Parker said he had a blind spot when it came to Betty, a pin in a grenade, and maybe it was true. He stared straight ahead as he walked, barely aware of cozy couples as they passed or laughing groups milling by. He and Betty had so much history together—as friends, as family . . . He swallowed hard to dispel the shame in his throat. *As lovers.* His shoulders slumped as he slowed his pace. That was the brunt of the blind spot, he supposed—a guilt so deep and raw, he couldn't be rational when it came to her. He had wronged her, used her, the best friend he'd ever had on the streets, and the guilt ate at him like a case of Nehis bubbling in his stomach. And to add insult to injury, she was still in love with him, and he knew it. All the more reason to protect her, defend her, he thought with a firm press of his jaw. And he'd start tonight by making Leo wish he'd never been born.

He rounded the trash-littered corner of Berthold and Humphrey with its flickering streetlamp and shards of broken glass, and had no qualms whatsoever about being in the wrong part of town. Weedy lots and ramshackle flats had been his lot in life, and tonight felt almost like coming home. He glanced down Humphrey, dark and menacing, shadow-garish with broken streetlamps and the flash of neon. He slowed his gait like a cat on the prowl with muscles loose and motion fluid as he scanned each address. A feral smile slid across his lips when he spotted 14 Humphrey, dark and foreboding—the perfect place to extract a pound of flesh. Luke mounted the first step, and his muscles tensed at a movement of shadow in the alley between the flats. He eased off the step and flexed his fingers, every nerve itching for release.

The shadow shifted, moving into the moonlight. "I can't let you do this, Luke."

Shock paralyzed Luke's muscles. "What are you doing here?"

Brady strolled forward, hands in his pockets like a walk in the park, but his jaw was as steeled as if he thrived on the streets. His eyes were calm, and there was the barest of smiles on his serious face. "Parker called. Seems he thinks you plan to kill somebody tonight."

A swear word hissed from Luke's lips as naturally as if he still belonged in this part of town. "Go home, Brady. It's none of Parker's business, and it's none of yours."

With a casual air, Brady perched on the chipped stone top of a brick column that showcased the concrete steps, cracked and littered with weeds. He folded massive arms, bulging with muscles as tight as Luke's, then squinted up, the faint smile still in place. "You see, that's where you're wrong, Luke. Caring about you makes it my business, just like it does Parker's. Just like you care about Betty, making her welfare your business."

Luke took a step forward. A tic pulsed in his cheek as he clenched his fists. "Betty *is* my business, and I'm going to do everything in my power to protect her."

Brady assessed him through veiled eyes, his voice low and unhurried. "And what about God's power, Luke . . . you doing everything in his power to protect her?"

With a curse and a violent thrust of his foot, Luke kicked a stray bottle into the concrete step. It struck with a sickening shatter, and chards of glass exploded onto the walk. "Don't peddle your talk of God to me, Brady. He hasn't done a whole devil of a lot to protect Betty tonight." His chest heaved with anger as he thought of Katie, and pain seared a hole in his gut at the notion he was in love with a woman who would never love him back. "Or me, for that matter," he said with a sneer. "Go home and leave me alone. I'm going to handle this my way, with a fist instead of forgiveness. That lowlife raped her, and he's going to pay."

"It's your word against Betty's, and you don't know that for sure."

His eyes bulged with hate. "No, but I know lowlife scum like him—using her body for his own vile release, taking what he wants with no happily ever after."

Brady's jaw shifted before he pinned Luke in a probing stare. "You mean like you did?"

Rage exploded in Luke's brain and he lunged, his deadly fist coiled in fury. It clipped Brady on the jaw, toppling him into a spindly yew bush at the side of the steps.

He rebounded quickly, circling Luke in ready stance. His fingers clenched and unclenched at his sides as if he were just warming up, and the faint smile returned while he stared at Luke with that familiar white-hot calm. "I can't help but wonder, *Cluny*, where you and Betty would be right now if God had used a fist instead of forgiveness."

Brady's words stung his pride, detonating his temper. He

rushed again, hurtling a punch at Brady's face that earned Luke a fierce blow to his own gut, doubling him over and stealing his wind. Before he could catch his breath, an iron fist to his cheek sent Luke staggering back, momentarily stunned.

"Come on, Cluny boy," Brady said with a twitch of his fingers, "I whipped you as a snot-nosed kid, and I'll whip you as a man." The smile eased into a savage grin. "And it sure beats the stuffing out of boxing with Collin."

Luke studied the man who had saved his life, not to mention his soul, his muscled body crouched and ready and as powerful and menacing at the age of thirty-six as Luke was at twenty-two. Strength shimmered from his face and arms, now glistening with sweat.

"I don't want to fight you, Brady," he said, his breathing heavier than it should have been and moisture beading his brow.

White teeth flashed in the moonlight. "Afraid you'll lose?"

Luke flashed some teeth of his own. "Nope. Afraid I'll hurt you."

Brady's grin curled wide, taunting Luke with a gleam of a dare. "Or get hurt . . ."

Swallowing the bait whole, Luke pounced, landing a powerful thrust that sent Brady reeling back.

The blow seemed to ignite Brady's temper, launching him forward in a blur of muscled arms and fists. "Better me than Leo," he said with a grunt, delivering a clip to Luke's jaw that hurled him into the grass.

Rubbing his chin, Luke jumped to his feet and stormed forward, his good humor fading fast. "Don't worry, I have enough for you both," he rasped. He drove his fist straight for Brady's face.

With a duck of his head, Brady undercut him, blasting an iron jab to his ribs that felled Luke to his knees. "Not when I'm done with you, you overgrown street punk."

In a final thrust of his foot, Brady discharged a kick that slammed Luke flat on his back with a gargled groan.

Brady dropped to the grass beside him and yanked a handkerchief from his pants, his chest heaving as hard as Luke's. He wiped the sweat and blood from his face, then tossed it at Luke.

"Here," he wheezed with sputtering rasps, "you don't look so pretty anymore."

Luke sat up and touched the handkerchief to his jaw, wincing at the pain. "Shoot, Brady, what are you trying to do, kill me?"

Brady rolled his neck. The smile on his lips was as peaceful as the black sky above studded with stars. "Nope, bud, just beat a little sense into you, that's all." He looked up, moonlight sculpting his features with a quiet reverence that was uniquely Brady. His words, despite being carried forth on short, heaving breaths, were soft and low. "He's forgiven you, you know, and so has Betty. It's time you move on to be the man God has in mind for you to be. No more dancing around the edge anymore, Luke, living for God when it's convenient, living for yourself when it's not. Accept his forgiveness for what you did to Betty, and then give it back to those who need it. Like Leo. We're all sinners, bud, some of us more than others. And nobody knows better than me just how hard some sins are to forgive, especially in yourself. But I wasted years beating myself up, robbing myself of peace when forgiveness was as close as the repentance on my tongue."

Brady clutched an arm around Luke's shoulders, giving him a firm pat. He rose to his feet and extended an arm. "Don't make the same mistake I did, Luke. Refusing God's forgiveness only did damage to me and those I love. Don't do that to Betty if you love her." A nerve quivered in the hollow of Brady's cheek. "Don't do that to me if you love me."

Suddenly Luke felt all of fourteen again, his eyes misting at the only love he had ever known from a father. He gripped Brady's arm and sprung to his feet, eyes averted as he brushed twigs and leaves from his pants. With a hand to his head, he massaged the bridge of his nose, then dabbed at his eyes in a manner he hoped wasn't obvious. He sucked in a cleansing breath and released it again, the tension and fury finally gone from his body.

He shoved his hands in his pockets and stared at his feet. "Thanks, Brady," he whispered. Fists clenched tight, he fought the urge to embrace the man who had shown him the face of God.

Brady hooked a steady arm over Luke's shoulders, his touch warm and firm. "Don't thank me, Luke, thank God. I know I do. He's the one who put us together, you know." He grazed the side of his jaw with the back of his hand and flinched. "Painful as that may be at times."

Luke laughed and touched a hand to the tender side of his swollen lip. "You pack a mean wallop for an old man, you know that, Brady?"

Brady started walking toward the street. "Wait till you see my one-two punch . . . which, by the way, would go great with hot coffee at your place right about now."

"Your one-two punch?" Luke jogged to keep up, matching Brady's pace, stride for stride.

Neon blinked across Brady's features as he shot a sideways glance, sweat and eyes gleaming in the shadowed light. "Yep, pardon and prayer—guaranteed to make a new man out of you. And if you don't believe me, just ask Collin." Brady grinned. "He's got the drill down good."

John Brady yawned as he trudged up the moon-washed steps of the brick house where his wife and child were sound asleep, and almost hated to glance at his watch. Four o'clock in the morning! A groan rumbled in his chest at the thought of Teddy rising at six, pumped full of energy for another new day. The polished wood floor echoed his groan as he entered the foyer, smiling at the stuffed monkey astride the wooden rocking horse he had made for his son. Maybe Lizzie would keep him quiet before church so he could sleep in, Brady thought, although that was a monumental task, he knew. But Lizzie would manage, he was sure, and as always, he whispered a prayer of gratitude for the woman in his bed.

He moved down the hall toward their bedroom at the back of the house as silently as the creaky floor would allow, touching the side of his jaw that still throbbed from Luke's blows. He ducked in the bathroom and carefully closed the door, then grinned at the blood on his face when he turned on the light. But injury and lack of sleep notwithstanding, he wouldn't have traded a solitary moment of his evening with Cluny McGee. A pain in his shoulder suddenly vied with his jaw, and he winced. Well, maybe one or two that wouldn't have left such a mark on his tired body.

Tonight had been like old times—easy conversation with the boy who had become like a son, now a man who had become a good friend. Laughter, confession, prayer—hours of bonding between two men bent on serving God. Brady stripped off his shirt and turned on the water, grateful for the sore but solid muscles he saw in the mirror. They had won him a battle tonight, taking Luke all the way to the throne of grace. Gratitude eased their ache as he cupped several handfuls of water to his head and chest. He soaped his hair and under his arms, then leaned in and doused his head under the sink and then his torso. With another wide yawn, he dried off, wiped down the sink, then donned his old, ragged T-shirt that Lizzie always threatened to burn. After brushing his teeth, he flicked off the light and opened the door, the clean smell of soap following him down the hall. The very scent forced moisture to his eyes. Sweet mercy, how he loved being clean! Both in body and soul, and God had done just that, cleansing him of a past that had stained him far too long.

Though your sins be as scarlet, they shall be as white as snow; though they be red like crimson, they shall be as wool.

White as snow . . . just like him.

And now, Luke.

Brady took off his trousers and tossed them on the hamper before slipping under the coolness of the lone sheet that was the only cover Lizzie could abide. The bed radiated with the welcoming heat of the woman carrying his child, and once again tears pricked his eyes at the boundless blessings of God. He eased his feet to the edge of the bed to stretch his aching muscles, then turned and pressed in close to the back of his wife, her knees huddled up to her swollen belly. In a gentle caress, he rested his hand on her stomach, and she slowly turned in his arms, expending a good deal of effort to face him with a sleepy smile.

"Is everything all right with Luke?" she whispered.

The cumbersome mound between them brought a smile to his face as he pulled her close and brushed a gentle kiss to her lips. "More than all right. I finally got through tonight."

She shifted to stare in his eyes, her fingers grazing the bristly line of his jaw. "I thought you got through a long time ago."

A heavy sigh parted from his lips, and he idly traced the curve of her hip with the palm of his hand, her warmth seeping into his fingers. "I did, but tonight he was set free from his past, Lizzie, cleansed and ready to reap the blessings of God."

"Like you," she whispered. She moved in close to nuzzle the hollow of his throat.

"Mmm . . . exactly," he said with a sudden surge of heat. He tucked his head beneath her chin and explored her throat with his mouth.

"Ohhhh . . . ," she said with a soft moan. Her head drifted back to allow him full range. "All's well that ends well, I guess."

Brady paused, his fingers stilled as they traced the smooth line of her collarbone. "Not exactly," he said with a sigh against her chest. He lifted his head so his gaze could probe hers. "Luke's in love with Katie."

"What?" Lizzie lumbered to a sitting position as quickly

as she could, the bedsprings squealing from the effort. "What do you mean Luke's in love with Katie? *Our* Katie . . . with *our* Cluny? When? How?"

Brady chuckled and sat up himself, pulling her into his arms as he leaned against the headboard. "Over the summer, evidently, after a period of butting heads, I understand."

"Oh, Brady, what an answer to prayer!" Lizzie burrowed into her husband's hold with a soft giggle. "Faith, Charity, and I have been praying because none of us think Jack is right for her. And Cluny . . . I mean Luke . . . oh my goodness, he's a godly man, smart, good-looking, a lawyer, and certainly tough enough to handle Katie." She sighed. "A match made in heaven."

"It might be," Brady said with a wrinkle of his brow, "if she loved him back."

Lizzie pulled away, her eyes wide with concern. "She doesn't feel the same way?"

Brady's lips flattened into a tight line. "Well, Luke certainly thought so, because apparently our Katie has been melting into his arms at the drop of a hat. But when he approached her tonight, she turned him down flat, telling him she sees him only as a friend."

"But that can change!" Lizzie insisted.

"Not with Jack's diamond on her finger," Brady said in a droll tone.

"What?"

"According to Luke, Jack asked Katie to marry him tonight, and she said yes."

"Well, we'll just have to see about that," Lizzie muttered with a cross of her arms.

Brady tugged her back. "It's Katie we're talking about, Lizzie, and you know good and well you won't be able to sway her once her mind is set. And you can't say a word to Faith or Charity about Luke's feelings either, because he doesn't want anyone else to know."

"But you and I can pray about it, can't we?"

His chuckle feathered the top of her head. The familiar scent of lilacs drifted up to tease his senses. "Yes . . . which is exactly why I told you in the first place, Elizabeth," he whispered into her hair. "We need the power of two."

He felt the warmth of her words against his throat. "'If two of you shall agree on earth as touching any thing that they shall ask—'"

"'—it shall be done for them of my Father which is in heaven,'" Brady finished. He lifted her chin with his finger, a proud smile edging his lips. "And that's why I married you, Mrs. Brady," he said with a playful kiss to her nose. "You're a quick study."

"No, you married me, Brady, because God answered our prayers." She leaned back into his arms and released a soft sigh. "Now let's just see what we can do about Katie."

Brady rested his head against hers and closed his eyes. "Dear God, your Word says that many are the plans in a man's heart, but it is your purpose that prevails. As long as I've known Katie, she's been a little girl of strong will and single purpose. And right now she has many plans in her heart—from law school and marriage with Jack, to achieving great things on behalf of women. But, Lord, what do you want for her? Lizzie and I both know that Katie's happiness—and Luke's—lies in your purpose and plan for each of them. Reveal that to them, Lord, lead them along the path you have for them both. And if that path leads them to join together as one, then open Katie's eyes to the truth, and give Luke the grace he needs to see it through. Deepen their relationship, Lord, not only with each other, but with you. In Jesus' name, amen."

Lizzie's gentle sigh merged with one of his own, and suddenly a rush of love flooded his heart. His eyes moistened at the touch of her warm body against his, carrying his child. He clutched her tightly in his arms, and when he spoke, his voice was rough with emotion. "What did I ever do to deserve you, Lizzie?"

He felt the curve of her lips against the stubble of his

skin. "Oh, not much, Brady, just love God with all of your heart."

With a raspy groan, he kissed her hard, sweeping the curve of her body with his hands.

"And what did I do to deserve that?" she breathed, pulling back with a hint of a tease.

His palm stroked the full of her belly, then slid to her waist to gently shift her close. "Figure it out, Elizabeth," he whispered in her ear, and proceeded to kiss the hollow of her throat . . . this time without interruption.

13

Katie dodged a flock of St. Mary's nuns, their flared white headpieces flapping in the summer breeze as she rushed to Dennehy's Department Store in the heart of downtown. Her pulse was racing faster than her feet as she hurried by, thinking the sisters looked more like a gaggle of geese than Daughters of Charity on their way to daily mass.

"Good morning, sisters," she called with a grin, and suddenly the thought of their "charity" warmed her heart as much as the heat of the day. Because of their devotion to God and compassion for mankind, these women provided a safe haven for thousands of infants and unwed mothers at St. Mary's Home, a godsend to those with nowhere to go. Katie's heart swelled with joy at the prospect of doing the same. Well, maybe not thousands yet, at least not until she was a lawyer or congresswoman who could wield influence on their behalf. But for now, she could certainly find a home or a job for one or two in need. Her grin softened into a smile. Like Alli.

A tanned workman repairing a cracked patch of pavement winked and shot her a grin, and she actually returned it with a brilliant smile, something she seldom did. Even the awful smell of his fresh asphalt couldn't wrinkle her nose today. No, today was just too special, too life-altering of a moment to not respond in kind. She slipped a hand into her skirt pocket to absently fondle her list for the day—now half completed—and the cool touch of the crisp, folded piece of paper brought an extra bounce to her step. All she had left to do was finish a report for Parker, drop off a donor's list to Vera at the BSCG *and* . . . pay a visit to Emma at the store, hopefully to secure a job for Alli. Katie's heart raced at being able to check that final glorious goal off her list—talking to Emma on Alli's behalf—and never had she felt such a sense of purpose or joy in the prospect of completing a task. She had found a home for Gabe, and in the process, had made both her mother and Luke McGee two of the happiest people alive, not to mention one salty-tongued seven-year-old who was sure to give Patrick O'Connor a run for his money.

The thought immediately produced another grin on her face and a rush of love to her heart. Nobody could reform a pistol like Gabe Smith better than her father, she finally realized with grudging respect, and for the first time, she was grateful for the tight rein he'd held all of her life. Although she'd been dead-set against it, banishing her to the Boston Children's Aid Society had been a blessing in disguise and a critical turning point in her passion for women's rights. Now more than ever, she wanted to be a part of giving women a voice, a hope, and a chance to escape the tyranny of a society that kept them pinned beneath its thumb—in schooling, in marriage, and especially in business. Her lips angled. Ironically, the very man responsible for helping to shape her dreams by punishing her with a stint at the BCAS—her father—was the same man who'd kept her under his thumb as a little girl, stoking her fire for independence with every tantrum curtailed. Her lips lifted in a tender smile. *I really should thank him someday . . .*

Dennehy's Department Store loomed large on the next block, and Katie's muscles twitched with impatience as she waited at the corner for traffic to pass. She had found a home for Gabe and now she hoped—and prayed?—she'd find one for Alli too. She absently scanned the colorful window display of a classroom with its stylized manikins dressed in the latest children's fashions for school, and her mind wandered to the prospect of prayer. Unlike the rest of her family, Katie wasn't prone to invoking the help of the Almighty, but some things, she supposed, were just too important not to pull out all the stops. The image of sweet Alli with her heart-melting smile and her childlike innocence tugged at Katie's heart, and she knew she would do whatever it took to brighten the girl's future.

Even prayer, she resolved with a lift of her chin, something she wasn't sure would actually work. Faith and Brady were big on it, she knew, as were Luke, Parker, and the rest of her family, but to Katie, God had always seemed too far away, too distant, and too impractical in a world where reality called the shots. And yet, strangely enough, that mindset had been challenged by a simple young woman with childlike faith and steel braces on her legs. And in her spine too, apparently, Katie thought with a quirk of her lips. The day she had spent working in the kitchen with Alli had opened her eyes considerably. On the surface this frail, handicapped woman elicited pity, appearing to have no hope or prospects for her future. But inside, Katie had discovered a vibrant powerhouse of prayer who emanated a calm assurance that "Jesus will take care of me."

Katie's lips squirmed to the right as her gaze flitted upward. "Okay, Jesus," she muttered under her breath, "if you really are up there listening like Alli seems to think you are, please take care of her and help me to convince Emma to give her a job."

She yanked on the heavy glass door emblazoned with DENNEHY'S in graceful gold script and instantly felt a sense of peace. Whether it was from the cozy feel of one of Boston's most stylish department stores or the prayer was anybody's guess. Dominating half the block, Dennehy's had expanded from a quaint single storefront that Mitch had bought for Charity after they were married, to a charming emporium that rivaled the bigger stores in popularity. Not as large or as sophisticated as Filene's, which occupied an entire city block on Washington and Summer, Dennehy's catered to a simpler clientele. Here, those who appreciated the warmth and courtesy of a specialty store in a small-scale department store could browse everything from fashion and toiletries to home goods and more. Lily of the valley teased her senses, and Katie glanced at a young woman testing perfumes on her wrist at a glass counter that showcased the latest in Paris scents.

Across the way an intricately carved wood display featured a charming array of ladies' hats—from large-brimmed garden-party varieties to lavish veiled "celebrity hats" à la Joan Crawford and Clara Bow, several bedecked with sequins for evening wear. Still in vogue, there were plenty of beloved cloche hats that fitted tightly to the head and rested just above the eyes, tempting shoppers with an endless variety of styles, be it skull cap or turban. A bored-looking manikin modeled the latest eared cloche with tucks and swirls that swooped over her ears and up in front and the back. A pretty silk flower bloomed from the side of the hat, coordinating nicely with a tall vase of silk flowers in the center of the table.

Viewing the simple elegance of the displays, Katie once again marveled at the miracle that was Emma Malloy. Charity's best friend from Dublin ten years hence, Emma had co-managed the store with Charity that first year until her sister had gotten pregnant and Mitch insisted she quit. Since then, Emma had single-handedly transformed "Dennehy's Emporium" from a quaint mom-and-pop storefront into a thriving mercantile. She'd even talked Mitch and Charity into changing the name to Dennehy's Department Store to capitalize on the recent trend of larger, more sophisticated stores. A natural-born merchant, Emma had been given free rein by Charity and Mitch, an investment that had paid off handsomely for Katie's sister and brother-in-law, as evidenced by the people milling throughout the store. No, in Katie's mind, there was no doubt—strong, quiet Emma Malloy was just the person to take little Alli under her wing.

"Katie! What are you doing here today?"

She glanced up to see the woman in her thoughts bounding toward her with a stack of papers fluttering in her hands, the pretty tilt of the left corner of her lips contrasting with the mottled scar on the right. "Looking for a new dress for a date with Jack?"

Katie studied Charity's friend with sudden curiosity. Without question, Emma Malloy had been as beautiful as Charity at one time, before a philandering sot of husband had reshaped her features with a pan of hot grease. Her heart-shaped face lent itself to a delicate and graceful air with soft, grey eyes that evoked the gentleness of a fawn. A nose that could only be described as "classic" was strong and straight with the barest upturn at the tip. Rich, chestnut hair, shimmering from the crystal chandelier overhead, was styled in the latest Joan Crawford look, parted on the side and sleek from the crown until it curled below her ears. Wisps of bangs feathered her forehead, accentuating a perfectly manicured brow while the other arched over a scar long since faded with time.

As Charity's best friend, Emma seemed the perfect balance for Katie's mischievous sister—shy and demure rather than sassy and bold, totally content for Charity to shine while she herself faded into the shadows. And yet, despite quietly stepping to the background, Emma possessed a strength of character that was hard to miss, radiating joyous calm as surely as the sun radiated warmth. Without question, she was a stabilizing factor—not only for Charity, but for anyone Emma came in contact with. Even now, just a hint of a smile in those gentle eyes had the same calming effect as a cleansing sigh, relaxing the tightness in Katie's neck and stomach.

She sucked in a deep swallow of air and released it, returning Emma's smile with a bright one of her own. "Not really. I'm afraid I have more important things on my mind than Jack."

A twinkle lit Emma's eyes as she hugged the papers to her chest. "More important than Jack? Well, now you've piqued my interest."

"Good," Katie said with a tug of Emma's arm. "Do you have a moment to talk in your office, or is this a bad time?"

"No, now is perfect—I was just going to have lunch." Emma led her through the store and up to her office on the second floor while Katie studied her out of the corner of her eye. Although only inches taller than Katie's five foot two, Emma seemed almost willowy with her slow and graceful stride, as if she floated on air rather than always rushing as Katie was prone to do. Katie released another breath and matched her pace to Emma's, grateful for the calming effect of this woman.

Nodding at several employees on the way, Emma finally opened a bubbled glass door at the rear of the store and invited Katie in. She smiled at a big-bone, olive-skinned woman who seemed better suited as a warden in a women's prison than a secretary for one of Boston's most popular stores. Decidedly too large for the small, wooden desk at which she sat, the woman looked up with a scowl that rivaled Patrick O'Connor's on his worst disciplinary day.

"You know those three dozen Panama straws we ordered from DelMonico's?" The woman's scarlet lips flattened as she waved a paper in the air. Her mouth slanted into a caustic smile. "They forgot to send the pitchfork and tractor."

A heavy sigh drifted from Emma's lips, the closest thing to a complaint Katie had ever heard out of her. "Oh, Bert, no . . . They sent the farmer's straw instead of the boaters?"

"Yep. 'Course, I'm thinking we can always hurl a few hay

bales and a couple cow patties in the window and stage a hoedown." Bert slapped the sheet of paper on the desk with a slam that jolted Katie.

Emma seemed undaunted, either by the situation or Bert's crusty manner. "Well, we'll just have to send them back with a note explaining it's the straw boaters or nothing, which is a real shame. The salesman for DelMonico's has been so nice." She gave Bert's shoulder a comforting squeeze as she moved past the desk toward her office door, then paused to shoot a smile over her shoulder. "Oh, Bert, this is Charity's sister, Katie O'Connor."

"Hi, Bert," Katie said with trepidation. She stuck out a tentative hand, somewhat nervous that the woman just might crush it.

The warden grunted and offered a handshake that seemed more of a threat than a greeting.

"The Schiaparelli collection hasn't come in by chance, has it?" Emma asked. "Patrice tells me she's already had several requests."

Dark thunderous eyebrows dipped low over slitted hazel eyes. "Yep—bathing suits, skiwear, linen dresses, you name it. But dollars to doughnuts Filene's had their order first."

"Go to lunch, Bert," Emma said softly. "I'll cover till Cora gets back, okay?"

The woman lumbered up from the chair with a low rumble of words, and the slow rise of her wide girth reminded Katie of a volcano about to spew. "Heaven knows when that'll be," she mumbled under her breath. "Spends more time filing her nails than that stack of purchase orders on her desk. When she isn't making personal phone calls, that is."

Emma chuckled. "You know Cora has a lot to do in the next few weeks before the wedding. Besides, you're just hungry, and you know it. Go on—scoot. Tell Mario to give you that free lunch he promised us last week."

"Promised *you*, you mean," Bert emphasized with a lift of her formidable chin. Waves of black hair tinged with silver hugged her head in the slicked-down style of the day, doing nothing to soften her intimidating air. "I'm not takin' your lunch."

"Take it," Emma ordered with more force than Katie was used to. "I brought two hard-boiled eggs and an apple, so tell Mario to give the lunch to you, you hear? No arguments."

"Humph. That won't make him none too happy—it's you he'll be looking for." Bert turned at the door and aimed a menacing finger toward the stack of purchase orders on Cora's desk. "Don't let me catch you filing her orders, Miss Emma."

Emma grinned. "Go—eat your lunch and tell Mario I said hi. And come back in a better mood or I'll make Horace help you with inventory."

A reluctant smile flickered across Bert's wide mouth, and for the first time, without the nasty face, Katie could see that she was actually rather pretty for a middle-aged woman whose height and weight commanded respect. "You sic that old man on me, Miss Emma, and I guarantee you'll be looking for a new employee."

"You would never leave me, Bert, and we both know it," Emma said with a smile.

Bert's eyes narrowed. "I was talking about Horace. 'Cause if that man comes near me during inventory one more time, he'll be strung up in a hospital with both legs in a cast." She opened the door and shuddered. "Eat your egg."

The door slammed behind her, and Katie blinked. "My, what an . . . interesting woman."

A grin lit Emma's face. "That she is. Bert's been with me for almost ten years now, and she's nothing more than a pussycat with porcupine quills. But it's all a front, you know. She has a heart as big as she is gruff—wouldn't hurt a fly. I honestly couldn't run the store without her."

"Bert? Short for . . . ?"

"Bertolina, but she absolutely hates that name, so don't tell her I told you."

Katie glanced at the door with a lift of her brows. "Not on your life. I'd rather stay on her good side . . . if she has one."

Emma chuckled and sat in her chair behind a battered desk neatly piled with invoices and a mockup of a newspaper ad for the store. A warm breeze from an arched window behind her fluttered the back of her hair as she pulled a paper bag out of a drawer and released a weighty sigh. "So, Katie, what brings you to Dennehy's?" She glanced at her watch. "I assume you're on lunch hour at the BCAS? Have you eaten? I have two hard-boiled eggs I can share."

"No, no, I've eaten, but thank you." Katie slipped into the chair by the side of Emma's desk and locked gazes with Charity's friend. "But I do have something I need . . ."

With an inquisitive smile, Emma unwrapped a piece of parchment that contained a small pile of salt. She tapped the egg on the edge of her desk and began to peel, assessing Katie through curious eyes. "Really? What?"

"A favor actually, for a friend. One who needs a job pretty badly."

A wrinkle puckered Emma's brow indicating she was thinking as she finished peeling the shell. She tapped the white of the egg in the salt and took a bite. "What kind of job? Sales?"

"I'm not sure she could handle sales . . ." Katie fidgeted with her fingers, hesitating as she worked her lip. "You see, when she gets nervous or meets someone for the first time, she has a terrible stutter, and she's very slow of speech."

"Oh." Emma continued chewing, eyes squinted as she gave it more thought. "Well, then, what about janitorial?"

"No, that wouldn't work either, I'm afraid." Katie's gaze flicked up. "She had polio as a child and wears cumbersome leg braces. It'd be hard for her to get around the store, I'm sure."

The egg froze midair, halfway to Emma's mouth. Compassion softened the gray of her eyes as her voice lowered to a whisper. "Oh, God love her . . ."

Katie sucked in a deep breath and straightened her shoulders, determination steeling her words. "Well, that's just it, Emma. Alli—that's her name, Alli Moser—believes with all of her heart that God *does* love her and fully expects him to find her a job. But she turns eighteen in several months, you see, and the BSCG has to either place her in an apprenticeship with a family, find her a job where she can support herself, or . . ." The air seemed trapped in Katie's lungs before she released it in one arduous exhale. "Be turned out on the streets to fend for herself."

The hitch of Emma's breath was as harsh as the burn in Katie's throat at the thought of Alli on the streets, and when she saw tears glimmer in Emma's eyes, she had no power over those in her own. She placed a tentative hand on Emma's arm. "She has no family, Emma, and the worst part is she's epileptic. When people hear that, well, understandably . . . they're afraid."

Emma nodded slowly, then swallowed hard and placed the half-eaten egg on the parchment. "How is she with numbers, then? Things like filing, typing, general office work?"

A slow grin eased across Katie's face. "She's a champ. She may seem slow because of her speech, but I swear her mind is sharper than yours or mine. And she's a whiz at numbers."

The edges of Emma's mouth curled into a beautiful smile. "Is she, now?"

Both looked up at the sound of a timid knock. "Miss Emma?"

"Yes, Horace?" Emma smiled at a slight, balding man hovering in the door.

"Just received a box of what looks like dark eyeglasses from something called the Foster Grant company and, uh, well . . . I'm not real sure what to do with 'em."

"Oh, finally! Give those to Patrice, will you, Horace? They're sunglasses to add to the swimsuit display she set up last month. Apparently Sam Foster's new invention is selling like hotcakes on the beaches of Atlantic City, and we're lucky to get them. And, thank you."

"Yes, ma'am, will do." Horace disappeared as quickly as he had come.

Katie cocked a brow. "*Sun*glasses?"

"They're all the rage, apparently, and Sam Foster stands to make a killing, according to Mitch. But thanks to his connections at the *Herald*, we've been able to get our hands on a few even before Filene's." Emma dabbed the last of her egg into the salt and popped it in her mouth. She smiled and finished chewing. "So, Katie Rose . . . when can your Alli Moser start?"

Katie's heart stopped for the briefest of moments before she launched up with a squeal to give Emma a hug. "Oh, I knew it! The moment I heard about Alli's plight, I thought of you, Emma. With all the hardship you've been through in your life, I just knew you would understand. I can bring Alli by anytime—just give me the word."

Emma's smile edged into a frown. "The braces on her legs—is walking difficult for her? How will she get here?"

"It certainly seems cumbersome to you and me, I know, but Alli appears to take it all in stride. She moves slowly, but it doesn't hinder her mobility. As far as getting to the store, she lives at the BSCG until she turns eighteen, and that's just a trolley ride away."

"What happens when Alli turns eighteen—where will she go?" Emma asked, eyes sloped with concern.

Katie released a weighty sigh and sat down, her euphoria ebbing away. "We don't know yet. Miss Lillian—the director of the BSCG—is looking for a home for Alli right now, but she hasn't had much luck." Katie idly grated teeth to lip and looked up, desperate to win Emma's favor, and in the process, a home for Alli. Her breath stilled in her lungs. "Any ideas?"

Emma stared at Katie and for the first time saw a resemblance to Charity. Not so much in the physical sense, although both were beautiful women who turned their fair share of heads, but more so from the glint of steel in their striking blue eyes whenever they were on a mission.

Like now.

Emma knew that over the years Katie had challenged her parents and family with a headstrong nature and a drive to achieve whatever she set her mind to, much like Charity. Both were tough, stubborn women who seldom revealed their softer side. And yet one of the things that Emma loved most about Charity was her tender, vulnerable heart, once calloused and hidden well beneath layers of hurt. Studying Charity's sister now, Emma suspected it was much the same with Katie, but she wasn't sure why. Where Charity's demons had stemmed from a childhood trauma when she was small, Katie had always lived a charmed life, it seemed—Marcy's "baby" who was always catered to because of her demanding nature. Emma fought the quirk of a smile as she reached for her apple.

"Ideas?" she repeated quietly, apple poised at her lips.

Katie straightened in the chair and leaned forward, the intensity in her eyes as compelling as the strong jut of her chin. "Yes—ideas—*any* ideas. Perhaps a young woman at the store with whom she might share a flat . . . or a kind customer who'd consider renting out a room. Or even a landlord you know who would be fair and kind." Katie gripped the edge of the desk with fingers pinched pale, her gaze piercing Emma to the core. "*Anyone*, Emma, who possesses a heart as big as Alli's . . . who can help her, care for her, and love her like she deserves."

Emma stared, fully understanding the spell Katie O'Connor wielded, not only over Jack Worthington, one of the most eligible young men in Boston's social scene, but the group of friends that always flocked to her side. Although her stature was petite, there was nothing small about the confidence she exuded through every pore of her porcelain skin, from the sculptured lift of her manicured brow to the tight press of those full and determined lips. That same spell now brought a smile to Emma as she bit into the apple, a flood of flavor bursting onto her tongue. She chewed slowly, savoring both the sweet fruit in her mouth and the sweet fruit she saw in Charity's little sister. A little sister who had always seemed somewhat removed from the rest of her family because of her aloof nature, sassy tongue, and biting wit. And, Emma thought with silent gratitude, a sister who'd obviously taken great pains to guard a tender heart.

"Well . . . ," Emma said softly, "I suppose your Alli could move in with me for a while until we find her a room of her own. My flat is tiny and cramped, mind you, but it's only a few blocks away from the store, and the trolley covers the route—"

"Oh, Emma!" Katie shot up and, as tiny as she was, hoisted Emma from the chair in a jubilant hug. "I just knew it. I have to admit, I wanted this so badly, that I actually resorted to prayer, if you can believe that. And I swear that right off, something whispered your name in my ear—'go see Emma'—and it was right!"

Emma grinned and squeezed Katie back. "He always is," she said with a soft chuckle.

Katie released her hold and plopped back into the chair with a loud exhale. Her smile turned curious. "By 'he,' you mean God, I suppose."

Something about the skeptical slant in Katie's brow caused Emma's stomach to flutter. It was no secret Katie didn't share her family's allegiance to God, a concern voiced by both Faith and Charity on more than one occasion.

Emma eased back into her chair with a prayer in her heart, and gave Katie a shy smile. "I do—the Holy Spirit, in particular—that still, quiet voice."

The cool guard Katie always wore so well shifted into place, a ceramic mask with a tight-lipped smile. "It was nothing more than a thought, Emma. I seriously doubt that any deity was whispering in my ear."

Emma leaned forward to prop her elbow on the desk, chin in hand. "Really? Why?"

Katie blinked. "Because God doesn't intervene in people's lives like that—at least he never has in mine."

Her smile softened. "He just did, Katie. First when he brought you into Alli's life as an answer to her prayer . . . and then when he brought you to me, in answer to yours."

"Coincidence," Katie said in a clipped tone, her back pressed hard against her chair.

"Could be," Emma said quietly, "but it's been my experience that it's not. When coincidences start piling up, you start to notice a trend."

"A trend?" Katie folded her arms with a smile. "What, that some Being up in the sky is whispering in my ear?"

"Yes." Emma's tone softened with reverence. "And that there is a God in heaven who aches inside to love you and bless you and answer your prayers."

The smile faded on Katie's lips. "How can you say that, Emma? You, of all people—after all the pain you've suffered in your life?"

Emotion thickened in Emma's throat as she stared at the young woman before her, and her heart wrenched at the hardness she saw etched in her face. "It's because of the pain in my life that I can say that, Katie, because it's that same pain that brought me to him."

"But aren't you angry at God for what happened? Your marriage, your scars?"

"No, Katie, I get angry at sin—mine and Rory's, because it was sin that brought pain into my life and robbed me of the blessings of God—not God himself. You see, when I was not much younger than you, I fell in love with Rory against my father's wishes. He warned me to keep away from him, but I didn't listen." Emma sank back into her chair, memories from her past flooding her with regret. "I was young and naïve and so very much in love that I didn't care that Rory was prone to drink, didn't care that he didn't share my faith." A shiver rippled through her as her eyes trailed into a distant stare. "Didn't care that he lured me into sin . . ."

Emma straightened her shoulders to shake off the awful melancholy that still haunted her soul. "When I said I was going to marry Rory, my father cut me off—said I was dead to him and could never come home. So when Rory's true colors began to show with his drinking and temper and womanizing . . . well, I had nowhere else to go." Emma drew in a deep breath and locked gazes with Katie. "Nowhere but God."

Katie stared in silence, her arm limp on Emma's desk. Although her mask was still in place, her eyes were moist with compassion.

"So you see, when my family and Rory abandoned me, God did not. Yes, Rory beat me and scarred me and cheated on me, but God saw to it that I had favor at the shop where Charity and I worked, both with the clientele and the owner who taught me the skills I use in running the store today." A mischievous smile tugged at her lips. "That is, until your sister came along. But even that he worked out for my good. Not only did he give me the dearest friend I have ever known, but he blessed me with a life in Boston with her family and her store, both of which have allowed me more joy than I ever dreamed possible." Emma reached to touch Katie's hand. "He will do the same for your precious Alli, I'm certain. And if you call on him, he will do the same for you. Whatever your hurts or fears or scars, Katie—call on him. He's waiting to love you like you've never been loved before."

Katie slowly removed her hand from the desk and offered a nervous smile. "I don't know, Emma, it all sounds wonderful, but God . . . prayer, well, I'm the type of person who deals with facts, not fantasy, and to be honest, I'm just not sure that it's real."

Emma's smile was peaceful. "I understand, Katie, but I can tell you this—you won't know till you try."

A blush stained Katie's cheeks as she quickly rose, indicating her awkwardness with the discussion. "Well, I'm not sure I'm ready to turn my life over to another authority figure just yet, because as you know, my father already holds a pretty tight rein. But I will agree you have been an answer to prayer for both Alli Moser and me today, so I promise to give your suggestion some definite thought."

Emma stood to her feet. "Give it some thought if you will, but with your heart, Katie, not your head. That's where he resides, you know, when you invite him in—in your heart. And it's where faith grows to heal a wounded soul." After wrapping Katie in a tight hug, Emma smiled and led her to the door. "Now, when can you bring Alli by so I can meet her? I have paperwork she'll need to fill out."

"How about tomorrow? I can stop by the BSCG right now on my way back to tell her."

"Perfect!" Emma said, opening the door. "Have a good day, Katie."

"I will," Katie said, and then taking Emma by surprise, she whirled around and swallowed her up in a ferocious hug. "Oh, Emma, thank you *so* much—I am so excited! I'll tell you what—Alli Moser has no idea how her life is about to change."

A soft chuckle tumbled from Emma's lips as she returned Katie's embrace. "No . . . no, she doesn't, does she?" she whispered with a catch in her throat. A grin tugged at her smile while she squeezed with all of her might. *And neither do you, Katie Rose . . . neither do you.*

"Teddy finally asleep?" Filling a kettle for tea, Faith turned at the sink to smile at Lizzie who hurried into her kitchen, cheeks flushed and a hand fanning her face.

"Yes, thank heavens," Lizzie said, blowing her bangs out of her eyes. She gave Charity's shoulder a quick squeeze on her way to the cabinet where she kept her teacups and saucers. She shot a glance at the clock and toted the dishes to the kitchen table, clinking them down next to an African violet that looked as wilted as she. She sagged into a kitchen chair with a groan. "I really appreciate you two coming here to plan Mother and Father's anniversary party—it makes it so much easier for me. Do you think Mother suspected anything?"

"Nope," Faith said, "I dropped the girls off, and the woman was so thrilled to have children underfoot again, she didn't even ask where I was going. *And*, she even let Gabe stay home and play hooky from school today." She scrounged inside Lizzie's pantry for tea and then turned to squint at her sisters. "Earl Gray or Lavender?"

"Lavender—I suspect Lizzie could use the calming effect," Charity answered. She sighed and shook her head. "Father isn't going to like that—Gabe playing hooky—*if* he even finds out." An evil grin sprouted on her lips. "Mother is really something, though, isn't she? Married almost thirty-five years, and the woman still can't let go of raising children. You would think with all the trouble Steven and Katie have been, she'd welcome the change of life with open arms. But no, two children at home and six grandchildren underfoot are still not enough—she has to badger Father into a foster child too."

Faith grinned. "Gabe is as cute as a bug's ear. Even though I have a feeling she's going to make Katie look like a cherub." She made the sign of the cross. "God bless Patrick O'Connor."

"Speaking of Katie," Charity ventured as she picked at her nails, "is anybody else as tentative as I am about Katie's engagement to Jack?"

Fragrant steam misted Faith's face as she steeped tea in the kettle, her brows bunched in thought. "I definitely am. Not only has Katie never given any indication she's madly in love with Jack, but neither of them seem to have much of a spiritual base, you know? As if God is no more to them than Sunday morning mass." Faith sighed. "I guess I have to admit, it doesn't thrill me to the bones."

"Father, either, apparently," Charity said with a slant of a smile, "given the fact he's making her wait until she's out of law school."

"*If* she waits." Faith sniffed her tea, soaking in the sweet aroma of lavender. "Knowing Katie, she'll manage to harass him until he gives in." She folded her arms and leaned against the counter as she waited for the kettle to boil. "I just wish Katie had fallen for someone like Luke McGee, a man with a heart for God and the strength to stand up to her. Not always let her have her own way like Jack does. But as we all know—Katie *is* Katie, the hardest head in the lot." Her lips quirked into a smile. "Like I said, God bless Patrick O'Connor."

"Oops, I forgot the milk and sugar—" Lizzie bounced up.

Charity clamped a hand to her arm. "No, sit—I'll get them. I swear you're wearing me out just watching you. Being seven months pregnant is bad enough, but running after an overactive toddler to boot, no wonder you look so tired."

"Thanks, sis," Lizzie said with a weary smile. "We were up at four on Sunday morning and—" She shot a nervous look at both of her sisters, then gnawed on her lip and looked away. Color rose in her cheeks as she rubbed her swollen stomach. "Uh . . . I mean this little ruffian has been getting me up at the crack of dawn with its kicking and rolling."

"Four a.m.? Sounds like its father," Faith said with a dry smile. "Collin says Brady still gets to the shop by six in the morning, even with the extra help they hired." The teakettle whistled, and she snatched it up with a lift of her brow, proceeding to pour them each a cup. "Not that my husband would know, mind you, as he tends to roll in by nine."

Charity placed three spoons on the table, along with milk and sugar. "Likes to sleep in, does he?" she asked with a twinkle in her eye.

Faith tossed a pot holder on the table and set the kettle on top. She slid into her chair and gave Charity a patient smile. "Yes, but trust me, sleep is the operative word. Lately that man has been too tired to do much of anything else."

Both of her sisters blinked. Charity leaned forward, one

hand pressed to the table. "Collin McGuire? Too tired to try for a boy? What, has he given up his quest for a son?"

"No, he still wants a son, but he's been too tired to think about it like before. He works late almost every night, and even some Saturdays."

Charity eyed her over the rim of her cup. "With . . . Evelyn?"

A sigh parted from Faith's lips as she took a sip of her tea. "Sometimes. But I actually think that may be some of the reason he's not so driven about having a son anymore. You see, Evelyn has a sick boy that Collin has met a few times, and I think he . . . well, I think he feels drawn to this boy, protective of him."

Charity's cup met her saucer with a sharp clink. "You don't think the boy could be—"

"No! No, I don't. In fact, it's impossible. The boy is thirteen and Collin hasn't . . ." Heat stung her cheeks and she took a quick gulp of tea. "Well, he hasn't been . . . close to her in almost twenty years. So, it's not that."

Lizzie stirred cream into her tea with a pucker of concern. "You're not worried that it could be an attachment to Evelyn that's driving him, are you?"

Uncomfortable with the conversation, Faith jumped to her feet and hurried to the cabinet. She pulled a plate out and proceeded to fill it with cookies from Lizzie's ceramic cookie jar. "No, of course not. Collin has always had a big heart, especially when it comes to children who can't fend for themselves. I think this little guy has just won his affection, that's all." She set the cookies on the table and took a deep breath. "Besides, I trust my husband."

Charity shoved a cookie in her mouth. "I wish I did," she said with cheeks bulging.

"You don't trust Mitch?" Lizzie's tone bordered on shock.

"Oh, I trust him all right—to be a man. I mean, I love my husband, you all know that, but let's face it, Mitch Dennehy is a bona fide bully. Even though the kids are in school every day and I have nothing to do, he has this antiquated notion—along with Collin, I might add—that women shouldn't work. So while Emma's overloaded with work at the store, what do I do? I stay home day after day and twiddle my thumbs . . ." Her eyes narrowed considerably. "While Mitch keeps me under his."

"He won't let you help Emma for even a few hours a day?"

Charity's jaw angled up. "Absolutely not. Says his children need a mother, not a woman with a career—case closed." She slumped back in the chair and sulked with a pout. "I'll tell you what, if I had known what a tyrant he'd be, I would have thought twice about saying yes."

Faith couldn't help but chuckle. "Sure you would have. Face it, sis—that man had you so lovesick you were nothing but a pile of mush. You thought twice all right—'yes, I'll marry you,' and 'yes, I'll marry you tomorrow.'"

Her pout tilted into a sheepish grin. "I know. He's lucky I'm so crazy about him or I'd go at him with both barrels blazing. As it is, I'm biding my time and wearing him down day by day so he has no idea that I'm actually going to win this battle. And don't think I don't have devices to get my way with an amorous man like Mitch Dennehy, because I do. And then we'll see just who has whom under their thumb." A sultry smile surfaced on her lips as she wiggled her brows with a gleam in her eyes. "Although I must admit . . . there are times I rather enjoy being under his."

"Well, that certainly won't be Katie's problem," Lizzie said quickly, obviously hoping to steer the conversation into a safer direction. "Jack seems pretty content to give Katie whatever she wants, as far as I can see. She told me he's letting her have her way on everything—when they get married, how they get married, and even where they'll live after." Lizzie sighed and took a sip of her tea. "Maybe it's just me, but I don't think I could be happy in a marriage like that. Brady is so solid and strong and wise, that I just naturally defer to him."

Charity's lips skewed into a dry smile. "That's because you have as many stars in your eyes as I do in mine, Lizzie."

Faith tasted her tea and wrinkled her nose. "Yes, well, we all know there's a lot more to a marriage than stars in your eyes."

"Easy for you to say," Charity said with a jut of her brow. She leaned in, elbows flat on the table. "You could blind somebody with that constellation blazing in yours whenever Collin enters a room, same as Lizzie and me. But the truth is, I see nothing flickering in Katie's eyes but burning ambition. Have you noticed how she always shoos Jack away when he hovers over her, trying to hug her or hold her hand? Sweet mother of Job, if Mitch pulled his nose from the grindstone long enough to fawn over me like that, I would die a happy woman."

"Not everybody is as needy as you, Charity," Faith said with a squirm of her lips. "Katie's a lot more private, so maybe she's just not comfortable with Jack's displays of affection in front of the family."

"Maybe," Charity said with a tilt of her head, "but I have this sinking feeling deep down inside that Jack may not be the man that Katie needs. Call me a hopeless romantic if you will, but I think we need to pray about this engagement daily and often, before this ship sails." One brow shot up. "Or something tells me this is one marriage that could very well hit the rocks."

"I'm inclined to agree," Lizzie said quietly. "And Brady does too."

Faith pursed her lips as her gaze flicked from Charity to Lizzie and back, disappointed that she hadn't thought of it herself. She scooted her chair in and clasped her hands on the table, giving Charity a slatted look that held both tease and approval. "I just hate it when you're right."

14

Katie shifted on the love seat. Her legs were stiff and sore from stockinged feet tucked beneath her for well over an hour now. A quiet sigh rose and fell in her chest. She honestly hadn't thought it would be this difficult. She glanced at Luke's chiseled profile as he sat with Gabe in his lap, their eyes focused on the chessboard before them, and her heart did its usual annoying flip. If she had taken the time to realize Gabe living here would bring Luke to visit, she would have rethought the whole idea.

She watched his thick arms twine around the little girl as he moved his pawn, then she flipped another page in her *Harper's Bazaar* with a tight press of her lips. The clock on the mantel chimed nine, and relief oozed like balm to her aching limbs. The evening had finally come to an end—Gabe's bedtime! Her expectant gaze flitted from her father, whose grim concentration told her he hadn't noticed the time, to her mother, beatific as she knitted a sweater for Gabe. Katie ground her jaw in frustration.

Go home, Luke McGee, and leave me alone.

She unfolded her legs and lumbered to her feet with a

grimace. Maybe she could move this along. "Anybody need a drink?" she asked sweetly. She slipped her shoes back on and glanced at the clock. "Oh . . . maybe not. Look at the time—it's nine."

"Mmm . . ." Her father said without looking up.

"No, thanks, dear," her mother quipped with a smile.

"I'll have a root beer," Gabe volunteered.

"No root beer," Patrick said, eyes glued to the board.

Katie sighed. She stared at the Greek god with the child in his lap and narrowed her eyes, noting only silence from the thorn in her side.

Katie plunked back down on the love seat and wished she could go to bed, but the "thorn" had made that rather prickly as well. And what good would it do? She'd only stare at the ceiling, sick to her stomach over her gnawing guilt for leading him on. She jerked the *Harper's Bazaar* open once again and began at the beginning, staring at pages she really didn't see.

Her jaw hardened. Could she help it if the man raced her heart like a jog in the park? Caused more flutters inside than a flock of hummingbirds? It wasn't her fault he'd kissed her in the first place, was it? Not the first time . . . nor the second . . . nor even the third or fourth. She closed her eyes, and the memory of each and every kiss flashed through her mind like a summer heat wave. Heaven help her, even ten feet away with a child in his lap, the man could heat her blood to a simmer. She put a hand to her eyes, shame warring with attraction as it flamed in her cheeks, then released a breath that merged with a shudder. And each and every time she had responded by returning his affection with a passion she had never even shown Jack. Her breathing thinned to a tenuous thread. It had to stop—all of it.

The heat of attraction.

The cold slither of guilt.

His subsequent indifference which was clearly *Luke*warm.

Her lips bent in irony. No, she had to stay up tonight, if

only to talk to him one more time, clear the air so she could clear her life. A dozen times she'd tried before she'd left the BCAS, but he'd made sure they were never alone, never made eye contact, never gave her the chance to tell him how sorry she was.

"Checkmate!" Patrick leaned back in his chair with all the smug satisfaction of a miser who'd recounted his money. "And that, young man and young lady," he said with a splayed hand to his chest, "is how a doddering old fool regains his pride." He rose to his feet with a smile on his face. "Gabriella Dawn Smith, your bed awaits."

"But I'm not tired," she whined with a clutch to Luke's arm, "and besides, Luke promised checkers."

Patrick adjusted his vest and gave her the eye. "People without children promise a lot of things, young lady, all stemming from woeful inexperience and a desire to appease. None of which," he said with emphasis, "you will find here." He glanced at his wife as she worried her lip, and a heavy sigh prompted a heave of his chest. "At least, not on *this* side of the room."

Gabe spun around. "Mrs. O'Connor—please, it's only a little after nine. Can't I please play a quick game of checkers with Luke, *please*?"

Luke nudged Gabe from his lap and started to rise. "Gabe, no—"

"Now, Patrick, thirty more minutes won't matter, will it?" Marcy's eyes registered a plea.

Katie watched the familiar rise of her father's shoulders, the set of his jaw, the flex of fingers that twitched at his sides—all signs of a storm brewing she'd seen a million times before.

"The girl is tired, Marcy . . . ," Patrick began.

"No! I'm not—"

A firm hand gripped Gabe's shoulder as Patrick gave her a tight smile. "*Yes.* You *are.*" His words were pinched, like his hold on Gabe. "Aren't you?"

Katie hid a smile as Gabe's lips flattened into a hard line—not unlike her father's at the moment—then folded her arms with a thinning of eyes. "I suppose."

"Good, because I have to leave anyway," Luke said. He shoved his chair in, and more relief exuded from Katie's pores. "Great game, Mr. O'Connor. I hope for a rematch sometime."

"No!" Katie groaned, which earned her one of the few glances Luke had spared her all night. Heat flooded her cheeks. *Did I really say that out loud?*

"Will I see you soon?" Gabe asked, hope brimming in her eyes.

Luke ruffled her hair with a tender smile. "'Fraid not, Gabe. Remember the orphan train that almost stole you away? There's another this week, which means long hours and not much sleep."

Spindly arms clutched Luke tight around the middle. "Rats! Oh, well, I love you, Luke—thanks for everything."

He chucked her on the chin. "Don't thank me, thank the O'Connors." His gaze flitted to Katie a second time, causing her heart to flip. "Especially, Katie. Without her, you'd be chugging along to the Midwest right about now with ten other orphans."

Gabe spared Katie a faint smile from the folds of Luke's Oxford bags. "Thanks, Katie."

"My pleasure, sweetie." Katie flipped her magazine on the love seat and rose with a stretch. She buffed her arms out of nervous habit. "It'll be nice to have somebody to snuggle with when the weather gets cold, won't it?"

A puckish grin lit Gabe's face. "Yeah, especially if it's Luke."

Katie blinked. *Oh, my!*

"Gabe!" A wave of scarlet splotched the back of Luke's neck.

Katie's too, only it traveled clear up to her bangs and beyond.

Marcy saved the day with an extension of her arm. "Come on, Gabe, I'll bring you milk and cookies in bed after your bath."

"Can I use some of Katie's rosewater again too? Luke says he likes it."

More color bled up Luke's neck, settling in his face.

"Of course," Marcy said with a grasp of Gabe's hand. She flashed a warm smile. "Luke, we hope you'll become a regular fixture on Wednesday nights—we enjoy having you." Her gaze shifted to her daughter. "Katie, would you see our guest out while I put Gabe to bed?"

Patrick shook Luke's hand. "Wednesdays work for us, Luke, if they work for you."

Luke's pause was long enough for Katie to notice. "Actually, Mr. O'Connor, I'm afraid next week is going to be difficult—we have a train departing on Thursday."

Gabe wheeled around with fear in her face. "But, Luke, you have to come—please?"

"I see," Patrick said with a scrunch of brows. "Well, Friday then? Gabe is anxious to have you back and so are we—especially if you bring this chess prodigy you've bandied about."

"Please, Luke?" Gabe was relentless.

Luke laughed, but when his gaze flicked in Katie's direction, she noted a crimp in his brow. "All right, Mr. O'Connor—thank you. And I'm sure Parker would love to come as well. Mind if I bring Betty along too? She's our secretary at the BCAS and one of my closest friends."

"The more the merrier, I always say." Patrick's lips zagged into a smile. "An obvious conclusion, I suppose, with six children to our credit." He strolled to drape an arm around Marcy's shoulders. "Come on, Mrs. O'Connor, you'll need to tuck me in after Gabe. Good night, Luke." He winked at Katie as he ushered Marcy and Gabe to the stairs.

Luke wasted no time taking his leave. He strode to the door and put a hand on the knob. "Thanks again, Mr. and Mrs. O'Connor. Good night, everyone."

"Wait!" Gabe broke free to bolt down the stairs and fling herself into Luke's arms.

"Whoa, little girl," he said with a chuckle. He pried her loose and squatted before her. "We already said goodbye, remember?"

"Just one giggle kiss, please?"

He expelled a stern sigh, but his eyes softened along with his smile. "Just one," he whispered, then whisked her up and held tightly, his lips burrowing into the curve of her neck.

Shrieks and giggles rose to the rafters, but all Katie heard was the sound of her own ragged breathing at the memory of those same lips grazing her throat the night in the kitchen. She blinked at Gabe and shivered, unsettled at the thought that she wished it were her.

Luke set her back down and tousled her hair. "Good night, all." He opened the door and left with a wave, shutting it firmly behind him.

"Good night, Katie," her father said. "Mind dousing the lights and locking up? I'm afraid trouncing Luke took all the energy I have."

Katie hurried to the door with a nervous smile. "No problem, Father. I'll be right up."

"Hurry," Gabe said with a giggle. "I wanna snuggle."

The trio disappeared around the landing, and Katie wasted no time opening the door. She flew down the steps and out to the street, fingers shaking as she unlatched the gate. "Luke!"

In a halfway turn, he halted at the corner, hands buried deep in his pockets. Streetlight and shadows defined pensive features, reflecting the surprise in his face as he stared.

She hurled the gate open and ran, grateful for the breeze that cooled the clamminess of her body. Her chest was heaving when she finally reached him, and with a deep intake of air, she put a hand to her throat. "Goodness, you'd think you were training for the Boston Marathon."

He folded his arms and slacked a hip, his look as glaring as the tungsten lamp overhead. "What do you want, Katie?"

She sucked in more air in an attempt to humble herself—something she seldom did unless coerced by her father. "I was hoping we could talk . . ."

"We have nothing to say to each other." His tone was cold—like the moisture at the back of her neck in a sudden wisp of wind.

Her humility waffled with a slight jut of her chin. "Well, maybe you don't, but I certainly do." She tried again, tamping down her temper with a softer voice. "Luke, I can't stand this—your disdain, your coldness, acting like I'm not even there." She released a whispery sigh. "I . . . need you to forgive me." She swallowed the pride in her throat. "And I want to be friends again."

He looked away, and she saw a muscle pulse in his cheek. "No."

"No?" She blinked, all humility floating away with the breeze that fluttered her hair. "You won't forgive me? You won't be my friend?"

His eyes shifted to pierce her straight through. "That's right."

"But, why?"

"Because I don't *want* to be your friend, *Katydid*."

It was her turn to cross her arms, which she did with a thrust of her chin. "A little uppity for a brat from the streets, don't you think?"

An almost imperceptible flicker softened the hard line of his mouth, and she felt her stomach relax. He straightened his stance and propped muscled arms on his hips. Annoyance pinched at his brow. "Yeah? Well, I had a good teacher."

She pursed her lips to fight a smile, never more sure of a win. "Well, you don't have a choice, Luke McGee, now do you? We have to be friends—for Gabe's sake. So, there!"

The shift of his jaw told her she was wrong. "No, Katie, we don't." He turned and walked away.

"Wait!" She ran to grasp his arm in a death hold, fingers clenched as tight as her stomach. "Don't do this, please—

don't just walk away. I care about you, Luke, and I need your friendship. And you need mine."

His gaze fixed on her hand where Jack's diamond glittered in the lamplight, then slowly rose to her face, his blue eyes almost black. "No, Katie," he whispered with a thread of pain in his voice, "I need your love."

Her heart crashed to a stop. She removed her hand and lowered her eyes, her gaze fused to the fringed tongue of his brown leather shoe. "I . . . care about you, Luke, I do." Her voice trailed off, fragile and reedy with regret. "But please . . . why can't we just be friends?"

Taut fingers gripped her chin and jerked it up, the dominance of his hold matched by the anger in his eyes. "Because it will be lovers or nothing, Katie Rose. The choice is yours."

Air seized in her throat as heat rolled through her body. She faltered back and put a hand to her cheek while warmth radiated through her fingers.

"I thought so," he said in a harsh whisper. He spun around and strode away.

She raised her voice, fists clenched at her sides. "Then what about God, McGee? Brady says you're a changed man. Is all that love and forgiveness for real . . . or only a façade?"

He stopped, arms and back suddenly rigid with tension. Seconds passed before she saw his shoulders slump and a hand press to his eyes.

She moved to stand behind him then, her voice a plea barely spoken aloud. "Not undying devotion, Luke, just civil friendship to carry us through." She drew in a halting breath. "For Gabe's sake, please . . . and mine."

It seemed as if moments passed before his broad back finally rose and fell in consent. "All right, Katie Rose," he whispered. "You win." His labored sigh carried on the breeze. "You always do."

She watched as he walked away, her eyes in a hard stare long after he'd turned the corner, seeing nothing but his face on the walls of her mind. She'd won again—he'd said so himself—

won a battle over Cluny McGee. She drew in a harsh breath and turned to go, then suddenly wondered . . .

So why did it feel like she'd lost?

This was not good. First he'd agreed to a friendship he didn't want, and now he'd forgotten his key. Luke was tempted to kick the door in, but settled for a choke-hold on the knob to rattle it senseless.

Senseless. An accurate term at the moment—at least for him. What had he been thinking? Certainly not about a friendship with the woman who'd stomped on his heart. He jiggled the knob a second time, his frustration mounting by the moment. Her final day at the BCAS hadn't come soon enough to suit him, and if he had his way, Katie O'Connor might just as easily fall off the face of the earth. But Gabe had begged him to come, and Mrs. O'Connor had begged him to stay, and now he was stuck. He slammed a palm against the door and then gave it a kick for good measure. Stuck in weekly dinners with a woman he didn't want to see.

And she wants to be friends?

He frowned, tenting his fingers to squint into the glass side panels of Mrs. Cox's front door. The parlor was as dark as his mood and the foyer as empty as his patience, but at least a stream of light filtered out from the kitchen. He ignored the front steps and vaulted off the side of the porch, clearing Mrs. Cox's rhododendron to land on a sidewalk between the buildings. He strode to the back of the house with head down, a scowl on his face and his mind mired in thought. Why had he agreed? Said yes to a woman he didn't want in his life, much less in the same room? He didn't want to talk to her, to look at her, to see her for who she was—the girl who had his heart by the throat. Why had he given in? He swallowed hard, sweat beading the back of his neck, then stopped to put a hand to his eyes.

Why? Because he needed to forgive her before he could ever let her go. He drew in some air and released it again, sagging against the brick wall with a groan. Brady had convinced him—he could do this. If God had given him the grace not to bash Leo's head in, he could certainly give him the grace to be friends with Katie again.

Week after week. Desire after desire. Ache after ache.

He blasted out a sigh and rounded the corner, grateful for the kitchen light that lit up the weedy backyard. Luke peered in and saw Parker hunched at the table, pouring over papers with a pen in his hand. He pressed his nose to the screen. "Hey, open up. I forgot my key."

Parker looked up in surprise and smiled. "Again? I told you to carry a spare."

"Yeah, yeah, just open the door, Parker, I don't need any grief." Luke jostled the knob till the door swung wide, then pushed past to head to the sink. He pulled a glass from the cupboard and filled it with water. After taking a long, hard swallow, he turned and butted against the counter, eyeing Parker as he took another sip. "Betty in bed?"

"Yeah, she wasn't feeling great. Another headache, apparently, and so exhausted, she practically fell asleep in her dinner. Went up about an hour ago."

"Why are you still up? I thought you had an early meeting with Carmichael tomorrow."

Parker sighed and slanted back in his chair. "Yeah, well, it's the early meeting with Carmichael that's keeping me up. He wants all the budget numbers first thing."

"What a jerk. Never mind you're working sixty-hour weeks while he's home in bed." Luke drained the glass, then slammed it down on the counter. "Wouldn't it be great if we could tell people what we really thought?"

Compassion glimmered in Parker's eyes. "Rough night?"

Luke pulled out a chair and straddled it with arms loose over the back. "Yeah."

"Not Gabe, I'm guessing?"

A grunt rolled from Luke's lips. "Nope. For once, Gabe's not the problem. She loves it there." He folded his arms on the back of the chair and then rested his chin. "She's actually learning to play chess, if you can believe that."

"No kidding? Who's teaching her?"

"Katie's father—he's pretty good too. Took me to task tonight, like you usually do."

Parker hiked a brow. "Really?" He grinned and entered numbers on his sheet. "Maybe I'll get the chance to play him and redeem your pride sometime."

"I was hoping you'd say that. You free next Friday?"

Parker squinted in thought. "I think so, if we don't have any problems this week."

Luke straightened, then stood up from the chair. "Good. Then plan on dinner at the O'Connors at six. Betty, too. G'night, Parker." He turned to go.

"Luke . . ."

He glanced back, his body exhausted and his mind even worse.

"The hurt over Katie? It won't last forever."

He stared, giving Parker the benefit of a tired smile. "Yeah, I know. Thanks, Parker."

A headache started to throb as he lumbered up the steps, his fingers pressed hard to the ache in his temple. He needed to put his body to bed . . . not to mention his feelings for Katie. And he would, he thought with a grim press of his lips, whatever it took. He'd get on his knees before God day and night if he had to, to be her friend and nothing more. And he'd become immune—to the lift of that pretty chin that signaled a battle would be waged, the playful smirk on that soft and sensuous mouth. Resolve tightened his jaw. By the grace of God, he'd survive the surge of his pulse whenever she entered a room and forget that vulnerable look in her eyes whenever his mouth had taken hers. Because that's what she wanted—to be friends and only friends. He stopped and braced a hand to the railing, stricken by a hollow feeling in his gut.

I can't do this.

All at once he thought of Brady and his words from the other night. Saying no to self and yes to God. And loving someone so much, you lay down your desires for theirs.

Greater love hath no man than this, that a man lay down his life for his friend.

His friend. Pain seared through his chest, and he closed his eyes. Could he? Lay down his life—the "life" he had hoped to have? The woman he wanted . . . as his wife, by his side, in his bed? Love her enough to be her friend and nothing more? He sucked in a harsh breath and opened his eyes. *God help me, can I really love her that much?*

He saw her then, in his mind's eye, a stubborn sprig of a girl, feisty and funny and so full of dreams, it made his heart ache. And that's when the truth struck—a realization as brutal and sharp as the pain in his throat.

Katie O'Connor would be his friend till the end of his days.

And somebody else's wife.

She hated to admit it, but Katie was grateful Father insisted she stay home tonight. The sound of katydids and crickets buzzed outside the dining room window while a pleasant mid-September breeze infused the room with the earthy scent of grass and mulch recently dampened by rain. Despite the Indian summer, she could smell the hint of fall in the air, and she expelled a silent sigh as she took another sip of lemonade. How she wished summer could go on forever! Or at least this night, she thought with a glance around the table. Who would have thought a game of Pinochle could be so much fun? And yet, here she was, her stomach aching from laughter and her heart warmed by the presence of people she loved.

Maybe it was seeing Gabe so happy, giggling and huddling close to Luke's chair on a stool of her own. Or the gloat on

Luke's face, rivaled only by Sean's, who tallied their points as Betty and Parker looked on. Katie took another sip of her drink, warmed by the crooked grin on her brother's handsome face. It was a rare occasion, indeed, to spend time with Sean since he'd moved out of the house four years ago, and she suddenly realized just how much she had missed him. As the eldest O'Connor, he had always provided a buffer between her and Steven, his ready humor and easy manner the perfect foil to Steven's brooding and her own demanding ways.

And, she thought with a secretive smile, he apparently did wonders for Luke as well. She watched as the two shook hands and noted that Luke's hardened mood over their coerced friendship last week was nowhere in sight. He was the old Luke once again with teasing quips and unwavering self-assurance, and Katie was greatly relieved. There were glimmers of the boy he used to be in the twinkle of his blue eyes, and she marveled that she was finally friends with this pain from her past, a boy she had vowed to hate.

"You know, McGee, we'd like you a whole lot better if you didn't gloat quite so much," Betty said with a roll of her eyes.

Luke's grin was positively annoying . . . and classic Cluny McGee. "Come on, Bets, this isn't gloating, it's sheer joy and celebration of my mental triumph over Parker."

Her hazel eyes narrowed. "So we all suffer because Parker beats you at chess?"

"Yes," Parker said with a veer of his lips. "The man's ego is attached to every game he plays, which is why he always challenges me to basketball after I annihilate him at chess."

Sean glanced up as he shuffled the cards. "Chess, huh? Have you played my father?"

Parker's grin was sheepish and definitely more humble than Luke's. "Afraid so, which explains why I've been banned to the dining room for Pinochle."

Sean chuckled. "Good to know—I'll put off asking him for that loan I had in mind." The blue of his eyes sparkled with humor as he offered Katie the cut of the deck. "Patrick O'Connor doesn't lose well, you know—a trait he passed on to this one over here."

Katie gulped her lemonade and jutted her chin. "Hey, Mr. I-Don't-Care-If-the-Sky-Is-Falling—can I help it if I like to win?" She parted the deck with focused precision and gave him a superior smile. "Besides, I've only won one game, but you don't hear me whining, do you?"

He picked up the cards and gave her a quick squeeze at the back of her neck. "That's because you're not concentrating, Sweet Pea. Your head's in the clouds, probably over Jack." He shuffled the cards a final time, then began to deal. "By the way, where is Jack tonight?"

Katie's gaze flitted to Luke, then back to her brother. "Out with the gang. Poker's his game, not Pinochle."

"His loss," Betty said. She folded her arms on the table and gave Sean a curious look. "So, what do you do for a living, Sean?"

An easy smile curved the corners of his mouth as he divvied out the cards. "I manage the second Kelly's Hardware store on Lancaster Street. Not as glamorous as these two legal minds here, I'll grant you, but if you're looking for the right pliers to fix a leaky toilet, I'm your man."

A gleam lit Betty's hazel eyes as she took a sip of her lemonade. "Mmm . . . do you make house calls?"

Sean's eyes rallied with a twinkle of his own as he studied her, his smile as easy as his manner. "Well, I can't say that I do, but I guess there's always a first time."

Katie rose to her feet with a grin. "Mmm . . . maybe before we start another game, we ought to cool off with more lemonade." She pinched Sean's shoulder and headed for the kitchen.

Plucking several lemons from a basket on the counter, Katie reached for a knife from the drawer and commenced to cutting. She grinned, thinking of Betty's flirtation with Sean. At thirty-three years of age, her brother could certainly use a woman in his life, although Katie knew that was the last thing he wanted. Still, Betty was a beautiful girl, and Sean was a man, after all. Humming softly to herself, she cut the last lemon clean through.

"Katie?"

She whirled around with a tiny squeak, fingers gripped tight on the knife in her hand.

Luke grinned, and his steady gaze sent a familiar rush of heat to her cheeks. "Uh, with that knife in your hand, I'd like to remind you we agreed to be friends."

She sagged against the counter, palm to her chest, and gave him a wobbly smile. "You scared the daylights out of me, Luke McGee, friend or no." She wagged the knife in a tease. "I suggest you keep your distance."

"Well . . . that's why I'm here, as a matter of fact," he said slowly, the smile vanishing from his lips. He took a step forward, eyes intent. "Katie, I . . ." He paused, drawing in a deep breath and exhaling again while his fingers chafed the back of his neck. "I . . . I owe you an apology for not keeping my distance at the BCAS. It was unprofessional, uncalled for, and totally unfair to both you and me. I regret it more than I can say."

She blinked, the air suddenly thick in her throat.

Averting his gaze to the floor, he buried his hands in his pockets and continued. "I regret the attraction, I really do, as well as the damage it did to our friendship. And I want you to know . . ." He looked up then, his eyes as earnest as she'd ever seen. "It will never happen again. I want you to feel at ease with me, Katie, not on edge because of anything . . . stupid . . . that I've done."

A lump bobbed in her throat.

"So please know that I'm praying for you and Jack, that God will bless you with the marriage you need, and I'm praying for myself too. That you and I can become good friends. You know, like Betty and me?" A smile finally tilted the far edges of his mouth and his voice took on that little-boy drawl from his past. She smiled when one blond brow edged up, just shifting toward cocky. "Friendship with women seems to be something I'm good at, I guess. Like Pinochle."

Her smile faded to soft. "That's because you're the best there is, Luke McGee, bar none. I never want to lose your friendship."

He smiled, then reached for the empty pitcher and strolled to the icebox to fill it with ice. The annoying grin was back in play as he shot a glance over his shoulder. "You won't lose my friendship, Katie Rose," he said with a smirk, "but you *will* lose at Pinochle." He gave her a half-lidded smile that assured her she was in trouble, then winked. "And that, my good friend, is a money-back guarantee."

Marcy dabbed perfume behind each ear and then to the hollow of her throat. She stared into the bathroom mirror with a tremulous smile. Adjusting the thin straps of her new satin nightgown, she drew in a deep breath, feeling every bit a young girl on a first date. A hint of rose crept into her cheeks as she thought of Patrick lying spread-eagle on their bed, eyes closed and muscled arms relaxed at his sides. And probably half asleep.

But not for long.

She smiled again and turned out the light, hurrying down the hall to their room. She eased the door closed and glanced at their bed, adrenaline skittering through her. Patrick O'Connor was a handsome man, but never more so to Marcy than now. Suddenly, in the last few weeks, she'd felt so alive and so young, her energies rekindled like the strike of a match. Since Gabe had come, it was as if her life was finally back on track once again. She had children that needed her, a husband that wanted her, and a houseful of laughter one floor below. Her sigh was pure contentment as she slipped into bed, on top of the sheets next to Patrick.

"Are you asleep?" she whispered, one arm tucked to his waist.

"Mmm," he muttered and rolled on his side. "Good night, Marcy."

She stared at his back, surprise parting her lips. Scooting close, she trailed her nails down the muscled curve of his arm. "Are you tired?" she asked, punctuating her words with soft kisses to his shoulder blade.

No answer.

"Patrick?"

"Go to sleep, Marcy."

The hiss of his tone was like a slap to her face. She jolted up in bed, anger sharpening her mood. "I don't want to go to sleep, I want to talk."

"I said go to bed, I'm in no mood to talk."

She gripped his shoulder and jerked him flat on his back. Fear tightened her stomach. "Oh, no—you're not doing this again, shutting me out with your coldness." A shade of hysteria crept in. "You swore, Patrick, after that time that Sam came to call—you promised you'd never hurt me like that again."

She stared at his face in the moonlight, and saw the hardest of rock, chiseled in anger. A nerve pulsed along the stiff line of his jaw, and his chest expanded as he sucked in a calming breath. "I'm sorry if you think I've been cold, but don't pretend you don't know why."

"I . . . don't know why," she whispered, and the half-truth weighted uneasy on her tongue.

He pushed up on one arm, bicep bulging from the effort. His voice was cool. "We all make 'promises' we don't keep, darlin', like the one you made to me regarding Gabe."

She swallowed hard to clear the guilt from her throat. "What do you mean?"

One brow jagged high. "Where is she right now?"

Marcy avoided his eyes. "Downstairs."

Patrick lashed around to snatch the alarm clock from the

nightstand. He held it up, lips in a tight line. "And what time is it?"

Marcy peeked up at the clock. "Almost midnight."

"That's right, an hour beyond when that girl should be in bed."

"But, Patrick, it's Friday night, and Luke is here with all her friends."

He reached for his pillow and stabbed it with a few hard jabs. "Which is why I allowed her to stay up past nine. But, Marcy, you knew I wanted her upstairs with us, in bed by eleven, but apparently what I want doesn't matter a whit to you anymore."

"That's not true—"

"No?" He shoved the pillow hard against the headboard. "Since that girl has arrived in this house, you've defied me at every turn, spoiling her like you've spoiled Katie and Steven."

Her breath caught in her throat, colliding with anger. "I do *not* spoil Katie and Steven, or Gabe! You're far too stubborn a man to let me have the final say in this house, and you know it."

"Only because I refuse to see our children ruined. But in the process, I am the ogre, the monster who doesn't love them quite as much as their mother."

"You're being ridiculous! Why don't you go down there right now and yank her upstairs if your authority is so abused?"

"Oh, you would like that, wouldn't you, now? Then I would be the villain once again, and you sail through unscathed." He leveled a stiff finger in her direction. "Mark my words, Marcy, things are going to change or you will have a villain as a husband as well as a father."

The breath seized in her lungs. "Don't you dare threaten me—"

He turned away, his back a wall of granite effectively shutting her out.

With a swell of anger, she lunged, allowing her fury to take control.

He disarmed her with a tight grip before he shoved her away. His voice was savage. "Go to sleep—our talking is through. We'll discuss this in the morning when cooler heads prevail."

He bludgeoned his pillow and edged away once again. Tears spilled as she stared, the muscles of his body as rigid and hard as his words. With a broken sob, she fell on her pillow, forcing violent heaves to shiver their bed.

Painful seconds elapsed before she felt him move beside her. Her body jerked at the touch of his hand, and like a wounded animal, she curled her knees to her chest.

"Marcy—" The pull of his hand drew her close, and she fought him with flailing arms. His hold became like steel casing, crushing her close, and the chaotic beat of his heart pulsed in her ears. "Marcy," he whispered into the curve of her neck, "I'm sorry. We'll talk this through, I promise. But please, darlin', no more crying—you're breaking my heart."

Moments passed before her sobs finally stilled and all energy drained from her body. With soothing whispers, Patrick kissed her brow, her cheek, her lips—gentle brushes all, laden with repentance. He cupped her jaw in the palm of his hand and fondled her lips with a gentle caress, then pulled away to plead with his eyes. "Marcy, I was wrong. Blame it on poor temper from a bad game of chess or the dip in the stock market, but I overreacted badly, and I'm sorry. But we need to come to terms over Gabe, or I worry we may have more than a fight on our hands."

She sniffed, and he leaned back to retrieve his handkerchief from the nightstand. He handed it to her, and she blew her nose, all anger finally diffused. "I-I know, and I'm s-sorry too. We need to work in tandem, I realize, but sometimes it's so hard because I just want to love her."

He gently pushed the hair from her eyes. "You're a loving woman, darlin', which comes in handy with a lout like me, but with a strong-willed child like Gabe, it needs to be coupled with discipline." He lifted her chin with his finger. "We have to present a united front, my love, and you need to learn to say 'no.' Or I'm afraid with Gabe, there will be a heavy price to pay."

She nodded and sniffed again.

With a tight squeeze, he buried his head in her neck before pulling away with a lift of his brow. He stared at her new satin gown, then slowly fanned his hands down the sides of her waist. "And speaking of a price to pay—so you've taken to wearing perfume to bed, have you, Mrs. O'Connor?" He bent to caress the curve of her throat while his fingers grazed the strap of her gown. "And a new satin gown, surely not just for sleep." With a slow sweep of his thumb, the strap slithered from her shoulder. "Oh, I'm afraid this is going to cost you, darlin'."

He kissed her full on the mouth, and heat shivered through her. "I suppose this isn't one of those times when I need to say no," she whispered, her breathing ragged against his jaw.

"No, darlin', it's not." And clutching her close, he fisted the satin gown and moved in to deepen the kiss, his husky words melting in her mouth. "For all the good it would do."

15

Katie groaned and tossed the pencil on the kitchen table. It spun and rolled off, plopping onto the floor. "Why do I have to take accounting? I want to argue cases, not tally numbers."

Luke smiled and patiently retrieved the errant pencil. He rolled it back across the table with a gentle push that tucked it neatly against Katie's elbow as she lay facedown, head in her arms. "Hate to tell you, Katie, but most of your work will not be in the courtroom. The majority of your time will be spent researching facts, analyzing case studies, and determining a course of action for the best possible results. The law entails all aspects of life, so a lawyer has to be well-rounded, well-versed, and prepared for anything." He reached for her textbook and gave it a gentle skid in her direction, jolting her arm. "Including finance, my friend, especially in this economy."

She groaned again, her expression pure Sarah Bernhardt with head flung back and brows crimped in pain. "But numbers are not my strength, Luke! I've been at this over a month now, and it's not sinking in. Poor Jack had to practically carry me through algebra last year."

His mouth quirked as he gave her a slatted stare. "So let Jack 'carry' you again. I'm sure he'd chomp at the bit to see you more frequently since your father's restricted him to weekends only."

She gave him a pitiful look, manicured brows sloped high while full lips jutted in a pout. "Come on, Luke, I can't study with Jack—he's got a one-track mind. I need someone on a regular basis—like you, who's been to law school and will focus on the books instead of on me."

Luke exhaled and leaned back in his chair. Well, he'd been to law school, anyway, he thought as he studied Katie with a narrow gaze. He finally blew out a sigh and closed his eyes, scrubbing his face with his hand. "Okay, when?"

She actually squealed. "Oh, I could just kiss you!"

Hand to face, his fingers parted as he eyed her with a tight smile. "Please don't."

The brat actually had the nerve to prop her chin in her hand and wiggle her brows. "Really? Why not?"

Focus on the books, McGee, not the girl.

"Hey, what's going on in here?" Patrick said with a swoosh of the swinging door. "There is entirely too much levity here to constitute any viable studying." He entered the kitchen with a stern look that was edged with a smile. He made his way to the cabinet next to the sink and pulled out a glass, then glanced over his shoulder as he filled it from the tap. "So, who's the culprit here, I wonder—Luke or you, Katie Rose?" He reached for a bottle of aspirin and tossed two to the back of his throat. A brow shifted up as he took a quick drink of water. "As if I have to ask."

"Luke has offered to study with me every week, Father—isn't that wonderful?"

"Offered?" Luke leaned in, elbows flat on the table. He squinted with mouth ajar. "Railroaded is more like it." He gave Patrick a sideways glance. "She actually resorted to the protruding lip, if you can believe that."

Patrick set the glass down and put the aspirin back into

the cabinet. He turned to commiserate with a tired smile. "Inherited from her mother, no doubt, who has given me a fair amount of lip over the years." He started for the door. "Don't let her ride roughshod over you, Luke. She has a tendency to do that, you know."

"Uh, yeah, since she was in pigtails, Mr. O'Connor."

"Father, wait—aren't you feeling well?" Katie's smile lapsed into concern.

"No, darlin', but it's just a headache coming on, that's all. This downturn of the market has me on edge, I suppose, chipping away at our investments." He put a hand to the door and then shot them a thin smile. "Of course teaching chess to a bit of a thing who could be your twin, Katie Rose, might be at fault as well. God help me," he said as he plowed through the door.

Katie laughed and tugged a paper from her book, pencil in hand. "Okay, McGee, I made a list of what we need to accomplish tonight, so let's get started."

Luke grinned and glanced at his watch. "You and your lists. Well, I hope it's not too long because I promised Miss Lillian and the girls I'd stop by on the way home."

Katie opened the textbook with a flourish. "I swear, as much as you love kids, if you don't have a slew of your own someday, it will be a crying shame."

He rolled up his sleeves. "Oh, I'll have a houseful, you can count on that. Eight, at least."

With a casual flip of pages, Katie settled on the right chapter, then looked up, her eyes suddenly widening with shock. "*Eight?* You want eight? Sweet mother of Job, you better find a woman who's partial to babies."

"All women are partial to babies." Luke sloped back into the chair and folded his arms, giving Katie a crooked smile.

She leaned forward with a lift of her chin. "Not me."

He blinked. "You don't want babies someday?"

"Oh, I want babies, of course, but not until my thirties.

And definitely not an orphanage full. One or two is a nice number, I think."

He sat up, mouth gaping. "One barely constitutes a family, Katie Rose. What are you thinking?"

"I'm thinking I want a life other than washing diapers and cooking for a man."

His jaw dropped. "Tell me you're not one of those suffragettes that idolize Alice Paul and her cockeyed notion of an Equal Rights Amendment."

Her chin elevated to new heights. "I most certainly am—and you already know that."

"No, no I don't. It's a news flash to me. Does Jack know how you feel?"

She tapped the pencil against her lips, which were clamped in a tight line. "Yes, he knows how I feel. We're getting married, for pity's sake. Don't you think we've discussed this?" She averted her chin and doodled on the paper. "One child—that's all we're having. We've both agreed."

Luke sagged back into his chair and shook his head. "I had no idea you were so radical."

"Well, you're not marrying me, so what do you care?"

He sat up and slapped both palms on the table, shuffling his chair in. "You got that right—you're Jack's headache, not mine."

"Gee, thanks, McGee."

He smiled. "Start reading, kiddo, we don't have all ni—"

"Hey, Katydid—" Jack stood on the threshold, palm to the door and smile on his face. He saw Luke, and instantly the smile deteriorated into a scowl. "What's he doing here?"

"Well, hello to you too, Mr. Grouch." Katie jumped up and gave him a quick kiss. "Luke and I are studying."

Luke smiled, all but blinded by the glare. "Evening, Jack."

"What are you doing here, anyway?" Katie asked. "I thought you had an open house at Harvard Law tonight."

His eyes flicked to Luke with a cold stare, then back to Katie. His gaze softened. "I did, but I cut out early. Had a sudden urge to see my best girl. And your father said it was okay." He wrapped his arms around her waist and bent close to give her a kiss. "I missed you."

She shoved him away. "Not now, Jack, I'm busy," she whispered, her gaze fluttering to Luke and back. "Besides, Luke's here."

"Yeah, I know." Jack pulled her close again and glowered at Luke. "Why don't you run along, Soda Jerk, and let me spend some time with my fiancée?"

Luke rose to his feet, nerves twitching in more places than he could count. He trained his eyes on Katie. "Let's call it a night, Katie. We'll pick up next week, okay?"

"No, Jack is leaving—"

"No, I'm not, doll, I'm just getting comfortable." He snatched a chair from the table and sat down, pulling Katie onto his lap.

"Jack!" She shot up faster than the spasm pulsing in Luke's jaw. She crossed her arms and broiled her fiancé with a look. "Jack Worthington, you are leaving this instant, do you hear? We have studying to do."

"Actually, Katie," Luke said with a glance at his watch, "I really need to be going."

"But when will we study?" The pretty pout was back.

He unrolled his shirtsleeves with a serene smile. "I'll give you an hour next Wednesday, when I come to see Gabe, okay?"

"But an hour's not near enough! I told you I'm awful at math."

"I'll help you," Jack said with a swipe of his arm, attempting to pull her back to his lap.

She dodged him with a scowl while her eyes negotiated with Luke. "An hour on Wednesday, and two hours on Thursday," she countered.

"Why can he come twice during the week, and your father balks at me even once?"

She dismissed him with a wave of her hand. "Please, Luke, for me? As a friend?"

He braced hands low on his hips and gave her a lidded stare. "Two hours on Thursday, take it or leave it."

She beamed, the smile on her face positively radiant. "Thanks, McGee, you're the best."

"Yeah, yeah." He smiled and headed for the door, his heart a bit heavier than before.

"Good night, Luke," she called.

"Good night, Katie," he said with a forced smile over his shoulder. The smile died at the sight of Katie in Jack's arms, his mouth devouring hers as if he were a man starving to death. Hunger pains of his own rumbled within, roiled with regret.

Yeah, he thought with a hard push through the door, he knew the feeling.

Mornings are coming earlier all the time. Luke tossed his towel over his shoulder and yawned, half coherent as he scrubbed a slack hand across his bare chest. Of course, it didn't help he had a meeting with Carmichael at the crack of dawn. He rubbed the sleep from his eyes and plodded down the hall to the bathroom. What was it with that man, anyway? Meetings—first thing in the morning or last thing at night—didn't he realize people had lives to live?

A groan trapped in his throat when he rounded the corner and saw the bathroom was already occupied. He turned back to his room, then stopped at a frail noise, his senses instantly alert.

There it was again—a fragile moan and then . . . Luke winced at the sound of someone vomiting, and it made him want to retch himself. He leaned close and lightly rapped his knuckles on the door. "Betty? Is that you?"

Betty's low moan sent cold chills down his back, and he

sagged against the door, head bent and heart aching. "Are you okay? Can I get you anything?"

"No. Just go away."

"I'm not leaving."

"Luke, I'm fine. Just a touch of the flu. Go back to bed."

"Can't. Got an early meeting with Carmichael." He straightened and forced a light tone. "And after a midnight game of basketball with Parker following a very short game of chess, I'm guessing he'd want me to take a shower."

Another groan was followed by the flush of the toilet. He waited while the faucet ran, then pasted a smile on when she opened the door. "This is not a ploy to get out of work, is it, Galetti? Because I can't type that report by myself—Carmichael will fire me for illiteracy."

She looked like death, and it took everything in him not to panic, not to let her know how worried he was. But the ashen cheeks and red-rimmed eyes didn't make it easy. "Aw, Bets," he said, instinctively drawing her close in a protective hug, her robe-clad body stiff against his.

She pushed him away while color skimmed into her pale cheeks. "Ow . . . I'm sore. You better stay back. I don't want you to catch what I have."

He pressed a hand to her forehead. "Can't be the flu, you're cool as ice. Did you eat something that didn't agree with you?"

"No." She dodged his hold with a step to the side.

He clamped a hand to her wrist, forcing her to turn around. "What'd you eat last night?"

Her impatience puffed out on a sigh. "The chili that Parker made." She scrunched her nose. "Although come to think of it, it did taste like pure indigestion. Remind me to never eat it again."

"But you love Parker's chili," he said, feeling a touch of indigestion himself as concern churned in his gut.

"Not anymore. The smell made me sick to my stomach." She gave him a patient smile and patted his arm before peeling his hand from her wrist. "I'm fine, Luke, really. It's probably just a bug. Go back to bed." She turned to go.

He paused, heart thudding in his chest. "You're not . . . late . . . are you, Bets?"

She stopped, her back stiff as she rotated slowly. Her hazel eyes were mere slits in a pale face, warning him not to say another word. "We are *not* having this conversation, McGee." She spun on her heel and hurried to her room.

He was right behind her, shoving his fist in the door as she tried to slam it. "We *are* having this conversation, Bets, so you may as well accept it."

"You are not my keeper—get that through your thick head!"

"No, but I'm your friend, and I'm not leaving till I get the truth." With minimal effort, he pushed past her into the room and ignored the scowl on her face as he closed the door. He folded his arms and slanted back, eyes locked on hers. "Are you?"

She slammed her arms on her hips and glared. "That's not a question most males would ask a female friend, you know."

"Yeah? Well, most friends haven't been through what we've been through." He tried to rein in his own frustration, but his words still came out clipped. "Answer me—are you?"

Her eyes shimmered with anger as she clutched her arms tightly to her waist, the picture of vulnerability despite the stubborn bent of her jaw. Her voice was a whisper. "Yes."

His heart sank. "How late?"

A bitter laugh spewed from her throat. "Late enough."

He put his head in his hand, shock numbing his body. *Why didn't I hurt Leo when I had the chance?* "Maybe it's a false alarm," he said quietly, not at all convinced that it was. He knew she'd been having headaches lately and Parker had said she'd been fatigued. Her favorite food—Parker's chili—made her nauseous, and he suddenly realized she'd had enough mood swings lately to cause a strong breeze.

He released a slow, tenuous breath. "Have you thrown up before this?"

She spun around, her eyes on fire. "Yes!" she screamed. "Are you happy?"

"Absolutely giddy." He rammed his fist against the door. "Why didn't you tell me?"

Tears started to seep from her eyes. "And what was I supposed to say? Here's the report I typed for you, Mr. McGee and, oh, by the way—I'm knocked up?"

He took a step forward, his hands clenched at his sides. "Why'd you lie to me, Bets—you said he didn't rape you."

She turned and gave him a cold stare, tears glazing her eyes. "Because you would have killed him, and you know it." Her tone was as bitter as the taste in his mouth. She lifted her chin, stubborn to the core despite tears trailing her cheeks. "Besides, he didn't rape me, McGee. All it took was one slap for old time's sake, and I laid down without a fight."

He rushed forward and gripped her arms. "Stop it! This is not your fault. If it's anybody's, it's mine, for being late that night and for not hurting that lowlife when I had the chance—"

She hurled his hands away, eyes crazed. "No—*you* stop it! I am *not* your responsibility, Luke, so it's none of your business. I don't need you or your pious hovering, do you hear? I'm a grown woman, I can take care of myself."

Her words stung. He pierced her with his gaze as a nerve twitched in his cheek. "Yeah, I've seen how well you can do that."

She stared. Water filled her eyes as quickly as grief filled his heart. Her shoulders fell, and as if in a trance, she slowly lowered herself to the bed and put her face in her hands. Her weeping all but destroyed him.

"Forgive me, Galetti, *please* . . ." He rushed to her side and swallowed her up in his arms, soothing her with his words as he stroked her hair. "We'll get through this, Bets, I promise. I'm not going anywhere, whether you like it or not."

With a piercing sob, she clutched him back, her body wracking with heaves. "Oh, L-Luke . . . I-I'm s-so sorry and I'm . . . s-so . . . s-scared . . ."

He gripped her in a fierce lock, then closed his eyes to thwart the wetness in his own. "I told you, it's not your fault, so get that type of thinking out of your mind right now. And you have nothing to be afraid of. Parker, you, and I are in this together, and we'll figure something out, okay?" He pulled away to palm her tearstained face while his thumb stroked her cheek in gentle motion. "It still could be a false alarm. Have you ever been late before?"

She stared into his eyes, and he saw his own pain reflected there. "Just that once . . . when you and I . . ."

He swallowed hard. "Well, if you are pregnant, you won't be showing for another couple of months, at least. Did the lowlife happen to mention when he'd be back?"

A shiver rippled through her. "He's back," she whispered. "Pop called to say a 'nice young man' came by the diner looking for me. Left his number . . . so I could call."

"Pop didn't—"

"No, he told him that I quit, and that he wasn't sure where I was."

Luke exhaled the breath he had been holding and dropped his hands. He cuffed the back of his neck. "God bless Pop. But it's only a matter of time before Leo tracks you down." He hesitated before his gaze melded with hers. "We gotta get you out of Boston, Bets."

She shrank back, the fear evident in her eyes. "I'm not leaving you and Parker. And why would I even have to—Leo may never find me."

He lifted her chin with a gentle hand. "That's a risk I'm not willing to take. That monster robbed you of one baby, he's not going to rob you of another. You still have an aunt in Philly?"

"Yes . . . but I don't want to leave you and Parker." Fresh tears threatened.

He stood and tugged her to her feet, securing his hands to her arms. "Look, Parker and I both got offers from the Philly Children's Aid Society a while back, so who knows? Maybe I'll go with you. Carmichael has been getting on my nerves anyway." He grinned, hoping to lift her spirits. "So has Parker, for that matter—he's almost as bad as Carmichael."

A semblance of a smile trembled on her lips. "You would do that for me?"

He grew serious as he stroked her jaw with the pad of his thumb. A rush of love thickened in his throat, making his voice gruff. "You're in trouble, Bets. I would do anything for you."

She shot into his arms with a shuddering sob. "Oh, Luke, I love you!"

She squeezed so hard, it forced a chuckle out of him. "They probably don't have room for both Parker and me, of course, but I doubt I could pry him away from Carmichael anyway. And Philly's not all that far—he can always visit on weekends."

He peeled her away with a grin, then swabbed a palm across his bare chest. "Now I'm gonna take a shower, although heaven knows you've shed enough tears to do the job." He grabbed her chin and placed a kiss to her nose. "And then I suggest you get ready for work, Galetti, that is, if your stomach settles down. 'Cause if I have to type my own report today . . . that's the kind of trouble you *don't* want to be in."

"Sweet mother of Job, what a day. Sure glad it's over." Collin finished drafting the last of the invoices and rose from his chair. He strolled over and tossed them into Evelyn's tray.

She looked up with a tired smile, her eyes as fatigued as he felt. "I think we delivered a record number of jobs this month, if my books are any indication. And with the new pressman you hired and you and Brady pulling extra hours, this month looks to be quite healthy."

A smile quirked on his lips. "Yeah, well, I'm glad something's healthy around here, because my body's sure not." He dropped in his chair and put his feet up, pinching the back of his neck with his fingers. "My neck is killing me."

She pulled her purse from a drawer and rounded the counter, stopping in front of Collin's desk with concern in her eyes. "Would you like me to massage it for you? That always helps Tommy at the end of the day." She smiled a mother's smile. "He says I have magic fingers."

Collin sat up with a grunt. "Sure, can't hurt. Magic fingers, eh? This I gotta see."

She placed her purse on his desk and moved behind his chair. "Take a deep breath and relax." He complied and she went to work, kneading his neck with nimble fingers that produced an immediate moan from his lips. "Sweet saints, Tommy is right," he muttered. Closing his eyes, he noticed the silence from the back of the shop and raised his voice. "Hey, Brady, call it a day, will ya? Everybody's gone except Evelyn and me, and we can't keep up with you anymore."

Footsteps made their way to the front room and stopped. Collin squinted one eye open, unleashing another moan. "We need to give this woman a raise—she's way too valuable."

Evelyn laughed. "Except I wear out fast." She flexed her fingers, then propped her hands on Collin's shoulders and leaned forward. "How's it feel now?"

He rolled his neck and grinned. "Like spaghetti. Thanks, Evelyn—Tommy's a lucky boy."

She picked up her purse and shot Brady a smile. "Maybe not. We're having spinach tonight. Tommy's hoping it will make him strong like Popeye." She moved toward the door and unlatched her coat from the rack, then put it on with a tentative smile. "Goodness, I hope you like spinach, Collin. I didn't even think to ask." She buttoned her coat with a worried slope of her brows. "You are still coming tonight, right? Tommy finished that woodcarving you helped him with, and he's kind of anxious to show it to you."

His own smile grew stale as he shot a nervous glance in Brady's direction. He cleared his throat and nodded. "Sure thing, Evelyn. And tell him to set up the board."

"Great!" she said with a bright smile. "Good night, Brady—see you tomorrow." She hurried out with a merry clash of bells that stiffened Collin's neck all over again. He sucked in a deep breath and turned to face the wrath of God.

Which was pretty much right on target. Brady stood there, jaw slack and hands on his hips, enough energy pulsing off his body to run a two-ton press. "You're going to Evelyn's tonight?" It was more a statement of shock than a question.

Collin felt his hackles rise. He straightened his shoulders and prepared for battle, his stomach as tight as the press of Brady's lips. "Yeah I am, why?"

Brady folded his arms and strolled forward. He stopped just short of sitting on the edge of Collin's desk, where most of their friendly chats took place. "Why?" he asked with exaggerated emphasis, causing a nerve in his cheek to twitter faster than the clip of Collin's heart. "It's Wednesday night, and you want to know why?"

Collin blinked and then sagged back in the chair with a low groan. "Blast—the gym! I completely forgot." He tried to ward off Brady's anger with a sheepish smile. "Sorry, Brady, I meant to tell you this morning after Evelyn asked, but I guess it slipped my mind."

"How convenient."

Collin's grin dissolved into a scowl. "What's that supposed to mean?"

"It means," Brady said through clenched teeth, "that Faith is under the impression you and I will be at the gym tonight. Have you even bothered to tell her you're going to Evelyn's, or has that slipped your mind too?"

Collin shot to his feet, the fire in his eyes matching his partner's. "You're way out of line, Brady, and I suggest you back off."

Brady moved a step closer and stared him down. His tone

was deadly quiet. "No, Collin, you're the one out of line, and I'll back off when you stop jeopardizing your marriage."

"So we're back to that again, are we? For your information, my marriage is better than it's ever been. Because unlike you, Faith actually understands the situation with Evelyn."

Brady never blinked. "What she knows of it, I guess."

"I don't have to take this." Collin shoved past Brady and headed toward the door.

"Call her then. Tell her where you'll be." Brady's voice lost some of its fire, sounding more like himself—a friend who was closer than a brother.

Collin's hand paused on his jacket, which still hung on the hook by the door. He released a weighty breath and lowered his head, the jacket now limp in his hand.

"You can't, can you?" Sorrow laced Brady's question, and shame warmed Collin's cheeks.

He turned to face his partner. "I can, Brady, but I'd rather not. Faith has been . . ." He looked away. "Well, more understanding than I have a right to expect." The muscles worked in his throat. "I just don't want to give her any more reasons to worry."

Brady stared, his eyes a mix of compassion and conviction. "I understand, Collin, but she needs to know the truth. If she learns that you're over there more than the Friday evenings you've told her about, it will wound her." He shifted and blew out a weary breath, then rotated his neck while he watched Collin through tired eyes. "You want my opinion?"

Collin glanced over, one corner of his mouth edging up. "No, but does it matter?"

Brady smiled and eased onto the corner of Collin's desk. "Not really." He drew in a deep breath and then exhaled slowly, arms folded across his chest. "I think chess with Tommy once a week is more than enough. I think it's more than any other woman alive would even allow. And I think any more than that is downright irresponsible. Going over there creates a dependence on you, not only for Tommy, but for Evelyn."

"Brady, the boy's dying—"

Brady's gaze softened. "I understand that, Collin, but he's Evelyn's son, not yours. It's not your place to be there. It's your place to be with Faith and the girls." He reached to lift the phone off the receiver and held it out. "Call her, Collin, please?"

Collin balked. He shifted on his feet and stared at the floor. "I will, Brady, but from the phone booth by Evelyn's house, not here, all right?" His gaze lifted to Brady's face. "If I call now, her tone may deter me from going . . . and I . . . well, I promised Tommy I'd be there."

Brady nodded and replaced the phone, his eyes resigned. "Okay, Collin. But promise me you will call—Faith deserves that much."

Collin exhaled and opened the door. "I will, I promise. See you tomorrow." And slipping his jacket on, he headed out the door . . . to Evelyn's house, to Tommy, and to a promise he fully intended to keep.

Patrick lay in his bed, as wide awake as if strong coffee percolated in his veins. He glanced at the clock on the nightstand and groaned, jaw twitching along with the muscles in his legs. Heaven help him—three o'clock in the morning and sleep was nowhere in sight. He shifted from one side to the other, spooned Marcy and then not. But nothing—not positions of comfort or the sweet warmth of his wife's body—seemed to calm the restlessness in his bones.

With a sigh of defeat, he rose from the bed and reached for his robe, grateful that Marcy never stirred as he slipped from their room. He tied the sash of his robe and lumbered down the hall to the bathroom, then wondered which of the problems in his life was responsible for his insomnia tonight. The list seemed endless—from Marcy butting heads with him over Gabe to Steven defying him at every turn, or even

Mitch's squabbles with Charity over her desire to return to work. He sighed and filled a glass of water. Of course, Katie's situation was no prize either with an engagement to Jack, nor was the declining stock market that slowly sucked the life from their savings.

He took a swig of water and hung his head, certain that his concerns over the market bore the bulk of the blame. Marcy had been skittish about his investing to the extent that he had, but in a rare override of her counsel, he had done so nonetheless, certain that wisdom and good fortune would weigh in on his side. And for a while, it appeared that it had—he'd more than doubled their money over the course of a year. His stomach suddenly skittered, as twitchy as his limbs. He set the empty glass down and frowned. The market had continued to climb all summer, but then quickly dwindled in September, fluctuating wildly. And now October shaped up to be bleaker yet. Patrick sighed, not sure what to do about this dip in the market that doomsayers were convinced would end up as a bottomless hole. He shuffled from the bathroom toward his bedroom, then stopped, his shoulders slumped and his spirit too.

He closed his eyes and exhaled a halting breath. "Please, Lord, give me wisdom. Guide me, and show me what to do. Whatever path this economy takes, please, hold us in the palm of your hand. And thank you, God, for your mercy and your love."

Feeling somewhat better, he started back down the hall and then stopped again, ears pricked at the sound of something below. He moved to the landing and listened, head cocked and hand pressed to the rail. His pulse picked up as he descended the stairs, slowly, quietly, uneasiness as close as a shadow. A muffled noise drifted from the parlor, and his foot froze to the step. *God, help me . . .*

With breath suspended in his lungs, he eased toward the parlor door and flipped the switch. Light flooded the room, and he gasped.

Steven jolted up from the couch, blinded by the light while Maggie Kennedy lay beside him. Shock glazed Patrick's eyes as he took in Maggie's disheveled clothes. Rage paralyzed the words on his tongue, rendering him speechless.

"Father!" Steven stumbled to his feet, shirt unbuttoned and face blanched white. His eyes met Patrick's with shame as thick as the shock in Patrick's throat. "Father, we were just—"

"Spare me the details, Steven, I'm fully aware of what you were *just* doing . . ." Patrick's voice returned with a vengeance, eating away at Steven's excuses like the hard-grain alcohol his son was so partial to.

Typically calm and defiant in the face of his father, Steven was suddenly reduced to stammering. "M-Maggie was supposed to spend the night at Celia's, but she got locked out—"

Patrick took a step forward, the tightness in his chest nearly choking him. He stabbed a rigid finger toward his son, and the heat in his face all but suffocated the air from his lungs. His voice was savage. "I don't want your excuses, Steven, I want your hide, and I'll have it, so help me. You take this woman home now, and if I ever so much as see her face around here again, I will throw you both out on your ear. Is that clear? And we will discuss this tomorrow, you can count on that—both your despicable behavior and your future at college. Now, get out!"

Silence prevailed as a hard veneer settled on Steven's face. He buttoned his shirt and stared, his eyes glinting with the same fury that burned in his father's. Handing Maggie her shoes, he sat beside her to put on his own, and then turned and helped her up from the couch, her blouse now smoothed and tucked in her skirt. She avoided Patrick's eyes as Steven looped a protective arm around her shoulders, challenging Patrick with a final thrust of his jaw. "I love her, and where Maggie goes, I go."

Patrick extended his hand toward the foyer. "There's the

door, Steven, be my guest. But don't plan on using it after tonight if you defy my wishes."

A nerve pulsed in Steven's hard-chiseled cheek as he glared, ushering Maggie to the hall. He plucked their coats off the rack and helped Maggie on with hers, then slipped on his own as he opened the door. He stared back at Patrick from the threshold—a study in sedition with slitted eyes and a sullen stance that fairly shimmered with defiance. His voice was that of a stranger rather than a son's. "Goodbye, Father. I'd wish you good night, but then I'd be lying. And heaven knows I don't want to add to my sins."

He slammed the door hard, his anger shivering the windows while his hate shivered Patrick's soul. Grief bowed his shoulders as he swayed on his feet, one steadying hand knuckled white to the wall. Tears pricked, and he put a hand to his eyes. Steven's sins, yes, he thought with a slash of pain that divided his soul. And his. He hung his head.

The sins of the father . . .

"Mother, I'm worried." Katie looked up from the skillet she was washing and saw her own concern mirrored in her mother's eyes. She dipped it into the rinse, then shook it out hard, wishing she could do the same with this uneasy feeling at the pit of her stomach. "Father's mood—it scares me. I've never seem him like this before."

Marcy took the pan from her daughter and began to dry, her shoulders slumped as if weighted with worry as heavy as the cast-iron skillet in her hand. "No, Katie, I can honestly say that I haven't either, not even during the war."

"It's a frightening time, I know, especially for those invested in the market like Father. My finance professor said the market dropped 33 points, which constitutes a selling panic according to him. He claims it's sent shock waves all over the country, even though President Hoover assures us U.S. business is sound." She scrubbed a final pot with fierce determination. "But Father is a smart businessman, and he'll land on his feet." She rinsed it, then handed it to Marcy before pulling the plug in the sink. Her eyes stared hard as both water and soap swirled away down the drain. She shivered and glanced at her mother. "How much did he lose today?"

Marcy pushed at a limp strand of hair with the back of her hand. "Enough to snap at Gabe when she picked at the roast before dinner, and enough to eat only a quarter of the food on his own plate—one of his favorite meals, no less." She sighed. "I don't suppose it helped when he learned I let Gabe play hooky again today—we butted heads over that when he came home."

Forcing a smile, Katie tossed the dishrag in the sink and laid a gentle hand on her mother's arm. "Which is why you called Sean, I suppose?"

Marcy hung the wet dishtowel over the rack to dry out, her lips skewed in a near smile. "Unlike Steven, who drives your father to distraction, Sean has always had a calming effect, it seems, especially when Patrick beats him at chess."

Katie looped an arm around her mother's waist, hoping to lighten her mood. "I wondered if Sean's lack of skill at chess had anything to do with it." She grinned. "Has he ever won?"

Her mother finally smiled. "Once or twice, I suppose, although your father beats everyone regularly except Parker and Luke. Which," she said with a lift of her brow, "is why Luke is relegated to checkers tonight, unless you think he'd be willing to throw a game?"

Katie chuckled. "Luke McGee? Throw a game? The man is a compulsive winner, prone to maniacal activity and diabolical mood if he even comes close to losing."

Marcy shot her a secret smile and pushed through the door. "Thus the reason Sean is our sacrificial lamb tonight. Shall we put on our best smiles, Katie Rose, and liven the mood?"

Had it been any other night, the warmth and the glow of

her mother's intimate parlor would have been the perfect place for an evening of family fun and laughter. Gabe, as cute as a pixie in her pigtails and plaid school jumper, sat cross-legged on one side of Marcy's flame-stitch sofa while Luke lounged on the other, legs crossed on the ottoman before him. He studied the board with intense concentration, arm cocked against the sofa back and hand to his temple. A cozy fire crackled in the fireplace beyond, providing the perfect backdrop for Sean and Patrick's game by the hearth. Even Marcy's candles on the mantel seemed to flicker and sway, keeping time with the husky strains of Louis Armstrong from the radio as he sang "When You're Smiling."

Katie moseyed over to where her father sat, gaze glued to the board and a pucker in his brow. She stooped to give him a soft peck on his cheek. "Who's winning?" she asked.

Sean leaned back in his chair with a crooked smile. "Who d'ya think? The man who shows no mercy."

"You really ought to let him win now and then, Father—it's good for his self-esteem."

Patrick grunted and moved his pawn.

She strolled over and ruffled Gabe's hair, giving Luke the eye. "So, McGee, you almost done? We've got studying to do, if you recall."

Focused on the board, Luke's head remained fixed, but his eyes flicked up with a half-lidded smile that took her by surprise when it fluttered her stomach. "When I'm good and ready, Katie Rose, and not a moment before."

She blushed and folded her arms, wishing the attraction she still felt for this "friend" wasn't quite so friendly. She angled a brow and squeezed Gabe's shoulder. "Take him down, Gabe honey, will ya? The man is in dire need of humility."

Gabe looked up. The freckles on her face parted into a devious grin. "Wanna help?"

Adrenaline rushed through Katie's veins at the prospect of demoralizing Luke McGee in a game of checkers. Tongue in her cheek, she nudged Gabe's arm. "Move over—you and I are going to put this boy in his proper place."

"Whatever it takes, Katie Rose. Two against one is fine by me." A slow smile eased across Luke's lips, and much to her annoyance, her stomach did another flip.

It wasn't long before Luke reached prime gloating mode. "Crown me, Katie—*again*."

Katie pursed her lips, head bent over the board. Nothing moved but her eyelashes as they flipped up, eyes scorching him with a look. "Don't tempt me, McGee. I learned about voluntary manslaughter this week." She slapped a second checker on his and made her move.

He grinned. "Good. Now if you can just learn that I always win, you'll save yourself a lot of heartbreak." With lightning speed, he made a triple jump and leaned back against the sofa with that irritating smile that always riled her as a kid. A muscled arm loomed over the board to offer a handshake, which she completely ignored. "Congratulate me, Katie Rose—I just won my third game."

"Gosh, Luke, you are so good!" Gabe said in awe. She pumped his hand with respect.

"Hear that?" He gave Katie a wink and lapsed into his annoying Cluny drawl. "Gabe thinks I'm 'gooooood.'"

Katie's chin hiked several degrees. "I'll say—particularly at getting under my skin."

He flashed some teeth as he reset the board. "Yeah, I know."

"Lemonade, anyone? I have a sudden urge to wring something," she said with a pointed look in Luke's direction, "and it's probably safer if it's lemons."

"Oh, me, me, me!" Gabe said, bounding in the air.

The neat little checkers that Luke had just set up bounced like Tiddlywinks, flipping onto the sofa and floor. "Now look what you did!" he said with a mock groan, then dove across the board and pounced on Gabe. He tickled unmercifully until her giggles ricocheted off the walls.

"Lemonade sounds wonderful, Katie," Marcy said with a pile of knitting in her lap.

"Yeah, sis, it does. I'll need something after Father grinds me into the dust."

Katie smiled and headed to the kitchen, humming under her breath. Within minutes, the back door squeaked open, and Steven peeked in. "Where's Father?" he asked in a hushed tone.

"In the parlor. You want some lemon—"

"No." He stepped in and carefully closed the back door. His eyes flicked to the swinging door and back while his tone softened to a slur. "Can ya do me a favor—please?"

"What?" She plucked several lemons from the basket on the counter.

"I need some things from my room."

"What kind of things?" she asked, brow puckering as she studied him. His speech was slow and thick and his eyes were tired and spidered in red. She squinted. "Are you drunk?"

Steven licked his lips. "A little, but forget about that. I need clothes, textbooks. Father and I got into a fight last night, so I need to lay low. I'll be staying at Jeff's for a while."

She cocked her head. "You and Father always fight. Why is this any different?"

He swallowed hard. A wash of color filtered into his pale face. "This was worse than before. He threatened to kick me out."

"What?" The lemon in Katie's hand slipped from her fingers, rolling onto the counter. "What in the world did you do?"

A knot ducked in his throat as he looked away, thumbs latched in the pockets of his trousers. "He caught me with Maggie . . . on the couch."

Katie gaped, unable to believe the sheer stupidity of his action. "No! You weren't—"

He scowled. "We were just necking, okay? Give me a break, I'm not that stupid."

She folded her arms. "I don't know, sounds pretty stupid to me, in your own house."

A nerve twitched in his jaw. "Yeah? Well, I'm not looking for your opinion, Katie Rose, I'm looking for your help. Will you get my things or not?"

Her lips pressed tight as she sliced a lemon in two. "Not. If I get caught, I'll be in as much trouble as you, and I'm too fond of Jack to risk it. Just go—nobody will even notice."

A blast of air expelled from his lips as he stormed to the swinging door. "Thanks a lot."

"Steven, wait—" She turned, her guilt prompting second thoughts, but he was already gone, the door slowly squeaking to a stop.

Within seconds, her blood curdled at the sound of her father's voice. "Steven, get in here—*now*!"

She winced. Not a good evening for Steven, she thought with a grimace, or any of them, given Father's state of mind. Expelling a weighty breath, she proceeded to cut the lemons, only to drop the knife midair at the frantic sound of her mother's voice.

"Patrick, no!"

Katie rushed to the parlor, body numb at the scene before her. Her father was enraged as she'd never seen him before, knuckles fisted white on Steven's shirt as he pushed him to the wall. His face was scarlet while his chest pumped air faster than Katie could catch her own breath.

"You're drunk!" her father screamed, his voice that of a total stranger.

"Patrick, stop!" Marcy pulled on his arm, but her father only ignored her. His gray eyes darkened to black as he glared at his son while Sean stood behind, his face pale and tight. Across the room, Gabe shivered in Luke's arms with tears in her eyes.

"Answer me! Are you? Are you going to follow my rules?"

Steven remained silent.

"Answer him!" Sean rasped.

"Steven, please!" Marcy stroked a palm to Steven's face.

Patrick butted her aside with a jerk of his arm. "Leave him be, your coddling is the reason he's the way that he is."

Sean steadied Marcy when she stumbled back, and needles of shock pricked Katie's heart as she ran into the room. "Father, stop, *please*!"

Gabe started to cry, and Luke held her tighter, his own face sculpted in stone.

"Answer me, you punk!" Patrick slammed Steven hard against the wall with another angry thrust, and a gilded family portrait crashed to the floor. Gabe screamed and Marcy started to sob. Her father's voice was hoarse with rage. "Are you going to stop seeing that whore?"

Something deadly flickered in Steven's eyes and with a stab of his steeled arms, he shoved their father back.

Marcy's cry shattered the room.

Patrick stumbled. Sean steadied him with a clasp to his arm. With ragged breaths, her father flung it away and charged forward.

"Patrick, no!" Her mother's shrill plea pierced the air.

Sean gripped Patrick from behind in attempted restraint. As if empowered by madness, Patrick slashed an elbow. The force of it broke Sean's hold for the briefest of moments, but it was more than enough. Patrick lunged, delivering a blow that split Steven's lip with a splatter of blood.

Marcy screamed.

In a surreal blur, Steven drove his fist into his father's gut. Patrick doubled over.

Luke locked Steven's arms behind while Sean held onto Patrick as he wheezed uncontrollably. With a gasping breath, Patrick finally looked up, his eyes brutal with rage. "Get out! I never want to see you again—"

"Patrick, you don't mean that!" Marcy's voice bordered on terror.

Steven wiped blood from his mouth with the back of his hand while a dark mix of shock and anger glittered in his eyes. A hard smile curled the corners of his lips. "Well, what do you know, Pop? For once we feel exactly the same."

Patrick jerked forward, then seized up with a guttural groan. Shock glazed his eyes while he flinched hard, as if suspended in air. And then in one paralyzing moment of horror, he slumped forward, his body lifeless in Sean's arms.

"Patrick!" Marcy clutched at his shirt, panic bleeding all air from the room.

Katie stood like stone, her face and fingers chilled to the bone. In her brain, the room stilled to a nightmare state, sounds and movement coagulating into slow motion. Her mother sobbing, Gabe weeping, and Sean's fractured calm as he clutched his father in his arms. She saw Luke jerk Patrick's tie free and loosen his shirt, then press two fingers to his throat. Her body snapped to attention at the harsh command of his words as they rang in the air.

"Katie, get your mother's coat and the keys to your father's car. Gabe, bring me that blanket from the couch. Sean, you and I will carry him out." He braced his arms beneath Patrick's back and knees, joining with Sean in creating a hammock for his limp body. "Ready?"

Katie bolted in the hall to grab her mother's coat from the rack in the foyer, then frantically searched her father's coat pocket for keys. Sean's face appeared chiseled in white granite as he held his father's body close, while Luke bundled Patrick in Gabe's blanket at the door. Marcy's weeping filled the foyer with their grief.

Snatching the keys from Katie's hand, Luke leveled his gaze on Steven. "Call Sacred Heart Hospital immediately and tell them we're on our way, a possible stroke or heart attack. Then call your sisters. There's not enough room in the car, so one of them can bring you and Gabe to the hospital." He positioned his arms beneath Patrick's body, rejoining Sean in their makeshift stretcher. "Katie—the door!"

She flung it open with trembling hands. Luke and Sean carried Patrick through while Marcy sobbed on their heels.

Luke glanced back, his gaze fused to Katie's in a transmission of calm that defied the situation. "We'll get him there on time, I promise. Just bring your mother's coat out to the car, and get your father's too."

Nodding, Katie grabbed the coats and flew outside to reach her father's Model T before Luke and Sean. She hurled the back door open, and Sean got in first, cradling his father's head against his chest. Marcy climbed in after, sobbing as she held her husband's limp body on her lap. Her weeping stilled to frail heaves, fingers shaking with every gentle caress of his leg.

Katie was numb as she slid in the front seat and turned, her eyes locked on her father's body that was as still as death in her brother's arms.

No! her mind screamed—he couldn't die. He was their life . . . their pillar of strength . . . Fear rose like bile in her throat, as bitter as the tears that blinded her eyes. *Oh, Daddy . . .*

Luke started the car, and she finally broke into sobs—all of her hopes and dreams worthless in the face of losing her father.

Dear God, what can we do?

It came to her then—as soft as a whisper—the caliber of man that her father truly was. A man bent on serving God and family. And in one violent swell of hope, she suddenly realized.

They could pray.

16

Marcy stared at the sterile walls, all tears momentarily depleted from her eyes. Her gaze wandered aimlessly from the dingy black-and-white linoleum floor to the floral framed prints carelessly hung, no doubt in a pathetic attempt to infuse life where death often thrived. Polished wood chairs replaced splintered benches of yesteryear, and the garish glow of the overhead light was now softened by lamps on tables here and there. Piles of magazines were littered throughout, obviously meant to distract or pass time, neither of which Marcy had any inclination to do. She did not want to be distracted from the task at hand—beseeching God on behalf of her husband—nor allow time to pass without Patrick as her primary focus.

She closed her eyes to pray, vaguely aware of Faith hovering on one side while Charity squeezed her hand on the other. They had only been here for a little under an hour, but it seemed like years since that fateful moment her heart had been severed in two. And now the most cherished half—the man she loved and needed—possibly lay at death's door. While she, a woman in dire need of mercy, lay at God's feet.

It was almost too much to comprehend and certainly too much to bear, the notion that the strong and virile man who had lain by her side last night—held her, loved her—would not be there tonight. The very thought slashed through her with such anguish, it sucked the air from her lungs in a painful gasp. She slumped forward, head in her hands. *God, please, no . . . I love him! I would be lost if you took him . . .*

And partially responsible? On the heels of her pain, guilt took a shot, niggling in her brain as she suddenly remembered. She'd butted heads with him again tonight, right after he'd walked in the door, never realizing the kind of day he had had. And all over Gabe. She shivered. When would she learn? Moisture pricked her eyes, signaling the tears were back. *Oh, Patrick, forgive me . . .*

Movement stirred her, and she looked up into the worried countenance of her youngest daughter. "Lizzie and Brady are on their way," Katie whispered and offered her a cup of water. "They had to take Teddy to Brady's sister's, and she lives across town."

Marcy nodded and sipped, grateful to replenish with water rather than weeping it out.

Katie bent to kiss her mother's cheek, then searched her sisters' worried faces. "Would either of you like a drink? I'll be happy to get it."

"No, thanks, Katie. I finally got Mitch at the *Herald*, and he's on his way with coffee." Charity massaged Marcy's back with the heel of her hand, eyes rimmed as red as her mother's.

Faith shook her head, offering Katie a strained smile. She glanced at the oversized clock on the wall and laid a protective hand on her mother's arm, her thumb absently kneading. "I wish I could get ahold of Collin, but I . . . I don't know where he is." Her voice broke.

Marcy squeezed her hand. "It's almost seven-thirty, Faith, and he'll be home soon. When he does, your neighbor will tell him to come straight here."

"I know," she whispered, and then her eyes flitted to the

clock once again. "It's been almost an hour now—can't they tell us something?"

"He regained consciousness in the car," Sean said in a gentle tone from his chair across the way, "and the nurse told us that was a good sign."

Faith sighed and leaned her head back. "I know, I'm sorry. I'm just worried."

"I wonder why," Charity said, her tone acidic. "When a man as vital and strong as Father has a heart attack—"

"Possible heart attack," Sean corrected. "We don't know for sure that's what happened."

Katie eyed Steven where he sat, slumped in his chair with a glassy stare. "No, all we do know for sure is that something upset him badly enough to cause a problem."

"Katie . . ." Luke's tone held gentle warning as he glanced up from his game of tic-tac-toe with Gabe.

Steven's eyes flicked up, and his dark gaze glinted with accusation. "Don't hang this on me, Katie Rose, you could have avoided all of it by doing me a simple favor."

Katie spun around. "Yeah? And you could have avoided it by staying off the couch—"

Marcy's stomach constricted.

Katie halted, as if suddenly aware she'd said too much. She swallowed hard at the look of shock on Steven's face, then quickly started for the door. "I need a drink of water."

Marcy grabbed Katie's arm, halting her cold. "What do you mean he could have avoided this by staying off the couch?"

Heat washed into Katie's cheeks. She trained her gaze on the black-and-white floor instead of her mother's face. "Nothing."

Marcy slowly rose, her tone laced with a steely quality that her children seldom heard. "Don't you dare sidestep me, Katie Rose. Explain what you mean—*now*!"

Chewing her lip, Katie shot a quick glance in Steven's direction. She sucked in a deep breath and faced her mother head-on. "Father was angry because Steven had been drinking, yes, but also because he caught him with Maggie last night . . ." She swallowed hard. "On the couch."

Steven lunged forward with a curse. "You little—"

Marcy's hand rose with lightning speed. Her slap echoed in the silent waiting room, stunning Steven—and everyone else—into shocked silence. "Don't you dare use that kind of language in front of me. To think that I have defended you to your father, giving you the benefit of the doubt, over and over again. And now to find out that your lewd behavior—under our very roof, no less—may have been responsible for—" Her voice cracked on a sob.

Faith jumped up to cradle Marcy's shoulders and usher her back to her seat. "Mother, we're all pretty upset right now—"

With an angry shove to Katie's shoulder, Steven bolted from the room, and Sean quietly rose to follow. Katie tightened her jaw and started after them, retribution foremost on her mind.

"Let it go, Katie," Luke whispered, staying her arm with a quiet command.

She flung his hand away, all of her tension and fear rising up to spill like acid. "Leave me alone, it's none of your business. You're not family."

He latched on and practically dragged her to the other side of the room before shoving her into a chair. His eyes burned into hers, pinning her to the seat as surely as his massive hands pinned her to the wooden armrests. "No, but I'm a friend who's trying to stop you from making a bad situation worse. Your mother didn't need to deal with that right now, Katie, nor did Steven need any more guilt slung his way. It's pretty obvious he already blames himself as it is."

Teeth clenched, she tried to jerk free. "Good! He is to blame, as far as I'm concerned, defying Father like he always does. Let me go, you bully, you're hurting me."

His hold tightened, along with his voice. "Oh, and you're

the golden girl, I suppose? I'd be careful about throwing stones, Katie Rose . . . not with your reputation for breaking curfew left and right, drinking alcohol, and if I have my guesses right . . . ," a nerve twittered in his cheek, "your own fair share of necking in the car with Jack." He removed his hand from her arm and sat down, his eyes defying her to argue. "Not to mention kissing me behind your boyfriend's back."

Heat infused her cheeks and she looked away, ashamed that his aim was dead-center. Tears pricked her eyes, and she lowered her head. "Gee, thanks, McGee, I feel so much better."

The warmth of his breath brushed her cheek as he leaned in close. "Katie, I'm not trying to make you feel guilty here, but you need to understand that this isn't anybody's fault. It's just one of those awful things that happens in life. Blaming your brother is not going to help, and to be honest, it hurts your chances at the only thing that really will."

His words were calm and low, helping to ease the anger she felt inside. She looked up, tears blurring her eyes. "What are you talking about?" she whispered.

The soothing stroke of his fingers against her cheek drew her eyes closed. "Prayer," he said in a voice so sure and so still that peace lighted upon her soul. "Bitterness and unforgiveness are sins, Katie, and a luxury you can't afford right now. The Bible says if we regard sin in our hearts, the Lord will not hear our prayers. And if ever there were a time you wanted him to hear your prayers, I would think it would be now."

Tears spilled as she opened her eyes. "Oh, Luke, I want to pray, but I'm no good at it."

He smiled and braced a sturdy arm to her shoulder, pulling her close as they sat back, side by side. He pressed a kiss to her head. "Well, you're with the right friend, then, 'cause I've spent enough time with John Brady to get it down right. But first, you need to forgive your brother."

"How?" She sniffed. "I'm so angry with him right now, I don't know if I can."

"You can. It's not a matter of feeling it, Katie, it's a matter of doing it—making the decision to bend that iron will of yours in God's direction so that he can hear your prayers and unleash blessings." He hesitated, a note of levity in his tone. "But since that's something totally foreign to you, how about I pray, and you just agree in your heart?"

She nodded and rested back against his chest with eyes closed.

"Lord God, we need your help right now on behalf of Katie's father and her family. But first, we want to make sure all barriers are out of the way, so Katie asks you to forgive her for her anger toward Steven and to help her let it go. Whether she feels like it or not, she knows you've commanded that she forgive, so help her to do that now. And bless Steven too, Lord. Help him to find your peace in all of this and to forgive himself, Katie, and his father. We ask you to be with Mr. O'Connor—please stabilize and heal him. Wrap Patrick, Marcy, and their children in your peace right now, peace given in the midst of a storm as your Word promises. And finally, Lord, give the doctors wisdom and bring good from this situation on behalf of this man who serves you with all of his heart. Thank you, Lord." He squeezed her arm. "Feel better?"

She drew in a deep breath and released it again, shocked at how much calmer she actually felt. She turned and squinted up at him. "Yeah, I do. How did you do that?"

He laughed and massaged the nape of her neck, lulling her eyes closed once again. "I didn't, Katie, you did. It's called prayer, and when you mix it with faith and a clean heart—you can move mountains."

"Katie, will you take me to the bathroom?"

She looked up to see Gabe squirming before her, a pained expression on her face.

"Sure, honey." Katie stood and grabbed Gabe's hand, sparing Luke a half smile. "You—" she said with a pointed finger to his chest, "don't move."

She steered Gabe out the double doors to the bathroom,

past Steven and Sean who were sitting butted against a wide window ledge overlooking the parking lot. Steven's look was caustic, and with a press of her jaw, Katie escorted Gabe to the restroom down the hall, then doubled back to where her brothers sat.

"Steven?" She stood several feet away, hands clasped and heart pounding.

His head, slumped forward, suddenly jerked up.

She sucked in a fortifying breath. "I'm sorry. It's not your fault, you know, not anybody's, really. Although," she said slowly, her gaze avoiding his, "I bear a fair share of the blame for driving Father crazy." She looked up then, her eyes entreating his. "We're blood, Steven, and now more than ever, we need that connection, that closeness . . . to get through this."

She paused, arms clasped to her waist while tears sprang to her eyes. "W-when that happened to Father tonight, nothing else mattered—not Jack, not law school, not even my lofty dreams to make a difference in this world. I suddenly realized our time with Mother and Father is short. You'll be graduating next year, and I'll be planning a wedding to Jack." Her voice wavered and she lifted her chin to ward off a sob. She looked at Sean then, unable to fight the quiver in her lips. "And when I saw Father go limp in your arms, it crushed me to think that . . . every time we see him—see *them*—it could be the last time."

Her sob broke free, and Sean stood to pull her into his arms. She squeezed him tightly, grateful for the strength of his support. With a nasal sniff, she turned to look at Steven, her eyes beseeching his. "Steven, we need to love them—and each other—like every moment is our last. Because it could be . . . and it will be . . . someday. And I don't want any regrets. Do you?"

Steven stared, moisture softening the hardness in his eyes. He looked away, not trusting the grief that ached in his throat. "No," he said with a painful swallow. "I don't."

With a broken heave, she launched herself into his arms, and for one paralyzing moment he was struck numb with the realization of how everything had shifted with a single beat of their father's heart. He closed his eyes and stood, crushing her so tightly that tears escaped despite his determination to remain removed. He wasn't removed, he suddenly realized, no matter how far he had strayed from his father's love. He was Patrick O'Connor's son, and for the first time in a very long time, that awareness brought him a sense of pride along with more than a little guilt. He had battled his father at every turn, abandoned his father's values for those of his own, which in the face of this tragedy, suddenly had no value at all.

Katie pulled back and smiled, wiping her eyes. Gabe approached, and she tucked an arm around the little girl's shoulders and pressed a kiss to her head. "Come on, Gabe, let's go annoy Luke."

Steven watched as they disappeared through the double doors and exhaled slowly. He sat on the edge of the sill and leaned back, head against the window and eyes closed. He was silent for a long moment, and when he finally spoke, his voice sounded as far away as his thoughts. "I don't know when it all happened, Sean . . . the exact moment when Father and I parted ways."

His brother's husky chuckle broke his melancholy. "I'm going to take a shot here and say it was the moment you ruined his best tie for a magic trick with invisible ink."

Steven actually smiled. He shot a sideways glance at his brother. "To this day, I still don't know what went wrong. Father threw out that magic book so fast, I didn't have a chance to figure it out." His smile faded. "No, I think the rift happened much later . . . when I met Maggie."

Sean sighed and rested a hip on the sill. "I think you may be right. It's no secret to any of us that she hasn't exactly been a great influence on you."

The muscles in Steven's stomach tightened, but not like

they would have if it had been his father speaking. He studied his older brother through wary eyes, knowing full well that he would listen to what Sean had to say. Eleven years his senior, Sean had always been the anchor in Steven's world of sisters, a man he could look up to, along with his father. His calm, easy manner, and fun-loving personality always worked wonders in drawing Steven out of his shy and pensive ways, often warding off confrontations between Katie and him.

Steven blew out a blast of air, frustrated that as a man who wanted to live his own life, he was forced to agree that his brother was right. Maggie Kennedy had been anything but good for him over the last two years. She was a rebel of a girl who fit into the wild lifestyle of the twenties as snugly as a hand in a kidskin glove, and yet she drew him like no other woman ever had. Or at least her body drew him, he thought with a wry bent of his lips. Although he knew his moral decline had begun long before Maggie, she had been the one to actually steal his heart—along with his body—making it nearly impossible to turn her away. And there were times when he wanted to—badly—to alleviate the guilt that was eating him raw. The same guilt that flared out of control every time he looked into his father's face.

"I know," Steven began, his voice defensive, "but it's a different world now, Sean, you know that. Women today throw themselves at men, and to be honest, it's pretty hard to resist."

Sean folded his arms and leaned back on the sill, long legs crossed and head rested against the glass. "Can't argue with you there."

"And let's face it—there's no way Father can understand what we're up against today."

"He understands more than you think. He wasn't always married to Mother, you know."

Steven glanced up. "Oh, yeah, I'll bet he was a real live wire."

With a hint of a smile, Sean scratched the back of his head

and closed his eyes. "As a matter of fact, Collin told me once that the only reason Father agreed to let him come courting in the first place was because of Mother. Apparently she convinced him that at one time, he'd been just like Collin."

A smirk lifted Steven's brow. "You mean lousy at sports?"

Sean grinned. "Nope. An affinity for loose women."

"No kidding?"

"No kidding. According to Collin, Father's wild ways caused many a row with his parents." Sean opened his eyes to look at Steven point blank. "*Especially* his father."

Steven stared and then broke into a grin. "What goes around comes around, eh?"

"Apparently. Which I suppose is why Father rides you so hard. I think he's scared silly you won't end up as lucky as he did in finding a woman like Mother."

Steven let that sink in and knew that Sean was right. He needed to break it off with Maggie, something he'd known for a while now. Too bad it took a fight with his father to drive it home. A fight that could have taken his father's life. The reality stung so hard and so fast that Steven jerked to his feet.

He drew in a shaky breath and looked at his brother. "Thanks, Sean, for talking this through with me. I'm going to check if there's anything new. You coming?"

Sean smiled, hoping the worry churning in his gut didn't show on his face. "In a minute. I think I might stay here and say a few." He watched his brother leave and then sagged forward, elbows on his knees and head in his hands. He pinched his eyes tight to fight off the fear, but it was no use—water streamed his face and his hands as he heaved with his grief.

"Please, God, let him live—*please*! I can't imagine my life without him." His voice broke on another rasp of pain, and he wept for the first time since he was a boy. His heart bleeding now like his nose had bled then, hit in the face with a baseball. His father had been there as always, lifting him to his feet, then carrying him home, drying his tears and nursing his wounds. Restoring him with the healing balm of a father's pride. He was grateful for the release, the emptying of his emotions before he faced his family again. They needed strength and calm, not fear and foreboding. And he needed this time alone.

All at once his body froze at the touch of a hand, and he shot to his feet, quickly fumbling for his handkerchief. "Emma!"

"Sean . . ."

He stared at Charity's friend who had become like a sister to them all and suddenly had no inclination to bury his true feelings. If it had been anyone else, he would have met them with a warm smile and a ready quip, blinking away his grief as easily as he shooed away a fly. But something in the gray depths of this gentle woman's eyes released him to be who he was at the moment—a man laden with sorrow and riddled with fear.

She said his name again, and the tide unleashed when she embraced him in her arms. His silent weeping shuddered her body as he clung, desperate for the comfort she offered. When his emotion was spent, he pulled away to wipe his eyes with his handkerchief.

A faint smile shadowed his lips. "Did I get you wet?"

Her misshapen lips tilted up, and never had he seen a more perfect smile. "It'll dry," she whispered, "as will your father heal. Just a feeling I have, Sean, born of a prayer."

Hope flooded his heart and he gripped her hand, bringing it to his lips. He closed his eyes and kissed her fingers, then released them with a grateful smile. "Thank you—you're an angel of mercy, Mrs. Malloy." He saw the rise of rose in her cheeks, and his eyes softened. She reminded him of a shy and gentle fawn, ready to bolt at the slightest attention drawn her way.

"Sean, Emma—how is Patrick?"

They turned at the rumble of Mitch's voice, echoing down the hall as he hurried toward them with a box in his hands.

"We haven't heard anything yet," Sean said, "but he regained consciousness in the car, and the nurse indicated that was a very good thing."

Mitch screeched to a stop with joy pumping in his chest. "He did? That's wonderful! Either of you want a coffee? I brought six, half with cream, half without."

"No thanks, Mitch," Emma said with a smile, "but you'll have a lot of takers in there."

"My wife at the top of the list, I'm sure. See you inside." He butted through the double doors and honed in on Charity, sitting next to Marcy on the far side of the room. Her back was to him, but her body looked tired, arm limp around her mother's shoulders as her head rested against Marcy's.

His heart plunged. The moment she'd called, his anger over her push to work at the store suddenly fell away, his only thought for the well-being of Patrick. *And* his wife. He'd been a fool, he decided. *Again*. Charity was his life, his passion . . . at least until their bitter fight last week when she'd tried a new tactic—denying him her charms as a means of getting her way. Shame stabbed inside at how he'd lost his temper, berating her for manipulation and making her cry. In his acute frustration, he'd deserted her, choosing to sleep in his study until she came to her senses. He had wanted to punish her, hell bent that she would not force his hand. She'd pleaded and begged, explaining Emma needed help and she needed an outlet with the children in school, but he'd been too thick-headed to listen.

His jaw hardened. Well, he was listening now—and wondering why it took a tragedy to realize how very stubborn he had been. He'd given her the cold shoulder ever since, although she'd been nothing but kind, and he knew as sure as the ache in his heart that he deserved every prick of guilt roiling in his gut.

With a heavy heart, he rounded the bank of chairs to stand in front of his wife. "How is he?" he asked, lowering the box so she could distribute the coffee.

She looked up with gratitude in her gaze, and his heart turned over. How had he missed the dark circles under her eyes?

"A nurse told us just minutes ago that the danger is past and he's resting comfortably. But they're still observing him, so we're waiting on the doctor." Her eyes flitted to her mother as she handed her a coffee. "Anybody else?" She passed them out, then looked up with a nervous smile. "Thanks, Mitch. This'll help because we have no idea how long we'll be here."

He tossed the empty box on a chair and squatted beside her. "Charity, I'm so sorry."

Tears welled in her eyes and she nodded, quickly taking a sip of her coffee.

He glanced at Marcy and reached to touch her hand. "He's going to be fine, you know. I'm convinced the man has an iron heart with the pace he keeps at the *Herald*."

Her lips quivered into a smile. "That's our hope, Mitch."

"Are you going to head on home to relieve Mrs. Dean?" Charity's eyes were tentative over the rim of her cup. "I hate to impose, having her stay too late with the children."

Her look of trepidation—over her father, over him—pierced his heart. He took her hand in his and stroked her palm with his thumb. "No, Charity, I'm staying—my place is with you. Mrs. Dean will be fine."

"But, Mitch—"

He took the coffee from her hand and pulled her to her feet, his gaze welded to hers. "We need to talk," he whispered. "Marcy, we'll be right back." Without another word, he took Charity's hand and led her out into the hall, which was finally empty once again. He ushered her toward a bench at the far end, then sat down beside her. He handed her the coffee and exhaled, his eyes never leaving her face. "Charity, I'm a fool. There's no other explanation."

She blinked, her beautiful features momentarily stunned.

"You knew when you married me how thick-headed I was, and apparently I haven't changed all that much." He shifted to take her hand in his. "I miss you. Will you forgive me?" She swallowed hard, lips parted in shock, and he moved in close. "If you don't say something soon, little girl, I'll be forced to coercion." His lips hovered over hers. "Say you forgive me."

With a pitiful cry, she lunged in his arms, almost spilling her coffee. "Oh, Mitch, of course I forgive you." She pulled back, worrying her lip. "And you forgive me?"

He set her coffee on the floor, then bundled her in his arms. "I won't say you didn't make me mad, Charity, because you did. I don't think I've ever been angrier in my life, but in the face of something like this with your father, our squabble seems pretty insignificant." He tucked a finger firmly beneath her chin. "But you're my wife, little girl, and I love you. I want to express that as often as I can . . . *without* you using our marital love as a bargaining chip."

"Yes, sir," she whispered, leaning in to sway her lips against his.

He kissed her back with a hoarse groan, shaken by just how much he'd missed her. He pulled away and searched her eyes, his voice tender. "I realize now that for you to resort to such blatant manipulation, it must mean a lot to you to help Emma out at the store." He leaned in and feathered the edge of her mouth with a gentle kiss. "You haven't done that since before we were married, little girl," he whispered, remembering all too well the woman she used to be. "It drove me to distraction then, and it drives me to distraction now, so if it's all the same to you, I'd rather not start it back up again." He cupped her face in his hands and exhaled a weary sigh. "That said, if you want to work at the store, Charity, I'm not crazy about it, mind you, but you have my blessing."

She leapt into his arms with a squeal. "Oh, Mitch, I love you so much!"

He held her at bay with a faint smile on his lips despite the clear warning in his tone. "But only two days a week to start, and you're to be home when the kids leave for school and return. And *no* summers."

"Yes, yes, Mitch, anything you say."

He edged her chin up with the pad of his thumb, a dangerous smile hovering at the edges of his mouth. "And the first sign I see of you wearing down, or the kids suffering in any way, *or* . . . ," his gaze settled on the fullness of her mouth, unleashing a familiar heat, "being too tired to tend to your bullheaded husband . . . then you're fired from the store, understood?"

She reached up on tiptoe and gave him a kiss that made him forget where he was. "You have my word, Mr. Dennehy," she said with a tender smile, then pressed a soft palm to his jaw. Almond-shaped eyes fringed with heavy lashes blinked up, gleaming with both tears and tease. "And I will personally handle any and all complaints you may have, sir . . . day *or* night."

He grinned and gave her nose a gentle tap. "See that you do, Mrs. Dennehy. I would hate to go over your head . . ."

"How is he?" Lizzie bounded toward them as quickly as pregnancy would allow, a waddle in her walk and her breathing labored. She absently pressed a palm to an ache in her stomach, only vaguely aware of the pain. All that mattered at the moment was her father.

Brady locked a firm hand to her arm. "Lizzie, slow down or you're going to have that baby right here and now." He kissed the top of her head. "It may be the right place, but it's the wrong time, sweetheart. You've got two weeks to go."

"Thank goodness you're here." Charity jumped up and gave her a tight hug, then pulled away to touch Lizzie's cheek. "Good gracious, did you run all the way?"

"Yes, from the parking lot, at least," Lizzie said, hand to

chest to catch her breath. She grabbed Charity's arm. "How's Father?"

"He's resting and they're observing him, but it sounds like he might be okay. Mother's anxious to talk to the doctor, so we're all just waiting. Everyone but Collin, that is." Her lips pressed into a thin line as she glanced up at Brady. "He's at Evelyn's, apparently, and Faith doesn't know the number. Do you?"

Brady frowned. "No, she has no phone, but her house is not far, so I can go get him."

Lizzie spun around. "Oh, would you, Brady? I know that would be a huge relief to Faith."

He kissed her nose. "Sure, Lizzie, tell her it shouldn't be more than twenty minutes."

He sprinted down the hall, and Charity took Lizzie's arm to usher her through the double doors. Lizzie tried to bolt ahead, but Charity slowed her with a chuckle. "You're bound and determined to have that baby tonight, aren't you?"

"Any word on Father?" Lizzie's voice was breathless as she kissed her mother's cheek.

"Nothing more except that he's resting and out of danger," Faith said. She rose and gave Lizzie a hug. "Where's Brady?"

"He went to get Collin at Evelyn's," Charity said with a pointed look.

Relief eased across Faith's features as her lips lifted into a grateful smile. "Bless him. Does Evelyn live close?"

"Twenty minutes," Lizzie said, the anxiety lines pronounced on her face. She started pacing back and forth, hand to belly. "Oh!" A tiny squeak eked out of her mouth as she rubbed her stomach.

"What's wrong?" Katie shot to her feet, nerves as ragged as Lizzie's breathing. She glanced at her mother and sisters, noting their calm, and was somewhat annoyed. Apparently she was the only woman in the room not overly concerned.

"Nothing, Katie," Lizzie said with a smile. "Just a friendly kick. I guess sprinting all the way from the parking lot got this little guy worked up."

Katie clamped a hand to Lizzie's arm and steered her to the chair she'd just vacated. "Well, for pity's sake, Lizzie, park it, will you? We don't need any more excitement tonight. At least I don't." She blew out a sigh and glanced at Luke. "I need Life Savers. Do you have any change?"

His lips curved into a familiar smile. "I wouldn't take the name literally, Katie Rose, they're just candy, not likely to take the edge off."

She plucked the pencil out of his hand and handed it to Steven, then dragged Luke to his feet. "Here, Steven, mind finishing this game of Gallows with Gabe? We'll bring candy."

"Oooo . . . for me too?" Gabe said with a squeak.

Katie tweaked her pigtail. "Of course, you too. You're the whole reason we're going."

"Liar," Luke said as she dragged him toward the double doors.

She seared him with a mock glare. "I am not lying, Luke McGee. That little girl has been sitting there patiently for almost two hours now. Don't you think she deserves some candy?"

"Yes, I do." His smile went soft. "But not as much as you. This is tough on you, I know."

Katie swallowed hard and made a beeline for the candy machine, his sympathy pricking her eyes. She lifted her chin and patted a palm to the machine. "I suggest you empty your pockets instead of your mouth, McGee, 'cause the only thing I want from you is candy, not pity."

He strolled forward with a gleam in his eyes. "Is that a fact?"

With a regal lift of her brows, she folded her arms. "Yes, and I want five rolls, please."

"Five rolls?"

"You heard me."

His grin widened as he deposited his change in the machine,

obviously remembering the similar "Life Saver" memory when he'd been fifteen and she, eleven. He repeated the procedure until five rolls of gold and blue candy glimmered in his palm. She reached to take them, and he jerked them away, slipping them into his pocket with an annoying grin. "Not so fast, Katie Rose. How you planning on paying for these?"

She blinked, their little game suddenly gone awry. Her smile faltered. "W-what d-do you mean?" she stammered.

He gave her a slatted stare that sent heat to her cheeks before he casually strolled away with hands in his pocket, rattling his change. *And* her Life Savers.

She flew after him and jerked his arm to spin him around. "Okay, McGee, spill it. What do you want?" She smiled, well aware he wanted to continue the game from their past.

"Vindication, Katie Rose, for a ragtag little guy named Cluny McGee. An experiment—to see if you can say anything nice about him."

A smile tugged at her lips as she folded her arms. "Something nice. About Cluny McGee?"

He chuckled, giving her a sideways glance. "Yeah. I want to see if being nice to the little beggar will crack your face."

She squinted as if deep in thought while he reached into his pocket to produce the five rolls.

He bounced them in his hand with a little-boy glint in his eyes. "Come on, Katie Rose, this is our chance to clean the slate. You game?"

With a scrunch of her nose, she spun on her heel and headed for the door. "I don't think so, McGee. Can't shoot for the moon, you know."

Luke blocked her, hand to her arm and a wicked grin on his face. He prodded her to the wall with a lift of his brow. "One measly compliment, Katie Rose, and if Life Savers were money, you'd be a wealthy woman."

It was meant no more than a tease, a game from their past to get her mind off the present, but all at once his heart started pounding and his mouth went dry. Those blue eyes blinked up at him, and basic instinct kicked in, sending heat through his veins. He grazed her arm with the pad of his thumb, and he knew his eyes conveyed more than they should. Hovering too close, he teetered on a dangerous precipice, eyes fixed on her lips. He was a friend who wanted to be a lover, and for the first time in weeks, the desire was so strong, he had to physically pull away. He took a step back. *God help me, what I wouldn't give . . .*

She stared at him then with a lump in her throat, and her eyes met his piercing gaze with a soggy one of her own. "I'm already a wealthy woman," she whispered, her voice so low he had to strain to hear it. "Cluny McGee is the best friend I've ever had."

He blinked, the flow of air stilling in his throat. A bittersweet smile lifted the corners of his mouth as he took her hand and placed all five rolls in her palm. "Thanks, Katie Rose," he said in a quiet voice. "I needed to hear that." He looped an arm around her shoulders and gave her a quick squeeze. "Come on, kid, let's get back before Gabe calls out the cavalry."

"Katie?"

She glanced back, peering over Luke's arm, which was snug around her shoulders. "Jack?" Relief echoed in her voice as she pulled away and hurried to give him a hug. "Oh, I'm so glad you're here. I didn't think you would make it."

A frown shadowed his face as his gaze lashed to Luke and back. His voice was tainted by the slur of alcohol. "Come on, doll, you know I would be here at a time like this."

"I know, but I just thought you'd be out till late and wouldn't get the message I left."

He brushed a strand of hair away from her face and gave her a kiss. "How's your father?"

"Better, although we still don't know what happened. We're waiting on the doctor."

His eyes narrowed as they settled on Luke. "What's he doing here?"

Katie shot Luke a conciliatory smile, then turned back to Jack. "Luke was over to see Gabe when it happened."

"Gabe? Or you?"

The smile faded from her tone. "What?"

Jack took a step forward with a glazed look, and even several feet away, Luke could see the red in his eyes. "I want to know why he's always around." He glared at Luke. "You trying to steal my girl, Soda Jerk?"

Katie pushed him back. "Luke is my friend, Jack, and Gabe's. He comes to see her and to help me with homework, and that's all."

"Yeah, right. Then why was he hanging all over you when I just walked in?"

"Trust me, Jack, Katie and I are friends and nothing more." Luke's tone was hard.

"Trust you? Not on your life, Soda Jerk. I want you to stop hanging around my girl."

A nerve twitched in Luke's cheek. "That's Katie's call, not yours."

"Jack, stop it—now!" Katie grabbed his arm, but he slung her off.

He moved toward Luke with hate in his eyes. "It's my fiancée and my call, you slum rat, and I'm telling you for the last time—stay away from her."

"I said, stop it!" Katie jerked his arm and stood in his way. "So help me, Jack, if you don't apologize right now—"

Luke had to fight the impulse not to knock the punk down. His voice was strained. "Katie, I'm going in to say goodbye to your family, and then I'm heading home."

"Running away?" Jack's voice was hard.

Luke cauterized him with a look that should have sobered him on the spot. "No, rich boy, I just care about Katie too much to cause a scene when her father is lying in there sick." His gaze shifted to Katie and softened. "I'll call you tomorrow to check on him, okay?"

She nodded and watched as he left, feeling strangely bereft when he disappeared through the double doors. She turned to Jack with temper singed. "How dare you come in here and make a scene when my father is sick!"

Humility came quickly at the sound of Katie's voice. "Babe, I'm sorry, but that guy gets on my nerves."

"And you get on mine, Jack Worthington, when you embarrass my friends." She took a step forward and sniffed. "And you had the nerve to come here drunk?"

He pulled her close, contrition written all over his face. "Come on, Katydid, I'm sorry, but I came as soon as I heard, didn't I?" He nuzzled his lips into the crook of her neck, and she felt herself relent.

"Yes, you did, and I appreciate that. But you need to go home."

"But, babe, I came to be with you tonight."

She stroked the side of his cheek. "I know, but you're feeling no pain right now, and I'd rather you go home and go to bed, okay?"

"Okay, doll, whatever you say." He kissed her again and molded her close, eliciting a silent groan in Katie's chest when Luke walked by.

She held Jack tightly until Luke had time to leave the building, then pulled away and patted his arm. "Now, you go straight home, you hear?"

"I will, doll, I promise. I'll call you tomorrow."

Jack ambled down the hall, and suddenly Katie was overwhelmed with the sense of being alone, swallowing hard when she realized it was Luke she missed and not Jack. Drawing in a deep breath, she headed back to the waiting room and the comfort of family, where hopefully, she thought with an ache in her throat, she would purge this awful loneliness from her soul.

Brady knocked on Evelyn's door with loud, forceful strokes, his fury kindled on the ten-minute walk to her house. He loved Collin, closer than if they had the same blood in their veins, but right now it was all he could do to keep from bloodying that pretty face of his, a face that spelled trouble with women, ring on his finger or not. Collin had no business with this boy or his mother, a woman whose gratitude would obviously know no bounds. He blasted out another impatient sigh and bludgeoned the door once again before it swung open.

"Brady!" Evelyn stood there, the glow in her face the picture of hearth and home. She smiled, green eyes bright with surprise and wisps of auburn hair framing her pretty face, and for the very first time he noticed how much she looked like Faith. "What are you doing here?"

His eyes cut past her to where Collin sat on one side of a couch, hovering over a chessboard on a breakfast table between Tommy and him. Brady sucked in a harsh breath, ill-prepared for the sight before his eyes.

Tommy seemed so sallow and thin since he'd seen him last, his bony back hunched and propped against pillows on the side of the couch. Beneath the stilted table, his matchstick legs appeared flat and frail, peeking out beneath the remains of a blanket that had mostly slid to the floor. The boy looked up, and Brady's heart wrenched in his chest. Dark eyes sunken in a pale face were surrounded by bluish-green circles that looked like shiners he'd gotten in a fight. His skin, almost translucent, gave him an eerie, ethereal glow, as if he were spirit instead of flesh and blood. Brady swallowed the shock in his throat at the sight of a purplish lump protruding from Tommy's neck, and with a press of his jaw, he tore his gaze from the boy to Collin.

One look at his partner put all his fears to shame. The same haggard look in the boy's eyes could be seen in Collin's, right down to the hint of dark circles under his eyes, which now held an element of surprise. He straightened broad shoulders that had been hunched like Tommy's and squinted at Brady from across the room. "What are you doing here?"

Brady's gaze swept the room, taking in Evelyn's mother knitting by the hearth where a fire crackled and spit, and Evelyn with an apron tied to her waist and the scent of apple pie in the air. He focused on Collin, his eyes full of regret. "They took Patrick to the hospital tonight—a possible heart attack or stroke. He appears to be doing fine now, but Faith needs you."

The news obviously depleted what energy Collin had with a quick sheen of moisture that sprang to his eyes. His throat worked hard as he stood, his gaze settling on Tommy. "I have to go, bud, but I'll see you in a few days, okay?" He squatted to carefully embrace the boy, and Tommy clutched him tightly around the neck.

"I love you, Collin," he whispered, and Brady shifted on his feet while emotion stung in his eyes.

"I love you too, bud," Collin said in a hoarse voice. He ruffled the boy's hair as he rose to his feet. His eyes lighted on Evelyn and then on her mother. "Thanks for dinner. I'll see you tomorrow, Evelyn." He moved toward the door and lifted his coat from the rack, glancing at Brady out of the corner of his eyes. "You're sure he's okay?"

Brady gripped Collin's shoulder with a reassuring squeeze. "We think so. The nurse said he's resting comfortably."

Collin nodded and slipped out the door, letting Brady close it behind him. They walked in silence for several blocks before Collin ever uttered a word. When he did, his voice was raspy and nasal, and Brady suddenly realized he'd been weeping. "I'm sorry you had to come get me, Brady. What happened tonight?"

Brady filled him in on the little he knew while Collin listened with a dead stare ahead.

"How's Faith?" he whispered, his pace picking up as they approached the front doors of Sacred Heart Hospital.

"Worried about Patrick . . . and you."

Collin heaved the doors open and started to sprint down the hall, ignoring the look of surprise on the night watchman's face. Brady nodded at the man and loped behind, following Collin into the waiting room as he heaved the door wide.

"Collin!" Faith jumped to her feet.

In several long strides, she was in his arms, his head buried in her neck. "Forgive me, Faith, I am so sorry I wasn't here." He jerked back, his arms still clutching hers. "How is he?"

She studied the worried gray eyes now spidered with red, and her heart swelled with love, nearly trumping the hurt she harbored inside. "He's weak, of course, the doctor said, but he expects him to recover with lots of rest. The good news is he suspects something he called 'angina' rather than a heart attack, which he says results from a lack of oxygen to the heart. Once the demand for oxygen abates, so do the symptoms, apparently, and no permanent damage is done. Mother saw him briefly before they shooed her out. He'll be here for a week, which is going to rile him something fierce."

"Are they sure it's not a heart attack?" Collin's tone begged reassurance.

Faith stroked his cheek at the look of fear in his eyes. "No, not 100 percent, but reasonably so. The doctor feels a regimen of less stress, reduced activity, and nitroglycerin to reduce his blood pressure will help, and hopefully in a few months, he can return to a near-normal lifestyle."

His shoulders slumped in a weary sigh as he rubbed her arms. "Near normal, eh? Knowing Patrick, there'll be no 'near' about it. Your mother'll have her hands full, I'm afraid."

"I heard that, Collin McGuire," Marcy said behind his back, and he turned to face her, one arm still cradling Faith. Marcy snatched her coat from the back of the chair, and then her purse, her jaw as tight as Faith had ever seen. "After the scare Patrick O'Connor gave me tonight, I'm afraid it will be him who will have his hands full. There will be no work for three months, no steps to scale, no activity if I can help it, and no argument." She gave Collin a thin smile as he helped her on with her coat. "I suggest everyone go home and get some rest. We have a monumental task ahead with your father."

Mitch grabbed Charity's coat and held it while she slipped it on. "No work for three months? During this financial crisis?" A smile hovered at the edges of his mouth. "You may need a length of rope, Marcy, to tie the man down."

She buttoned her coat with a tight press of her lips, which held just a hint of a smile. "Don't think I won't." Her eyes lighted on Sean. "Bring rope home from Kelly's, will you, Sean? The strongest hemp you have." She walked over to Steven and put a gentle hand to his cheek. "And you—you're forgiven, but only if you develop a passion for chess with a tightly bound man. Now, let's go home—I'm exhausted."

"Oh, me too," Lizzie said as she rose to her feet. She suddenly lurched forward. "Oh!"

Katie looked up from her chair with Gabe asleep against her shoulder. "Another kick?"

Lizzie blinked while her mouth rounded in a soft "o." She skimmed a hand across her belly. "I . . . I don't know."

"What do you mean, you don't know?" Brady said, shooting to his feet.

She scraped her lip and looked down, worry etched in her face. "I think my water just broke."

Eleven sets of eyes focused on Lizzie's feet where a pool of liquid puddled on the floor.

"Sweet mother of Job," Katie whispered, "this baby stuff is not pretty."

A grin parted Marcy's lips, infusing new energy into a face that was no longer tired. She unbuttoned her coat and slapped it over her chair. "Sean, Steven, Katie—take Gabe home and put her to bed. I'll call when I'm ready."

"I'm not going anywhere," Katie said with a thrust of her chin.

"Me, either," Faith said, giving Collin a peck on the cheek.

"Go home and relieve Mrs. Tang, and get some sleep—you look spent."

Mitch sighed and stood to his feet, caressing Charity's neck with the palm of his hand. "I guess you plan on staying too, don't you?" He glanced at Brady. "How long did it take with Teddy, do you remember?" There was the faintest trace of hope in his voice.

"Twelve hours," Marcy answered, "so hopefully this one will go faster."

Mitch groaned, and Charity reached up to kiss him lightly on the lips. "Go home, darling. Babies have a way of taking their sweet time." She patted his cheek and gave him a tired smile. "Like you, when you're being stubborn."

17

"I liked you better before when you weren't such a crab." Gabe flopped her arms on the table and studied the chessboard with the same grumpy look on her face Patrick felt on his own.

He shoved up the sleeves of his charcoal gray pullover and mirrored her mood, jaw to jaw. His eyes narrowed into the disgruntled look he'd worn for the last blasted week, ever since he'd begun his prison term at home. "Well, I liked me better too, for your information, when my wife didn't hover over me with a stick and I could sleep in my own bed."

Gabe's eyes narrowed right back. "You are sleeping in your own bed—"

A tic vibrated in his cheek as he leaned in. "In-my-own-room, next-to-my-own-wife!" He peered at the twin bed that Marcy insisted her sons bring down to the parlor, and was certain that if looks could singe, it would erupt in flames.

Gabe glanced over her shoulder at Marcy who was knitting with all the calm of a saint. "Do I really have to play chess with this guy? I'd rather do dishes."

"That can be arranged," Patrick said with a grind of his

jaw. "Take your time with your next move, Gabe—I'll just hop in my bed over there and take a nap while I'm waiting."

"Patrick, stop it! You're being a baby—*again*. Gabe, it's Katie's night for dishes, and although I'm sure she would love the help, you need to finish your lesson in chess."

"You mean agony," she mumbled under her breath.

"I heard that," Patrick said with a lift of his chin. "And if you want to get good enough to beat Luke, I suggest you make a move, little girl, at least while I'm still in the land of the living." He reached for his pipe out of sheer habit and scowled. "If that's what you call it."

Marcy shot to her feet and had the pipe whisked from his lips before he could light it with the match he'd just struck. "How did you get that?" she demanded, her voice considerably less calm than before. "You know the doctor said no pipe, at least for the foreseeable future."

Gabe yawned. "He bribed me," she said in a matter-of-fact tone, squinting at the board.

"Snitch," Patrick mumbled under his breath.

"Patrick O'Connor, so help me, I will kill you myself if you don't shape up and do what the doctor says. I will not be left a widow, do you hear?"

"Marcy, I'm fine, and I would get over this weakness soon enough if you wouldn't coddle me this way. I can handle the stairs if I take them slow."

"Dr. Williamson was adamant—no stairs, no pipe, no activity, and no stress . . . which means no work, no radio, no newspaper, and no finances until you're stronger. Case closed."

"And no life," he muttered. "For pity's sake, it's been two weeks without any pain."

"And I want two more weeks, and two more weeks after that, and so on. The doctor said three months of total rest, and I aim to see you get every blessed second."

"Is he giving you trouble again, Mother, because I can carry him up to the bathroom, if you like." Steven sauntered into the room, lips twitching as if a grin waited in the wings. "After all, he's due for a full-blown shower about now, isn't he? After a week of sponge baths?"

"You lay one hand on me, Steven, and you will be putting yourself through college."

Steven grinned and pulled up a chair, then slapped Patrick on the back. "Come on, Pop, you know I'm kidding, don't ya? You two almost done? I'm itching to take a shot at the grouch."

Gabe blasted up like a Roman candle. "He's all yours, Steven, take him down."

Patrick grunted. "As if I could sink any lower."

Steven claimed Gabe's vacated chair and studied the board for several seconds before glancing up at his father. He suddenly rose and moved to Patrick's side, squatting to grip his arm. His voice was quiet. "I know this is killing you, Pop, but you're tough, and the recovery won't last forever. But the good from this will."

Steven shifted and lowered his voice for Patrick's ears only, facing his father with a rare humility. Patrick's muscles stiffened in shock at the moisture in his son's eyes, and when Steven finally spoke, tears pricked his own.

"Being your son is something I took for granted, Pop, a privilege I didn't respect until it was almost too late. Well, I want you to know, it will never happen again. I only hope and pray I can make it up to you. I'd like to make you as proud of me as I am of you . . . if that's even possible."

Patrick blinked hard while emotions clogged his throat. Steven stood to his feet and swabbed an arm across his eyes, then offered a grin obviously meant to deflect the awkwardness he felt.

All at once, he bent to clutch Patrick tightly, a heave choking his voice as he embraced his father. "I love ya, Pop," he whispered, "and I'm so sorry."

Patrick patted his son's back, the rasp in his tone betraying his own emotion. "I love you too, Steven, more than a stubborn old man can possibly express. You're my son, my blood. And truth be told, I'm grateful for this wretched angina, if only for the fact that our relationship has been restored. I love you, son, and I always will. And I'm proud of you too."

Steven grinned, his eyes still sporting a sheen of tears. "Yeah, well, let's see how proud you are when I kick your backside in a game of chess."

"In your dreams, college boy," Patrick said in a gruff tease. "It's my heart that's ailing, you little punk, not my brain. Set it up."

Katie strolled into the parlor with a textbook in her hand and a smile on her face. "Whew, finally done! Mother, I think you may have used every pot in the kitchen tonight. Anybody want anything before I recline on the love seat and lose myself in the thrilling world of finance?"

Patrick grunted in jest. "Yeah, I'd like my old life back."

Marcy's knitting dropped to her lap. "This is not easy for any of us, Patrick, and if you don't stop whining and show some gratitude to this family who loves you, I'll be forced to break down and cry."

Terror struck as Patrick stared, unnerved by the threat of his wife's tears. He sucked in a deep breath. "Marcy, don't cry, please. I'll do my best to behave, I promise."

She gave him a sweet smile. "That's my boy," she said with a hint of victory in her eyes. "No, Katie, I'm fine, thank you. But I'll bet Gabe would like something."

"Root beer!" Gabe said with a shout.

"Milk," Patrick bit out, hunkering down in the chair.

"She had milk for dinner, Patrick. A small glass of lemonade will be fine, Katie."

"One lemonade, coming right up." Katie glanced over her shoulder. "Is Brady stopping by for that casserole or are we supposed to deliver it?"

Marcy looked up from her knitting. "He said he wanted to stop by to see your father."

"Oh, speak of the devil," Katie said at the sound of someone at the door. She hurried to give Brady a hug as he entered. "You're just in time for lemonade. How are the girls doing?" she asked, taking his coat from his hand. "Has little Molly gotten the hang of nursing yet, I hope?"

Brady threaded a hand through his hair and grinned. "Yeah, finally. We've gotten her four and half pounds up to a hefty five. As far as the girls?" He grinned. "They're tired and crabby." He shot a quick glance in the parlor. "Much the same as here, I imagine."

"Don't start, Brady," Patrick called. "The battle for my pride has already been won."

Brady grinned as he gave Marcy a hug. He wandered over to slap Patrick on the back. "Well, you look good, if it's any consolation. How are you feeling?"

Patrick attempted a smile. "Does it matter? I'm confined to house arrest for the next two and a half months whether I like it or not."

"Mmm . . . let me see if I can drum up some sympathy here." Katie tapped a finger to her chin and pursed her lips. "That's shorter than my confinement this summer, if I'm not mistaken."

A smile twisted on her father's lips. "Yes, but you forget that you deserved it, and I don't. And at least you got out of the house every week, to work at the BCAS."

Katie's gaze shifted to Brady. "Speaking of the BCAS, do you have any idea what's going on? Luke's been downright evasive lately. I talked to him on the phone several times, but we haven't seen him for almost two weeks. And now he says he has to work late every night this week and won't be able to visit Gabe or tutor me."

The smile in Brady's eyes instantly sobered. His gaze shifted to Gabe and back. "He's got a lot on his mind right now, I think." He hesitated, then squeezed Patrick's shoulder before heading toward Katie with concern in his eyes. "I'll help you get those lemonades."

Her smile stiffened as Brady ushered her through the swinging door. As soon as she was on the other side, she spun around. "What's wrong?"

He studied her with pensive eyes, as if gauging how much to say. "I thought you knew. Luke told me he was going to tell you."

"Tell me what?"

Brady drew in a deep breath and released it. "He gave his notice to Parker last week."

"What? Why?"

"He's taken a job with the Children's Aid Society in Philadelphia."

Katie just stared, her heart thudding to a stop.

"I can't go into any detail, but Luke's taking Betty to live with her aunt because of personal problems here in Boston."

"For how long?"

Brady moved to the icebox to pull out the lemonade, then fished two glasses from the cabinet. He filled each with ice slowly, assessing Katie from across the room. "For good."

Katie tried to gasp, but the air welded to her throat.

"I didn't want to say anything in front of Gabe because I think Luke should handle it. But as close as you two have gotten, I thought you should know."

Pain like the thrust of a knife almost doubled her in two, gutting her good mood as she glazed into a hard stare. *No, God, he couldn't . . .* She closed her eyes, envisioning the man who had given her so much through his friendship. Didn't he know she needed him? Relied on him? He was everything to her—the tutor she depended on, the cohort she confided in, the friend she cared for. Her eyes suddenly flipped open in shock.

And the man I love?

The air thinned in her throat as the awful truth struck. She put a hand to her head, dizzy with the realization that it was Luke she relied on, not Jack. Luke who quickened her spirit with prayer, and Luke who stirred her pulse with the lift of his smile . . .

And the heat of his kiss?

She swallowed hard, comprehension seeping in to numb both her body and her brain. Luke—always Luke—by her side when she'd needed him most . . .

The cold grip of reality strangled in her throat. How could she have been so blind? She moved to the counter like a zombie and closed her eyes again, unwilling to see the truth for what it was, and yet unable to escape its painful presence. Images of Cluny McGee and the man he'd become flashed before her, and with a quickening in her spirit and her pulse, the truth she'd evaded so long finally set her free. *God, help me . . . could I be in love with Luke McGee?* And then suddenly nothing mattered more. Not Jack, not law school, not rising to the top for whatever cause she held dear. From the moment that her father had flirted with death, everything had shifted in her brain. She opened her eyes, and like a lens to a blind eye, it all came into true focus. Her heart started to race. She was in love with Luke McGee! And he was in love with her.

"Katie, are you all right?" Brady studied her with concern.

She nodded and then glanced at the clock. Six-fifteen—she could still catch him at the office. Working her lip, she hurried over to pour the lemonade, then grabbed her mother's pot holders. She removed the casserole from the oven and put it in the box her mother had prepared, next to the rolls. She retrieved the salad from the icebox and partitioned it with several of Marcy's dishtowels. Her mind—and her heart—were racing as she lifted the lemonades from the counter and handed one to Brady with a shaky grin. "Your dinner is all ready—don't forget it when you leave. And give Lizzie my love, okay?"

He took the lemonade and smiled, a curious look in his eyes. "Thanks, Katie. Mind if I ask why you looked like death a few minutes ago and now you're glowing?"

She made her way to the door with Gabe's lemonade in hand, shooting a smile over her shoulder. "Sure, Brady. You might say I'm looking forward to giving Luke McGee a healthy piece of my mind, that's all." She butted through the door, pulse racing. *And my heart.*

"You don't have to do this, you know—kill yourself for the cause." Parker plunged his hands in his pockets and cocked a hip against Luke's door, his voice wistful. "Once you and Betty leave, I won't have anything better to do than work."

Luke glanced up from the legal documents he was determined to finalize and managed a tired smile. "Sure you will. I'll bet Betty's replacement has lots of ideas of things you can do."

Parker groaned and lumbered in, dropping into the chair in front of Luke's desk. He passed a hand through sandy hair normally so neat and manicured, and muddled it with an uncustomary gouge of his fingers. "It's bad enough I have to lose my two best friends, but I have to put up with Carmichael's niece on top of it. I don't think the woman can even spell."

A grin creased Luke's lips as he signed a document with a flourish and tossed it in the basket. "Come on, Parker, what she doesn't have in brains, she makes up for in looks. And she certainly likes you. Who knows, maybe you can marry her and hire somebody who can spell."

"Very funny, McGee." He rested his head on the back of the chair and closed his eyes. "If only I could hire somebody like Bets or Katie." He paused, his eyelids opening a fraction of an inch. "And speaking of Katie . . . have you told her or Gabe yet?"

Humor faded quickly from Luke's mood. His jaw tightened as he reached for another stack of contracts. "Not yet, but I will."

Parker didn't even blink. "When . . . after you leave?"

Luke's eyes narrowed. "I've been busy."

"Yeah, I know—avoiding the inevitable. You're leaving in three days. Don't you think it's time?"

A sigh loaded with guilt rolled from his lips. He glanced away, absently taking in the clutter of sports paraphernalia he still had to pack. "Yeah. I just didn't think it would be this hard." He kneaded his temple with the heel of his hand. "I'm taking Gabe to Robinson's on Saturday afternoon. I'll see if Katie can join us and tell them both then."

Parker nodded and rose to his feet. "That would be good—I know you two have gotten to be close friends. You almost done? I've got papers to go over yet and Betty ran the monthly report up to Carmichael, but as soon as we're both through, we'll be heading home."

"Yeah, just let me know when you're ready, and I'll head out too, okay?"

"Ahem . . ." A feminine voice drifted in from the door.

Parker spun around while Luke froze, signature mid-scrawl.

"Parker Riley—are you working this man to the bone before he leaves you high and dry?" Katie stood on the threshold with arms crossed and lips pursed, a definite glint in her eyes. Her gaze shifted to Luke and narrowed. "And speaking of leaving, how were you planning on breaking the news, McGee—in a Christmas card?"

Parker shot him a glance of sympathy before heading to the door and giving Katie a hug. "It's good to see you, Katie, it's been too long. How is your father doing?"

She hugged him back. "Weak, but he's improving every day, Parker, thanks." Her lips veered to the right. "His health, that is." She folded her arms again and scalded Luke with a look. "His disposition is failing, I'm afraid." Her manicured brow lifted to hazardous heights. "Kind of like mine at the moment."

Parker smiled and eased out the door. "Uh, well, I'll let

you two talk, then. Don't be a stranger, Katie." The door shut behind him with an ominous click.

"I was going to tell you, Katie, I promise, but I've been so busy . . ."

She strolled forward with hands on her hips and sparks in her eyes, her petite frame actually daunting as she loomed over his desk. "I'll say. It's hard work lying to your friends."

"I didn't lie—"

She leaned in, palms splayed wide on the edge of his desk. "You didn't tell the truth!"

"That's not fair. You've had a lot on your mind with your father. I just didn't want to add to the mix." He dropped his pen on his desk and pressed his hand to his eyes, massaging his forehead. "Besides, I was going to tell you and Gabe on Saturday."

She straightened her shoulders and nodded slowly. "Oh . . . I see, Saturday, yes, that would be good." She lunged forward, knuckles white on his desk once again. "If it wasn't two weeks after the fact!"

He shot to his feet, his own temper on the rise. "Look, Katie, we're friends, but I don't need your permission for what I do with my life."

"And just exactly what are you doing with your life, Luke? Tell me, as your *friend*, am I entitled to know that?"

He exhaled and, his head down, worked the back of his neck, his eyes lidded with guilt. "Yes, yes, you are, and I apologize for not telling you and Gabe sooner, but I've . . ." He looked up then, facing her square on, determined to get the truth out. "I've taken a job in Philadelphia."

"So I've heard. What I haven't heard is why."

He stared at the proud lift of her chin and the blue eyes that glinted with anger and more than a little hurt, and a dull ache throbbed in his chest. "Betty's in trouble. I have to get her out of Boston, so I'm taking her to live with her aunt." His gaze returned to the document beneath his hand, studying it without really seeing it. He snatched his pen up and signed the bottom line.

"What kind of trouble?" Worry threaded her tone.

He glanced up, unwilling to divulge the depth of Betty's problems, but well aware of Katie's bulldog tenacity. "Ex-boyfriend trouble. The slime has a tendency to beat her up."

Concern lighted in Katie's eyes, and she swallowed again. "So take her and come back."

"I can't do that," he whispered.

"Why?"

"Because she needs me." He scratched his signature hard and fast, like a blind man with pen and paper, his name as unreadable as the stone expression on Katie's face.

In the next slash of his pen, she rounded the desk and stood by his side, her hand trembling as it rested on his arm. Shock coursed through him as he looked up to see that indomitable chin start to waver and those steady blue eyes begin to blink with moisture. "I understand, Luke. So take Betty and get her settled in and come back. Because I need you too."

Something clutched in his chest and he put the pen down and stood, skimming her arms with his hands. "Katie, I'll visit you and Gabe whenever I can, I promise. Philadelphia's only a little over five hours away by bus and less than four by train. Besides, I have a feeling you're going to be so busy with school and the wedding, you won't even miss me."

In nervous habit, she scraped her lower lip with her teeth while a tiny wrinkle puckered at the ridge of her brow, actions he'd long become familiar with whenever wheels were turning in her head. All at once, a death knell rang in his brain at the lift of her lashes, revealing a scared and skittish little girl with a glimmer of hope in her eyes. That deadly look of vulnerability that always took him down. A look that jerked a hook in his heart and reeled him in, confirming what he'd always hoped for, prayed for—tough, independent Katie O'Connor needed him, wanted him. The realization pasted his tongue to the roof of his mouth, dryer than dust.

His pulse seized as she slipped tentative arms around his waist, her manner shy, and then took off in a frenzy when she moved forward, her body grazing his. Her eyes held gentle promise, offering gifts he'd only dreamed about. "Luke," she whispered, "don't leave me, please. I need you . . ."

Blood pounded in his body like a tide surging through his veins, hot and hungry as her hands drew him close. His breathing was heavy and his reflexes slow and sluggish, as if she had cast a spell, paralyzing him with her touch. In slow motion, her gaze melded to his lips and she slowly lifted on tiptoe to take his mouth with her own.

"Katie, no!" He gripped her arms so tight, she winced, and his body shook as he held her at arm's length. "I can't stay! I wish I could, but I can't." His voice rushed from his lips, desperate to make her understand. "Betty's pregnant . . . her ex-boyfriend raped her, and he'll hurt her if she stays. She's in serious trouble, Katie, and I can't let her do this alone."

Hurt swam in her eyes. "But I'm in trouble too, Luke." Her hands bent to grasp the arms that held her at bay, thumbs stroking his wrists. "You can't leave now, *please*, not when I—" With a broken sob, she fell against his chest, clasping him tightly as she wept.

"What do you mean you're in trouble?" He held her away, his pulse pounding in his brain like a painful echo warning of doom. Other than the night he'd taken her father to the hospital, never had he seen Katie O'Connor cry before, but she may as well have lanced him with a knife—he was bleeding all the same.

She looked up then, her body quivering with short, little heaves while tragedy pooled in her eyes. "I . . . I think I'm in love with you, Luke, and I don't want you to go . . ."

His body went to stone.

"Please say something," Katie whispered. Her fingers curled against his wrists once again and her eyes begged him to respond as he had once before. But he only stared, his eyes glazed with shock and those wide lips—the lips she longed to kiss—parted with shallow breaths.

He released her too quickly and backed away, eyes steeped in pain. "Katie, I . . . I'm sorry, but everything's arranged." A lump shifted in his throat. "We're leaving on Sunday."

Fear iced her skin. "But you said you loved me once, told me you wanted me." Panic rose in her chest, quivering her voice and betraying her alarm. "Was that a lie?"

A nerve pulsed at the edge of his jaw. "No, it wasn't a lie."

Terror restricted the flow of her air, making her feel faint. She forced the words from her tongue, frail as they drifted from her lips. "But you . . . you don't love me like that anymore, is that it?" Her gaze fell to the stretch of floor between them, unwilling to witness the truth in his eyes.

"I can't answer that."

Her head jolted up. "You can!" she cried, hysteria tingeing her tone. "Tell me now, Luke—tell me if it's true. Do you still love me?"

He looked away, shoulders bent. "Yes."

"Then stay!" she said, every nerve and muscle straining within. She took a step forward, her voice an impassioned plea. "Take Betty to Philadelphia and come back to me, please."

He stared, breaking her heart with his eyes. "Katie, I can't."

"But you can—" She stepped forward to clutch him with a sob.

His hands were warm when he grasped her arms, but the dread they instilled was as cold as death. "No, Katie, I can't," he whispered. "I'm taking Betty to Philadelphia for good . . ." His eyes shimmered with grief as he braced her. "As my wife."

Her world slowed to a stop, body numb and all air depleted from her lungs. She couldn't feel her skin or her limbs, only a dull ache in her chest that seemed to grow as his face blurred before her. She was vaguely aware of his hands on her arms, caressing her, comforting her, and her eyes trailed to them in a daze, almost seeing the gold band that would sever their love. She closed her eyes, and her heart reeled at the shock. Luke McGee wed to another—the man who had stolen her friendship and captured her heart, wooed her with prayer and stirred her with passion. A strange buzzing filled her brain, and her tongue was paralyzed, unable to release the agony of her soul.

His wife.

Betty, not her . . . wearing his ring, sharing his bed, bearing his children.

A soul mate lost forever.

She swayed on her feet, and he steadied her, his voice fading in her ears . . .

"Parker!" He picked her up and set her in a chair. Words, distant and faint, pierced her consciousness as her eyelids weighted closed. "Get me a wet rag. She's white as a ghost."

Movement . . . hovering . . . voices tugging as something heavy pulled her toward the dark.

"Katie!" Her eyelids flickered open at the touch of cool to her cheek. "Are you okay?"

She licked her lips and struggled to focus, her eyes expanding at the sight of blue eyes that pierced and freckles she now loved. And that was when she knew.

She would never be okay again.

There was nothing more to say. He had wanted to walk her home, but she couldn't bear it. And so he asked Parker to take her back instead—to a life now void of Luke McGee. It was all arranged, Parker said—Father Mac was to marry them on Sunday following mass, a simple ceremony with only Parker and Bobbie Sue in attendance. And then Luke and his bride would board their train for Philly, where Luke would start work the next day.

Katie put a hand to her eyes, every step home taking her deeper into an abyss, a dark, gaping hole where she drowned in her own tears, salty with sorrow. She wept for blocks before uttering the phrase that had ruined her life. "I-I l-love him, Parker," she said with a heave, her voice nasal and her words mere steam that drifted away like her hope into the frigid night air.

"I know, Katie," he said. His voice girded her with the same tenderness as the strong arm that now braced her, holding her tightly as he led her through the dark. "And he loves you."

"Then, why?" The warmth of that awful word billowed into the November night to die in the cold.

Parker's answer was spoken with kindness, but its meaning was cruel. "Luke knows the pain of an illegitimate birth, Katie . . . He's determined Betty's baby will not." He paused then, perhaps hesitant to add to her grief. His grip tightened, as if to prop her to hear the truth. "And he felt he had nothing to lose since you were to marry Jack."

An icy gust slapped her hair across her face. She stared at the diamond on her finger, its gleam as cold as the shivers that traveled her spine. The wind whistled through the trees, and its eerie sound seemed to mock her for the fool that she'd been. She took the ring off and dropped it into her pocket with a violent shudder. "Nothing to lose . . . ," she said quietly, a chasm of grief splitting her heart. "Except a cherished piece of our souls."

They walked in silence for a while, until Parker broke it with a monotone voice, low and edged with intent, as if pleading her case to a jury. "Don't blame yourself, Katie. Luke has other demons to wrestle as well."

She gave him a sideways glance, his sculpted jaw blurred through her tears. "Like what?"

He tightened his hold around her shoulders. "Like guilt." His eyes met hers. "You know anything about Luke and Betty's past?"

She shook her head.

"Well, they've been like blood since they met on the streets of New York almost seven years ago, two throwaway kids with no family of their own, or at least any who cared."

Katie sniffed. "But what about Betty's aunt? Doesn't she care?"

"Yeah, she'll give them a roof for a while, but not for long, and Luke knows that. And the last thing he wants is for Betty to find herself on the streets again. He feels too responsible."

"But, why? She's a friend, not a responsibility."

His low chuckle echoed in the air, the sound too harsh for Parker. "Yeah, well, with Luke, it's one and the same, I'm afraid. And like I said, there's the guilt. She was a sister to him, although that changed for Betty as they got older. And one night a few years back, she proved it, when both she and Luke were too drunk to care—she slept with him."

Katie's breath caught in her throat.

"Luke felt awful, but guilty too, enough to keep the relationship the way it was for a few months, hoping it would work. But it didn't because he wanted her as a sister, not a lover, so he broke it off, both their intimacies and their friendship. It nearly killed them both, of course, but especially Betty. Which is why scum like Leo was able to draw her in so easily. And when Leo found out she was carrying Luke's baby—"

"No!" Katie stopped, her feet grafted to the sidewalk in shock.

Parker squeezed her again and started walking, tugging her along. "I'm afraid so. Even though she and Luke finally patched up their relationship, Luke could see that Leo was no good for her, but Betty refused to leave him. You can imagine how Luke felt when he discovered Leo was not only beating up on Betty, but that he'd caused her to miscarry a baby—a baby Luke didn't know was his until two years later. Suddenly protecting Betty, making it up to her, became the most important thing in his life. You see, Katie, family is everything to Luke. He's never had any to speak of except Betty, Brady, and me."

"How . . . did it happen—this pregnancy?" Her tongue was thick in her throat, as if reluctant to pursue the truth. She swallowed hard. "I know it was Leo, but how . . . when?"

Parker's sigh swirled up and away into the cold, cold night. "It was Luke's turn to pick her up from Robinson's that night—she worked there some evenings, you know, which is why Luke was jerking sodas the night you two met—he was filling in for her. Apparently Roberta—Leo's cousin that we met that night at Kearney's—told her friend Dot all about Leo and Betty. Unfortunately, Dot has a thing for Leo and used the information as a means of getting him down here. He came to town then with the intention of getting back with Betty, only she turned him down." His voice hardened considerably. "So he raped her." Parker's voice, suddenly so foreign, made her shiver. "And unfortunately, Luke, who usually has a phobia about being on time, was actually late for once in his life."

"Why, God? Of all nights, why then?" she whispered, not really expecting an answer.

The hand on her arm tightened while the pressure of his thumb grazed back and forth as if to numb the pain of his words. "Because," he said, his voice so low she barely heard it, "he was with you that night, Katie, the night he told you he loved you."

A gasp shuddered in Katie's throat, and her body froze to the spot. Tears welled in her eyes as a hand flew to her mouth. "No, please . . ."

Parker pulled her close. "I only tell you, Katie, to let you know—guilt had Luke by the throat, and in his mind, he has no choice but to marry Betty."

She felt depleted when they finally arrived at her house, as if her grief had robbed her of all sensation, all energy, all hope. Parker quietly opened the gate and walked her to her porch, his arm steady and solid around her shoulder. At the door he reached into his pocket and handed her his handkerchief, watching her through tender eyes as she blew her nose.

With a final sniff, she gave him a weak smile. "I'll wash this and get it back to you."

"I have more," he said softly, studying her with concern. "Anytime you need them."

She nodded and looked up, finally seeing the man whose losses were as great as hers. She placed a trembling palm to his cheek and blinked to clear the blur from her eyes. "I'm so sorry, Parker—your hurt must be as deep as mine."

He cupped a warm palm over hers, pressing her hand to the bristle now shadowing his jaw. "Not quite, Katie, but it's there."

Her lips trembled. "Oh, Parker, what are we going to do?"

He blinked, and she saw a glint of moisture before he pulled her to his chest and rested his head against hers. "We're going to pray, Katie—for Luke, for Betty, and for ourselves. And we're going to survive and move on. And do you know how I know?"

She shook her head, her cheek rubbing against the rough weave of his coat. The low timbre of his voice was gentle and kind and sure—like the man who now stroked her hair.

"Because God answers prayer," he whispered, "and he takes care of his own." He kissed the top of her head and opened the door. "I'll be praying for you, Katie. And if you ever need a shoulder to cry on—or anything—you know where I am. Good night."

"Good night, Parker." She slipped inside and closed the door, tears welling anew.

"Katie? Is that you?"

Her heart skipped a beat. The anxiety in her mother's words drove every other thought from her mind. She rushed into the parlor, alarmed to see her father dressed in his pajamas at this early hour and lying on his bed. "What is it? Is Father all right?"

"I'm fine, Katie Rose, just tired," her father said in a voice that confirmed his weariness.

Marcy's eyes sought hers, clouded with worry. "He had another incident tonight."

"Marcy, it was probably just heartburn—"

"You had pains in your chest for almost five minutes, Patrick, you were dizzy and sweating and couldn't catch your breath—that's not heartburn."

Katie rushed to the side of his bed, her manner as nervous as Marcy's. "Did you do something, Father? Attempt the stairs, smoke your pipe?"

Marcy's tone was stern, in stark contrast to the gentle quiver of her hand against his brow. "He bribed Gabe to give him the newspaper after I went upstairs to ready her bath. The next thing I know, she's flying up the stairs screaming that he was having another attack."

"I tell you, I'm fine—" The gray pallor of his cheeks defied the truth of his words.

"You're not fine!" she shrieked. Tears pooled in her eyes as she worked to soften her tone. "Your heart is weak right now, Patrick, and you refuse to take that seriously."

"I do take that seriously—"

"No—you don't! Did you take your pill today?"

His lips gummed into a straight line.

"Have you even taken it any day this week?"

His jaw, dark with stubble, hardened along with his voice. "I tell you, I don't need it—"

"You do need it!" Her fist slammed the bed, jostling his leg. "Am I to be your warden every minute of every day? Is your love so insignificant you refuse to see how this destroys me?"

"Marcy, I'm sorry—the pill makes me dizzy and restless, and I didn't need it before."

"Well, you need it now, and if you don't start following the doctor's orders, it will kill me as well as you." She started to cry, and he attempted to rise from the bed, his face pale from the effort. She pressed him back with a firm hand. "No! You will not rise from this bed tonight unless you need to use the bathroom, is that clear?" She shot Katie a look tempered with steel. "Katie, get me the family Bible from the bookcase, please."

Katie handed the book to her mother, and Marcy laid it on Patrick's chest. She jerked his hand up and placed it on top. "Swear to me now, Patrick, before God and your daughter that you will take your medication every day for the rest of your life . . . that you will not use the stairs, exert yourself with any undue activity, smoke your pipe, listen to the news or read the paper—"

"Marcy, I'm the editor of the *Herald*, for pity's sake, I have to read the paper—"

"Which triggered your angina when you saw the extent of the market crash, did it not?"

He seemed to sink into the bed at the pain of her words. He closed his eyes and swallowed hard, the realization obviously sapping his will.

"Swear, Patrick—*now*—no radio or newspaper until Dr. Williamson releases you."

Katie stared at her father—so handsome and so strong—and yet now so much older than he'd ever seemed before. All at once she saw the glint of silver in his hair, the slight sag of his jaw, and dark shadows that circled beneath defeated eyes. When he finally spoke, his voice was barely a whisper.

"I swear, Marcy, before God and you—I will do everything the doctor says."

She removed the Bible and stood, clutching it in her arms. "I trust you, Patrick, something you've not made easy for me these last few weeks. But I know you will not lie to God, so I take my peace from that." She set the Bible on the coffee table and tugged at the blanket folded at the bottom of his bed, tucking it in and pulling it up to his chin. "Do you need a drink or have to use the bathroom before Katie and I head up?"

He didn't answer, but simply jerked the cover loose and pushed it away before closing his eyes and resting clasped hands on his chest.

Marcy leaned to press a kiss to his lips, and her heart clutched at his lack of response. "Good night, Patrick. I love you."

"Good night, Father, I love you too," Katie whispered, brushing a kiss to his cheek.

"Good night, Katie Rose," he said quietly before turning on his side and shutting them both out.

Tears stung her eyes as Marcy doused the lights and mounted the stairs with her daughter.

"I guess Gabe's in bed?" Katie asked, her voice sounding as drained as Marcy felt.

"Yes, the poor thing was so guilt-ridden over sneaking the newspaper to your father that she disappeared rather quickly, sound asleep before I could even kiss her good night." Marcy gave her a sideways glance. "Did you get to talk to Luke like you'd hoped?"

Katie nodded.

The puffy eyes and mottled cheeks suddenly caught Marcy's eye. She put a hand to Katie's arm. "Is everything okay?"

Katie shook her head, dislodging several tears from her lashes.

Marcy halted her on the steps. "Tell me what happened."

Katie whisked away the tears as she squared her shoulders, attempting a smile. "Nothing that can't wait till morning, Mother. We both have enough on our minds right now with Father. But I'll fill you in tomorrow, I promise."

Marcy touched a palm to Katie's cheek, too fatigued to argue. "It will all work out, Katie, trust me. God has never failed us yet."

Katie nodded and gave her a hug. "I know. I've always depended on your and Father's faith, but I suppose it's time I learn for myself. Good night, Mother. Try to sleep, okay?"

With a depleted sigh, Marcy watched as Katie headed to her room, then forced herself into the bathroom where she went through the motions of brushing her teeth and washing her face. She put her silk nightgown on, the one she'd taken to wearing since the awful change, and then welcomed the cool of the sheets as she slipped into her lonely bed. Laying her head on the pillow, she was suddenly overcome by Patrick's scent, strong in the room. She closed her eyes, and tears dampened her cheeks as musk and pipe tobacco taunted her senses.

So much more than her body temperature had changed of late. Chaos reigned—not only in the tumult of her emotions, but in the well-being of her family and the stability of the world as they knew it. Bent on keeping Patrick from the stress of the dire economy, Marcy had taken to hiding the *Herald* from her husband daily, only reading it herself, with trepidation, in the confines of their bedroom. But the news tightened her stomach and rattled her faith. She knew little about the stock market or Patrick's dalliance with it, but on October 29, while her husband lay weak in the hospital, her knowledge expanded considerably, along with her fear.

More than 16 million shares had been traded that day, culminating in a paralyzing drop in the market in less than two months, and overnight, a frightening pall had settled over the country. Prominent companies and financial institutions collapsed, their company stock worthless and their futures bleak. The financial world was in crisis, and from the knots in Marcy's stomach, she knew that her family was too.

Dear God, what does the future hold? Worry leaked from her eyes, staining her pillow and weighting her heart. Like many others, her husband had invested—and lost—a fortune and was now out of work, at least for the next two and a half months. Their savings had been bled dry, and their future hung in the balance. Fear skittered her spine like the deadliest of parasites, threatening to suck the life from her soul. She tucked legs to her chest while dread stifled her air.

Though I walk in the midst of trouble, thou wilt revive me . . .

Marcy stilled on her pillow, the passage from her morning missal lighting upon her mind as quietly as the near-silent tick of the clock, whose steady rhythm now matched that of her heart. *Thou wilt revive me . . .*

She breathed in the thought, inhaling it deeply, thoroughly, desperate for the calm of God's Word . . . his promises.

I will never leave thee, nor forsake thee.

Fresh tears swelled in her eyes, rushing forth from a well-spring of hope. She clutched her pillow, overcome with his peace. *Oh, God, what would I do without you?*

Her mind strayed to Patrick, downstairs and alone, and her heart seized in her chest. Hurling the covers aside, she bounded from the bed and raced down the hall. Cheeks flushed with warmth, she chewed on her lip as she scurried down the steps like Gabe so often did. Her bare feet were silent as she padded to where he lay, a shadowed lump facing the wall. With a rush of love, she eased under the covers on a sliver of bed, spooning him close with arms to his waist.

He jolted from his sleep with a grunt. "Marcy? What are you doing?"

She pressed a gentle kiss to his neck, reveling in the scent of him, the man God had blessed her with for better or for worse. The worse may well be upon them, but they would not face it alone. No, they would have each other, two frail human beings clasped tightly to the hand of God. *A threefold cord not quickly broken.*

"Patrick, forgive me, please—I just want to hold you a while."

He turned in the bed then, shifting to make room for her as he pulled her close. With a low moan, he buried his head in the crook of her neck, his lips tender and his words thick with emotion. "God knows how I love you, Marceline."

The warmth of his words brought a smile to her lips. "We

will get through this, Patrick, we will—one day and one prayer at a time."

"I know, darlin'," he whispered. Peace settled as they lay in each other's arms, the sound of Patrick's prayers warm in her ear. When he finished, they rested a long while, her body languid and lazy as it molded to his.

Drowsy with relaxation, her eyes popped open when Patrick jerked in her arms and snorted in his sleep. A tender smile tugged at her lips as the snoring rose in volume, warming her heart with the blessed sound. "I love you, Patrick O'Connor," she whispered in the dark, her words drowned out by the nasal rasping from her husband's open mouth. "And as far as your snoring, I give you my word . . ." She sidled closer and breathed in the scent of him, his body lulling her to sleep with its glorious warmth. "I will never complain again."

18

Luke stared out his bedroom window, body numb and eyes glazed in a hard stare. The lamppost across the street blurred into a halo of light, foggy and out of focus—like his mind at the moment—and as dim and surreal as this nightmare that wouldn't end.

The scene in his office replayed, and the tragic turn of events twisted his gut once again.

"I . . . I think I'm in love with you, Luke . . ."

He slumped at his desk, hand to his eyes, never believing those words could have caused him such pain. She wanted him to stay, but he had promised to go. Two women who stirred the love in his heart . . . but only one who stirred his passion.

He closed his eyes, and thoughts of Betty were immediate, producing an ache so deep, more tears welled beneath his lids. Like him, she had lived in the gutter all of her life. Not just in the streets of New York, but in the littered ruts of destiny as well, where life denied her any chance at happiness. A father killed in the war and a destitute mother, a stepfather who thrived on abuse, and a lover who took it a step further.

The result was a baby destined to be born a bastard, and a friend who had vowed it would never happen. Betty and he were blood, not in the literal sense of heritage, but in the true sense of all they had shared . . . as friends . . . as family . . . *as lovers*. Grief pierced anew, and the emotion shifted in his throat. Brady and the O'Connors had taught him well. Luke had little or no experience with family, but one thing he knew to the core of his being—family didn't desert family . . . not in their time of need.

He opened his eyes, and Katie's image filled his thoughts, unleashing a slash of sorrow in his heart unlike any he'd experienced before. She was everything he'd ever wanted . . . and now something he could never have, and the reality of that bitter truth settled on his mind like a mantle of despair. He had hurt her, and the realization cut him to the quick. But the scales had been weighed, and justice demanded its balance—Katie had a family to get her through this . . . while Betty had none until his ring was on her hand. Katie had a fiancé to make her dreams come true . . . while Betty had a friend who might just keep her nightmares away.

A knock sounded, and Luke jerked in the chair, knowing full well that Betty waited on the other side. He rose and rolled his shoulders to shift the kinks from his neck, then drew in a deep breath and strode to the door. He opened it with a practiced smile that was wide and relaxed, perusing Betty's housecoat from head to toe. "Hey, you're supposed to be in bed—we have a big day tomorrow."

Ignoring his smile, she slipped past him, turning only when she reached the middle of his room. When she did, the agony on her face matched that in his gut, and he took an abrupt step forward. "Bets, are you all right . . . is the baby . . ."

She halted him with a hand in the air, eyes rimmed red and a quiver in her lip. "Fine, Luke, we're both fine."

He moved forward. "Then what's wrong—"

"No!" The harsh sound of her voice froze him to the spot

as she waved him away. "Please, don't come any closer . . . this is hard enough as it is."

Sweat beaded on the back of his neck. He slammed the door shut. "Bets, you're scaring me—what's wrong?"

She put a fist to her mouth and began to shake her head while tears glimmered in her eyes. "It's no good, Luke . . ."

"What's no good?" he whispered, and strain cracked in his voice.

A single tear trailed her cheek. "You and me—married. It won't work."

He ignored her protest and charged forward, steering her to sit on his bed. When she started to sob, he sat down beside her and swallowed her up in a hug. "It will work. I love you, Bets, and I'll love your baby. We can do this, we can make a life for your child."

She jerked from his embrace and jumped up, then distanced herself several steps and turned to face him, arms gripped to her waist. The chin lifted and the tears slowed. "Katie . . . she left crying tonight. Why?"

"What?" He stood to his feet, heart pounding and heat gorging his neck.

"You heard me. Something upset Katie pretty badly at the office tonight. She was sobbing in Parker's arms when I passed them in the hall. I want to know why."

He stared, heat bleeding into his cheeks. Moving forward, he raised his hand to touch her shoulder, then halted when she took a step back. With a deep swallow of air, he forced his body to relax, absently flexing his fingers. "She's just upset, Bets . . . we're all good friends, and she's not happy we're moving away." He shoved his hands in his pockets, avoiding her gaze. "Besides, I've been going to see Gabe every week and tutoring Katie as well, so naturally we've gotten pretty close."

"She's in love with you, isn't she?"

The heat in his cheeks swallowed him whole, burning up into the roots of his hair. His throat constricted and he looked up, unwilling to lie, yet loathe to confirm her statement.

"I thought so," she whispered.

He winced at the anguish he saw in her face.

She moved to the window like a sleepwalker, staring into oblivion like he had only moments before. "I never really saw it, I guess, because she hides her feelings so well . . . but then maybe I really didn't want to either." She turned, her composure intact once again as she stood, straight and tall, eyes fused to his. "This changes everything, Luke."

"Why?" His voice was a choked rasp as he took a step forward. "You still need a friend to get you through this, and your baby still needs a father. Katie will get over this. She has Jack—she'll move on."

She stared, her eyes betraying her hurt despite the proud lift of her chin. Her voice was a fragile whisper. "Will you?"

Her question took him by surprise and he blinked, desperate to put her off. He straightened his shoulders and folded his arms. "Katie and I are friends, Bets, nothing more."

"That doesn't answer my question, Luke. Are you in love with her?"

He sucked in a deep breath, the casual manner he'd been striving for suddenly crashing to his feet. With a heavy sigh, he mauled his face with his hand, then slacked his stance, propping his hands low on his hips. He studied her through lidded eyes, a touch of frustration in his tone. "Of course I love her, Bets . . . just like I love you, which is why I refuse to let you do this alone."

Tears welled in her eyes. "No, Luke, not just like you love me. Oh, yes, I know you love me, and I know how much. Enough to give your life for me—which is exactly what you're doing."

"You're being ridicu—"

"No!" she screamed, her eyes brimming with pain. "You forget I know you, Luke, every hair on your head, every mole on your body . . . every thought in your brain." She shook her head, her gaze tender with affection. "Don't you know, McGee? One look at your face, and I can read you. I didn't want to face it, but deep down I knew it was true, and you never even had to say a word. You've been in love with Katie O'Connor since she first walked through our door."

"Bets—"

She cut him off, her eyes glazing into a hard stare. "Of course, at first I was hurt . . . and then I found myself hurting for you because I knew she had her sights set on Jack. Then you offered to move to Philadelphia with me, and I thought—yes! This could be good for him, spare him the torment of being around someone he wants but can't have." She looked up then, her eyes naked with love. Her voice dropped to a feeble whisper. "Because I know what that's like, Luke, and I love you too much to watch it happen to you."

He swallowed hard, unable to speak for the ache in his throat. He'd always known she loved him that way, but he hadn't realized the pain she'd endured. Tamping down her own desires to extend friendship instead, making it easy for him, comfortable. Just like he'd done for Katie. Realization throbbed inside like an exposed nerve, and his shoulders slumped as he put a hand to his eyes.

"So you see, McGee, as bullheaded as you are, it won't work. I can't let you marry me when it's Katie you love." A whispery sigh wavered from her lips as she attempted a sad smile. "Not when she's in love with you too."

He shook his head. "You weren't there, Bets. You don't know that she loves me."

A corner of her lip edged up. "Sure I do, McGee. I badgered Parker till he spilled. And from the sound of it, the woman's even further gone than me." She managed to hike a brow. "What can I say? You're a bona fide lady-killer." She strolled over and patted him on the cheek, her poise almost fully restored. "Come on, Luke, for once in your life, embrace the moment."

She started for the door, and he tugged her back, leveling both palms on her shoulders. He made a poor attempt at a confident grin. "I am embracing the moment, Bets. I'm going to marry my best friend and live happily ever after with her and our baby."

Tears welled in her eyes, and he pulled her into his arms and buried his head in her neck. "Aw, Bets, I love you, and you love me. Maybe we're not where a marriage should be yet, but we'll get there, I promise. And in the meantime, your baby will have a father." He closed his eyes tightly, shutting thoughts of Katie out at the same time. When he spoke, his whisper was gruff with emotion. "And with God's help, Galetti, for the first time in our lives, you and I will have a real family."

She pushed him back and shook her head, the glimmer of tears once again glazing her eyes. "No, Luke, I can't let you do that."

He cocked a brow. "Yeah? And just how are you going to stop me? I have a train ticket with a seat next to yours and a job at the Children's Aid Society in Philly starting Monday. And if I'm the lady-killer you say I am, I'm pretty sure I can coax Aunt Ruth into letting me stay with her too . . . especially since she's expecting her newlywed niece and her husband.

A ghost of a smile shadowed her mouth despite the tears streaking her face. "Luke . . ."

He pressed a palm to her lips, stilling her with a look. "No argument, Galetti—I'm still your superior till the end of the week." He leaned in to press a kiss to her cheek, then wriggled his brows "And come Sunday, I'll be your husband, and then you'll never have any say."

She flicked his hand away with a smirk. "Now why would I marry a tyrant like you?"

He tapped a finger to her chin. "Because you need me, Galetti."

Her eyes softened, and she traced a hand along his jaw, her tone suddenly serious. "I do need you, Luke, I won't lie. I'm scared to death to go to Philly by myself, to face Aunt Ruth and to . . ." A lump shifted in her throat as she skimmed a hand across the burgeoning mound of her abdomen. "To bring new life into the world." She shivered, and he bundled her in his arms, stroking her hair. "I . . . I don't think I could do this alone . . . ," she whispered.

"Well, you won't have to. I'll be there every step of the way."

She twined her arms around his waist and squeezed hard, her fingers clenched to his back. "Oh, Luke, I love you so much, and I need you, I do." She pulled away to look him dead in the eye, her smile as tight and firm as her grip. "But only as a friend, understood? No marriage. Aunt Ruth will put you up while you see me and the baby through. But when it's over, McGee, I'll have Aunt Ruth kick you out on your ear so fast, you're gonna think *you* went through labor." The edge of her mouth curled up. "And then you can hightail it home to Katie . . . that is, if she'll still have you."

He threaded his fingers through her auburn hair to cup the back of her head, his smile tempered by her refusal to marry him. "We'll see, Galetti," he whispered. "Your baby needs a father, and unless you can pull one out of your hat between now and his birthday, you're going to be Mrs. Luke McGee whether you like it or not." His jaw stiffened, underscoring the seriousness of his tone. "I came into this world as an outcast, Bets—I'll be bound and gagged before your baby will."

She quirked a brow. "Bound and gagged? Don't think it can't be arranged."

He bullied her toward the door, brows lifted in challenge. "You threatening me, Galetti?"

"Nope, just letting you know how it's going to be, McGee. You get me through these next six months, and then you're back on a train to Boston. Ya got it? That's the deal."

He opened the door, lips crooking into a wry smile. "Like I said—we'll see. Now I suggest you get yourself to bed, young lady, because we've got a busy couple of days ahead." He gave her a soft peck on the cheek. "G'night, Bets—sleep well."

"Good night, Luke," she whispered, then cocked her head with a squint of her eyes. "I won't marry you, you know."

He cupped her face in his hands to kiss her nose before he

butted her out of the door. His lips parted in a cocky grin. "Wanna bet?"

"Good night, sweet Jesus, the one I love best. I have finished my work, and now I must rest. You have blessed me this day, now bless me this night, and keep me from danger till morning is light. Amen." Abby's cherub face puckered into a sweet, little yawn. "When is Daddy coming home?"

Faith glanced at her watch and worried her lip. She bent to plant a kiss on the tip of her youngest daughter's nose. "Soon, Abby, although you girls may be in Dreamland by then."

"But I don't want to go to Dreamland. I want to wait up for Daddy," Abby insisted. She shoved her tiny thumb into her rosebud mouth, her scowl looking so much like Collin when he was mad that Faith chuckled.

"Well, hopefully Daddy will be home soon," Faith said with a grin, tucking the little tyke in bed. "And when he is, I'll send him up for kisses straightaway, okay?"

Abby's gray eyes, so like her father's, sparkled with unshed tears. "No, it's not okay—I miss him."

Faith sighed and pressed a final kiss to her daughter's brow. After months of extreme patience with Collin over his long hours, she was starting to feel a lot like Abby. More and more, it was becoming less and less "okay" all the time.

"I miss him too, Mama," Laney echoed from across the room.

"Why does he have to work so much?" Bella asked, her voice sluggish with sleep.

"Daddy has a lot to do right now, girls, so we just have to be patient. But it won't always be this way." *I hope.* The smile stiffened on her lips as she made her way to the door. She blew each girl a kiss. "Good night, Bella, Laney, and Abby . . . and good night, angels."

Her daughters giggled and snuggled down in their beds

while Faith turned out the light and made her way down the hall. She yawned and glanced at her watch again, and her stomach tightened. Nine-thirty. Surely inventory couldn't take this long, could it?

She lumbered down the stairs and into the kitchen to put the kettle on to boil, wondering what Brady and Collin could possibly be inventorying at this late hour. Collin had mentioned it would be a long night and not to wait up, but that did little to calm her nerves now. With a shiver, she reached for her sweater on the hook by the door, then tossed another log into the beloved pot-bellied stove Collin had given her for Valentine's Day. "To keep the home fires burning," he had said with a hungry kiss to her neck, and she had giggled in his arms, quite certain they would never need a stove to accomplish that. But the fire after dinner had long since waned, and Faith found herself jostling the embers with a flicker of frustration. Ivory tongues of fire licked at the log, its crackling and spitting as agitated as Faith's mood was proving to be.

The jangle of the phone startled her, and she rushed to answer it, her voice breathless. "Collin?"

"No, Mrs. McGuire, this is Mrs. Toomey . . . the editor for the church bulletin at St. Stephen's?"

Disappointment soured her stomach. "Yes, Mrs. Toomey, of course. How are you?"

The voice hesitated. "Fine, Mrs. McGuire, thank you. Is . . . Mr. McGuire home?"

"No, I'm sorry, he had to work late tonight. Is there anything I might help you with?"

"No . . . but perhaps I may be able to help you."

Her cautious tone set Faith on edge. The teapot whistled, and she jumped. "Mrs. Toomey, may I ask you to hold for a moment, please?" She set the phone down and whisked the teapot from the stove, then poured some and steeped her tea. Cup trembling in hand, she pulled a chair to the phone and sat down, allowing the comfort of a warm sip before returning to the conversation. "I'm back. Forgive me, but my tea was on the boil. Now, you were saying?" She blew on the tea and took another taste.

"Yes, Mrs. McGuire, well, let me say right off that this phone call is not easy for me."

The tea pooled in Faith's mouth, burning her tongue.

"You see, I live next door to Evelyn Raeburn . . . do you know her?"

Faith started to cough as the hot liquid obstructed her air.

"Are you all right, Mrs. McGuire?"

"Yes, fine, thank you." Her voice was hoarse. "Yes, Mrs. Toomey, I'm familiar with Mrs. Raeburn. She is my husband's employee, you know."

"Yes, so I've heard. But are you aware, Mrs. McGuire, that your husband visits Mrs. Raeburn at her home quite frequently?"

Her temper suddenly steamed, hot as the blasted tea. "Yes, Mrs. Toomey," she said in a voice as cool as her tea was hot. "I am well aware of my husband's visits to Mrs. Raeburn's home. On Fridays, he enjoys playing chess with her son who is ill."

"Usually on Fridays, yes." The languid voice paused as if savoring its power. "Although lately, he has taken to coming more frequently. Shall we say . . . every day?"

The teacup quivered in Faith's hand. She lowered it to the floor where it clattered and spilled across the tiles. "Every day?" she whispered, her fury at this woman cooling as quickly as the tea spilled at her feet. Her mind raced through the last few weeks, when Collin had worked late almost every night, coming home spent and deprived of his usual appetite—both for food and for her. She closed her eyes, shock and anger surging through her body like poison.

"Yes, I thought perhaps you might not be aware of that," the smug tone confirmed. "Which is why I felt it my duty to call when Mr. McGuire arrived again tonight. Why, it's almost ten o'clock, and the boy would obviously be in bed."

Tonight? Faith struggled to draw air, all words wedged in her throat.

"Now, I live on a respectable street, Mrs. McGuire, and not only do I not wish to see your reputation sullied, but—"

"Excuse me, Mrs. Toomey, but I really must go—" Faith hung up the phone too quickly, fingers trembling and fear ramming against her ribs. *No!* The woman had to be wrong—Collin was working with Brady tonight, he'd told her so. Panic heaved in her chest as she fumbled to dial the shop's number, her strangled breathing raspy in her ears. She closed her eyes, each unanswered ring of the phone an eternity in her mind. *Pick up the blasted phone, Collin!*

No answer.

With a violent slam of the receiver, she dialed Lizzie's number, tears welling in her eyes.

"Hello?"

Relief flooded at the sound of her sister's voice. "Lizzie, is Brady home?"

"Faith? Yes, of course. Are you all right?"

"I need to speak to him, Lizzie—now, please." Her voice cracked with strain.

There was a nervous lull. "Sure, Faith, just wait and I'll get him."

Faith sucked in a deep breath, desperate to force some semblance of calm into her body. "God, give me peace, please," she prayed under her breath, squeezing the receiver so tightly, her palm ached.

"Faith, what's wrong?"

Her fingers relaxed at the sound of Brady's steady voice. "Brady, you and Collin had inventory tonight, right?"

"Of course. Why—isn't he home yet?"

"No, no he's not, and I was just wondering . . . when did you leave?"

He hesitated. "Around seven, I think. But Collin said he had a few things to wrap up before heading home. Did you call the shop?"

She squeezed her forehead with her fingers. "Yes, of course, but there's no answer."

"Well, maybe he's on his way home."

She bit her lip, tears welling once again. "Maybe." She put a hand to her eyes. "Could he be . . . could he be at Evelyn's?"

Dead silence.

"Brady? Could he?"

Her brother-in-law cleared his throat. "It's possible, Faith, but I think he would have let you know. Are you sure he didn't say something this morning?"

"No, just that he had inventory with you and not to wait dinner." She chewed hard on her lip, suddenly tasting the metallic tang of blood in her mouth. "Do you have Evelyn's number?"

His heavy release of air carried over the phone. "She doesn't have one. Collin says she saves every dime for Tommy's medical expenses." He paused. "But I'm sure he's okay."

"Are you, Brady?" Hysteria rose in her tone and her mind was frantic, roaming the possibilities. This was a dire economy where crime was on the rise—wasn't the St. Valentine's Day Massacre proof of that? And Collin could find himself in danger through any number of threats—desperate people on the loose, gangsters, street gangs . . . Faith swallowed hard. *Another woman's arms*.

"Evelyn doesn't live far. I'll be there in twenty minutes, and he'll be home in forty."

"No! Please, no." She put a hand to her chest, willing herself to be calm. "I've obviously had a little too much tea tonight—I suppose my nerves are on edge. Please don't bother. I think I will simply say a prayer and go take a bath and relax. But, thanks, Brady, for the offer."

"Faith?"

She closed her eyes, her breathing heavy. "Yes?"

"Everything will be okay. The man is desperately in love with you."

Tears sprang to her eyes, and she nodded, spilling them down her face. "Thanks, Brady. Tell Lizzie I'll call tomorrow. Good night."

"Good night, Faith."

She hung the receiver up and sagged against the wall, suddenly feeling more than a little foolish. A quick glance at the clock told her it was ten-thirty, and she drew in a deep swallow of air. She stooped to pick up her cup and pushed the chair back into the table. Releasing a weary breath, she put the cup in the sink and wiped up the spill on the floor before dousing the lights on her way to a much-needed bath.

She soaked and prayed until eleven, her body as limp as her mood when she finally stepped from the tub. Drying herself off, she got ready for bed, trying to keep her mind focused on prayer. With tight-lipped determination, she dove into her Bible. When the grandfather clock in the foyer struck midnight, she turned out the lights and closed her eyes.

And then the evil began. A painful barrage of thoughts—Evelyn's son and mother long gone to bed while she and Collin chatted on the couch. A comforting arm, an accidental kiss, a young love rekindled till the flame was hot.

No! Faith jolted up in bed, eyes wide, and yet the vision remained. She saw Collin's eyes, sensual and moody and heated with desire, muscled arms drawing her close, wayward lips with a mind of their own. *No, God, please!* Her heart rate escalated as moisture beaded her brow. With ragged breaths, she seized her Bible from the nightstand and clutched it tightly to her chest. "For God hath not given me the spirit of fear; but of power and love and a sound mind." Her whisper was harsh in the dark as she repeated it over and over until that holy quiet finally entered her soul, sealing God's Word deep in her heart. *Power . . . love . . . a sound mind . . .*

She fell back on the pillow, her body exhausted and slumber weighting her eyes while Scripture still moved on her lips, lulling her into a weary peace . . .

The clock chimed three when she jolted awake, all sleep suddenly gone from her eyes. She sat up in the dark, the Bible still open in her lap. And then she heard him—his key in the door, the click of the lock, the groan of the steps as he made his way up. She vaulted from the bed, and the Bible crashed to the floor.

Three o'clock? He chooses to waltz home at three in the morning? Anger seethed in her chest. How dare he! She heard his footfall on the landing and ran to the door, flipping the bedroom light as he entered the hall. His body froze, hair disheveled and clothes unkempt as if he'd spent the night doing who knows what. He stared, obviously blinded by the light, eyes worn and jaw dark with stubble. He took a faultering step forward, and she flew at him, rage rising as she pelted him with her fists. "How dare you do this to me!"

"Faith, please—" he whispered, but she only struck harder, her vision too blurred to see anything but his sin.

He grabbed her then, hands anchored to her wrists as he held them to her sides. "Faith," he said, his voice steeped in pain, "Tommy died tonight."

Her body went stiff beneath his hold, and it was then that she finally saw the grief in his soul. Eyelids rimmed with red and face mottled by tears. The awful look of desolation in those tragic gray eyes. His chiseled jaw, so fine and so strong, now trembled with pain as pale lips formed his words. "Faith," he whispered again, "I lost my son tonight."

The air seized in her lungs as she stared, her body going numb with cold. With a violent heave of his chest, he clutched her close, the weight of his agony heavy against her frame.

Her body stilled to stone, shock stealing everything—her breath, her pulse, her love. *God, no, please . . . his son?* The realization seared through her with a pain more cruel than anything she'd ever felt. Another woman had given him the son he craved, not her. The man of her heart, tethered to a woman he'd loved by a child who bound them forever. The agony was too much to bear and she staggered back, unable to see his grief for the tears in her eyes.

"Faith," he whispered, "forgive me, please . . ."

She stared, his face a distorted blur of the man she loved. With another step back, her breath suddenly caught in her throat. Maybe . . . maybe it wasn't true . . . Maybe it was just a lie to win her husband's affection . . .

She felt him shudder, even two feet away. He seemed little more than a lost soul, shoulders slumped and eyes wandering into a blank stare, glazed with mourning. His arms, so strong and so able, now hung limp at his sides while his voice broke with repentance. "I didn't know, not until tonight. Evelyn called to say it was time, and I . . . I swear, as God is my witness, I never suspected."

"How, Collin?" she whispered. "How could it be?"

He closed his eyes, fingers kneading his temple and face weary with regret. "Before the war, when I was engaged to Charity, Evelyn came to Brannigan's periodically, but I always avoided her because I knew she wanted to get back together, and I wasn't interested. And then one night, I drank too much and passed out, a rare occurrence for a man who could hold his liquor." His eyes flickered open. "But it was that night Charity found me with you, and I was so devastated by the pain I caused, that I drowned my troubles in the drink. I swear I hadn't touched the stuff in almost six months. But it got the best of me, I guess, and when I passed out at the bar, Lucas hauled me into his back room to sleep it off. I didn't know, but he told Evelyn I was back on his cot, despondent over a broken engagement." He swallowed hard and looked away. "I swear I don't even remember her slipping into my bed . . ."

Her eyelids fluttered closed, and the hurt was so sharp, she swayed on her feet. He reached for her then, his voice hoarse as he pulled her into his arms, clinging like a man drowning in a sea of anguish. "Forgive me, Faith—I'm sorry for the pain I'm causing you, but I can't be . . . I won't be . . . sorry about Tommy. He was everything I'd ever hoped for in a son . . ." She felt his heave against her chest as he tried to stifle a sob. "A boy like I've always dreamed—so smart, so witty, so strong. A good boy, like I used to be before my own father died. A boy with a deep faith in God . . . just like you. And I swear, Faith, from the moment I met him, I wished he were mine."

His words pierced her, finally dislodging the bitterness from her soul. A deep faith in God.

Just like me.

With a harsh draw of breath, she fought off a shiver, begging God for the strength to do what she needed to do . . . what would be impossible for mere flesh and blood to do. *Help me, God*, the thought came, and with it, she reached deep in her soul, clinging to that faith that would see her through. A faith that would carry her past this crisis with her husband . . . and then heal their souls when it was over and done.

He wept in her arms, and in one anguished sob, she swallowed him up with a love so fierce, their quivering shadow became as one. "Oh, Collin," she cried, and their bodies clung as her sorrow melded with his. "I'm so sorry! And how I wish I could have met him." She pressed in even closer. "Did he . . . know?"

His voice was a shell, hollow and still. "No, Evelyn never told him. Her husband Frank adored Tommy. He thought he was his, and Evelyn kept it that way." Emotion thickened his voice. "I loved him, Faith, and I will never forget him."

Grief and forgiveness swam in her eyes. "No, my love, and he will never forget you, a father in spirit and flesh when he needed it most. Come to bed, Collin, and take your rest. God's Word says 'weeping may endure for a night, but joy cometh in the morning.'"

"Joy . . ." he whispered, his voice an echo of pain, as if he could barely believe it possible.

"Yes, joy, my love," she said, her voice as sure as the dawn. "The son of your heart is now whole and free, Collin, safe in the arms of our God . . ." She stood on tiptoe to press a kiss to his sodden cheek. "Watching, no doubt, over his sisters, to keep them safe in their beds." And with a steady hold to the bulk of her husband's back, she took him to the sanctuary of their room.

To pray . . . to sleep . . . and to enter God's rest.

19

Katie waved and flashed a smile. "Thanks, Meg. See you tomorrow." She watched her new friend from Portia Law School pull away from the curb, the maroon paint of her daddy's Model A roadster gleaming in the sun. Katie closed the door and drooped against it with a pile of textbooks in her arms. Her eyes wavered from the stack of mail on the foyer table to the empty parlor and back. The loneliness that had been her constant companion since Luke left over a month ago was as palpable as that of the empty house.

Eyes fixed on the mail, she moved forward like a woman toward a mirage, hope beating in her breast for something to quench this awful ache in her heart. Her breathing quickened as she unloaded her books on the table. She sifted through the letters and bills, fingers shaking with the need for his caress—a note, a letter, anything his hands had touched. The envelopes spilled from her palms back to the table, and she closed her eyes, her hope once again as dry and parched as the most brutal desert. The man she loved was no more than a mirage—his image ever-present and haunting, but as empty and out of reach as the love she'd hoped to have.

Tears pricked and she jerked her gloves and coat off, determined she would survive this final blow from the King of Misery. From start to finish, Cluny McGee had subjected her to pain, the ultimate strike being the joy he had given her and then taking it all away. Well, she vowed with an iron thrust of her chin, she would best the little brat once again. She'd move on with her plans and show him she didn't care, get on with her life with or without him. She stared at her left hand, so naked without Jack's ring, and her fury rekindled. The blasted street rat had even ruined that, robbing Katie of all desire to even be in another man's arms. Oh, how she hated him! She shoved her gloves in her pockets, then hurled her coat on the rack before pressing a shaky hand to her eyes. Her shoulders slumped in defeat. Oh, how she loved him . . .

Something clattered in the kitchen and Katie looked up. Steven had taken Mother and Father to the doctor and Gabe was spending the night with a friend—who in the world was here? She hurried to the kitchen and pushed through the door, jaw distended at the sight of her sisters. "What in blazes are you three doing?" she asked in a tone still tinged with anger at Luke.

"Nice to see you too, Katie Rose," Charity quipped, her manicured brow arched high. "Bad day in the courtroom?"

Katie shot her a narrow gaze. "Classroom, not courtroom, and I had a good day, why?"

Charity rolled her eyes and finished peeling a carrot. "Mmm, nothing." She bent close to Lizzie and lowered her voice to a loud whisper. "Remind me to avoid her on bad days."

"Ignore her, Katie," Faith said with a smile. She opened the oven to peek in at three whole chickens roasting with potatoes in her mother's turkey pan, then slammed it shut again.

Wonderful smells assailed Katie's appetite, reminding her that she hadn't been interested in lunch *again*—a frequent occurrence these days.

Faith opened a cabinet to retrieve a stack of plates. "She's just giddy because she gets a night out while Mitch is saddled with the kids."

"Amen to that!" Charity said, popping a carrot in her mouth. "Nothing like an evening with Henry—forcing him to do homework, take a bath, go to bed—to make the love of my life truly appreciate me." She glanced at the clock and grinned. "You mark my words—come nine o'clock, the man will be prostrate at my feet."

Katie folded her arms. "I'm ecstatic for you, Charity, but you haven't answered my question. What are you three doing here?"

Worry deepened the violet hue of Lizzie's eyes as she looked up from the bread she was kneading. "Sean thought it would be fun to surprise Mother and Father with a family dinner like we used to. You know, without all the husbands and kids? He thought it might lift their spirits." Her tone was edged with concern. "And speaking of spirits, Katie, are you all right? You seem . . . depressed."

Eager to avoid any probing, Katie tugged the stack of plates out of Faith's hands and piled utensils on top. "Oh, I suppose I'm a little out of sorts because of breaking up with Jack, but nothing law school and baked chicken can't cure." She hurried toward the door, forcing a bright smile. "Goodness, eight in the dining room again and only six drumsticks—could get ugly." She set the table, then returned to the kitchen where the conversation turned serious.

"How does Sean know they're in dire straits?" Charity asked quietly. At the stove, she dropped her final carrots into a bubbling pot without a smile, her good humor appearing to evaporate along with the steam from the boiling water.

Faith sighed as she tossed flour into the chicken drippings that would soon be gravy. "He says Mother asked for help with the bills and bookkeeping after all this started with Father. Apparently most of their savings were in the stock market, and we all know what happened there. Without Father's salary for three months and all the medical bills, it doesn't look good."

Expelling a soft blast of air, Charity returned to the table. "No, it doesn't. And to make matters worse, Mitch says Mr. Hennessey is looking to cut staff. The paper's profits have dropped dramatically." Her lips twisted. "Imagine that—nobody wants to read bad news."

"Nor able to afford it," Katie said in a dry tone as she plopped into a chair. She paused, then squinted up at Charity. "You don't think Father's job is in danger, do you? Or Mitch's?"

A sheen of moisture glimmered in Charity's eyes before she whisked the bowl of peelings away. "I don't know. All I do know is that Mitch was alarmed when Arthur commented about how one editor seemed to be working out just fine." Charity turned at the sink with a sour smile on her lips. "Of course it's working out fine—Mitch goes in at the crack of dawn and comes home after eight, totally exhausted. He's been covering for Father for almost a month now. The poor man falls asleep brushing his teeth."

"Goodness, then how did you get him home tonight to watch the kids?" Lizzie asked.

"I told him I'd make it worth his while," Charity said with a wry twist of a smile. "I'll let him sleep."

Faith chuckled. "Land sakes, the man *must* be exhausted."

Charity sighed. "No more than Collin and Brady, I suppose." She wriggled her brows in Lizzie's direction. "Although I imagine John Brady is pretty energetic these days now that the doctor has given you the go-ahead, eh, Lizzie?"

More color whooshed into Lizzie's cheeks. "Charity, I swear you have a one-track mind. I wish your interest in you-know-what was a little more discreet. And Katie's here too, so hush!"

"Katie's all grown up now, Lizzie. I'm sure she understands perfectly well all about the pull between a man and a woman . . ." She arched a brow. "As well as you-know-what."

"More like imperfectly," Katie muttered.

Lizzie gave her a sympathetic smile. "I'm sorry it didn't work out with Jack, but the right one is out there for you somewhere." She released a wistful sigh. "With all that Brady put me through, I never thought it would happen for me, but it did, and it will happen for you too—you'll find the man of your dreams."

Tears pricked Katie's eyes. *Yeah, the man of my dreams—too bad he's married to somebody else.* She jumped to her feet. "Tea, anyone?"

"Yes!" Charity and Lizzie chimed in unison.

"Sounds good, Katie," Faith said, her back to her sisters as she stirred the gravy at the stove. She gave Katie a sideways glance, and her smile faded enough for Katie to notice.

Turning away, Katie blinked to dispel the wetness in her eyes as she filled the kettle.

"But to be honest," Lizzie continued, "since Evelyn left, both Collin and Brady are working the same kind of hours as Mitch, I'm afraid. And believe me, between that, a jealous two-year-old, and a little girl who likes to exercise her lungs throughout the night, it doesn't leave much time nor energy for conjugal bliss."

Katie pulled four cups and saucers from the cabinet and set them on the table. "Evelyn's gone? When did that happen?"

"Last week," Faith said quietly. She put the lid on the skillet of gravy and turned down the heat, then rejoined her sisters at the table. "Too many bad memories here in Boston, she said. She and her mother are moving in with her uncle in Maine, to live in a lighthouse, of all places." A lump shifted in Faith's throat. "Collin says Tommy would have loved living in a lighthouse."

Charity squeezed Faith's arm. "How's Collin doing?"

A fragile sigh floated from Faith's lips. "Better, I think. He's been spending every waking hour at the shop or with the girls, of course, having breakfast with us in the morning, coming home for lunch and even dinner before going back to work with Brady." She looked up with a sad smile. "Evelyn was a wonder in the office, apparently, and now the two of them are lost, trying to catch up on paperwork." The kettle began to whistle, and Faith jumped up with a smile to steep the tea. "But not tonight, eh, Lizzie?"

Lizzie grinned. "Nope. It's kind of fun having them close the shop early for once. I have a feeling after tangling with Teddy when he gets up from his nap, Brady will appreciate his presses all the more."

Steam rose into the air as Faith poured everyone a cup. She fetched spoons, cream, and sugar, then sat down to sip her tea. "How does Father seem lately, Katie? Has he adjusted to life on the first floor without pipes, radios, or newspapers?"

Katie blew on her tea, then carefully sipped. "Pretty well, actually. Oh, he was bored as the devil the first few weeks, but after Sean repaired the pot-belly stove on the sun porch and Steven dragged all that old furniture up from the basement, Mother actually turned it into a cozy little den that Father seems to love. He's been doing a lot of reading and writing out there, even working on some editorials for Mitch here and there. Not to mention teaching Gabe how to write. They work together almost every day, and believe it or not, Gabe's grades in English have gone through the roof."

A smile softened Faith's lips, easing the worry lines in her brow. "Oh, I'm glad. Father needs total rest right now to get well. And he's taking his medicine, so no more attacks?"

A chuckle parted from Katie's lips. "Nope, no more attacks. He's taking his medicine faithfully . . . at least since Mother made him swear on the Bible."

Charity blinked, her cup stalled midway to her lips. "She made him swear? On the *Bible*?"

Katie nodded and grinned. "And then she tucked him in just like she does Gabe." Her brows lifted as she gave her sisters a knowing look. "Trust me, it was a rather chilly night on Donovan Street, as I recall." She blew on her tea again and took a drink, her smile shifting into a frown. "How bad does Sean say it is—their finances, I mean?"

The creases were back in Faith's brow. "Bad enough that he's going to ask Father if he can move back in—not because he needs to, mind you, but because he knows they need the rent. He plans to tell Father that Mr. Kelly has cut his hours, which he has, but I know Sean has more than enough saved to stay in his flat for a long time to come." She shot a nervous look over the rim of her cup. "Providing all the banks don't default first."

Katie's chest tightened. "You don't really think that could happen, do you? Why, President Hoover is talking of cutting taxes and raising government spending to stimulate the economy. Surely that will help."

"Don't hold your breath," Charity said in a grim tone. "Mitch says Hennessey has ordered him to put a positive spin on all the bad news they print, even things like referring to a 'labor surplus' instead of calling it 'unemployment.'" She paused, her eyes fixed on the cup in her hands. "I didn't say anything before, but trust me—a lot of jobs are in jeopardy." Her eyes flickered up, and her worry was evident in the hush of her tone. "Including Father's."

"That can't be," Katie said, her tone laced with shock.

Charity leaned forward. "Don't you dare breathe a word of this to anyone, especially Mitch, but Hennessey said . . . well, he *implied* . . . Mitch could have Father's job if he wanted."

Faith gasped. "No!"

"Yes, and after almost thirty years at the *Herald*, Father draws three times the salary that Mitch does, so don't think that's not attractive to Hennessey at a time like this. Trust me, loyalty goes out the window when money is involved."

"What did Mitch say?" Faith's cup quivered in her hands as she stared, open-mouthed.

"Well, he told him in no uncertain terms that if Father left, he would too."

"Oh Lord, help us . . ." Faith's cup clattered back onto her saucer. "I had no idea it was that bad. What did Hennessey say to that?"

"What could he say? He backed off. He knows how close Mitch and Father are."

"But what if he fires Mitch?" Lizzie asked, chewing on her lip until it was pink.

"Doesn't matter," Charity said with a toss of her head. "Mitch is a saver who has put a tidy bundle away, not to mention his inheritance in Dublin that he's hardly ever touched. And then there's the store, which is still doing well despite the economy, thanks to Emma."

Katie stared blindly ahead, the conversation swimming in her brain. Suddenly it all came into focus—Mother taking in laundry and sewing, leftovers three times a week, large family dinners happening less and less. Katie swallowed and closed her eyes. And now Sean talking of moving back home. She shivered, thinking of what a drain law-school tuition would be. With a clank of her cup on the saucer, she shot to her feet. "Well, it looks like you have dinner under control, so I really need to get some studying in before they get home." She glanced at the clock. "Mother said they'd be late because Dr. Williamson has a brand-new test he wants to run on Father—something called a cardiac stress test."

"As if Father doesn't have enough stress already," Charity mumbled.

Faith pushed her cup away. "Mother didn't mention when they'd be home, did she?"

Katie glanced at the clock. "She said something about six o'clock or so."

"Good," Faith said. "That's when Sean said he could be here too. It's five-fifteen now, Katie, so you better hurry if you want to get some studying in before dinner."

Katie gave Faith's shoulder a quick squeeze and headed out. "Thanks, guys," she said, then pushed through the door and vaulted up the stairs, tears stinging.

She closed her door and leaned against it with eyes closed. Fear writhed in her stomach. Her world was falling apart! First Luke, and now her parents. And who knows what that meant for law school. Sobs rose in her throat as she threw herself on her bed.

She froze at the sound of a knock on the door.

"Katie? Can I come in?" Faith's voice was a muffled whisper. The door opened quietly and closed once again.

Katie lay still, her face buried in the pillow while she waited for Faith to speak. The bedsprings groaned as her sister sat down, and when Faith touched her shoulder, a sob broke from Katie's lips. "Faith, what am I going to do?"

"Oh, Katie." Faith gathered her in a tight hug, her voice low against her ear. "My heart is breaking for you, and I am so sorry. But it's times like this that strengthen our faith. God says in our weakness, he is strong."

Katie lurched up to a sitting position, her cheeks sodden with tears. "But I don't have any faith—not like you. You've always focused on God, but I've barely ever thought about him."

A faint smile softened Faith's lips. "That doesn't mean he hasn't thought about you. You own a piece of God's heart, Katie, like a piece of a puzzle that's missing. A piece nobody else can fill."

Katie sniffed and wiped at her eyes. "But I'm angry at him too. I had my life all planned out—a long list that included law school, marrying Jack, and making a difference in the world. Now with this financial crisis, it looks like I'll probably have to quit school and maybe even get a job, if there's even a job to be had. I could be selling apples on the corner next week, for all I know." Her chin began to quiver. "My list and my life are in shambles, and on top of everything else, I've lost the man I love . . ."

Pulling her sister into her arms, Faith soothed her with a gentle massage of her back. "Shhh, Katie, hush . . . if you put your life in God's hands instead of your own, you'll be amazed at what he will do for you . . . including the man that you love."

"No . . . no, it's too late."

Faith stroked her hair. "Whatever happened between you and Jack, if he's the man God has for you, it will all work out."

Katie shook her head, her voice nasal with tears. "No, Faith, he can't. It's too late."

"But Jack—"

With a violent heave, Katie pulled away, her vision blurred as she stared at her sister. "No, you don't understand. I'm not talking about Jack—I'm talking about Luke."

Faith blinked, eyes rounded in shock. "*What?* You're in love with Luke?"

She nodded while heaves shook her body.

"Oh, Katie . . ." Faith tugged her close. "I thought you two were just friends."

"So did I," Katie said with a tremor in her tone. "Over the summer, he told me he was in love with me, but I wouldn't listen." She pulled away and pushed the hair from her eyes, her voice hard. "No, I had my life all mapped out, pretty as you please, and it sure didn't include a starving street lawyer whose only ambition in life was saving the next orphan."

"Did he . . . did he know you were in love with him when he . . ."

"Proposed to Betty?" Katie lagged into a cold stare, remembering with painful clarity everything about that fateful night. "No . . . no, he didn't. I could see it in his face when I told him—he was stunned beyond belief." She looked up then, the despair so potent in her eyes, it was bleeding down her cheeks. "He admitted it, Faith, admitted then and there that he was still in love with me, but his mind was made up. And that's when I knew—I had lost a soul mate forever, a man who's been the missing piece of my heart since as far back as I can remember. But it's too late now . . . even for God." Bitterness cut in her tone. "Because I may be the woman in Luke McGee's heart, but for the rest of my life, it will be Betty who'll be in his arms."

Faith grabbed her hand and held on tight. "Katie, I'm so sorry. But all the more reason to cling to God, because you have nothing to lose right now and everything to gain."

Katie pulled her hand away and closed her eyes, her voice dead. "I don't know, Faith. I know God is real to you, but to me, it's always been more of a fairy tale. You have faith in him, but I don't. Sometimes I even wonder if I believe in him at all. I pray, but I feel like he doesn't hear my prayers, like they're long-distance and lost in the shuffle. I don't feel any closeness with him, any desire to pursue him." Her shoulders slumped forward, weighted with despair. "I guess the bottom line is . . . ," a knot shifted in her throat, "I'm not sure he even exists."

Her sister's tone was gentle. "It doesn't matter, Katie, not one little bit. All you have to do is ask him to reveal himself to you, to prove that he's real and that he loves you and has a plan for your life. Just the frail consent of your will to invite him into your heart is all it takes. And you can have a living, breathing relationship with the God of the universe, overflowing with a love and passion as real as anything you ever felt for Luke. Go ahead, Katie, do it! And if you do, you have my word—your life will never be the same."

Katie's eyes widened as she stared, her sister's gaze aglow like a beacon of hope. She swallowed hard, knowing full well that no matter any storms in her life, this was the sister who carried a reservoir of peace wherever she went. The sister who had scaled every mountain, weathered every storm with her resilient faith in God. Katie blinked. *Could it actually be real?*

As if she sensed the shift in Katie's thinking, Faith placed a palm on top of Katie's hand, warm and stable, cupping it, shielding it, like an anchor of hope in this storm of her soul. "Katie," she whispered, "you say he's not real to you, that you're not sure he even exists. But right this minute, one of us is right and one of us is wrong."

Katie looked into her sister's face, as if compelled to listen by some strange force that pulled at her with a tentative thread of hope.

Wetness shimmered in Faith's eyes. "If it's me who is wrong, then I have lost nothing. Because even if I have believed in a lie or a fairy tale, then that lie or fairy tale has given me more joy, more hope, and more strength than anything I have ever encountered. But if it is you who is wrong, Katie, I tremble to think that you will have lost everything—his joy, his peace, his hope . . ." Her voice softened to a bare whisper. "His salvation." She straightened then, her manner as sure as the conviction in her tone. "I repeat, Katie, one of us is right and one of us is wrong. Do it now, I beg of you—invite him into your heart. Because truly, you have nothing to lose and everything to gain."

Katie stared while seconds ticked by like heartbeats, thundering increments of time in a reality she could feel, see, touch. She was a realist, a woman bent on the law, with a penchant for facts, statistics, and tangible proof. How could she lay all of that down to embrace an intangible God? A God her family had embraced all of their lives, depended on, lived for . . . while she herself had stood in the wings, master of her own future. She closed her eyes, grief piercing anew. A future that now lay in shambles at her feet. She swallowed the pride in her throat. *Nothing to lose . . .*

And then out of nowhere, Emma's words that day in the store haunted her thoughts, and in a catch of her breath, Katie's heart began to race.

"Whatever your hurts or fears or scars, Katie—call on him. He's waiting to love you like you've never been loved before."

"I don't know, Emma, it all sounds wonderful, but God . . . prayer, well . . . I'm just not sure that it's real."

"I understand, Katie, but I can tell you this—you won't know till you try . . ."

Till I try . . . Katie's breathing accelerated, and all at once, in the thud of her pulse or the trail of a tear, her decision was made. Gripping her sister's hand like a lifeline in a stormy sea, Katie lifted her face to the ceiling while water seeped from her lidded eyes. Her voice quivered, but her resolve was sure. "God, Faith says you're up there, that you care for me and have a plan for my life. If you are, and I'm not just talking to a ceiling, will you show me? Reveal yourself to me, your love, your purpose for my life. Please, God, come into my heart and make me the woman you want me to be."

She opened her eyes then, and somehow the room seemed different. The same ivy wallpaper covered the walls, and the lace-curtained windows still wore pretty green ribbons tied back in a swag. The scent of rosewater hovered in the air, and Miss Buford—the porcelain doll from her youth—still perched on her vanity like some regal judge presiding over her bench. And yet, in the beat of Katie's heart, everything had changed. She closed her eyes and breathed in the scent of her freedom, tears escaping as surely as her heart had escaped its gloom.

Dear God, can it really be this easy?

Her eyelids fluttered open and she looked at her sister, her words soft with wonder. "I never knew . . . never knew that it could be so easy . . . so real."

A smile lighted upon her sister's lips as Faith placed a gentle hand to Katie's face. "Believing in him is easy, Katie, because he gives us that tiny seed of faith. And loving him is even more so, because when you see how he moves on your behalf, your heart will spill over with joy. But unfortunately, living for him is not so easy. Feelings and doubts will come and go, but his Word stands forever. Study it, commit it to memory, learn through his Bible what he wants you to do. Because everything in this world will come and go—people we love, financial security, jobs—but God is a constant, and his promises endure forever."

Katie nodded, the memory of her father's hand on the Bible bringing a soft smile to her lips. All at once, she thought of law school, and the smile slowly dissolved. She drew in a deep breath. "I need to quit law school, don't I, Faith?"

Her sister studied her, a look of regret in the depth of those gentle green eyes. "Maybe not quit, Katie, let's just say postpone. Just until Father can get on his feet again."

A heavy sigh departed from Katie's lips, along with any sense of disappointment. She blinked, stunned that she actually felt relieved. "I . . . I don't understand," she muttered in confusion. "Law school was everything to me." She looked up, her eyes circled in shock. "Why do I suddenly feel like I don't care?"

Faith smiled. "Because your life is in God's hands now,

Katie, not yours. And when we cling to him and follow his precepts, his path is paved with peace."

Katie nodded, her amazement blooming into a grin. "Peace . . . ," she said, reveling in the feel and wonder of the word. "Sweet saints alive, he should market it!"

A grin spread on her sister's face. "He does, Katie Rose, every day. Through grateful pieces of the puzzle like you and me."

LEGAL DEPARTMENT. Katie blinked at the gold lettering on the bubbled glass door and winced at just how much it hurt to be here again. She pressed a hand to her stomach, queasy beneath the bulk of her camelhair coat, and closed her eyes to try to ward off the thoughts. But it was no use—she saw, heard, and felt them all in a movie reel in her mind. Betty's droll comments, Bobbie Sue's outrageous humor, Parker's solid friendship . . . and Luke's every kiss. She shivered. Ghosts from her past that she needed to face and move on. She opened her eyes, and her lips quirked to the right. *God, help me*, she thought, *I've never been fond of ghosts* . . .

At least there were no more "ghosts" in her closets, though, she thought with a grim smile. Not since Faith had introduced her to the ultimate "Ghost," the Spirit of God. From the moment her sister—and the Holy Spirit—had opened her eyes to God's personal love for her, Katie had become a changed woman. She sighed. *Well, almost*. She was still stubborn and headstrong to a fault, she supposed, and certainly ready to battle at the drop of a hat, but far more at peace and far more willing to include God in every decision she made. She stared at the door of the BCAS Legal Department and chewed on her lip. Like this one . . .

She closed her eyes and clung to the Scripture from Isaiah she'd memorized—the one that assured her that God would provide a shelter from the wind and a refuge from the storm. Never had she needed a refuge more, in the throes of the worst financial crisis the country had ever seen. Katie whispered the words, desperate for the comfort they offered. *And a man shall be as a hiding place from the wind, and a refuge from the storm; as rivers of water in a dry place, as the shadow of a great rock in a weary land.*

And the eyes of them that see shall not be dim, and the ears of them that hear shall hearken.

Peace flooded her soul, and she swallowed to relieve her parched throat. Licking her dry lips, she felt them lift into a gentle smile. Streams of water in the desert . . . still, quiet, and providing precious sustenance in her time of need. She sighed. Like Parker, she hoped?

Her grip on the knob was tentative, but when she opened the door and saw the woman at the desk, her confidence resurged. A far cry from Betty Galetti—or *McGee*, she corrected with a hitch of her heart—the girl before her appeared arrogant where Betty had appeared regal, cool where Betty had been warm. Even more attractive than Betty, this woman wore the look of a flapper and wore it well. Black hair, shiny and chic in a curly Clara Bow bob with shadowed eyes and a come-hither look. She was a stunning woman with a body to match, judging from what Katie could see, but it was all ruined by her condescending air. Katie stifled a grin. Not to mention the incessant smacking of her jaws from gum that rolled around behind those cupid-bow lips. She waited for the lips to speak. They didn't.

Closing the door behind her, Katie managed a polite smile. "Hello, I'm Katie O'Connor—the volunteer from last summer. Is Parker in?"

Darkly smudged eyes perused her from head to foot with a slow sweep of lashes, then settled on her face with obvious disdain. Gum popped in her jaws. "He's busy."

Katie blinked, her polite smile gaping. She snapped her mouth closed and lifted both chin and brow, giving the flapper a dose of her own medicine. "Excuse me, but is he in a meeting?"

The raccoon eyes narrowed. "I said he's busy, bimbo, scram."

Katie's ire rose, along with her height on the balls of her feet as she lifted to loom over the desk. "Would you be so kind to at least *ask* Mr. Riley if he will see me?"

The gum went silent as the woman glared. "Beat it—*now!* He ain't got time for you."

Katie leaned in, both hands propped on the edge of the flapper's desk along with her purse. She couldn't resist a sugar-sweet smile as she lowered her voice. "But you see, he left his keys on my nightstand this morning, and I'm just certain he'd want them back right away." Katie gave her a knowing smile. "I'm sure you understand . . ."

Miss Manners shot to her feet. "I'll give them to him," she snapped. She extended a hand dripping with scarlet nails that matched her lips.

"No, thank you," Katie said in a singsong tone, dodging her as she bolted for Parker's door and knocked.

"Wait! You can't go in there—"

Parker glanced up when Katie opened the door. "Katie! What are you doing here?"

"Parker, I told her you were busy but she—"

"It's okay, Gladys, I always have time for Katie."

Katie clasped her purse in her hands and awarded Gladys a smug smile as she slowly eased the door shut in her face. "Thanks, Gladys," she whispered through the crack. "Can you make sure we're not disturbed?" She smiled and scrunched her nose. "We'll be busy."

With a click of the lock, Katie shot Parker a grin as she sashayed to a chair.

Parker smiled. "Mind telling me what that was all about?"

Katie crossed her legs and adjusted her short skirt in an attempt to cover her knee. "Let's just say ol' Gladys doesn't have Betty's finesse with people." She angled a brow. "Does she even know how to spell?"

"No, as a matter of fact. How'd you guess?" Parker sighed and tossed his pen on the desk. He kneaded his forehead with the palm of his hand before threading his fingers through perfect sandy hair. The effect was a somewhat disheveled look so unlike the Parker she knew, that she grinned. It made him appear more dangerous—like Luke.

Her grin quickly lost its glow, fading into a half smile. "Oh, I don't know, maybe it was that gum slapping around on her molars or the Grand Canyon view of her . . . uh, shall we say, finer attributes?" Katie's lips squirmed. "She belongs in Arizona, Parker, not the BCAS. You should charge admission." She gave him a narrow look. "Not that any females would get in—I think she may have designs on you, my friend."

Parker groaned. "Don't remind me."

She leaned forward to launch folded arms on his desk. "Well, if it's any consolation, I did my best to convince her you were already spoken for."

Color bled up his neck. "What do you mean?"

She winked. "I told her you left your keys on my nightstand when you left this morning."

Other than Sean, Katie had never seen a man turn that red before. Parker started to cough and reached into his bottom drawer to pull out a grape Nehi. With one raspy hack after another, he opened it and took a fast swig, bottom up, his face a close second to the purple in the bottle. The guzzling stopped for air while he held it out to her, obviously still unable to speak.

She did her best to fight a grin, to no avail. "No thanks, Parker, but I see Luke bequeathed you his stash." She shook her head and settled back in her chair, arms flat on the armrests while the grin still beamed on her face. "He was a bad influence, that boy."

"Yes, he was," he finally said in a hoarse voice. He set his Nehi on the desk and sucked in a deep breath. His brown eyes, usually so gentle, held a stern twinkle. "And so are you, Katie Rose. I'm sure you've ruined my reputation forever."

She wriggled her brows. "Or helped it."

He blushed again, desperately trying to shuffle papers into a neat pile.

Parker liked things "neat," she remembered, even his conversation. She changed the subject. "I'm sure you realize this is not a social visit," she began, attempting to resume an air of professionalism. She sat up straight and folded her hands neatly in her lap. Her tongue suddenly felt like Jell-O. "Have you . . . heard from Luke and Betty?"

Gentle eyes assessed her, as if measuring the depth of her hurt. "Yeah, I have. They're all settled in at Aunt Ruth's, and Luke's knee-deep in orphans at the CAS. He's already started both a football and a basketball team while Betty works part-time at the five-and-ten."

She nodded. Her eyes flitted from his face to the hands in her lap. "I'm glad. I wish them every happiness." She paused before her gaze returned to his. "Parker . . . after Luke left, you told me that if I needed anything—a shoulder, whatever—that I should come see you."

The brown eyes softened to almost hazel in the bright afternoon light. "You need a shoulder to cry on, Katie Rose?" he whispered.

It was her turn to blush. She trained her gaze on the edge of his desk, cheeks hot at the innocence of his statement. "No, Parker, not a shoulder." She looked up, gaze skittish. "A job."

Surprise flared in his eyes, and the clean line of his jaw shifted the tiniest bit. He leaned back in his chair and clasped hands to his chest, sleeves rolled like Luke used to do. His height and build—similar to Luke's—seemed slight by comparison, revealing forearms corded with muscles more prone to chess than basketball. The barest of smiles toyed with his lips. "You want a job," he said, more of a statement than a question, and the twinkle in his eyes inspired hope.

She nodded, holding her breath.

"What about law school?" he asked.

She swallowed hard. "Postponed . . . at least for this year. The economy, you know."

He nodded and his gaze slid to her hands and back, his

look pensive as he studied her through cautious eyes. "And how does Jack feel about that?"

She hesitated, drawing in a deep breath. "Also postponed," she said with a swerve of her lips. She exhaled with a faint smile. "You might say, forever."

Compassion flickered in his face. "I'm sorry, Katie. About everything."

She nodded as tears stung. "Don't be. Luke saved me from a big mistake."

"You mean like me hiring Gladys?"

She grinned and pushed the wetness from her eyes. "Yeah, kind of like that."

He sighed and ruffled a hand through the hair at the back of his head, once again giving him that rumpled look that made her smile. "Yeah, well, she's Carmichael's niece, so enough said there, I guess." He looked up, deep in thought as he rubbed a jaw just beginning to shadow with beard. "My budget's pretty tight right now, but we did receive a grant we weren't expecting . . ."

Her rib cage froze, unable to expel air.

He sighed again, depleting her hope, then flashed a little-boy grin that revived it all over again. "When can you start?"

She shot up from the chair. "Oh, Parker, you won't be sorry, I promise!" She giggled and rounded the desk, her heels clicking on his wooden floor with the same giddy excitement she felt inside. She leaned to throw her arms around his shoulders as he sat in his chair and hugged him tightly, never more grateful for his friendship. "How does Monday sound?"

His low chuckle rumbled against her ear. "Like heaven." He paused, his voice hesitant with apology. "Now, I can't pay much, Katie—" he began.

"I know, and it doesn't matter. I just need a job, and there's nowhere I'd rather work."

"And you'll need to take over all my typing from Gladys . . ."

"Yes, yes, anything you say. At least it won't be Luke's chicken scratch—"

"And," he said holding her at arm's length, a twinkle in his eyes, "I want my keys back."

She grinned and kissed him on the cheek. "How 'bout I bring them on Monday?"

"Sure," he said, and she noticed his dimples for the very first time.

She snatched her purse from his desk and then stopped, hesitation in her tone. "I don't have to take orders from the gum flapper, do I?"

He laughed, and the husky sound warmed her inside. "Uh, no, Katie, I think the 'boss's girlfriend' should at least be office manager, don't you?"

The blush in her cheeks went head-to-head with his. She darted to the door and turned, managing a silly grin as she placed her hand on the knob. "Well then, as office manager, I'd better get busy." And with that, she opened the door and blew him a kiss in full view of the ice queen. "See you tonight, darling, and don't be late." She closed the door and clicked past the flapper's desk with a perky toss of her head. "Good night, Gladys. See you on Monday."

And the only response was the snap of her gum.

The grandfather clock in Aunt Ruth's parlor chimed two and Luke jolted awake, his breathing labored as he stared at the ceiling of the tiny bedroom he now called home. He massaged the back of his neck, which was beaded with sweat like always after one of these dreams. His eyelids sank closed in defeat. Dreams? *Nightmare* was a better word. A surreal world where he always seemed to be running, sweating, desperate to escape . . . From what, he was never quite sure . . . but he had his suspicions.

He slowly rolled on his side to avoid rustling the noisy

springs, careful not to waken Betty in the next room. She was a light sleeper, and the walls were paper thin. With a guarded sigh, he adjusted his pillow and stared in the dark, wondering when the dull ache in his chest would subside, the one connected to his dreams. He swallowed hard, closing his eyes. The one connected to Katie.

He knew it was sin thinking of her, because when he did, the want inside was so strong, it was a physical ache, and so he avoided it at all costs. Until moments like this, when his iron will was at the mercy of his subconscious, foisting her memory upon him when he had no say at all. And then in his weakest moments, depleted of energy, heart pounding and will still groggy from sleep, he'd be faced once again with the fact that he was in love with a woman who wasn't his wife.

His wife. Because that's what Betty was, as surely as if they had consummated the marriage with a diamond on her hand, and he refused to think of her in any other way. His commitment was unshakable, and the vows were just a formality once he managed to get her to say yes. And it was coming, he could feel it in his bones. In the two months they'd been in Philadelphia, they'd become so much closer, their friendship almost intimate. He closed his eyes. He needed that intimacy badly—anything to draw Betty closer . . . He swallowed hard. Anything to push Katie further away . . .

He heard Betty's soft snoring through the wall and wished she slept beside him instead. He longed to commit to her in every way possible—with his vows, with his name . . . with his body. But then in the shaky exhale of his breath, Katie's face suddenly lighted once again, and his eyelids jerked open, desperate to erase her image and the longing it produced. *God, help me to be free*, he prayed with a shiver. *God, help me to love my wife . . .*

Holding his breath, he eased from the bed as slowly as humanly possible, at the mercy of the springs as they squeaked beneath his weight. Sleep would evade him, he knew, at least until memories of Katie grew cold in his bed. And so he would seek solace in prayer down the hall, until slumber could take him far, far away. With a gouge of his hand through his hair, he hitched his pajama bottoms up a fraction of an inch and carefully opened his door, welcoming the cool draft against his bare chest as he silently padded to the parlor. He sank into the couch with a weary groan and laid his head back, eyes closed and thoughts focused on prayer until the clock struck the half hour . . .

"Trouble sleeping again?"

With a jolt against the sofa, his eyelids twitched open at the sound of Betty's gentle whisper. Worry lines puckered the bridge of her nose as she stared, arms folded at a waist that was now a compact mound beneath a tightly sashed robe. "That's been happening a lot lately, it seems. Do you . . . want to talk about it?"

The concern in her eyes touched him, and he reached out and tugged her to the sofa, scooping her close as she tucked her legs beneath her robe and rested her head on his shoulder. "As a matter of fact I do, Galetti. Just what do you think you're doing traipsing around at this hour of the night? You and the baby need your sleep." He pressed a kiss to her head with a touch of tease. "Of course, if you listened to reason and quit that job like I asked, you could get all the sleep you want during the day."

Her heavy sigh blew warm against his bare shoulder. "We've been over this before, Luke. You know I need the money."

"No, you need your rest. And so does the baby. Besides, I already told you that I make enough for all of us." He bent his head to tuck his mouth close to her ear. "Quit the job, Bets, we'll both get more sleep, I promise."

She squirmed free from his hold to give him a look that told him he was wasting his time. "You know how I feel about taking charity, McGee, so don't start with me now. I'm already having enough trouble sleeping as it is. Between endless trips to the bathroom, worrying about you roaming the halls all hours of the night, and this drafty house that keeps my teeth chattering, the last thing I want to do is butt heads with you over money." Her lips flattened into a tight line. "I'm keeping the job."

He grinned and hauled her back to his arms, gripping her close until she sagged into his embrace with a sigh of surrender. He kissed her nose. "A little testy, are we? Mmm . . . can't imagine how it's going to be after the baby's born and you don't get *any* sleep." He drew her close to warm her, palms massaging her arms to generate some heat. He paused, measuring his words. "But we both know I have the answer for most of your problems, Galetti . . . and mine."

She stiffened beneath his hold, but he didn't give her the chance to respond. "Everything solved in one fell swoop—your worries about me, your sleep, your finances, and the future of your baby." He nestled his mouth at the side of her neck, his voice husky with tease as he kissed her throat. "Plus keep you warm, all at the same time." With a nip of her earlobe, he breathed his next words hot in her ear. "Marry me, Bets—please."

"Luke . . ."

Her voice held pain as she attempted to pull away, but he stopped her and cradled her face in his hands. His heart clutched at the sheen of tears in her eyes, and his jaw tightened. Betty Galetti had certainly cried enough tears in her lifetime, he thought with a stab of grief, and it was time that it came to an end. He stroked her cheek and felt his resolve harden as he studied the woman who *would* be his wife. He brushed a stray tear away with the pad of his thumb, and the misery in her eyes told him he was doing the right thing. Her baby would have a father, and his best friend, a husband who would protect and take care of her all the days of her life. He felt his will harden to steel. And by the grace of God, his wife would know there was a God who loved her . . . just like Brady had taught him. He sucked in a deep breath. But . . . he had to convince her to marry him first. Even if it took a mountain of guilt to do it. He studied her through narrow eyes. "Do you have any idea why I haven't been able to sleep?"

She shook her head, more tears glinting in the glow of the streetlamp outside.

"Because my life is on hold, Bets. You see, you just don't need me . . . I need you. I lie in that lonely bed night after night, knowing full well that I'm going to marry you sooner or later, no matter what you say." He lifted her chin with a firm grip, his eyes burning with intent. "So because you're too pigheaded to see the way it's going to be, you lie there cold, and I lie there on hold, frustrated that I can't love you the way that I want."

Her lip began to quiver, and he pulled her to his chest, squeezing her tight while a smile edged his tone. "I love you, Galetti, and nothing has ever felt as right to me as this. So either you say yes and marry me now, or both of us are in for a lot of sleepless nights."

A heave quivered from her lips. "B-but, Katie . . ."

His teeth ached as he clenched his jaw. "Katie, nothing. She's in Boston engaged to Jack while you and I are here, about to have a baby." He arched a brow, then slowly fondled her lip with his thumb, burning her with a smoky look he hoped would hasten his cause. "And I told you before, Galetti, I'm not going anywhere." He fixed his gaze on her mouth. "So how long are you going to make me suffer?"

She collapsed against his chest with a broken sob, and he grinned, stroking her head with moisture in his eyes. "So . . . can I take that as a yes?"

"Oh, Luke . . ." Her voice wobbled with another doleful sob, prompting a chuckle from his lips.

She sniffed and swiped her face with the sleeve of her robe. There was a timid flicker of hope in those wet, sad eyes, and his heart skipped a beat. He'd been relentless—wearing her down with his proposals, day after day, night after night, hoping against hope that her emotional state of pregnancy would work in his favor. He knew he was taking advantage of her, what with the fragility of her moods, but he flat-out didn't care. This was too important, and she was being way too stubborn. She blinked now, causing several tears to skitter down her cheek as he held his breath.

"Are you . . . sure?" she finally whispered.

He pulled away to study the woman he had loved more and longer than any woman alive. First as a sister on the streets of New York, then briefly as a lover before she became the friend he would do anything for. Tears stung his eyes. "I've never been more sure of anything in my life, Galetti," he whispered.

With slow, careful movement, he pulled her close to brush his lips gently against hers, deepening the kiss until she moaned in his arms. She melted into his embrace, and he smiled, finally feeling his body relax. He burrowed his lips in the crook of her neck, breathing in deeply and enjoying her scent. He had no doubt a time would come when he would love her the way he should—religiously, faithfully, completely. Without another woman in his heart. Knew it as surely as he knew the power of prayer. And in his waking hours when dreams didn't haunt, he could feel it too—every day when their bond became closer . . . and every night when he prayed their love could become one.

"Oh!" She twitched in his arms with a faint cry of surprise, and his hands shielded her belly, colliding with her fingers.

"What's wrong?" he asked, his voice raspy with concern.

She cupped his hands and guided them across her stomach, gently pressing his palm against a particular spot. "Can you feel it?" she breathed.

He closed his eyes and focused, holding his breath as he waited for movement. Nothing. He finally stroked her belly with a gentle hand. "No, Bets, what'd it feel like?"

"Like a butterfly fluttering or a goldfish swimming around."

He fondled her earlobe with his fingers, giving her a wry smile. "Are you sure you're not hungry?"

She smacked his hand and shimmied in close. "Of course I'm sure, you goose. It felt just like the last time—I remember the doctor called it quickening." She blinked up at him with eyes full of wonder. "Oh, Luke, it's really going to happen this time, isn't it?"

Pulling her close, he kissed her on the nose. "You bet, Galetti—you're going to be a bona fide mother."

"And if you get your way, don't forget you'll be a bona fide father too."

He chuckled and lifted a brow. "*If* I get my way? And how can I forget when this little guy keeps getting bigger every day?"

She jerked again, this time with a giggle. "Oh! Guess what he's doing now?"

"What?" he said with a gentle stroke to her abdomen.

"Embracing the moment."

He grinned in the dark. "Naturally." His smile faded to soft as he bent to kiss her full on the mouth. "And guess what I'm doing," he said, tugging her lip with the edge of his teeth.

"What?" she asked, her voice suddenly hoarse.

"The same." He caressed her mouth again before feathering her throat with soft little kisses.

She giggled and buried her head in the curve of his neck. "You think so, huh, McGee?"

He pulled away to cup her chin in his hand, his eyes tender with affection. His voice was calm and sure . . . like his love for her. "I know so."

Tears spilled as she blinked several times, and then she thrust herself into his arms so hard, she forced him back against the sofa with a chuckle in his throat. Hungry hands swept the length of his bare back while she nuzzled his mouth with her own. "Oh, Luke . . . I want you . . . I've always wanted you."

Heat suddenly surged, driving every other thought from his mind but the taste of her lips. He kissed her hard, and she moaned in his arms, jarring his senses back to reality. He jolted up straight and held her at arm's length, giving her the stern eye. "So, you'll marry me, then?" he asked, wanting it etched in stone.

She nibbled at her lip and nodded. "Maybe."

"No maybes, Galetti. You're already committed, just like me, so you might as well warm up to the idea." He kissed her again, hoping to help with the warming process. "When?"

Her breathing was erratic as she pushed away, indecision clouding her eyes. "I don't know, in a few months, maybe. But definitely before the baby is born."

His jaw shifted, tightening with the motion. "Nope, tomorrow."

She shook her head. "No, Luke, you need more time."

Ignoring her comment, he eased her back to explore her throat with his mouth, finally nipping at her earlobe before whispering warm coercion in her ear. "Don't make me wait, Galetti—I need you *now*."

With a quivering hand to his chest, she studied his face a long, long time before a tentative nod finally signaled her consent. He watched as guilt worked its magic, dispelling her resistance with the soft exhale of a sigh. She caressed his scruffy jaw with the palm of her hand while a beautiful joy pooled in her eyes. "You're the love of my life, McGee—yesterday, today, and forever."

"Mine too, Bets," he whispered, then bent to kiss her again.

Yesterday and forever.

20

For Katie, Christmas Eve had always been magical, but never more so than now. True, there would be fewer presents to open under the tree this year and an economy that put a strain on their dinner budget, but somehow it didn't matter. Her father seemed his old self once again, teasing his wife that he could take the stairs two at a time if need be, while her mother glowed with the effervescent joy of family and faith.

Katie curled up on the love seat and drank in the sights and sounds before her, along with the eggnog in her hand. Adults laughed and played cards. Children giggled and played hide-and-seek. And all the while the tree shimmered with cone-shaped lights flickering like candles and tinsel swaying as children whisked by. The house was filled with the wonderful smells of Christmas—cinnamon from fresh-baked snickerdoodles and pine needles—while the family was filled with awe over the blessings they shared.

Unto them a child was born, and the effect of the Savior could be seen in the love and peace that abounded beneath their snow-drifted roof. From tender glances between her mother and father, to secret smiles between Faith and Collin or Charity and Mitch, Katie saw actions far more familiar to newlyweds than those married for so many years. Brady hovered and Lizzie cooed, the baby in her arms their primary focus, while through it all, cousins ran wild with cousins, all breathless with excitement. Katie smiled at Sean sparring with Steven over chess as Emma chatted with Mrs. Gerson, their blind neighbor who'd shared every Christmas that Katie could remember. And amid all the teases and giggles and happy shrieks of children, Christmas carols floated from her father's radio, heralding a season of hope for a country so badly in need.

The doorbell rang, and Katie eyed the clock on the mantel. Seven o'clock—Parker was on time, prompt as usual. Her father looked up from his newspaper—a Christmas allowance from her mother. "Finally—the competition is here! I get so tired of demoralizing my family."

"We heard that," Sean said, eyes focused on the chessboard between him and Steven.

"Maybe it's time we let the professionals take over," Steven countered, "although I *am* kicking your backside rather nicely tonight." He slanted back in his chair with a cocky grin.

"You're all lightweights next to Parker," Patrick said with a chuckle, "which I admit, pains me to say." He winked at Katie as she jumped up to answer the door. "We could use some of his skill in the gene pool, Katie Rose."

"Father, don't start," she said with a rush of heat in her cheeks. "For pity's sake, he's my boss, and we're friends and nothing more." She sidestepped a game of checkers between Gabe and Collin on the floor and hurried to the foyer, heaving the door open with the glow of Christmas in her cheeks.

Parker stood on the threshold with a bag of presents in his arms and a ruddy smile on his face. Between the twinkle in his eye and his red nose and cheeks, he reminded Katie of a handsome St. Nick.

"Merry Christmas!" he said as snowflakes lighted on his coat and hair.

She smiled at the man she'd spent every day with for the last month, if not at work, then for Saturday night dinners and mass on Sundays. Parker's loneliness was as keen as hers, she quickly discovered, bonding them in a way she had never expected. Their friendship had deepened over sack lunches in his office or doing dinner dishes in her kitchen while her father eyed his chessboard, a hunter awaiting his prey. Her smile edged into a grin when a snowflake melted into his dimple, drawing her attention to the fact that in his own quiet way, Parker Riley was an attractive man.

She took his arm and pulled him inside. "We're going to have to thaw you out by the fire, I suspect," she said with a chuckle.

He butted the door closed, then shifted the bag from one arm to another to slip off his coat before tossing it on the rack. He yanked his gloves off with his teeth and shoved them in his coat pockets, then pressed a red, chapped hand to her cheek. "You think?"

"Oh, goodness, you're like ice!" Clasping his hand between both of hers, she rubbed hard, trying to build heat with some friction. "Is that better?" she asked, blowing on his palm.

His eyes instantly took on that same dreamy quality she'd seen in Jack's, a kind of half-lidded stare that settled on her mouth. "Much," he whispered, and his fingers twined with hers.

She gulped. *Talk about friction!* Katie jerked her hand back as if his were an icy snowball, stinging her palm. Heat whooshed in her cheeks as she spun around to take refuge in the kitchen. "Put your presents under the tree, then put Father out of his misery and let him beat you at chess. Do you want eggnog?" she asked, shooting a shaky smile over her shoulder.

He stood in the foyer, a bit bewildered like a little boy who was lost, sandy hair askew from the bluster outside. "Sure . . . but let me help." He took a tentative step forward.

"No! You sit, and I'll be right back." She dashed through

the swinging door and stopped, hand to her chest as the wood thudded against her back. *Sweet saints in heaven, what just happened?*

"Ninety-six, ninety-seven, ninety-eight, ninety-nine, one hundred! Ready or not, here I come." Hope Dennehy, Charity's eight-year-old daughter and Henry's twin, whirled around from her corner in the kitchen and screeched to a stop, her gentle eyes wide with concern. "Goodness, Aunt Katie, are you okay? You look as white as the snowman Henry built."

Katie swallowed hard and forced a smile. "Yes, sweetie, I'm fine. Just a little dizzy, I suppose, from all the excitement." She peeked out the door, then turned to give her niece a mischievous smile. She crooked her finger, indicating for Hope to come close, then bent to whisper in the little girl's ear. "Don't say I told you so, but I think they all barreled up the stairs, and if I'm not mistaken, I may have heard mention of Grandma and Grandpa's room . . . I think from Henry."

A giggle as soft as an angel's breath fluttered from her niece's lips as her blue eyes sparkled. "Oh, won't Henry be mad? Thanks, Aunt Katie, you're the best!" She flew from the room as if she had wings.

A chuckle bubbled in Katie's chest and then quickly popped at the thought of Parker. Her breathing slowed as she hurried to the icebox to pour him an eggnog, wondering what in the world she was going to do. He couldn't be falling for her! *Could he?* She leaned against the counter and closed her eyes, reflecting on the last month that they'd spent so much time together. His gentle encouragement, so soothing and strong, or the occasional hug that provided comfort between friends. Surely nothing more than a shoulder to cry on or lips to encourage, right?

And kiss?

Her eyes flipped open. For him, apparently, given the look in his eyes. She poured the eggnog, watching as it slithered into the mug, slow and creamy and as thick as the shock coating her throat. She gulped again.

But for her?

Her hands shook as she hefted the pitcher of eggnog back into the icebox. She closed the icebox door and then her eyes, tentatively testing the waters by allowing herself to think about Luke for the first time in weeks. The pain was immediate—sharp and wrenching, stealing the breath from her throat with such force, she bent with a groan. She blinked quickly to stem the tears with a hand to her mouth. *Oh, God, help me, please!*

The door squealed open, and she spun around.

"Gabe says you're next up for checkers. Apparently Collin went down in flames." Parker leaned against the door, arms folded and a faint smile on his face.

She flinched at the guarded look in his eyes, as if he guessed what she'd been thinking.

He strolled in and lifted the mug from the counter. "Is this for me?"

She nodded and moved toward the door while he followed, managing a nervous smile. "Poor Faith—she just hates it when Gabe beats Collin at checkers. He tends to sulk, you know."

Before she could leave, he stopped her with a gentle hand to her arm. "Katie," he said in a quiet voice. "You don't have to worry. I value our friendship way too much."

A lump shifted in her throat as she turned to look up into his eyes, her heart buckling at what she saw—tenderness, compassion, and the faintest glimmer of hurt. "Parker, I . . . I'm just not ready for . . . anything right now . . . anything more."

He squeezed her shoulder, resignation softening the distress in his eyes. "I know, Katie, and like I said—your friendship is precious to me. I will never do anything to jeopardize that."

She nodded and exhaled slowly. "Thanks, Parker, I appreciate that." She sucked in a deep breath and gave him a crooked smile. "Now, if you're ready, I believe we both have some humility to impart, Mr. Riley. Shall we divide and conquer?"

The evening was all she'd hoped for. She beat Gabe soundly at checkers, as did Parker her father at chess, and Collin seemed none the worse for wear as he munched on cookies and nuzzled his wife in his lap. Katie and Parker all but embarrassed Charity and Mitch at Pinochle, which they didn't seem to mind, although their winning streak ended abruptly when Sean and Emma came to call. When the cookies and wassail were gone, sleepy-eyed children sagged against parents, protesting the chore of going home. The house finally stilled and creaked beneath a blanket of snow while the hearth flickered low and the scent of pine lingered on.

"Will you lock the front door, Katie Rose, after Parker goes home?" Her father shuffled out of the bathroom in his robe and slippers, stifling a yawn. "Always good to see you, Parker, although you'd make more points if you'd throw a game or two."

Parker chuckled as he slipped his coat on at the door. "Sorry, Mr. O'Connor, but if it's any consolation, I have to work a lot harder with you than I used to with Luke."

A grin spread across Patrick's tired face as he scratched the back of his head. "Yes, it is some minor consolation, I suppose, meager as it might be. But a day is coming, my boy—you mark my words—when your wins won't always come so easily."

Parker's eyes sparkled. "I look forward to the challenge, sir. Merry Christmas."

Patrick squinted at the clock in the parlor and yawned again. "I suppose it is. Merry Christmas, Parker. We'll see you tomorrow."

Katie hurried to kiss her father good night. "I'm going to walk Parker out, but I'll be right back, and I'll be sure to lock the door when I come in. Good night, Father."

"Katie, it's cold out and the snow is deep—stay inside." Parker pulled his collar up and tugged on his gloves.

"No, I need to tell you something," she whispered. She bundled up in her coat and gloves, then opened the door.

They stepped out into the night, and silence swallowed them up whole while soft swirls of snow feathered their cheeks. Katie breathed in the clean, crisp air, feeling as if she had stepped into a Currier & Ives print of a winter wonderland. Enormous snowflakes fluttered onto her lashes and she giggled, trying to catch them with her tongue.

"You better go in, you're going to freeze out here," Parker said, ever the sensible friend.

"I will, but there's something I forgot to tell you," she whispered, suddenly shy as her thoughts returned to when he'd arrived earlier in the evening. She had told him then that she wasn't ready for anything more, and she wasn't, but something had happened tonight in the warm cocoon of Christmas. As if a dormant yearning had somehow been awakened, she became keenly aware of the common landscape she saw every day of her life. Her father's squeeze of her mother's hand, or Collin's kiss at the back of Faith's neck. Mitch looking at Charity as if he wanted to devour her, and Brady snuggling Lizzie while their baby slept in his lap. And then, in the midst of children playing and family sharing, the unthinkable had happened. Luke's face had appeared as if he belonged—playing chess with her father and cutting up with Collin, teasing Gabe or talking with Brady. Suddenly tears had threatened, and Katie had fled—praying for release in the shelter of the kitchen.

Please, God . . . take him out of my heart.

Composing herself once again, she'd returned to the sofa to talk to Emma, giving her ample opportunity to study the man who played chess with her father. The man who would love her . . . if only she would let him. His chiseled profile was nothing like Luke's, serious and strong where Luke's was stubborn and proud and always a tease on those wide, full lips. Brown eyes that were pensive and bore the weight of her problems rather than a piercing blue that fluttered her stomach. A gentle man, solid and calm, contrasting a passionate one who stirred her blood with his kisses. And then, somewhere between Emma's account of a shoplifter at the store and her father's triumph at besting Parker with a move, she suddenly found herself wondering . . . could she be happy with a man like Parker Riley?

She stirred from her thoughts and returned to the present, a smile tilting her lips at the snow in his hair and the concern in his eyes. "Merry Christmas, Parker," she whispered, then lifted on tiptoe to brush her lips against his.

His manner stiffened for several seconds, as if the cold had iced him to the spot, and then in the time it took for a snowflake to dissolve against her cheek, he pulled her close with a low moan and deepened the kiss.

Suddenly he wrenched away, his labored breathing billowing into the night. "Katie, I'm sorry . . ."

She touched a hand to his cheek. "Don't be, Parker. I kissed you, remember?"

A smile pulled at the corners of his mouth as those serious eyes studied her, cautious and nervous and so full of love. "Why did you?"

She rested her cheek against his chest, drawing comfort from the steady beat of his heart. "I don't know. I had no intentions, as you know, but then . . . something happened tonight. Call it Christmas or family or the fact that Betty and Luke are gone and you and I are still here. But I watched you playing chess with my father and mingling with my family as if you belonged, and suddenly . . . I . . . wanted to know you better."

He held her away as his eyes searched hers. "What do you want from me, Katie?" he asked quietly. "Friendship or more?"

She licked her dry lips before her eyes met his. "I think I want more. Slowly . . . but more."

A smile curved at the edges of his mouth. "You're in luck, Katie Rose," he whispered, "'Slow' is my middle name." He gloved a hand to her cheek, his eyes suddenly serious. "But I think it's only fair to warn you—I'm falling in love with you, my friend."

The muscles in her throat worked hard. "I have to admit, that does scare me a little."

He suddenly grinned. "Me too." The grin gave way as he looked in her eyes, and the dreamy quality returned once again. As slowly as if time were standing still, he bent to caress her mouth with his own, and her body relaxed, gentled by his touch. He pulled away and she remained there, face lifted and eyes closed, thinking Parker's kiss was unlike any she'd ever had. Not hungry and tempestuous like Luke's or Jack's, but quiet and steady . . . like the man himself.

She opened her eyes and smiled. "Good night, Parker, and Merry Christmas."

"Good night, Katie. See you tomorrow." He opened the door and ushered her in, closing it again to leave her alone with her thoughts.

Tugging off her gloves, she shoved them in her pockets and hung her coat on the rack, then stomped her shoes on the mat as she glanced in the parlor. All was quiet and dark except for the glow of the hearth. With a deep sigh, Katie bolted the door and tiptoed in to where her father appeared to be sleeping. She bent to press her lips to his cheek, and his low chuckle took her by surprise.

"That was a cold, cold kiss, Katie Rose." He turned in the bed with a yawn and a stretch.

She grinned and blew on her hands. "Sorry, I thought you were asleep."

"As if I could sleep with the ice of your lips on my cheek."

"You think my lips are cold, wait till you feel my hands . . ." Katie grinned and attempted to tuck her fingers into the hollow of her father's neck.

Patrick lunged to the far side of the narrow bed. "You lay one frozen finger on my tired body, young lady, and you'll find coal in your stocking come morning, make no mistake."

"Come on, Father, you can do better than that. What, no confinement, no threat of taking law school away?" Katie butted him over and sat, her eyes tender with compassion. "Speaking of confinement, when is yours over? I thought Dr. Williamson talked about releasing you to normal activity if you were on your best behavior."

Patrick grunted. "Humph. The man is a regular Ebeneezer Scrooge, if you ask me. Best behavior, my eye. I've done everything he and *that woman*—" with a roll of his eyes, her father jerked his head in the direction of his bedroom upstairs—"have asked me to do, and where has it gotten me? Bunched up in a cold, cramped bed on Christmas Eve—all alone, no less."

Katie grinned. "Well, cheer up, Santa should be here before long, and besides, you forget that Mother is cold and alone too."

"Good," Patrick said with a sullen smile. He adjusted the covers. "And speaking of pushy women," he said with a quirk of his brow, "how's it working out with you and Parker at the BCAS? You're not trying to ride roughshod over that young man, are you, Katie Rose? I heard you bullying him tonight about changes you think he needs to make at the office."

Katie sighed and slumped against the headboard. "I don't know, Father—maybe."

Patrick eyed her through narrow eyes and finally sat up. He jabbed his pillow several times and tucked it behind both Katie and him, then drew her close with a firm arm to her shoulder. "Compromise, Katie Rose, is a not a profane word, you know. In some cases, it can actually be in your best interest, not to mention being an excellent means of expressing love. And Parker is your manager, young lady, so you need to respect that and honor his decisions."

A weary sigh drifted from Katie's lips. "I know, Father, and I'm trying, really I am."

He squeezed her close. "I know you are, darlin', and I'm proud of you. You've grown up a lot these last six months, Katie, and it gives my heart great joy, I can tell you that."

She leaned back against her father's shoulder and closed her eyes to ward off the sting of tears beneath her lids. It felt so unbelievably good to rest in the safety of his arms, this man whose authority she'd spent a lifetime begrudging. A father who loved her enough to steer her and guide her, no matter how difficult she had made it for him. A silent grief welled within at the sudden realization that her own blind rebellion had robbed her of years of fellowship with this man, this father, this incredible source of love and strength.

Not unlike God, she thought with a clutch of her heart. As a little girl, she'd done nothing but thwart all authority, bent on her own will and her own way, fighting those she loved and alienating herself in the process. *Oh, God, forgive me, how very foolish I've been . . .*

With a sudden rush of love, she gripped her father's waist. "Oh, Daddy, I love you so much, and I'm so sorry for bucking you at every turn. I didn't know . . . I honestly didn't understand that all along . . . you only did it for me."

His low chuckle vibrated against her face, forcing hot tears from her eyes. "You're my girl, Katie Rose, of course I did it for you—our last-born child, and my precious challenge from God." She felt the comforting weight of his hand, stroking her hair as another chuckle rumbled her cheek. "Of course, I fully intend to have words with the Good Lord one day, darlin', as to why he sent you last when my energy was near depleted."

Katie pulled back to cup her father's face in her hands, emotion thick in her throat at the gray in his temples and the lines etched beneath tired eyes. "To keep you forever young," she whispered with a catch in her throat, "for me, Father, because I need you that much."

She felt the quiver of his stubbled jaw beneath her palms, and as he spoke, the glimmer of wetness in his eyes unleashed more in her own. "And I need you, Katie Rose. From the moment you took your first breath, you claimed a piece of my heart that nobody else can fill."

A smile blossomed on Katie's lips, and Faith's words echoed in her mind.

"You own a piece of God's heart, you know, Katie, like a piece of a puzzle that's missing. A piece nobody else can fill."

Katie wiped her eyes with the sleeve of her sweater and gave her father a tender peck on the cheek. "Merry Christmas, Father. And it will be—because of you, still here with us for a long time to come." She rose and gave him a quick squeeze. "I love you. Sleep well."

"I love you too, Katie. Good night."

A warmth that defied the chilliness of the winter night infused Katie with a warm glow as she mounted the stairs. She reached the landing, and all at once Luke's handsome face flashed in her mind, the memory of the night he'd carried her to her room painfully real. And in one aching beat of her heart, the warm glow faded as she made her way to the bathroom, her thoughts suddenly as scattered as the delicate crystals fluttering outside.

With a melancholy heart, she brushed her teeth and washed her face, but when she stepped foot in her room and kicked off her shoes, an overwhelming urge arose to talk to her mother. A long-forgotten need to cuddle in her mother's arms and soak in her reassurance that everything would be all right. Katie turned and silently padded down the hall to her parents' darkened room. She paused at the door, listening for the sound of sleep.

"Mother, are you still awake?" she whispered.

"Katie? Of course—I'm too excited to sleep."

A swell of love rushed through her at the sound of her mother's voice, and she bounded for the bed like she had so many Christmases in the past. Marcy held the covers open while Katie slipped in, and the warmth of her parents' bed made her feel six again.

Scooping her close, her mother kissed her head. "It was a wonderful evening, wasn't it?"

Katie nodded, unable to speak for the emotion in her throat. She squeezed her eyes shut, and water seeped from her lids.

Marcy stroked her face and stopped, fingers slick with Katie's tears. She pulled away to study her daughter in the pale moonlight. "Katie? What's wrong?"

"Nothing, Mother, I'm just . . . a little scared."

Marcy blinked. "You? Scared? I don't believe it. What are you afraid of, darling?"

Katie drew in a deep breath. "I guess I'm afraid of what the future may hold."

A sigh drifted from her mother's lips as she pulled Katie close once again. "You've been thinking about Luke, haven't you?"

She nodded again and sniffed, sinking into the warmth of her mother's embrace.

"You will fall in love again, Katie," she whispered, "exactly when God wants you to. And believe it or not, when you do, Luke will become nothing more than what he's always been—a wonderful friend from your past."

Katie nodded and released a shaky sigh, her tone quiet. "Mother?"

"Yes, darling?"

"I overhead Faith and Charity once . . . when you had that awful fight with Father after Sam O'Rourke came into town . . ."

Her mother was silent for several seconds. "Yes?"

"Well, they said something that shocked me."

"What was it?"

"They said . . . that when you married Father, you were in love with Sam." Katie hesitated, almost afraid to ask the question. "Is that true?"

It was Marcy's turn to pause. Katie felt the warmth of her mother's sigh, soft against her ear. "Yes, Katie Rose . . . and no."

"What does that mean?" Katie sat up.

Her mother's tone was somber, but her face held a peaceful smile. "It means that yes, when I married your father, I thought I was in love with Sam O'Rourke. But Sam was not the marrying kind, no matter how much I wanted him to be. So when Patrick began to call, I put him off for a long time, too in love with Sam to consider another relationship. But I had a firm faith in prayer, and that's what I did. I prayed for God to open my heart to Patrick if he was the one, and something amazing began to happen. All at once, I relaxed and got to know him and thought to myself, 'This is a good man.' He treated me with respect and kindness, even though I'd known he'd had a reputation as jaded as Sam's. But where Sam would stir me with his kisses and try to push, Patrick waited patiently and took it very slowly, wooing me with his love. So when I said yes to your father, I did have passionate feelings for Sam that I thought were love, but it was your father—then and now—who taught me what real love between a man and woman should be."

Katie toyed with the collar of her blouse. "So when Father would kiss you before you were married, was it quieter . . . less exciting than it was with Sam?"

Marcy squinted as if deep in thought. "Yes, I suppose it was, but I think that's because my head was so in the clouds over Sam, that I couldn't feel everything I needed to feel for your father." She paused, her voice growing tender. "But I can tell you one thing, Katie Rose. I remember most clearly the morning that I woke up next to your father about a year into our marriage. He lay there by my side, asleep and looking so much like a little boy with those dark lashes and handsome face, that I remember thinking in shock, 'Dear Lord—how lucky am I? I married the love of my life.'"

A second round of tears welled in Katie's eyes and she pushed them away with a grin, noting the same in her mother. "Oh, I want that so badly. Do you . . . do you think . . . I mean, could that be possible for Parker and me?"

Marcy sat up, eyes wide with surprise as she took Katie's

hand. "Oh, Katie, has something happened between you two?"

A sigh quivered from Katie's lips as she nodded. "He said he's falling in love with me, Mother, and I . . . well, I told him we could take it slowly."

With a faint cry of joy, Marcy hugged Katie tightly. "Oh, darling, he's a wonderful man, and I just know he would treat you well."

"I know it too, and I care about him a lot." She hesitated. "But the spark . . . like it was with Luke . . . well, it's not there yet."

Marcy stroked her daughter's cheek. "My grandmother wrote me a very wise letter once that I will never forget. I'd written her that your father had asked me to marry him, and her approval was quite obvious in her response. You see, she knew the heartbreak Sam had caused, and although she wasn't enamored with Patrick either, given his reputation, she told me she felt a peace about it. But she also knew the struggle I had for the very reason you mention—the 'spark' for your father was not what it was with Sam."

Her mother's eyes took on a faraway quality, as if she were traveling back in time to read her grandmother's letter once again. "I remember her words exactly. She said, 'Marceline, if you remember nothing else I say, remember this—always marry a man who loves you a little bit more than you love him.'" Tears glimmered in Marcy's eyes as she squeezed Katie's arm. "And she was right. Trust me, Katie Rose, if Parker is the man God has for you, the spark will come. Sometimes with attraction, all that fire and smoke just sting your eyes, keeping you from seeing those white-hot embers that will truly keep you warm. Just pray, darling, and you'll find your answer. God is the ultimate romantic, you know. You just have to have faith."

Katie hugged her mother's shoulders, content in the peaceful shelter of her arms. How she wished she had spent more moments like this rather than thwarting her parents' will as a self-sufficient little girl, bent on her own stubborn independence. She smiled and relished the moment, enjoying the feel of her mother's arm wrapped securely around her waist while her breathing feathered her face. With a sigh of relaxation, she closed her eyes, and all at once she thought of Parker.

White-hot embers. Her lips quirked into a smile at the thought, and with very little difficulty, she let herself dream of the possibilities . . .

Marcy lay next to her daughter with a smile on her face, listening to Katie's even breathing as she slept by her side. Her heart clutched at the memory of the little girl who had always seemed so aloof, as if being the baby had kept her too far removed from her sisters and brothers. *Thank you, God, for the woman this daughter has become* . . . "Guide her," Marcy whispered, "protect her, and open her eyes to the man you have for her."

Longing for a few moments more before waking Katie to dress for bed, Marcy wished she could just let her daughter sleep here, even in her clothes. It got so lonely without Patrick by her side, and no more so than on Christmas. She let her mind wander over the last two months, and felt an instant tightening. The thought of ever losing him was a constant threat which often flared into fear that clawed in her chest. She squeezed her eyes shut, the doctor's words echoing from two weeks ago.

"Marcy, the tests are back, and everything looks good. I don't want him going back to work just yet, but as far as the stairs and additional activity, marital or otherwise, if he just takes it slow, he can resume his normal life." There had been a tease in his tone. "And that includes, Mrs. O'Connor, the man's pipe, papers, and radio."

Her eyes blinked open in the dark, well aware she could give her husband the best Christmas present he ever had . . . if only.

You just have to have faith. Her statement to Katie returned, mocking her for her fear. She bit her lip hard, ashamed of her deception. Patrick had a right to know, but what if something happened? What if the pain returned when he mounted those steps? What if his heart faltered when he returned to her bed? Patrick O'Connor was a passionate man who'd been deprived of her love for over two months now. *Dear God, what if . . . ?*

No! She closed her eyes while the air thinned in her throat. She just wouldn't tell him . . . not yet. *Just one more month, God*, she pleaded. *I love him too much, and I'm just so afraid . . .*

Perfect love casteth out fear . . .

A silent groan rose in her throat as she opened her eyes. "Please don't make me . . ."

And he that feareth is not made perfect in love.

She exhaled slowly, as if to expel her apprehension. "Forgive me," she whispered as she sat up in the bed. "And *please*—give me strength to put him in your capable hands."

Drawing in a deep breath, she shook Katie from her sleep. "Come on, darling, I'll walk you to bed." She ushered her groggy daughter to her room and gave her a hug. "Good night, Katie Rose," she whispered with a soft kiss.

"Good night, Mother."

Marcy closed Katie's door and padded down the hall. Her steps slowed at the stairs as indecision railed in her mind. *I should really let him sleep, Lord . . . he needs his rest . . .*

Conviction pierced. *Perfect love . . .*

Squaring her shoulders, she made her way down the stairs and into the parlor, and the moment her foot touched the threshold, she was overcome by such a rush of love that her throat ached. Ornaments and tinsel twinkled in the waning light of the flickering fire, bathing her husband's bed in shadows that shimmered and danced across his thin cover. She heard his soft grunt as he snored on his back, legs spread-eagle and hands folded on his chest. Strong, capable hands that rose and fell with the beat of the heart that was so connected to hers. She hesitated. *But he looks so peaceful, Lord . . .*

Do it, Marceline. She smiled then, almost hearing God's voice, so like her husband's.

"Yes, Lord," she said and moved toward his bed. She bent to brush a kiss to his lips.

He jolted awake and blinked. "Marcy?"

"Merry Christmas, darling. I have a surprise."

A sleepy grin curved on his lips as he lifted the covers and pulled her in, nuzzling her neck. "What's it this time, darlin', a Christmas hug because you pity your husband?"

"Yes, and more," she whispered, snuggling close. "For starters, Katie and Parker may get serious. He told her he's falling in love with her."

"Ah, thank you, God, the gene pool!" His chuckle was sleepy. "How does she feel?"

"Well, her feelings for Luke are still a factor, I think, but I hope I convinced her that if Parker is the man God has for her, it will all work out."

"Amen to that," Patrick said with a yawn. "What else?" He tucked her close.

"Well, I spoke with the doctor and . . ." She kissed his jaw, the bristle tickling her lips.

He gripped her arms and held her away. "And?"

With the tip of her toe, she slowly trailed his leg with a gentle tease. "He said your tests all looked good and although he doesn't want you back at work before the three months are up, you can . . . if you're able . . ." She paused to feather a kiss at the edge of his mouth.

The fingers tightened on her arm. "Marceline!"

"Resume normal activities," she finished with a grin. Her finger traced his lips in a playful caress. "Such as stairs, your pipe, newspapers, and radio."

With a low groan, he pressed her to his pillow and devoured her with his lips. He jerked back, his breathing uneven. "Normal activities . . . does that mean . . . *everything*?"

She stared up at his handsome face and knew then that not only was God giving her husband a gift tonight, but he had given her the greatest gift of all, aside from his Son—Patrick's love. Tears pooled in her eyes. "Everything," she whispered.

"Thank you, God," he rasped, kissing her so deeply, his moan melted in her mouth. "I love you, Marceline . . ." He pulled away and grinned, brushing the hair from her eyes. "I hope those are tears of joy, darlin', and not that you have to share a bed once again and put up with my snoring."

A tear trickled down her temple as she smiled. She put a hand to his scratchy jaw. "I'll gladly put up with whatever you dole out, Patrick O'Connor—your snoring, your kisses, your love . . ."

A throaty chuckle rumbled against her ear as he fondled the lobe of her ear with his mouth. His hands and lips explored, and her breathing accelerated. "Heaven help me, darlin', do you have any idea just how much I've missed you?" He kissed her again, stealing her grin away.

Yes, she thought with another shiver of heat, *I do.*

And they never made it back to their room.

"Have you heard from Luke and Betty lately?" Lizzie asked. She patted six-month-old Molly on the back, a chub of a thing who sat on her mother's lap with Gerber baby food ringing her mouth. Pink cheeks hung like overripe peaches as she sat hunched, quivering with every tap of Lizzie's hand.

The essence of spring drifted into the partially open window over the sink, bringing with it the chatter of birds and children in the backyard and the earthy scent of mulch. A balmy May breeze fluttered both the tiny chestnut curls on Molly's head and the pretty spray of lilacs that graced the table, mixed with Marcy's creamy tulips in a crystal vase. An impressive burp bubbled from the baby's mouth, and everyone looked up from their sewing.

Charity arched a brow. "Goodness, she could give Henry a run for his money."

Lizzie grinned and returned her focus to Katie. "Brady talks to Luke every month or so, of course, but they never talk about important things like the names they've picked out or if she's carrying high or low. Does Parker give you any details, Katie?"

Katie squinted at the hem she was basting and smiled, grateful that the mere mention of Luke's name no longer caused a sharp stab of pain. Almost six months had passed since she'd seen Luke McGee, and between Parker and prayer, her heart was finally healing. She had wanted to take it slowly with Parker at first, but that had all changed when she'd discovered how safe and comfortable he made her feel. *Safe from the pain of Luke.* So when he had asked her to marry him last month, she had said yes, working hard to focus her thoughts only on him. And it was working—she was finally happy again. She drew in a deep breath and exhaled slowly, offering silent gratitude.

She looked up with a hike of her brow. "Parker? Details? Not unless they're attached to an adoption report or nailed to a chessboard."

"Really? I would think Parker would be good at details," Faith said, threading a needle. "He seems so sensitive about stuff like that, like helping you pick out china and things."

Katie's lips quirked. "Sensitive, yes, about details that relate to me. But details relating to a baby? Uh, no. There's nobody more sensitive than Collin, Faith, but can you see him gleaning details about baby names, the color of the nursery, or if a baby is carried high or low?"

Faith smiled. "I guess not. I suppose they're all a little too male to focus on the really important things. So when is Betty due again?"

Katie's eyes flitted to Marcy's calendar hanging on the cupboard door. She squinted. "I'm not sure of the exact date, but I would think any day now." She glanced out the window, anxious to change the subject. "Don't look now, Charity, but Henry has a stick—"

Charity jolted to her feet, hands on her hips as she stood at the screen door. "Henry, drop that stick right now—and *not* on your sister's head—or so help me, I will come out there and slobber you with kisses." She closed the door and peered out the window. "Men," she muttered, "what is it with power, taking control every chance they get?"

A husky chuckle tripped from Faith's lips. "Well, in Mitch and Henry's case, I'd say it's because they so seldom get to."

Charity shot her a narrow gaze. "I've gotten better at that. Just ask Mitch."

"With or without you in the room?" Katie teased.

Charity plopped back into her chair and picked up the trousers she was mending. "Without," she said with a shift of her lips. "After all, I don't want to tempt the man to lie."

Faith grinned and then glanced up at her mother. "So, how are things at the *Herald*, Mother—are there still rumors of staff cuts as far as you know?"

Marcy sighed. "Yes, apparently. And now Patrick tells me that he and his editors have agreed to take a pay cut for the time being, just until things pick back up."

"Which may not be all that long, according to Father," Katie said, trying to put a positive spin on the conversation. "He says he's encouraged that the stock market is climbing again. And government and business actually spent more in the first half of this year than the same time last year, so that's got to help too."

"Except according to Mitch, most consumers have cut way back on their spending, especially those who lost heavily in the market." Charity sighed. "And believe me, we've certainly felt the pinch at the store."

Marcy plucked a blouse from her basket and examined the tear that needed mending. "I'll vouch for that. With Patrick's pay cut and our savings all but wiped out, we'll be watching every penny for a long time to come. Which," she said with a weary release of her breath, "is why I'm becoming a rather handy seamstress." She smiled at her daughters. "With your help, of course."

Lizzie had Molly draped over her knees, swaying her to sleep while sewing buttons onto a jacket. "Katie, I thought you and Parker were going to spend the day scouting apartments."

A frown puckered Katie's brow as she glanced at the clock. "We are, but he's late for some reason, which is odd because Parker is never late." She squinted at Marcy. "He didn't call this morning when I was out, did he?"

Marcy shook her head with another needle tucked in her mouth. "Not that I know of, but Steven or your father could have taken it, I suppose, and forgotten to tell you."

The doorbell rang, and Katie popped up. "There he is now. Mmm . . . engaged for a month and he's already taking me for granted." Humming to herself, she opened the front door with a hand on her hip. "Goodness, Parker, I was getting ready to comb the streets." She stopped, her heart toppling at the deathly look on his face. "What's wrong— are you all right?"

"No, Katie, I'm not." He reached inside and grabbed her jacket off the coat rack, then draped it over her shoulders with a glazed look. His lips were as white as his face as he steered her out the door. "Can we talk on the swing, please?"

She started to tremble and he quickly helped her on with her wrap. His hands were cold, not unlike the sick feeling in her stomach. "Parker, tell me what's wrong, please."

They sat on the swing and he drew her close. The muscles in his throat worked hard as he struggled to form the words. "Katie, Betty had the baby late last night, a little girl . . ."

Katie turned and clutched his hands. "Oh, Parker, did the baby die . . . is that it?"

She'd seldom seen Parker with tears in his eyes, but she saw them now. "No," he said in a strained voice that sounded nothing like him at all. "Not the baby, Katie . . . Betty."

She blinked, the words not registering in her brain. Betty?

Gone? No—it was impossible! Her eyelids drifted closed and she could see the lazy curve of that beautiful smile, the faint sprinkling of freckles on that alabaster skin. In her mind's eye, she saw hazel eyes that had always held a twinkle, framed by that auburn hair that so often turned a head. Bile rose in her throat, and she thought she might be sick. Betty . . . *dead? No, God, please . . .*

She stared at Parker, so pale and so stunned, and felt tears spring to her eyes. She forced the words from her mouth, her throat aching from the strain. "How? Why?"

"Severe bleeding," he whispered. He stared, eyes stark with grief. "She died this morning."

The breath seized in her lungs. She closed her eyes and fell into Parker's arms, sobs rising in her throat. How could this be happening? To Betty? To Luke? Suddenly she thought of Luke and what he must be experiencing, and the anguish in her soul was almost unbearable. She needed to go there, to be there for him. *Now!* She clutched Parker's arms. "We have to go, we have to be there for him. I'll call the train station and then go pack—" She shot to her feet.

"Katie, no," he whispered, clasping her arm and easing her back into the swing. "I came to tell you that I'm leaving for the station now, and I'm going to stay with Luke for several weeks. There's no reason for you to come, and I need you at the office."

She blinked, not comprehending. "No reason to come? I love Betty and Luke—of course I'll come. I'll just make sure Bobbie Sue is in all week, and Gladys will be there too. I won't stay for longer than a few days, I promise, but I need to be there for him."

Parker gripped her wrists, his face as solemn as she had ever seen. "No, Katie, I'm sorry, but Luke specifically asked that I keep you away."

She flinched, as if he had slapped her. She sank back against the swing, eyes wet with shock. Her voice was a pained whisper. "But why, Parker?"

He pulled her into his arms and stroked her hair. "I don't know, Katie. All I do know is Luke is in a place he's never been before—broken, defeated, angry at God. He doesn't want to see anyone right now, even me, but I told him I was coming whether he wanted it or not. I called Brady, and he's going with me for a few days, at least until the funeral." He cupped her face in his hands. "Katie, listen to me. Luke's world has fallen apart—the last thing he needs right now is to see the joy you and I have—the woman he loved, now engaged to his best friend."

She nodded dumbly, all energy depleted from her body. "All right, Parker," she whispered hoarsely, "but tell him that I love him, will you? And that I'm sorry . . . so sorry."

He stood and pulled her to her feet, then squeezed her in a desperate hug. "I love you, Katie, and I'll call you when I arrive." He kissed her gently on the lips, then took her hand and led her to the door. He stroked a thumb along the curve of her jaw, his eyes raw with grief. "I need you to pray, as hard as you've ever prayed before. And don't stop."

She watched as he strode down the steps and out through the gate, the mourning in her heart almost choking her air. He needed her to pray. She put her face in her hands and wept. As if there were anything else she could do. Her body trembled with sorrow and pain while anxiety clawed in her mind. "Oh, God, help Luke, please," she whispered, her heart breaking for this man that she loved. "Be with him every step of the way and give him your peace . . ."

Though I walk through the valley of the shadow of death, I will fear no evil: for thou art with me; thy rod and thy staff they comfort me.

A heave shuddered from Katie's body as she sagged against the door. "Yes, your comfort, God, please . . . for Luke . . . and for us all."

21

December 1930

The day was bitterly cold, but Katie was wonderfully warm. She tucked the valet carrier that contained Lizzie's bridesmaid dress close to her body, barely aware of the occasional snowflake that swirled in the brisk December air. A biting breeze lashed against her, but she never felt a thing other than pure contentment. And all the while, a smile bloomed beneath the plaid scarf wrapped around her head and mouth. In three weeks, she would be Mrs. Parker Riley, and Parker had just told her last night he wanted her to go to law school in the spring.

The smile eased into a grin as she thought of her future husband. Since that very first kiss last Christmas, her feelings for him had deepened and grown from a dear friend to a dear man who quickened her pulse and spoiled her shamelessly. When she'd argued that the salary for the director of the BCAS could not possibly afford law school, he calmly informed her that it wouldn't be his salary sending her, but his inheritance from his grandfather, which despite the dismal economy, was still considerable.

Katie had been shocked. She'd had no idea he was a wealthy man because evidently it had slipped his mind to tell her. To Parker, it wasn't important, apparently, but to Katie it certainly was. Sweet saints, a wealthy man who lived like a pauper! She shook her head, amazed at this man who was so full of surprises—all of them good. Over the months they'd been engaged, she had learned so much about him—about his passive relationship with his father, his keen dislike of confrontation, and his strong desire to serve others. Her smile tilted. Especially her! There was nothing Parker Riley wouldn't do for her. She stopped, realizing with a touch of embarrassment that she'd gotten what the "old Katie" wanted all along—a rich man who was eating out of her hand.

A gust of wind blew her scarf off her head and she tugged it back on, her warm feeling dissipating somewhat, but not from the chill in the air. She frowned as she continued down Harper Street toward Lizzie's house, a niggle of guilt stealing her warmth. True, Parker let her have her way most of the time, but he was still in charge, she argued to herself, like at the BCAS. She quickened her pace to sprint across the street, determined to beat the car that was approaching. She huffed to the other side and shot a menacing glance at the man who had immediately honked his horn. With a lift of her chin, she returned her thoughts to the man she would marry.

No, at the BCAS, Parker was definitely the boss, and she usually did what he said. She slowed her pace to catch her breath, nodding at a postman who hurried by. *Well, some of the time*, she supposed, and worried her lip again. She halted at the next street to wait for several cars to pass and sighed. *None of the time, actually*, she finally realized. But could she help it if Parker was just so wonderfully easygoing, so gloriously permissive, so unlike her father?

Thoughts of Patrick O'Connor softened the sting of her guilt. It was her father who'd kept her from total ruination as much as she hated to admit it. His stubborn personality had always gone head-to-head with hers and usually won, which had only hardened her determination to be in control—of her life, her heart, and her money. She shuddered to think what might have happened if he hadn't reined her in, a spoiled brat that nobody could love.

The sun crept behind a billow of clouds, and a faint shadow of regret crept into Katie's heart. Regret that Parker wasn't just the teeniest bit like her father in telling her no. As much as Katie had hated her father's dictates, there had been a strange measure of comfort in the restrictions he'd imposed. As if she was being protected and cared for in a way she didn't quite understand. Tears pricked her eyes as she dodged a man on a bike. Well, she understood now. *For whom the Lord loveth he correcteth.*

"Thank you, Father," she whispered, and her heart swelled with love for the man she respected most in the world. "And thank you, God, for giving him to me." The wind died down, and her good mood returned. *And thank you for Parker*, she thought with a smile, *a wonderful man who showers me with everything I could ever want.*

Picking up her pace, she turned the corner onto Lizzie's street. Arched with oaks laden with ice, limbs merged over the cobblestones like a crystal canopy glinting in the sun. No, things were definitely perfect, Katie concluded with a lift of her chin. And for the first time in her almost twenty years, she was completely, undeniably content.

Almost.

The thought shocked her enough to halt her in her steps, frozen on the sidewalk in front of Lizzie's house. For the second time that day, the sun ducked behind the clouds, taking with it the warm glow in which she had basked. Her mood suddenly darkened along with the gray pallor now tingeing the sky. She pressed the valet carrier to her chest and closed her eyes, hoping to shut out the one imperfection in her otherwise perfect world.

In three weeks, she would see *him* again. It had been over a year since she'd laid eyes on Luke McGee . . . or twelve months, three weeks, three days . . . She took a quick glance at her wristwatch and frowned. "And seven hours to be exact," she muttered, but then who was counting? Obviously she was, she thought with a groan. She vented with a sigh and mounted the steps to the front porch, her spirits suddenly lagging despite the festive reindeer and holly-berry wreath on Lizzie's front door.

Katie pressed the doorbell, glowering at the button-eyed reindeer as if it were all his fault. "I don't want to see him again, God," she whispered, knowing full well in her heart that she had no choice. He was Parker's best friend and had been hers once as well, so why did it scare her so much to see him again? She closed her eyes and released a frail sigh, no longer pretending she didn't know why. The simple fact was that she wasn't sure—sure that the feelings were dead and gone. The feelings that had haunted her dreams for months until Parker's ring had finally pushed them away. And even now, against her will, there were those rare occasions when her mind would play tricks on her—she'd turn a corner and see his powerful arms launching a basketball into a net while chatting with kids on a weedy parking lot. Or worse yet, those infrequent dreams where those same arms held her close, forcing the breath from her lungs so hard she would always wake up with a jolt.

No! She could do this—for Parker, if not for herself. She would face him again and be done with it once and for all. Her spirits lifted along with her jaw. And in three weeks, it would all be over. She would say "I do" to Parker and "goodbye" to Luke McGee.

She pushed the doorbell again and pressed her ear to the door, suddenly aware that Molly was crying. Katie grimaced at the sound, hoping the little tyke wasn't hurt. At thirteen months, she was walking sooner than Teddy had and falling down more too, with plenty of scrapes and bruises to prove it. A grin lifted the corners of Katie's mouth. Poor Lizzie—two active babies under the age of four. Good thing she and

Brady seemed to have the patience of Job. Unlike her, Katie thought, as she rammed her finger to the doorbell for the third blasted time.

The door opened a smidge. "Katie—what are you doing here?"

Katie blinked at Lizzie, who appeared as white—and gray—as the burp rag draped over her shoulder. She held the valet up and arched a brow. "Your dress? For the wedding? Mother hemmed it, and I thought I'd bring it over so you could try it on." Katie grimaced, trying to see past Lizzie as Molly howled in the next room. "Can I come in, or would you prefer I stay out here in the cold?" She squinted at Lizzie as she tried to wedge in the door. "Is Molly okay?"

Lizzie clutched her arm, her whisper barely audible over the wail of Molly's lungs. "She's fine," Lizzie said in a rush. She snatched the valet from Katie's hand and tried to close the door. "Thanks, Katie, no need to stay. Tell Mother I'll bring it back tomorrow, all right?"

Katie butted the door open and frowned, brows puckered and mouth parted in surprise. "No, it's not all right, Lizzie." She pushed her way in and pulled off her gloves, shoving them in her pockets. "For pity's sake, I could be frozen to the bone outside, waiting on you to let me say hello to my niece." She started to unbutton her coat as she barged into the parlor and then stopped mid-stride, all air effectively trapped in her throat. And at that precise moment, "frozen to the bone" was only the tip of the iceberg.

"Hi, Katie . . . it's good to see you again."

Her jaw dropped like a rock. *Good?* To see Luke McGee standing in Lizzie's parlor? With a baby slung over his shoulder as naturally as a sweat rag after a basketball game in the street? Katie tried to breathe. She couldn't. To speak. Impossible—her tongue was welded to her mouth. She blinked. Good, at least something worked.

Massive hands calmly rubbed the back of a pink bundle draped over his broad shoulder, obviously having no effect given the thrashing of two fat, little legs. Katie stared, amazed at his air of calm despite the ear-splitting wail of the child he held. Without question, Luke McGee was all male and easily one of the most athletic men Katie had ever seen, but for some reason she couldn't ascertain, he looked as natural with a baby in his arms as he did with a basketball. The piercing blue eyes softened with apology as a hint of a smile flickered on his lips. "Katie's hungry, I'm afraid. Lizzie was just going to feed her."

She blinked. *He named his daughter Katie?*

Lizzie hurried over while Luke lifted the screeching bundle from his shoulder. He deposited a tender kiss on the baby's head, which was little more than a riot of red curls, and the innocence of that one simple action stirred something deep inside of Katie. Something she'd seldom experienced except with her nieces—a warm feeling that felt so strange as she studied the look of abject misery on the baby's face. *God bless her, the little tyke is starving*, Katie realized, and her stomach rumbled in sympathy.

Lizzie shot Katie a nervous look as she took the baby from Luke. "I'll feed her in the kitchen while you and Katie catch up. Come on in when you're ready, Katie, and I'll fix you some tea." She bolted from the room, hand fluttering against the baby's bottom like she was putting out a fire. The door swung shut with a whoosh, and in mere seconds, there was silence. A silence so thick, Katie wished the baby were back.

He pinned her with a solemn gaze. "You look good," he whispered.

She finally found her tongue. "Katie? You named her Katie?"

A sad smile edged his mouth. "It was the name Betty chose early on, I'm afraid. She thought it sounded strong." He threaded a hand through his hair and grinned. "Just so you know, I'm thinking of calling her Kat."

Katie nodded, still not able to believe he was standing before her, flesh and blood instead of a whim of her subconscious, haunting her during restless nights. He seemed leaner and certainly fairer than before, the smattering of freckles that had always faded into a tan now more pronounced against pale skin. Katie thought of the endless hours he'd spent outdoors all seasons of the year, and suspected he now spent them inside, caring for his daughter. The blue eyes still had the power to unsettle her, as evidenced by the racing of her pulse, although now they appeared tired and worn, as if he had aged years in the span of only one. She drew in a deep breath and laid a hand over the valet, which Lizzie had draped over a chair, then forced her gaze back to his. Her hands were sweating despite the cool of the room, and when she spoke, her voice shook. "I'm sorry, Luke, about Betty. It devastated all of us."

He nodded and for a moment, wetness glimmered in his eyes, but then he smiled, the effect warm and sad at the same time. "Congratulations. I'll bet Parker spoils you rotten."

Heat braised her cheeks, but she managed a sheepish grin. "Well, he does have a problem saying no, I'll admit, but I like to think I've grown up too and am, hopefully, not as demanding."

A twinkle lit his eyes. "I'll believe it when I see it, Katydid."

She chuckled, suddenly aware she'd been holding her breath. Drawing in some air, she leaned against the chair for support, absently fingering the leather seam of the valet that held Lizzie's dress. "I didn't expect to see you until the wedding. Does Parker know you're in?"

Luke's jaw shifted and he took several steps forward, holding out his hand. "Here, let me take your coat, and you can sit down."

"No!" It came out too sharply as she took a step back, and heat flooded her cheeks. "I mean, I can't stay." Air locked in her throat, and she swallowed hard. *God, help me . . .* She hadn't expected this—labored breathing, the threat of tears, this awful sinking feeling deep in her chest. Her eyes flitted to the clock on the mantel, the window, the kitchen door—anything but his face.

She heard his weary expulsion of air. "Yes . . . Parker knows I'm here."

She looked up then, eyes spanned wide. "He knows? That you're here?" She swallowed again, as if to clear the confusion in her mind. She made a feeble attempt to keep her voice light. "Funny, he didn't mention it. When did you arrive?"

He looked away, swabbing the back of his neck with his palm before the blue eyes locked on hers. A nerve fluttered in his cheek. "Last month," he said quietly.

She blinked. "Last month?"

"I couldn't take Philadelphia anymore without Betty." Muscles shifted in his throat. "So when Lizzie and Brady offered a place to stay while I looked for a job and help with the baby, I thought I'd take it."

She was in full gaping mode now, ire heating her cheeks to match the fire in her eyes. "You've been staying here . . . in my own sister's house . . . *for a solid month* . . . and nobody bothered to let me know?"

"We didn't want to upset you . . ."

She slapped two hands on her hips. "Oh well, that ship has sailed, now hasn't it?"

"Katie, we talked about it, and we thought it would be best—"

She marched up and stabbed a finger into his chest, glaring at him with the full force of her hurt and fury. "Best? Oh, I see—best for the pitiful little girl who got her heart broken, is that it? What, you were all afraid the poor little thing would fall to pieces?"

He quietly disarmed the finger probing his chest and curled his hand over hers, his eyes steeped in sorrow. "No," he said in a quiet voice that stole the wind from her wrath. "Not best for you, Katie . . . best for me."

The blood stilled in her veins as she stared, and in a painful heave of her lungs, she saw the truth in his gaze—the hurt, the regret, the love. A chasm of grief over his loss and hers opened up inside and tears spilled down her cheeks.

"Katie . . . ," he whispered, agony in his face as he caressed her arm. "Please don't . . ."

She squeezed her eyes shut, the gentle touch of his hand sending shock waves through her. *Don't what?* Cry? Feel like death now that he was back? Don't bleed at the prospect that he would never be hers? Fury rose in her throat like bile. How dare he! How dare he come back and ruin her life!

With a strangled cry, she raised her fists to strike him, only to collapse against his chest when he restrained her with his grip. His arms swallowed her up then, her body quivering while the touch and scent of him taunted her with a cruel reminder of all she had lost. Clarence Luke McGee—the little boy she loved to hate, was now the man she hated to love. But love him she did, to the core of her being, and the reality crushed her. She thought of Parker, so kind and so good, and the pain of ever hurting him was too much to bear. With a pitiful heave, she pushed Luke away, staggering back on her feet.

He reached to steady her, but she flung his hand away. "No! Don't touch me—ever!"

"Katie, please . . ." His voice bled with pain.

Without a backward glance, she rushed to the door, her tone nasal and her body shaking. All at once, she stopped and put a hand to her eyes, sick with regret. "Forgive me, Luke . . . for losing my temper. It's not your fault, not really. Will you please tell Lizzie I had to go?"

"Katie . . ." The sound of that one word was an aching plea.

But she wasn't listening. All she could hear was the door slamming behind her and the ridiculous pounding of her blood in her brain. She fled down the steps and then down the street, acutely aware that her whole world had just radically shifted. Gone was the warm glow of her engagement to Parker. Gone was her hope of happily ever after. And gone was the sun from the sky. Tears blinded her eyes as she ran, her fingers and hands strangely numb. And all at once—for the first time that day—she was painfully aware of the cold.

For all anyone knew, he was just another pedestrian milling in the rush-hour crowd, bundled in a black woolen coat with cheeks ruddy from the cold. But inside, Luke was a million miles away—or wished he were. All around him horns honked and police whistles blew while gasoline fumes and snowflakes drifted in the air, blanketing crowds who pushed and bumped, anxious to be home. Somewhere a bell was ringing, obviously a starving St. Nick hoping for a few pennies in his pot. But to Luke the peal of Christmas bells seemed more of a death knell, signaling the expiration of his hope the minute he had seen Katie's face.

There was no way he could stay and no way he would. Loneliness and mourning had driven him home, but it had followed him to Boston, it seemed, and would drive him away once again. He absently turned his coat collar up while he and the crowds waited at an intersection, eyes focused on the traffic cop as he waved burly arms in the air. The officer jerked a hand, and the crowd streamed forward, leading Luke like a lamb to its slaughter. He pinched a gloved hand to the bridge of his nose, wondering what in the world had possessed him to come home again. He had a great job in Philadelphia, and he and Betty had made some good friends. But then, everything had changed when Betty had taken her last breath. His best friend was dead, and suddenly so were all of his hopes, his dreams, and his passion for life. And he couldn't risk that, not with a daughter to raise. So when Brady had called and offered his home . . .

Someone dropped a set of keys, and Luke bent to retrieve them while the crowd swarmed around him like so many ants scurrying home.

Home. *Boston.* Just the sound had quickened his spirit, and Luke had felt Brady's invitation calling him back to the city that was more of a home than he'd ever had. And so he said yes, partially because Aunt Ruth was too old to care for an infant and Luke needed to work, and partially because he needed the comfort of family. Moisture blurred his view as he and the crowd surged forward, "home" foremost in everyone's mind. He hunched into his coat with hands buried in his pockets and blinked to clear the wetness from his eyes, knowing deep in his soul that it was "family"— Parker and Brady . . . *and* Katie—that had drawn him back.

And God? He sighed, parting from the crowd as he turned down Franklin Street to make his way to the Boston Children's Aid Society. He had certainly thought so at the time—that is, when he was finally speaking with God once again. Luke jogged across the street, waving at a vehicle that had slowed to let him pass. After Betty had died, he had railed at God, wanting nothing to do with him. Until John Brady had paid him a visit. And then, once again, the man who emulated Jesus Christ more than anyone Luke knew had picked him up and dusted him off for the umpteenth time in his life, leading him back to his Savior. Melancholy struck as Luke spied a group of boys shooting a ball into a hoop. He swallowed hard. A Savior who—he had believed at the time—had also led him home.

Wishful thinking. Obviously that's all it had been, not Divine Providence as he assumed. Parker had begged him not to take the job offered by the tiny pro bono law firm he'd found but to return to work with him at the BCAS instead. Katie would be in law school, he argued, and he needed Luke in the office. They could all be good friends again, he'd said, just like old times.

Yeah, old times.

Luke paused at the steps of the BCAS, craning his neck to study the second-floor offices where he knew she would be waiting . . . for Parker, not him.

"Come to dinner with us tonight," Parker had pleaded when he'd met him for lunch. "I'm supposed to pick Katie up at the office after my meeting across town, but I have a feeling it's going to run late. Do me a favor and pick her up and I'll meet you both somewhere."

"I can't," Luke had said, but Parker wouldn't back down. He pulled out the big guns and laid a hand on Luke's arm, his voice that of a skilled attorney going in for the kill. "I'm getting married, Luke, and I need you and Katie to be friends."

Luke stared up at his old office window, and a bitter laugh grunted from his throat. Yeah, pie-in-the-sky ideas that he and Katie could be friends. That he and Parker could work side by side, day in and day out, knowing full well that it was Katie's lips Parker would kiss each day and Katie's bed he would warm each night.

Well, maybe Parker believed it was possible, but Luke knew better. From the moment Parker had asked for his blessing regarding his growing feelings for Katie, Luke had done everything in his power to cheer Parker on. He was determined that his best friend would have the happiness he deserved, and so Luke convinced him that his feelings for Katie were part of the past. An Academy Award performance, apparently, that could have earned him Best Actor.

He exhaled hard, his breath curling into the frigid air in a cloud of resignation. And from what he had seen at Lizzie's between Katie and him, it appeared Katie would have nabbed Best Actress as well. Steeling his jaw, Luke mounted the steps, determined to do what he needed to do. Survive until the wedding, and then get out of town.

The door was ajar, and so he peeked in. She was all alone, of course, bent over an open file cabinet against the far wall. He took a moment to study her as she worked, admiring shapely legs with perfectly straight seams and a petite body small enough to belong to a young girl, but curved enough to ensure she was a woman. She was such a little thing, a pistol whose courage and spunk was way taller than she, this frail little girl he'd always wanted to protect. A nerve pulsed in his jaw. Yeah, well, here was his chance.

He knocked on the door and she whirled around, hand and papers splayed to her chest. Her shock was obvious from the gape of her mouth, and when her brain registered who it was at the door, a pretty shade of rose invaded her cheeks. Her throat worked several times before she was able to speak, and when she did, it was with a faint stutter. "P-Parker's n-not here."

He would have laughed at the way he could rattle her if it wasn't so tragic for them both, but he took no joy in her discomfort now, nor his. He cleared his throat and opened the door wide, careful not to close it again. "Parker sent me to pick you up. Said his meeting will probably run late. Wants us to meet him for dinner, The Union Oyster House, six o'clock."

Her throat bobbed again. "He didn't mention you coming to dinner." The papers clutched to her chest were bent from her white-knuckled grip, coaxing a half smile to his lips.

"Yeah, well, he pretty much strong-armed me at lunch today when I told him I saw you at Lizzie's." The smile faded on his lips. "He says he wants us to be friends."

"You didn't tell him . . . ?" she said, her face as white as the expanse of her eyes.

He mauled the back of his neck with his hand, offering her a bleak smile. "No . . . no, I lied actually—to both Parker and Lizzie, something I usually try to avoid. I told them you were thrilled to see me and everything was fine."

Her body seemed to sag in relief, the papers in hand finally fluttering to her side. She looked up with moisture in her eyes, and it took everything in him to stay where he was.

"Thank you," she whispered. "I couldn't . . . wouldn't . . . do that to him."

"I know, Katie," he said quietly. "I wouldn't ask you to." He exhaled and massaged his temple. "Nor would I. Parker is one of the finest human beings I've ever met, and the best friend I've ever had. The very last thing I would ever want to do is hurt him."

She nodded and slowly shut the file drawer. It closed with an ominous click of finality . . . like their relationship was about to do.

"So . . . what do we do?" she asked weakly.

"Well, for starters . . ." He stared beyond her as he absently rubbed his fingers against his mouth, thinking about the deception he'd planned. He drew in a deep breath and met her gaze once again, and the vulnerability in those blue eyes almost undid him. He looked away. *Focus, McGee—people you love are at stake here.* He strolled over to sit on the edge of Betty's desk, which he now assumed was hers, and a stab of grief revisited him all over again. He forced his thoughts to the present and unbuttoned his coat. "I think we need to go to dinner tonight and show Parker we can be friends—"

Her head was shaking before the last word ever crossed his lips. "No . . ." She clutched arms to her waist, crumpled papers fanned at her side, looking like the scared little girl he so wanted to protect. "I can't."

His jaw tightened. "You can and you will, Katie Rose. One night, that's all I'm asking for. If one of us doesn't show tonight, he'll know something is up, and we can't afford that."

With a shiver of her body, she walked to the desk and threw the papers in the basket. Her hand shook as she put it to her eyes. "I can't, Luke . . . please."

Desperation arose, and he grabbed her arm, fisting it tightly, coldly. "Yes, you can! We both love this man, Katie, and he's too important to let our feelings get in the way. I know what you're made of—tough mettle that tells me you can do this. I've seen you do it. You fooled me—convinced me you didn't care—you can fool him."

She jerked her arm free, and her eyes all but scalded him,

relieving some of the tension in his chest. *Finally* . . . a spark of anger!

"That's because I fooled myself," she cried, fists clenched white at her sides. But then all at once, the fury died on her face as her body crumpled and her eyes swam with tears. A hand quivered to her mouth. "Oh, Luke, forgive me, please—I was too blind to know that I loved you . . ." Her voice trailed off. "Too stubborn to know that I needed you . . ."

The urge to hold her was so strong, his teeth clenched in his jaw. He couldn't let her do this to him, unravel him with what might have been. He drew in a deep breath and eased back on the desk, keeping his tone firm. "That's over and done with, Katie, and our lives are headed in different directions now. We need to focus on Parker, join forces in our allegiance to him."

She finally nodded. Squaring her shoulders, she wiped the wetness from her face with the back of her hand. "So . . . ," she said with a shift in her throat, her voice as frail as the air that quivered from her lips. "Our hearts are to be joined after all . . . through our mutual love for Parker."

Her words lighted upon him like a gentle mist beneath a scorching sun, cool and comforting. A common bond . . . to seal their love forever. He sighed and folded his arms, a final barrier to ensure their decision was made. "I guess so, Katie."

Moving toward her chair, she sat down and crossed her legs, arms clutched to her waist. Her expression shifted into nonchalance as she focused on her desk. "So, what's the plan?"

Exhaling his relief, he put his head in his hand to knead the stress from his brow. "We go to dinner tonight, we talk, we laugh, we act like the best of friends." He looked up, a faint smile on his lips. "Because we are, Katie, and will be in the future." He rolled his neck to get rid of a kink. "Then I tell Parker I can't take the job here because I've got a better one in New York."

She blinked. "You're leaving Boston?"

He hiked a brow, shooting her that annoying smirk that always got under her skin. "Would you rather I stay?"

"No . . ." Blood gorged her cheeks, and she swallowed hard.

"I didn't think so," he said with a grin.

She squinted up at him. "You're going to lie again? About the job in New York?"

"I beg your pardon," he said with an indignant air. "I lied the first time because I had to save you, Little Miss Sass, but I don't generally make a habit of it. It just so happens that Parker's father sees me as a second son, and when I called yesterday to tell him I needed a reference, he offered a job instead—at the Children's Aid Society office on Staten Island." His lips quirked. "Lucky for me the director's pay is lousy—the turnover is terrible."

Her shaky smile only made the wetness in her eyes all the more painful.

"And Lizzie has been kind enough to offer to keep Kat while I go and settle in and look for someone to watch her while I'm at work. So rest assured, Katie Rose, after tonight, you will be well rid of me." He stood to his feet. "Are you ready to go?"

She pulled her purse from the bottom drawer, then rose and walked to the time clock. He watched her punch out, and the memory of her first day in the office washed over him like a wave of want, stinging his eyes. Dear God, what a brat she was. Dear God, how he loved her.

She tugged her coat from the rack, and he strode over to help her put it on, his hands trembling as he slipped it over her shoulders. She turned and looked up at him then, her eyes as soft and full of love as they were whenever she haunted his dreams. "Just for the record, Luke McGee, I love you. And I will love you until the day I die."

He swallowed hard and bit back the words he wanted to say, cloaking them with a sad smile instead. "No, you won't, Katie, at least not this way. Not with the caliber of man that

Parker Riley is . . . and not with the power of prayer." He lifted her scarf up to cover her head, then carefully tucked it around her neck. "We have to go, it's almost six." With a tight press of his lips, he moved to the door and flipped the lights off, then put his hand to the knob. "Ready?"

For several paralyzing moments, Parker stood pressed against the wall in the shadowed entryway of the next office, the sound of Luke and Katie's voices fading down the stairs. He finally moved toward the elevator like a zombie, oblivious to the cool touch of the steel button as it lay beneath his hand. And then with a slash of grief, he stumbled back from the doors with a hand to his eyes. The elevator opened, and Carmichael blinked.

He looked at his watch, then squinted up at Parker as he stood in a daze. "It's almost six. I thought you had a meeting across town and weren't coming back." He glanced at the darkened glass door to the Legal Department. "You coming or going?"

Parker just stared, his mind too numb to answer.

"Riley? Are you all right?"

He nodded, and his breathing was so harsh, it seemed to echo in his ears. He licked his lips. "I . . . forgot something and came back."

"Nothing important, I hope?"

"No . . . not anymore." Pain shifted in his throat.

"Well, you coming or going? I don't have all night."

Parker waved him off. "I think I'll take the stairs after all, thanks—I'd rather walk."

The elevator slammed shut, and his eyes trailed into a hard stare. He shifted his briefcase from one sweaty hand to the other, unprepared for the swell of anguish that overpowered him. His shoulders sagged and he put a hand to his eyes, knowing exactly what he needed to do.

He would walk.

22

She missed him. He'd only been gone three days, but it was lonely in the office without him because he so seldom traveled. He preferred the quiet life—working on behalf of children behind an old, battered desk rather than hobnobbing with the brass in New York. Much to his father's disdain, Parker Riley was a simple man, with no aspirations to rise to the top of the Children's Aid Society like his father wanted him to do.

Katie glanced up at the clock. "Uh-oh, you two better scoot—or Mr. Riley may show up and give you something to do."

With a scrunch of brows, Bobbie Sue shot a lopsided grin. "Sweet tea in the morning—are we talking about the same boy here? That man has a giant-sized marshmallow for a heart, and everybody knows it. And nobody knows that better than you, Miss Sass."

Katie grinned and inserted a piece of paper into her typewriter. She spun the platen with a lift of her chin. "That's right, Mizzzz Dulay, and don't you forget it. In two weeks, it will be me running the show—as Mrs. Parker Riley."

"Humph, you do now. Ain't that right, Mizzzz Carmichael?"

Gladys finished applying her lipstick and gave Katie a droll smile. "Sure . . . ever since she stole the boss out from under my nose, that is." She rose to her feet and winked, putting on her coat. "Tell me, Katie, has he left his keys on your nightstand lately?"

Katie chuckled to deflect the heat in her face. "I've already told you, Gladys, that was only a ploy to get into his office. Parker is completely committed to doing things the right way. For pity's sake, the man barely kisses my cheek, much less leaves his keys on my nightstand."

"Mmm . . . doesn't sound like the right way to me," Gladys said with a sultry grin. "I think she's trying to shoo us out so she can be alone with her sweetie. When does his train get in?"

Another blush warmed Katie's cheeks as she eyed the clock. "Around five-thirty, so he should be here about six. And I'm staying, Bobbie Sue, so if you want, I can finish that report."

"Be my guest." Bobbie Sue dropped papers on Katie's desk along with Carmichael's notes, then wrestled into her coat and clocked out, right behind Gladys. "Thanks, sassy girl." She followed Gladys to the door, then turned and winked. "Give that boy a kiss for me, ya hear?"

"For me too," Gladys called, her giggle echoing down the hall.

Bobbie Sue winked and closed the door, leaving Katie with a smile on her lips. She hummed to herself as she made a half pot of double-strong coffee—as stout as she liked since no one was there to complain—then returned to her desk to finish the report. The office was so quiet with everyone gone and ice-frosted windows to block out the street noise, but Katie didn't mind as she typed away. The rattle of the radiator and the purring of the coffeepot almost relaxed her, which was something she needed as she waited for Parker.

The dinner with Luke before Parker had left town had been strained, although Katie was certain that she and Luke had played their parts well. She stared at some of Carmichael's unreadable notes and frowned, her face squinted in thought. True, Parker had seemed rather quiet, but then, Parker had always been the quiet one.

Hadn't he?

A few moments later, the coffeepot spit and steamed, indicating the cycle was through, and Katie rose with the same unease she'd been wrestling with all day. Feeling somewhat stifled, she pushed the sleeves of her sweater up and poured a cup of coffee. Not unease over Luke—no, after their dinner out, that hurt had been pushed aside to focus on Parker, she and Luke determined he would never know the pain that festered in their hearts. Luke had been right—she had the mettle to see this through, to say "I do" to Parker when it should have been Luke by her side. She took a quick sip of the steaming liquid and returned to her desk, her resolve as strong and hot as the coffee that coated her throat. And somehow she knew—as sure as the diamond that glittered on her hand—that the power of prayer and that of Parker's love would transform her . . . into the wife Parker Riley truly deserved.

The door creaked open, and she looked up, a smile tilting her lips at the sight of the man who would be her husband. She rose to her feet and hurried to where he stood, a suitcase in his hand. "All right, this settles it—you are never going anywhere without me again. Do you have any idea how much I missed you, Parker Riley?" She stood on tiptoe to brush her lips against his.

"I missed you too, Katie," he whispered, his eyes worn and tired.

She pressed a hand to his cheek. "You look exhausted. Didn't you sleep well?"

His hand was cold from the weather as it covered hers, pressing it against his bristled jaw. "No, not really. Too much on my mind."

She reached up to kiss him again with a tease in her tone. "I suppose now you're going to tell me you're having second thoughts about marrying me."

He didn't answer, and she took his hand. "Parker?"

A lump shifted in his throat as he sandwiched his palm over hers. "I am, Katie."

The air locked in her throat and she stared, not willing to hear the rest of this conversation. She hurried to her desk to pull a swatchbook of fabric from her top drawer. "Look, I found the perfect material to recover that old sofa Mother and Father are giving us—"

The serious brown eyes, usually so calm and tender, now held the same look of grief as when Betty had died. "It's no good, Katie . . . ," he whispered.

She blinked, denial thickening in her throat. "Well, I know it's a bit busy—"

"No," he said in a voice that lanced her heart. "Not the swatch . . . us."

Her legs buckled and she sagged against the desk, heart pounding in her throat. When she found her voice, it was little more than a croak. "What are you saying, Parker?"

He moved forward with a firm bent to his jaw that she seldom ever saw. Without saying a word, he took his coat off and placed it on her desk and his suitcase on the floor, then looked up, his eyes pools of pain. The wind had wreaked havoc with him, ruffling that soft, sandy hair he tried so hard to keep combed, and he wore the stylish jacket she'd picked out, the tweed one that she loved. He was several feet away, but she could still smell the familiar scent of Bay Rum, and she closed her eyes, trembling at the prospect of losing this man that she loved.

Her eyes flinched open when his hands caressed her arms. "Katie, please forgive me, but I've prayed about this, and I feel our marriage would be a mistake."

Her eyelids flickered and closed as she swayed on her feet. He steadied her, hands clasped to her arms, and she felt the tender strokes of his thumbs as they grazed against her skin. Tears stung beneath her lids, and her breathing was shallow when she finally spoke. "No, Parker, please—don't do this. I love you."

His voice was as stricken as hers. "I love you too, Katie—I love your strength and your stubbornness and your passion for the things you believe in. But it's those same things I love in you that have taught me that I'm not being fair to you."

"Parker, no!" A sob broke from her throat as she opened her eyes. She clutched him, tears welling. "You just got back from a grueling trip—you're tired and need to rest."

"Actually, Katie, I returned early . . . and have been home several days now, thinking, praying . . ."

She stared, her eyes glazed with shock. "You've been home? And you didn't call?" Her voice was frail and reedy, matching the disbelief in her mind. She glanced at the suitcase on the floor. "But your suitcase . . . ," she whispered.

He looked away. "I'm leaving again . . . this time for good."

She wavered, unsteady as the blood rushed from her face. He blurred before her in a wash of tears. "Parker, I love you and I beg you—don't do this, please."

He caressed her cheek with the pad of his thumb, his calm eyes staring back with a sheen of tears. "Hear me out, Katie, please. After college, the desire of my heart was to serve God in the purest capacity possible. I knew deep in my soul that I had a calling, a vocation to live for him and only him. My father never understood that, of course, nor would he tolerate it." He drew in a deep breath, his fingers splayed against the side of her head. They threaded into her hair, and her eyes drifted closed again, memorizing every detail of this man she'd grown to love. "And being the dutiful son he expected me to be, I did what he wanted—I became a lawyer."

He sighed again and sat down on the edge of her desk, her hand clasped in his as he drew her close. "But I'm not sorry, because I met you . . . and Luke, and would you believe, he's the only real friend I've ever had, other than you and Betty and Bobbie Sue?" He closed his eyes and shook his head, wetness shimmering in his lashes. "He was so hard and so tough with others . . . and yet so kind with me." He wiped his eyes with the ball of his hand and laughed. "What an unlikely pair we made. Mutt and Jeff—polar opposites who became friends. The good-looking thug from the streets who beat people up . . . and the brainy rich kid who wanted to serve God."

He exhaled and opened his eyes, the calm taking control once again. His smile was peaceful. "I love you, Katie . . . and I love Luke, but I have to do what my heart is telling me to do." He swallowed hard. "What God is telling me to do."

She slumped against him, head on his shoulder and voice broken. "Oh, Parker, why . . . ?"

He grasped her face in his hands, his eyes intent. "As much as I love you, Katie," he said with quiet authority, "I'd rather have God's will than my own . . . for you, for me . . ." He paused, his voice betraying the barest trace of a waver. "And for Luke. Because therein lies God's best."

Her eyes spanned wide, swimming with tears. "Oh, no, Parker, w-why are you saying that? What do you know?"

He rubbed her arms slowly, eyes tender as he stared from where he sat on the edge of the desk, his gaze level with hers. "I know I'm not the man God has for you, Katie . . . as much as I want to be."

"No!" With ragged breathing, she kissed him hard, the taste of her tears salty on his lips. She heard a faint groan that seemed to come from deep within him before he swallowed her up in his arms, kissing her with more passion than he had ever shown before.

Hope sprang inside and she clutched him until her fingers ached. "Oh, Parker, please, I want you to marry me!"

He gripped her close, head tucked tightly into the curve of her neck. His voice, barely audible, held both peace and sadness. "Oh, Katie, it will be my privilege to marry you someday . . . but as the priest who performs the ceremony, not as your husband."

Someone cleared their throat at the door, and Katie jolted.

"Uh . . . sorry if I'm interrupting something here, Parker old boy, but you did say six . . ." Luke seemed ill at ease as he stood in the doorway and glanced at his watch. As if to deflect his discomfort, he slacked a hip against the door and plucked the leather gloves from his hands, flashing them a grin. "Of course, I can always go outside and walk around the block a few times . . ."

Parker smiled, eyes flicking to the clock on the wall before returning to Luke. He squeezed Katie's hand and rose to his feet. "Right on time, McGee, as always. I'll tell you, when it comes to punctuality, my friend, you're a credit to our sex."

"Only in punctuality?" Luke asked with a cocky grin. He strolled in and stuffed his gloves into his pocket. "What about basketball, baseball . . . chess?" His gaze flitted to Katie and sobered a degree, apparently noting the distress in her red-rimmed eyes. His voice lost its sparkle. "You two okay? I can come back if you—"

"No, come on in, Luke, and take off your coat, please. I have a favor to ask."

Katie exchanged a worried look with Luke, then gripped Parker's arm. "Parker, please, I'm begging you . . ." Her eyes filled with a second round of tears.

Alarm registered in Luke's voice. "What's going on here, Parker?"

Parker hooked an arm to Katie's waist and pulled her close, his hand stroking her hair as she wept against his chest. "I need you to take over as director of the BCAS."

Luke blinked, not sure he had heard correctly. The sound of Katie weeping wrenched in his gut and he swallowed hard, forcing a flip tone. "Love to, old buddy, but you forget I'm the new director for Staten Island." He attempted a wry grin. "I doubt your budget can lure me away from such a lucrative future."

Parker stared with his usual calm while Katie's tiny body shuddered against his. "I'm not joking, Luke," he said quietly. "I need to know things are in good hands before I leave."

Ice-cold prickles shivered Luke's spine. "No, Parker, you hear me?" His voice was hard, tinged with fear. "I don't know what game you're playing here, but I refuse to be a part of it. So hear me loud and clear—the night of your wedding, I will be on my way to New York."

"There isn't going to be a wedding," he said softly, and Katie cried all the harder.

"For the love of God, why?"

It was a dichotomy that Luke couldn't fathom—Parker's hand stroking Katie's hair with such tenderness and calm while she fell apart in his arms. "Because I fell in love with a woman who taught me about courage—courage to follow my dreams and to press on despite the most painful obstacles." His voice thickened with emotion. "And because I have a friend who taught me what real love is all about."

"That's crazy! You can't just walk out on Katie . . . on these kids—"

"I'm not," Parker said with a sad smile. "I'm leaving them—and her—in good hands."

Luke snatched his gloves from his pocket and jerked them on hard, fire burning in his eyes. "Well, I won't do it. You're just going to have to stay."

Parker glanced at the clock. "Can't, McGee. My train leaves in fifty minutes, and Carmichael's expecting you on Monday. He has a list of everything in progress that he'll fill you in on. And then later, when you have time, there's a list in my desk of pet projects I'd like you to handle, no hurry." He gently dislodged Katie from his chest and cupped her face in his hands, brushing his lips against hers. "I love you, Katie O'Connor. Thank you for the best year of my life."

Katie sobbed, and Luke stared in shock as Parker lifted his

coat from the desk and put it on, then picked up his suitcase and approached with extended hand. "You're somewhat lacking at chess, McGee, but as a friend, you're the best there is."

"No," Luke said, backing away. "You're not doing this, Riley. I refuse the job."

Smiling, Parker set down his suitcase and moved forward, ignoring Luke's refusal with a tight clasp of his shoulders. "No you won't, McGee. Contrary to popular opinion, you're the one with a cream puff for a heart, not me." He glanced at Katie with a solemn smile, then slapped the sides of Luke's shoulders with a misty grin. "I suggest a firm hand, Luke. She tends to run the show."

Luke's hand was trembling as he clutched Parker's arm. "If I take it, Riley, it will only be until Carmichael finds a replacement, and then I'll be gone. So you're leaving for nothing."

"I don't think so," Parker said, resting his hand on top of Luke's. "If you won't stay for my sake, Luke, then stay for hers." He moved to the door and shot Katie a tender gaze. "Talk him into it, Katie," he said with a faint smile. "We both know he's the man for the job." He grabbed his suitcase and walked out, closing the door behind him.

Katie slumped against her desk, and her sobs finished shredding Luke's heart. He rushed to pull her into his arms, his own voice rough with emotion. "How did he find out?"

She shook her head, quivering against him. "I don't know, but he knows . . . h-he has to."

He handed her a handkerchief and touched her cheek. "Well, he's not getting away with it. This is Parker Riley—the man we can talk into anything, remember? You wait here, okay?"

She nodded and sniffed, blowing her nose with another soggy heave.

Bypassing the elevator, he bolted down the stairs and out the front door, eyes scanning the street in the dark, lit only by streetlamps and storefronts still ablaze in anticipation of Christmas. He spotted him a block away, shoulders slumped and gray woolen coat flapping open in the breeze. Luke sprinted toward him, dodging couples and groups as they window shopped and milled on the sidewalk. Night had fallen, but the city was alive with the sounds of rush hour merging into the weekend with its cadence of traffic and horns blaring and music floating in the air. His stomach rumbled at the smell of steaks sizzling at Mickey Malone's, a favorite lunch spot of Parker's and his, and he could smell the fresh-baked bread from the bakery that Parker was just passing. His breathing was labored when he finally huffed to a stop twenty feet behind. He cupped his hands to his mouth. "Parker!"

He turned, and Luke could see from his stance in the lamplight that he would have a fight on his hands. "It doesn't matter if you leave or not," Luke shouted, his words heaving forth on halting breaths as they curled into the air like smoke. "I'm not going to marry Katie."

The edges of Parker's lips lifted in a weary smile. "That's a lie, Luke. But don't worry—I'll absolve you after I become a priest."

"Don't do this, Parker, don't give her up for me." Luke's heart pounded in his chest as he moved toward the man who was as much of a brother as if they shared the same blood.

"I'm not just giving her up for you . . . I'm giving her up for me." Air billowed into the night as Parker sighed, his shoulders slumped from the effort. He pinched the bridge of his nose with gloved fingers, head bent as if weighted with the task of rallying Luke to his side. "Truth be told, after you and Betty left Boston, I was so depressed I wanted to leave myself." He glanced up, his eyes filled with longing. "That's when I started thinking about what *I* really wanted, all those dreams I had tucked away when my father forced me into law. And I swear, Luke, for the first time in years, I felt glimmers of hope that maybe—just maybe—with you and Betty gone, this could be the time to follow my own path instead of my father's."

As if buoyed by a secret strength, his shoulders slowly rose, squaring strong with a peace and purpose that matched the calm in his eyes. "A path ingrained in me since I was a small boy—to devote myself to serving God as I always knew I was born to do." A faint smile edged his lips. "As a priest."

Luke gripped Parker's arm, his tone rife with annoyance. "I don't believe it, Parker, not for a moment. I know how much you love Katie. I see it in your face, and I read in your letters. You're grasping at straws here, trying to convince me you're doing the right thing."

Parker placed his hand over Luke's, his tone quiet. "Luke . . . have I ever lied to you before?"

With a shaky draw of air, Luke hesitated before finally shaking his head, the question depleting his hope in a frail release of air. He withdrew his hand. "No."

"And I'm not lying now." His throat shifted as he averted his eyes, the bright lights of the bakery illuminating his grief. His voice faded to a whisper, reedy with regret. "Don't get me wrong, McGee, I'm not saying that I don't love Katie or that this doesn't hurt like the devil." He looked up then, locking gazes with Luke. "But I could never be happy knowing I kept her from the man she really loved. I love her too much to do that, Luke . . . *and* you."

"I won't marry her, Parker, I swear . . ."

"Yes, you will. You were always meant to, not me. Betty knew that when she refused to marry you, and I knew it when Katie called you her 'soul mate' after you and Betty left. It about tore my heart out because I ached for all the pain she was going through." One side of his mouth flicked up into a sheepish smile. "Which is about the time I abandoned my true 'Soul mate' to fall in love with her. But she's a stubborn little thing with more spit and spunk than the law allows. She taught me not to quit when life gets in the way of your dreams, like I did with my father. I let him steer me off course, Luke, and God's given me a second chance—through you. She's in love with you, my friend, and you're still in love with her, and it doesn't take a genius at chess to figure that out. Don't blow it, McGee. Few of us get a second chance to go after our dreams."

For the first time in his life other than at chess, he found himself in a stalemate with the man he would go to the mat for, die for. For the last five years of Luke's life, Parker Riley had been there for him, supplying him with friendship, truth, and a loyalty so rare, he'd known he was a gift from God. Their commitment to each other was strong, so much so that Luke had always been able to talk Parker into anything . . . anything but this, apparently. But this was the most important thing of all.

With a lift of his chin, Luke felt his iron will harden into every bone in his body. "Then we're both going to walk away from her, Parker."

Parker exhaled, his breath drifting away like a ghost in the night. He gripped his suitcase tighter in his hand and smiled. "Then some lucky guy is going to discover the girl of our dreams, McGee, because I guarantee you, she won't last long." He glanced at his watch. "I may have to take the next train, but that's okay. The Seminary of the Immaculate Conception isn't expecting me till Monday."

Reality sank in. "That's where you went? When you went out of town?"

Parker smiled. "Signed, sealed, and delivered, my friend. I knew I'd need everything nailed down or you would try and talk me out of it."

Luke was desperate. "You talk about dreams, Parker, so what about Katie's? Her dream is to become a lawyer, and you know I can never give her that."

Parker smiled. "I know that, McGee, not on your salary. Which is why I opened an account in Katie's name at First National—tuition for law school or whatever her heart desires. Consider it a wedding present. After all, I'm taking a vow of poverty—what do I need with it?"

"You've thought of everything, haven't you?" Luke's voice was thick with frustration.

"Yeah, Luke, I have," Parker said with a melancholy smile, head bent. "Everything but how to make Katie fall in love with me like she's in love with you." He released a weighty sigh before his eyelids edged up, revealing a hint of tease. He arched a brow. "But if I had, all of us would have missed God's proverbial boat, so it's a good thing you're the lady killer, McGee, and not me." He shifted his suitcase with a tight smile. "Do me a favor, will you? Tell her family goodbye for me . . . and tell them I'm sorry. Then get your carcass back up there and get her through this. She needs you." He held out his hand. "I'll stay in touch."

Luke stared at Parker's hand and swallowed hard, water blurring his eyes. With a rush of emotion, he bypassed his hand and embraced him hard. "You better, Riley, because so help me, she's going to need you when I leave for New York."

Parker grinned. "You never were a good liar, McGee, not on your worst day." With a firm grip to Luke's shoulder, he turned and continued down the street, fading into the shadows as Luke's gaze followed in a bleak stare.

Luke closed his eyes and suddenly became aware of the bone-chilling cold, feeling more like a failure than he'd ever felt before. God help him . . . why hadn't he stayed in Philadelphia? He blew out a shaky breath and turned to head back to the office, determined to make this right. He'd stay until Carmichael hired a new man, but then he would leave. And Parker would have no choice but to come back. He would never leave Katie high and dry. Luke halted as a thought struck, and a chill skittered through him that had nothing to do with the weather.

Can I?

"Please, God—I can't go through another week like this." Katie's nasal whisper fell on deaf walls in a lonely office where she'd just spent the most miserable eight days of her life. She sat at her desk, shoulders bent and head buried in her arms, weeping for what must be the hundredth time since the man she was to marry had walked out of her life.

Her jaw hardened with intent. Well, it was time for the tears to end. There had been tears when Parker left, and tears when Luke returned. Tears over the weekend and tears in her bed. Tears in Parker's office during lunch hours and again on the lonely walks home. The result was red-rimmed eyes and a rusty voice that sounded like she was sick. And she was—heartsick over the pain she'd caused the two men she loved.

She wiped her eyes with a soggy handkerchief—the same handkerchief Luke had given her last week when he'd returned after trying to talk some sense into Parker. Katie had sobbed, and Luke had comforted, but his manner had been cautious and stiff, the steeled grief in his eyes fair warning that he would neither let Parker win . . . nor let Katie in.

"He's determined to do this," he'd said, teeth clenched as he hurled the door closed, rattling the bubbled window. "He's enrolled at the Seminary of the Immaculate Conception in New York. That's where he went this week." He gouged shaky fingers through his hair, his eyes stormy. "But we're not going to let him do this, Katie."

He turned away, head in his hands, and then shocked her when he slammed his fist to the wall, jarring both her and the few pictures that now hung in the balance. She'd been told he had a temper, but she'd never really seen it until then. On the walk home, he had ranted and raved, obviously venting his keen frustration over "ruining their lives." And then with no more than a stiff hug at the gate, he had left her, promising to do everything in his power to bring Parker back.

A promise he kept, but nothing more. He had clearly taken great pains to avoid her this week, spending his time behind closed doors or in meetings with Carmichael, approaching only Gladys or Bonnie Sue whenever he needed something done.

The few times he did speak to her, his tone was professional and his eyes distant and cool, as if connecting with her in any way would violate some life-and-death vow he had made.

She glanced down at Parker's ring, still on her left hand, and silently grieved over other vows that would never be taken. Eyes closed, she twisted the diamond on her finger, knowing full well she needed to remove it, but no strength or will at the moment to let the past go.

With a sodden sniff, she glanced up at the clock, noting that Luke's meeting with Miss Lillian at the BSCG was running longer than usual. It was half past six and Katie had been working and weeping since they'd left—Gladys and Bonnie Sue for the weekend and Luke for his meeting. Seldom had she felt this awful, her sinuses a mass of congestion and fluid and grief, but it didn't matter. Not tonight. Because tonight she needed to talk, if only for closure with the two men she loved. She hiked her chin with steel in her jaw. And talk she would . . . whether Luke McGee liked it or not.

Rising to her feet, she moved toward the window as if in a trance, eyes raw as she stared at the glass encrusted with frost. She blew her nose with Luke's handkerchief and wanted to start crying all over again.

Luke. Parker had suspected—whether she had tipped her hand, or Luke had, or both—somehow he'd known that their love was not finished. Katie thought of the man who had encouraged her, coddled her, saved her from the pain of heartbreak when Luke had left, and her heart squeezed with agony at the hurt he must have felt. She loved him, had been ready to spend her life with him regardless of any feelings she still harbored for Luke. *Why, Parker?*

But she already knew. It was simple, really. Because he loved her . . . because he loved Luke . . . and because, as Luke had said, that was the caliber of man that Parker Riley was. A sob broke as she put the handkerchief to her mouth and closed her eyes. "God," she whispered, "please tell me what to do."

But this one thing I do, forgetting those things which are behind, and reaching forth unto those things which are before . . .

The air stilled in Katie's lungs, and the cold slithered her spine. She opened her eyes, staring not at the whorls of ice etched on the pane, but at a passage in her mind, the one from Philippians she'd read that very morning. She blinked, and the breath in her throat parted from her lips in short, shallow gasps as her pulse quickened in her veins. Could Parker be right—could this be God's will after all?

"As much as I love you, Katie, I'd rather have God's will than my own . . . for you, for me . . . And for Luke. Because therein lies God's best."

A gasp broke from her lips as she swayed on her feet, Parker's words impacting her for the very first time.

God's best.

She closed her eyes, and as cleansing as a sigh, the burden of her grief lifted from her shoulders to God's. Could it be? His will—not Parkers, not Luke's, and not hers. *His*—the Lover of their souls? The One who ordained a specific path for each of them—knowing full well that his plan and purpose was not only why they'd been created, but for their ultimate happiness as well. At the thought, the knot unraveled in her stomach and peace drifted through her body like a gentle breeze, as warm and soft as the air that blew from the radiator below, caressing her arms.

Luke. The breeze fluttered in her stomach. Parker's gift to her . . .

And God's?

She opened her eyes and rubbed her arms, wondering if in the shadow of her sorrow, she could truly accept this as "God's will." And more importantly—could Luke?

"Katie?"

She turned at the window, and her throat tightened at the sag of his shoulders, the tragic look in his eyes. She wanted to run to him, to bury herself in those strong arms and ease their grief together, this man she loved more than life itself. But something stopped her—a stubborn bent to his chin, lips pressed pale with resolution . . . and an air that told her the tragedy in his eyes extended well beyond Parker's departure. She remained silent. *Oh, Luke . . .*

He glanced at the clock, his voice almost curt. "What are you still doing here?"

Releasing the breath she'd been holding, she slowly moved toward her desk, her heart surprisingly calm in the midst of Luke's rejection and her pain over Parker. With eyes focused on Bobbie Sue's report rather than Luke's face, she absently fingered the stack of papers, her thumb creasing along the bottom edge. "We need to talk," she whispered. "We can't go on like this forever, never speaking, avoiding each other like the plague." She glanced up, her heart in her throat. "Oh, Luke, what are we going to do?"

She heard his weary sigh and chanced a peek, watching him frown as he plucked his gloves off his hands and shoved them into his pockets. There was an edge of annoyance to the hard line of his mouth as he took his coat off and flung it on the coat rack. "Well, for starters, I told Carmichael I would stay on for a month, maybe two . . ." His eyes flicked up, and he frowned again. "Until he can hire a replacement."

"You . . . don't plan . . . to stay, then?" Her heart stopped, awaiting his answer.

The frown melted into compassion as he stripped off his suit coat and rolled up the sleeves of his pinstripe shirt. He jerked his tie loose as if in frustration, but his voice was quiet and calm. "No, Katie, I don't. Once Parker realizes that, he'll be back—I promise."

"I see." Her fingers made another nervous sweep along the edge of the papers. "Oh!"

"What's wrong?" He took a step forward.

She sucked on her finger while water blurred in her eyes. "Paper cut," she said with a sudden heave, unable to stop tears from trickling her face.

"Oh, Katie," he whispered, "please don't—this is hard enough for me as it is."

The taste of blood soured her tongue, merging with her frustration. "It's hard for all of us, Luke McGee," she said with a snap of her chin. "For Parker, who gave up our marriage, for you who said goodbye to a friend, and for me who not only lost a dear fiancé but has to work here day in and day out, wracked with guilt because I'm still in love with his best friend." She rose to her feet, obstinence and anger strengthening her bones. "Parker's not coming back, and we both know it. Take the job, Luke . . ."

Regret shadowed his eyes. "I can't, Katie. We have to give him the chance."

She rounded the desk slowly, heart racing as she walked toward him. "I know, and I feel the same way, truly. But I also know that for the first time in his life, Parker Riley is being a brick wall that neither of us will scale."

Alarm flickered in his eyes as she approached. "No, Katie, don't. My mind's made up."

Ignoring the sharpness of his tone, she moved in close, suddenly never surer of anything more in her life. Her gaze fused with his as she slowly took his hand in hers, his pale lips parted to emit tenuous breaths. She swallowed hard and caressed his palm. "Parker has given us a remarkable gift, Luke—a second chance to get it right. Take the job—please . . ."

"Katie, I can't . . ." His chest rose and fell with labored breathing, as if he had just run a mile, and maybe he had. She stared at those blue eyes now etched with pain. It took a lot of energy to run away from your dreams.

Despite the pounding of her heart, a rare peace prevailed as she lifted his hand to her mouth and placed a gentle kiss in his palm. Her gaze never left his as she curled his fingers closed with the embrace of her hand. "I love Parker Riley, Luke, and you know that. But God knows—and Parker knows—that I'm *in love* with you. And maybe . . . just maybe . . . it's what God had in mind all along."

He eased his hand away with a nervous shift of his throat. "I love you, Katie, you know that. But I'm not ready . . . for this . . . for us . . ."

"I'll wait," she said quietly. She lifted on tiptoe to cup his face with her hand while her thumb gently stroked the edge of his lip. "Take the job, Luke," she whispered.

He groaned and swallowed her up in his arms, squeezing her so tightly that the breath left her lungs. "We don't work well together," he rasped. "We butt heads, Katie, and heaven knows you don't take orders."

"I can, and I will," she gasped against the rough plane of his jaw. "Whatever you say."

Shock cooled the blood in her veins when he suddenly pushed her away, his fingers gouging her arms as he held her at arm's length. His hard, rapid breaths ticked away the seconds as he stared wild-eyed, a man caught in the crosshairs of guilt. "God, forgive me, what am I doing?"

Leaving her stunned and breathless, he quickly distanced himself, and all at once the stubbled jaw steeled again, along with the flinty blue of his eyes. "Don't tempt me like this, Katie, it's not right. Not with Parker's ring on your finger and the memory of his kiss still warm on your lips."

She swallowed hard and stared at Parker's engagement ring, shocked at the calm she felt. As if the innate calm of the man who'd given this ring had infused into her soul somehow, giving her his peace as well. *God's peace.* Closing her eyes, she drew in a quiet breath and slowly took the ring off. She looked up with a gentle gaze. "It was Parker's decision to end it, Luke, not mine. Because he knew—knew that you and I belong together." Longing misted in her eyes. "He wants you to marry me, Luke," she whispered, "and so do I."

As if his defenses had wavered, he sighed and plunged his hands in his pockets, his eyes suddenly tender. "As God is my witness, Katie, there is nothing on earth I would rather do, but I just can't." He exhaled again and slashed a hand through his hair. "Not now . . . maybe not ever."

"But, why?" She took a step forward, hurt dimming the hope in her eyes.

"Why?" His thick, blond brows angled high as disbelief furrowed his face. His tone was clipped. "Because Parker's been gone all of a week, and Betty barely over seven months, that's why. How can I even think of being happy when both of them—" His voice cracked, and he put a hand to his eyes.

Empathy swelled in her chest. "Luke," she whispered, "it's what Parker wants—for you to be happy—and Betty would too."

He looked up then, guilt glazing his eyes. "Maybe so, Katie, but I'm just not ready." A lump shifted in his throat as he looked away. "Maybe not for a long, long time."

She nodded and drew in a deep breath, deflecting her hurt with a hint of tease. "Well, goodness, jilted twice in one week—a girl could get a complex." She returned to her desk to retrieve her purse from the bottom drawer, then walked to the coat rack and slipped on her coat. "But it's all right, McGee—I'll wait." She moved toward the door and turned, buttoning her coat with a hike of her brow. "Just don't take too long," she said, tugging at her gloves. "I'd like to be young enough to land somebody else if I have to. You planning on being here a while? Because if you are, the coffee's still hot. Sludge, but hot."

He smiled the first smile she'd seen since Parker left—a tired one, but at least it wasn't riddled with guilt. "Yeah, I haven't been able to bring myself to go into Parker's office all week, but I think it's time. He mentioned some pet projects he wanted me to handle, but first I'll walk you home—"

"Nope." With a twirl of her scarf around her neck, she gave him a sympathetic smile. "You stay and finish. I'll take the trolley. There are a few stores I need to stop in on the way home, and with what's on your desk right now, you don't have time to spare."

"Thanks, Katie," he whispered. "For everything."

Her lips twisted. "Yeah, well, if I am going to make any

headway with the new boss, I have no choice but to be on my best behavior."

A grin tipped his lips. "So there really is such a thing?"

Her eyes narrowed. "Don't push me, McGee—you need me." She gave him her customary smirk. "See you Monday." And with an ache in her heart, she quietly shut the door.

Luke stared at the bubbled glass, seeing only a sassy smirk and blue eyes that had more of a hold than he'd like to admit. "You need me," she had said, and the words echoed in his brain like a prophecy of doom. He exhaled loudly and poured himself a cup of coffee—if that's what you called it. It looked more like the newfangled Bosco chocolate syrup, he thought with a quirk of a smile, remembering Katie's groans over Betty's "weak" coffee. He took a sip and scrunched his nose as he made his way into Parker's office, recalling the sugared coffee she'd delivered on her first day of work. He stopped and stared at Parker's empty chair, and his grief slashed anew. *Why, God?*

With a tight press of his lips, he opened Parker's top desk drawer and plucked out an envelope Parker had addressed to him. He headed into his own office, the feel of his old chair molding to his body with a measure of comfort and far fewer ghosts. He took another swig of hot coffee and ripped the envelope open, his heart heavy at first sight of the header—"Parker's Pet Projects," written, as usual, in a penmanship that was meticulous and precise. He stared at the first item on the list, and before he could swallow, the coffee spewed from his mouth.

1) Marry Katie.

Heat shot up the back of his neck as he hurled the list back on the desk. "You're a real comedian, Riley," he said with a grind of his jaw. He sucked in a deep breath, his throat as parched and dry as if he had just swallowed hot sand. He leaned back to rest his head on the back of his chair and closed his eyes to pray, thirsty for God's direction in his life.

"Help me, God," he whispered. "Help me to know what to do . . ."

Behold, I will do a new thing; now it shall spring forth; shall ye not know it? I will even make a way in the wilderness, and rivers in the desert.

His eyelids peeled open as his heart started to race. He licked his dry lips. *No!* He couldn't think that way. He needed to leave so Parker could come back. He sat up and put his head in his hands. This was supposed to be Parker's life here, not his. Katie and the O'Connors were meant to be Parker's family, never his. His life would be in New York with his daughter, where hopefully someday he'd realize the desire of his heart with a wife and family of his own.

Family. The very word had such a stranglehold on his heart that tears sprang to his eyes. It was something he had never really had, only glimmers here and there with Brady, Parker, and Betty. His craving for connection had driven him to street gangs once, a needy little boy so desperate to belong. So desperate for family.

God setteth the lonely in families . . .

And then all at once he saw Gabe setting the table for Marcy, and Patrick playing chess with his sons. He heard the chatter of Katie and her sisters as they giggled in the kitchen and the rumble of Sean's laughter when he'd finally beaten Steven at chess. He could feel the vibration of the stairs as the grandkids tore up and down, filling the house with their happy shrieks, or the thickening in his throat whenever Brady greeted him with a hug. Water filled his eyes, but he could still see them all, heads bowed in prayer as their father blessed the meal and their mother gripped his hand. And in the midst of his tears, he saw Katie, the love of his life since he'd been a little boy.

He closed his eyes, and Betty's words came to him along with her crooked grin, always trying to convince him to let go of the past and glory in the present. *"Come on, Luke—make me a happy woman just once—embrace the moment."*

Air seized in his lungs, and his head shot up as tears blurred his eyes. Seconds slowed into eons. Was it possible? Could it be?

His love? His family?

A gift from God—and the best friend bent on serving him?

Luke jumped to his feet so fast, the chair rocked on its legs with a loud clatter. Heart hammering in his chest, he bolted out the door, not even stopping as he snatched his coat along the way. He burst through the downstairs glass double doors with such force that a woman passing by released a startled shriek.

"Sorry," he said with a sheepish smile, "but I'm late getting . . . *home*." The very word tingled on his tongue, forcing more tears to his eyes. He started to jog, his long legs passing the crowd as he scanned every face. "Parker, I'm such a fool," he muttered, desperate to get his hands on Katie once again. His coat flapped open in the wind, but he never felt the cold, and when he saw a tiny blond in a red coat step out of Woolworth's two blocks down the street, his heart caught in his throat.

"Katie!" he shrieked.

She didn't turn and he kicked up his speed, grateful for basketball and baseball in the streets and the occasional night at the gym. His heart was pumping in his throat as hard as his legs were pumping down the street, and when he saw her move toward a streetcar with a shopping bag in her hand, his heart seized in his chest. "Katie!"

She turned then, and her body stilled on the sidewalk like the statues on Commonwealth Avenue Mall, all expression lost in the distance. He started to sprint, a pain in his side and his heart feeling as if it might explode, but he didn't care. Within a quarter block, he saw her begin to move toward him and then break into a run.

"Katie!" he rasped, and when he grabbed her arms, he almost knocked her over on the spot, his breathing so ragged, he couldn't utter a word.

Her chuckle filled the air with beautiful music. "That's great, McGee, why don't you just kill yourself so I have to run the office by myself?"

A grin tugged at his lips, but he forced a sobriety that defied the hope in his heart. "Katie, listen to me—I'll stay, but I can't promise anything more right now. Please understand that my heart aches for Parker and you, and I have to do everything in my power to make sure . . ."

Her smile softened to serious. "I understand, Luke, and I agree."

He sucked in a fortifying breath. "But, that said, if Parker remains pigheaded and doesn't come back . . . then maybe . . . maybe down the road, after the air clears and if things change between you and me . . ." With gentle urgency, he suddenly cupped her face in his hands, all his fears spilling forth like the tears on her cheeks. "Katie, I have a daughter," he said, his voice choked with emotion.

She stroked a gentle hand to his face. "I know that, Luke, but I'm pretty sure she could use a mother."

"But it wouldn't be easy . . ."

"I know that too. But nothing has ever been easy with you, and I'm still here, aren't I?"

"I'll never be rich," he argued, gently pushing the hair from her eyes.

A smile tilted her lips as she blinked away her tears. "I've learned that at times, money can be highly overrated."

"I intend to wear the pants in my family . . ."

Her lips quirked. "I look so much better in a skirt, or haven't you noticed?"

"But I want lots of kids . . ."

She hesitated. "We'll talk."

He thought of Parker, and his smile dimmed. "And I need time, Katie . . . maybe six months or more . . . to adjust . . . to get past Betty's death and your engagement to Parker." A lump shifted in his throat. "To make sure this is the right thing to do . . . and to pray."

Wetness glimmered in her eyes. "Like I said, Luke, I'll wait."

He paused, searching those blue eyes that held so much hope, so much love, so much desire. He swallowed hard, almost shy for the first time in his life. With a nervous shift of his throat, he plunged his hands in his pockets and gave her a shaky smile. "Okay, then," he said with a loud exhale of air, "until then . . . friends?"

She caressed his stubbled cheek. "Forever and a day, McGee."

He cleared his throat and stepped back to distance himself, desperate to steel his feelings. "Which means, Katie, I can't handle anything more right now—not expectations on your part, not attraction on mine, and not badgering to get your own way. We both need friendship to get through this. And I won't take the job unless you can promise me that's all there will be and nothing more. No flirting, no plots of seduction like your sisters did with Brady, and no romance. Just good friends, pure and simple—like we were before." He extended an awkward hand, determined that for once in her life, Katie O'Connor would follow his lead. "Deal?"

A kaleidoscope of emotions shifted across her beautiful face, from a flicker of hurt, to relief, and finally respect. She squared her shoulders and placed her hand in his to give it a firm shake. "You have my word, McGee," she said with a somber nod. She bent to retrieve her shopping bag and then shot him a crooked smile. "About the friendship, that is. As far as the BCAS? No guarantees, *Mr. Priss*. See you on Monday."

She turned and made her way to the trolley while he watched with his heart in his throat. "Be on time, Katie Rose," he called. "We have lots to do, and I don't want you to be late."

She paused on the step of the trolley and turned, stealing his breath with a mischievous smile. "I'll be there, McGee, probably before you. But it's time you learn . . . it's never too late." She gave him a jaunty wave and disappeared inside the car, and Luke felt as if his heart might burst. With a silly grin, he turned and shoved his hands in his pockets, her final words flooding his soul with peace.

Never too late. Water rimmed his eyes as he forged his way through the crowd.

No, with God, apparently not.

23

May 10, 1931

"Okay, what's wrong with this picture?" Katie's lips squirmed as she shucked the corn with a vengeance. She cocked a hip against the counter, accentuating the scalloped layers of her floral sundress as it flared at her calf. "It's Mother's Day, and the men are outside playing horseshoes while the 'mothers' are stuck in a hot kitchen."

"True . . . ," Charity said with a slow drawl and a quick peek out the kitchen window. A breeze fluttered both the cream eyelet curtains and the sheer ruffle of Charity's pale blue organza blouse, infusing Lizzie's spacious kitchen with the scent of fresh-mown grass, newly hewn mulch, and smoked meat. The ping of horseshoes could be heard above the rumble of men's laughter and the squeals of children, creating the perfect spring day. "But keep in mind that the children belong to the fathers for the day." She cracked a hard-boiled egg on the counter with a diabolical grin and began to peel it for the deviled eggs. "And with the shenanigans that Henry's been pulling lately, that sure says 'Happy Mother's Day' to me."

"And they *are* handling the barbecue," Lizzie defended, closing her eyes as she sniffed the aroma of grilled meat. "Although Brady would do just about anything for barbecue." She popped an olive in her mouth from the relish tray she'd just finished and shot Charity a grin. "Short of watching Henry, that is."

Marcy chuckled as she shredded slaw at the sink. "He sounds like your father. Insists he wants his tombstone to read, 'He loved barbecue.'"

The spicy smell of pepper drifted in the air as Faith seasoned the potato salad with a hefty dose. "Oh, that's Collin too. Must be a primal thing, left over from the days when cavemen bopped their woman over the head and cooked game over an open fire."

Charity sneezed and then glanced up with a squint of her eyes. "Ooooo . . . now there's an idea to keep Henry in line."

A soft chuckle that could only be Emma Malloy carried on a breeze as she finished squeezing lemons for the iced tea. "Or you."

"Nice one, Emma," Katie said with a grin. She dropped an armful of corn into a boiling cauldron of water. "Talk about 'grilling' and putting someone's feet to the fire."

With another sharp crack of an egg, Charity charred her sister with a mock glare as a smile twitched at the corners of her mouth. "Speaking of 'putting one's feet to the fire,' Katie Rose . . . I'm guessing our Luke McGee likes his barbecue smoked a long, *long* time?"

Heat that had nothing to do with the steam from the pot blasted Katie's cheeks with an uncomfortable warmth. "Luke and I are nothing more than friends, Charity, and you know it. And I refuse to even think of the possibility of anything more until it's a reality in that man's mind, *if and when* that ever happens. Besides, he's my boss, and neither of us are looking to complicate things right now."

"Mmm-hmm. I'd say things are pretty complicated already," Charity said with a slant of her lips. "Given the fact you work with the man day in and day out and he still comes for dinner two times a week."

"To see Gabe and nothing more," Katie argued. She slapped a wilted strand of hair from her eyes, wondering why her stomach was suddenly in knots.

Marcy tucked an arm around Katie's shoulders and gave her a gentle squeeze. "Yes, Gabe, certainly, but also you," she said quietly. "Luke will come around, Katie . . . when he's ready."

Katie swallowed hard and straightened her shoulders, fighting the threat of moisture in her eyes. With a press of her jaw, she hefted more corn in her arms and dumped it into the scalding pot, wishing it were Luke McGee instead. "I'm not so sure he'll ever be ready, Mother. It appears friendship suits the man just fine."

Lizzie laid a gentle hand to her sister's arm. "Betty's been gone only a little over a year, Katie, and I think that was a milestone for Luke, I really do. Since he and Kat moved in with us last year, I've learned just how hard losing both Betty and Parker has been for him, not to mention the guilt he feels over coming between Parker and you." Lizzie ducked her head to smile into Katie's eyes. "But he's also told us just how much your friendship has meant to him, especially these last six months."

Katie nodded and put a hand to her eyes, embarrassed by the sting of tears.

As soft as a whisper, Lizzie eased Katie's hand to clasp it in her own, forcing her sister to look at her. She gave her palm a reassuring squeeze. "But two weeks ago, after Luke took Kat to visit Betty's grave on the anniversary of her death, he told us he also went to spend time with Parker. And I'm not exactly sure what happened that weekend, but when Luke returned home, I swear he was a different man. Lighter, happier, as if a huge weight had been lifted." Lizzie touched a palm to Katie's cheek. "Trust him, Katie . . . and trust God. I promise, neither will let you down."

Katie sniffed and pushed the wetness from her eyes. "I know you're right, Lizzie, because Luke's told me so himself—over and over—how much our friendship has meant. But it's just so hard, loving him like I do and wanting it to be more."

Massaging her shoulders from behind, Faith leaned forward to give Katie a sympathetic smile. "It is hard to be patient, I know. We've all been there, Katie, each of us with the men in our lives, including Mother." Her lips curved in a crooked smile. "Apparently God thinks nobody teaches patience better than Irish men. Must be a gift."

"Or a curse." Charity banged the last of the hard-boiled eggs on the counter with a particularly nasty crack. She glanced up through narrow eyes. "Hey . . . you don't suppose God's Irish, do you?"

Emma chuckled. "I suspect he might be, at least in this family."

Katie sucked in a deep breath and attempted a grin. "Thanks for the pep talk, everyone. I'm okay now, really." She glanced at the pot of steaming corn. "Guess I should turn it up to a boil, which," she said with a lift of her brow, "is exactly what I'd like to do to Luke McGee."

A devious grin sprouted on Charity's face as she pulverized the egg yolks with a fork. "Ooooo . . . a girl after my own heart. So, why don't you?"

Katie sighed and turned up the flame on the corn. "Because I want it to be his idea, not mine," she said with a pout, "which is something as foreign to me as patience, apparently." She turned and sagged against the counter with a fold of her arms. "Besides, I promised."

The fork in Charity's hand froze midair, egg yolk caked between the tines. "Promised what?" she asked with shock in her tone.

The edge of Katie's mouth crooked up. "No plotting, no ploys, no flirting, no seduction."

Charity's jaw dropped a full inch. "Sweet saints in heaven—Mitch would take my pulse."

Faith snickered.

"So, you see, my hands are tied," Katie said with a weighty sigh. "And believe me, I'm none too happy about it."

Dropping the fork into the bowl with a clatter, Charity hurried over to lock Katie in a tight hug. "Oh, honey, I am so sorry! Is there anything I can do?"

"Yeah," Katie said with a smirk. "Pray that God turns up the heat so I don't have to."

"Hey, when we gonna eat—me and the guys are hungry!" The screen door slammed as Gabe barreled into the kitchen with sweaty pigtails. She snatched an egg from Charity's platter on her way, earning her a playful swat.

"In the next ten minutes, as a matter of fact," Marcy said as she mixed the slaw. "Did you set the tables like Mr. O'Connor asked, Gabriella Dawn?"

"Yes, ma'am," Gabe said with a groan. "Took me forever, too, with all them stupid tables lined up clear across Lizzie's backyard."

"Good girl," Marcy said with a smile. "Now remember, he said you're to be in charge of the little ones, so you're the boss."

A gleam lit Gabe's eyes. "That includes Henry, don't it?"

"Absolutely!" Charity said with a wink of her eye. She plopped the last of the egg filling into the egg halves and carefully arranged them on the platter. "I'm hoping you can succeed where I've failed, Gabe Smith." Her eyes narrowed, glittering with conspiracy as she licked the spoon. She tucked the tray of eggs into the icebox, then peered over her shoulder with a threatening smirk. "Don't let me down."

Ping!

"Yes!" Collin's voice shot in the air along with his arms, effectively drowning out the groans of his competition. "The kid grinds 'em into the dust once again." He snatched the horseshoes from the spike in Brady's manicured lawn and delivered a cocky grin in Luke's direction. "So, McGee, it looks like it's time to stop hiding behind that baby and defend your title."

Luke smiled, enjoying the afternoon as he sloped back against a gnarled oak with Kat in his arms, her pink frilly dress fanned against dark suspenders and the crisp white of the rolled-up sleeves of his shirt. He latched a thumb in the pocket of his Glen plaid seersucker slacks and matched Collin's cocky grin, gleam for gleam. A breeze scented by lilac bushes heavy with bloom feathered both Luke's towhead and Kat's auburn ringlets as he shifted her in his arms. "Hey, McGuire, don't you worry, boy—I can teach you how it's played with a baby in my arms and a hand tied behind my back."

"Do it, Luke—it's the only thing that'll stop him from gloating." Brady glanced over from a massive stone barbecue pit where the mouthwatering aroma of grilled meat billowed into the air. He piled the last of the barbecue on a platter and slathered it with more sauce before joining Patrick, Mitch, and Steven at the cedar picnic table he'd built himself. Before he sat, he slapped Sean on the shoulder with a wry grin. "Heaven knows Sean and I did our best to humble the boy, but I suspect he recruited divine intervention."

Collin slacked a hip and grinned, bobbling the horseshoes in his hand. "You accusing me of cheating, Brady, is that what I'm hearing?"

Steven chuckled and fisted his drink. "I don't know, Collin—cheating or raw talent. Sounds like a clear-cut choice to me."

Brady rolled his neck and gave Collin a patient smile. "Settle down, Collin, you played a great game. But it wouldn't surprise me if you had your wife praying for you."

"Nope, wouldn't do that, ol' buddy."

Mitch laughed. "Don't have to. Faith's smart enough to pray on her own. That woman doesn't want to go home with a grouch."

"I'll show you grouch, Dennehy. Come on, one more game—put your money where your mouth is."

"No, thanks—I think we should let Luke have that honor, don't you, Patrick?" Mitch upended his ginger ale.

Patrick bounced Molly on his knee with a grin, looking the part of the doting grandpa as he shot Collin a wink. "Might be the wise thing to do. As I recall, the 'boy' is one of those who has to learn the hard way."

"Hear that, Kat? Daddy's got to teach somebody a valuable lesson." Luke ambled over with a sleepy-eyed baby in his arms and lifted her in the air, poised to deposit her in Brady's lap.

"Freeze!" Charity shot a mock glare, standing at the door with a tray of deviled eggs in her hands. "Don't you dare hand that baby off, Luke McGee. The food's ready, so the game has to wait."

"Saved by the bell," Luke said with a chuckle as he slipped Kat under his arm with the same firm hold reserved for a football. He strolled over to sit next to Brady and threatened Collin with a predatory grin. "You got a reprieve, McGuire, so enjoy your supper now, because after I'm done with you, it'll be giving you heartburn."

"You always were a little too big for your britches, Cluny my boy—I look forward to it."

Brady laughed and jumped to his feet, glancing at Collin over his shoulder as he grabbed a bowl of potato salad from Marcy's hands. "Yeah, ol' buddy, we all are."

The screen door squealed open to make way for a procession of women bearing platters and bowls of food. Their giggles and chatter filled the air, punctuated with the happy shrieks of apple-cheeked children, male laughter, and the surprisingly low boom of Gabe's directives, smug with authority.

"Momma, is it time for ice cream?" Teddy looked up with a tug of Lizzie's organza dress, leaving a sticky imprint on the yellow tea-rose pattern. She picked him up in her arms and planted a noisy kiss to his flushed cheek. "Nope, darlin', not till after supper. But first, we're going to wash those sticky hands."

Collin snatched Teddy from Lizzie's hold, unleashing wild giggles as he tickled his belly and hoisted him in the air. "I'll wash him up, Lizzie, you sit. It's Mother's Day." He plopped the toddler on his shoulders and bent to steal a kiss from his wife. "I'll be wanting one of these next year, Little Bit, because it's time for a little dirt and stickball around the house, don't you think?"

Faith pressed a hand to her husband's face with a tender smile, her voice brimming with affection. "I'm ready when you are, my love."

"I'm ready," Collin whispered with a gleam of hope in his eyes. He took his time with another lingering kiss before toting a squealing Teddy into the house.

When children's plates were finally made and mothers seated with a kiss, and even Henry had been bullied into a chair, Patrick rose and bowed his head in prayer.

With a gentle kiss to Kat's downy curls, Luke buried himself in the soft baby scent of Betty's daughter—*his* daughter—and closed his eyes. Kat was family . . . *his* family . . . and a daughter who needed a mother as much as he needed a wife. He chanced a peek at Katie across the red-and-white checkered table, her golden head bowed in prayer, and his heart turned over. She was everything he had ever wanted—friend, partner, and confidante. And now, since Parker had put his guilt to rest, not only with his spoken assurance, but with the peace in his eyes and joy in his face, Luke could finally admit that Katie was everything he'd ever need. A wife, a mother, a lover . . . and the key to a family he could call his own.

A lump shifted in Luke's throat as the prayer ended, and gentle chaos ensued with the passing of bowls and good-natured teasing and the jabber of children. With a full heart, his eyes scanned the table, taking in Charity wrestling with Mitch over the lightest roll, or Collin kissing Faith as she passed him the slaw. A smile shadowed his lips at the tender way Brady squeezed Lizzie's hand or how Marcy heaped barbecue high on her husband's plate. Beside him, Gabe chattered like a magpie while Emma and Katie giggled at one of Sean's jokes. And then, in the midst of these remarkable people he'd been so blessed to know, he felt the quiet confirmation in his spirit. He was finally *home*.

Gabe passed the beans and Luke glanced up to see Katie watching him. He grinned, his pulse accelerating at the cute smirk on those full, sassy lips, and for the first time since he moved to Philly with Betty, he let himself revel in the warmth that flooded his veins. He could feel the heat in his eyes as he stared her down, noting with satisfaction that a hint of color rose in her cheeks.

"There's trouble brewing in those eyes," she remarked with a lift of her brow, but he only grinned wider. *You have no idea, Katie Rose . . . how our lives are about to change.*

"Hey, why does *she* get to sit with the grown-ups?" Henry demanded, giving Gabe the evil eye as she sidled close to Luke. "I'm almost her age—I want to sit with the grown-ups too."

Patrick's chin elevated to assess the situation through slatted eyes. "Gabe, you were assigned to oversee the children—your place is with them, not the adults. *Move,* young lady!"

Horror expanded the whites of her eyes. "But Mrs. O'Connor said I could sit next to Luke, and she promised!"

With a grind of his jaw, Patrick seared her with a look before shifting his gaze to his wife. "I already told her no, Marcy. She's a child, not an adult, and only nine years old—"

"*You* said I was their boss," Gabe said with a hike of her chin, "and I'm almost ten."

Patrick stared her down. "*Nine* at the moment," he said with strong emphasis. "And keep in mind that while you're under my roof, Gabriella Dawn, *I* am the boss."

"I'm not under your roof right now," Gabe muttered, "I'm in Lizzie's backyard."

"Hush, Gabe," Luke whispered with a pinch of her arm.

Patrick's eyes flitted to his wife. "She's already too old for her britches, Marcy—the girl needs to sit with the children."

Marcy's face melted into a plea. "But, Patrick, you know how she loves to sit next to Luke, and it *is* Mother's Day . . ."

Luke bit back a smile as he straddled his dozing baby over his lap. He could almost swear Marcy had batted her eyes. A haze of ruddy color bled up the back of Patrick's neck as his lips clamped into a tight line. Silence shrouded the table at the interplay between husband and wife as Patrick sat back in his chair and snapped his napkin in the air with a loud pop. "Well, I suppose I have no authority whatsoever, given the occasion."

With a look of supreme victory, Gabe took "smug" to a whole new level. "Gosh, Mrs. O'Connor, you're the best . . ."

Something flickered in Marcy's cheek as she studied Gabe and then her husband. "Move to the children's table, please," she said quietly, finally turning her attention to Gabe.

Gabe's eyes grew. "But—"

"*Now*, young lady," Marcy said with steel in her tone.

"But, you said—"

"Not another word, or I will confiscate your stash of Dubble Bubble."

Gabe gulped, right before her lips flattened into a grim line. She rose to her feet with a lingering groan and cauterized Patrick with a glare.

"And wipe that look off your face this instant, young lady. Mr. O'Connor is your foster parent and, as such, will have your respect. Is that understood?"

Gabe gaped, her eyes circled in shock . . . not unlike Patrick's at the moment.

"Yes, ma'am," she muttered. She moved to the children's table where she plopped into the seat next to a gloating Henry.

As gingerly as possible, Charity leaned across the table to

address Marcy with a loud whisper. "Uh, Mother . . . do you think Henry could spend the week?"

Marcy spooned potato salad in her mouth and chewed, the barest of smiles hovering on her lips. Reaching for the salt and pepper shakers, she skewed Charity with a look. "Very funny, young lady, but I think your father and I already have our hands full, don't you?" She extended the seasoning to her husband, who sat watching her with wonder in his eyes. "Salt and pepper, Patrick? If I say so myself, my potato salad is rather bland."

He took her by surprise with a quick brush of his lips to hers before squeezing her hand with a grin. "Not at all, darlin', not at all. In fact, Marceline," he said in a husky tone that brought a trace of rose to her cheeks, "I think it may be perfect—just like my wife."

Luke popped barbecue in his mouth as a wail erupted from his daughter.

Katie started to rise. "I'll take her, Luke—you finish your plate."

He lifted Kat to his shoulder and hopped up before Katie could even clear her chair. "Nope, you stay and eat." He nuzzled her neck while her chubby legs thrashed against his chest. "Come on, little girl, we'll rock you and put you someplace comfortable."

Katie chewed on her lip, only half listening to Sean's story as she watched Luke cuddle and coo with his daughter on the way into the house. She startled at the touch of a hand on her arm and glanced up into the knowing eyes of Emma Malloy.

"He's a wonderful father," Emma said softly, her gaze trailing Katie's to the screen door as it slammed behind Luke and his daughter. "He'll make a wonderful husband."

A sigh of frustration puffed from Katie's lips. "Thanks, Emma. I agree . . . that is, if I ever get the chance to find out."

A smile curved the left side of Emma's mouth, almost

obscuring the faded scar on the right. "Something tells me you will, Katie. And sooner than you might think."

Katie squinted up. "You really think so?"

She nodded and rose, pulling Katie to her feet. "Come on, help me with ice cream?"

Katie followed her to the kitchen, reflecting on Emma's comment as they chatted and scooped bowls of ice cream. Like the gentle woman herself, her words had been so soft, so sure, oozing into Katie's spirit like a healing balm that helped to ease the frustration of Luke McGee.

When everyone had been served and Luke still hadn't returned, Katie quietly slipped away from the lively buzz and hum of family conversations to seek him out. She found him in his room on the far side of the house, the one he shared with his daughter. Katie paused in the doorway, content to stop and just study him a while, this man determined to be only her friend. All at once, the realization that this was where he lived and slept stirred a warmth within, and her lips compressed. A warmth that was obviously getting harder to ignore.

Eyes closed, he lay on his back in his narrow bed. His feet were bare and his long legs crossed at the ankles while muscled arms folded protectively across Kat's chunky little body as she slept on his chest. The rhythm of their breathing appeared as one, and the sunlit room was still except for the flutter of a breeze as it rippled the sheers of a large double window.

Katie released a silent sigh as she sagged against the doorframe, annoyed once again at the dangerous effect this man had on her pulse. The relaxation of sleep had no softening effect whatsoever on the firm jaw and finely chiseled profile that now sported a tan from time spent in the sun. She nibbled on her lip as she scanned his lean, muscled body, and heat suddenly steamed her cheeks at the thought of lying in his arms like that. With a catch of her breath, she quickly turned, suddenly anxious to leave.

"Don't go."

It was the faintest of whispers, but she whirled around, mortified at the blood that rushed to her cheeks. With a slow finger to his lips, his mouth eased into a half smile that caused her stomach to flip. Her pulse pounded in her ears as she watched him rise, graceful and strong like the athlete he was. With the gentlest of motion, he laid his daughter in the crib against the far wall, and then bent to press a soft kiss to her head.

Katie swallowed the emotion blocking her throat. *Oh, Lord, will we ever be more than friends . . .*

He reached for his shoes, then ushered her into the hall and silently closed the door behind, finally releasing a long, weary breath. "Poor, little girl—she gnawed on my finger forever, so I know she's teething. A nap will do her good." He stooped to put his shoes on before sloping back against the door and folding his arms, those blue eyes assessing her with a look that weakened her knees. "Did you . . . want something, Katie Rose?" he asked softly.

Her breathing shallowed as she lifted her eyes, swallowing hard when her gaze locked with his. "No, I mean, yes . . . I mean . . . do you want ice cream?" she blurted.

Everything slowed as he reached to brush a strand of hair from her face, and against her will, his touch quickened her pulse. "Not ice cream," he whispered, "but there is something I want . . ." The smile in his eyes heated several degrees as his gaze slowly dropped to her mouth, all but paralyzing her.

God, help me, this is it! she thought with a clutch of her stomach, and the notion almost buckled her limbs. "W-what?" she asked with a ragged breath, her lungs refusing to breathe.

He stepped forward and gently gripped her arms. "I need a favor, Katie. There's a board dinner this weekend, and for once, Lizzie can't watch Kat. Can you keep her on Saturday night?"

She blinked. *That's it?* Her pulse was hammering, he had that look in his eye, and her bones had softened to churned butter . . . and all he wanted was for her to watch Kat??? Disappointment slammed so hard that it was a physical ache, and when the stun wore off, her anger took over, tingeing her words with an edge. "Sure, Luke—anytime." Flinging his hands away, she turned to go, as angry at herself as she was at him.

A massive palm locked on her wrist, reeling her in with a dominant hold. Strong arms held her captive as he tucked his head close to hers, stealing her air. "I meant *forever*, Katie Rose," he said in a husky whisper that blew warm in her ear.

She jerked away with shock in her eyes, her pulse erratic. "W-what d'you m-mean?" she stuttered, too afraid her ears had deceived her.

He grinned and gently pressed her to the wall, pinning her there with a look that told her *exactly* what he meant. He bent to slowly feather her jaw with kisses. "I mean Happy Mother's Day, Katie Rose, and may it be the first of many."

Her gasp drew his lips to hers and then turned to a moan when he cupped the back of her head to consume her with his mouth. Heat came in waves as hungry hands drew her close, and with another weak moan, she managed to push him away. Her breath was as jagged as her nerves as she stood, back to the wall and palms hard against his chest. When she spoke, her voice was a rasp. "Plain English, McGee, I want plain English. Are you asking me to marry you or not?"

Reaching into his pocket, the smile never left his eyes as he unearthed a roll of Life Savers and bobbled them in his palm. He popped one in his mouth and offered the roll to her with a grin. "Have a Life Saver, Katydid, I hear they're your favorite."

"I don't want a Life—" She stopped, unable to utter another syllable. Hot tears swelled in her eyes as she blinked, the roll of Life Savers little more than a blur—a blur that held the ring that would seal their future.

Tugging the diamond from where he'd wedged it in the

roll, he placed it on her trembling finger. "Marry me, Katie," he whispered, "and make the King of Misery give up his throne."

She caught her breath and glanced up, a hand to her mouth. "Who told you?"

He brushed a strand of hair from her face and then stroked her jaw with his thumb. "Parker. Uh, I didn't know, but apparently you had a number of nicknames for poor, defenseless Cluny McGee." He gripped her chin as one blond brow angled high. "'The *King* of Misery'?"

She grinned, avoiding his eyes as she stared at the ring on her hand, hardly daring to believe. She swiped a tear from her cheek. "Yeah, well, when I was eleven, it certainly fit. You drove me crazy."

"Likewise, Sass," he said with that dangerous look in his eyes. He gathered her into his arms and gave her a slow, luxurious kiss that turned her stomach to Jell-O. "And if it makes you feel any better, I knew I wanted to marry you the moment you stuck that sassy, little nose in the air on an Easter I will *never* forget."

"Well, for somebody who wanted to marry me, you sure took your sweet time, McGee."

He kissed her on the tip of her "sassy, little nose." "Had to. You tend to be a pushy little thing with a knack for bulldozing your own way." The smile in his eyes sobered. "And I needed time, Katie—thank you for giving me that. I just couldn't rush into happiness with you in the face of my grief over Betty and the pain I caused you and Parker. I know it wasn't easy for you, but you honored your promise to me and to God, and for that I'm grateful."

"Luke! Be on my team, *please*?" Gabe shot down the hall, anxious eyes darting over her shoulder as Henry rounded the corner.

"Luke, no, she's already got Uncle Brady, so it's no fair!" Henry said with a gasp.

Gabe squinted her eyes, blocking the hall with two raised

fists that halted Henry dead in his tracks. "And you've got your dad, Steven, and Sean, while all I have is Collin, so back off, buster. Luke is mine."

"You're mean," Henry said with a sneer.

"That's right, and don't you forget it."

Henry ignored her and shot Luke a plea. "Please, Luke, huh?"

"Sorry, Henry, but Gabe did ask me first."

"Aunt Katie, can't you talk him into it, *please*?" Henry begged, reminding Katie so much of Charity that she stifled a grin. She folded her arms in surrender. "Sorry, Henry, the man is a mule. I have no influence whatsoever."

Luke arched a brow. "*I'm* the mule?" He tucked Katie under his arm and shot Henry a smile. "Tell you what, Henry, Father's Day is next month, so I'll be on your team then, okay?"

Gabe leapt in the air with a shriek while Henry puffed out a noisy moan. "Okay," he muttered, and Gabe dashed past him in a race to the backyard.

Luke gave a satisfied sigh. "I love kids, Katie Rose." He squeezed her shoulder and led her down the hall, planting a kiss on top of her head. "I want a houseful—at least eight."

The balls of her feet skidded to a cold stop. "Two, Luke McGee, and no more."

He turned and pulled her close. "Six, Katie Rose," he whispered, allowing his gaze to settle on her mouth. He bent to punctuate it with a slow kiss.

"Two," she repeated, despite the heat fogging her mind.

He leaned in and nuzzled her neck. "Five."

"Three."

"Four," he muttered, his mouth warm as it vibrated against her throat.

He kissed her again and she moaned. "You're taking advantage of me in a weakened state, Cluny McGee."

"I know," he said in a husky voice. He deepened the kiss,

then trailed his lips to her ear. "I suggest you get used to it, Katie Rose, because I plan to make a habit of it." He latched onto the small of her back and drew her in close, taking his time to kiss her thoroughly. "Four."

"Four, then," she rasped against his mouth, heat traveling her body like a steamy day in the devil's kitchen. She looked up at the man who checked every box on her list—and God's—then returned his kiss with a misty one of her own. "And I'd call *that* a definite maybe."

Acknowledgments

To my agent, Natasha Kern, and my editor, Lonnie Hull DuPont—two of God's many touches in my life—thank you for your faith in me.

To the great team at Revell, true professionals all—thank you for all you do. A special hug to Michele Misiak for her kindness and patience; to Cheryl Van Andel and Dan Thornberg for their great covers; and to the best copyeditor in the world, Barb Barnes, who makes editing an absolute pleasure.

To my brainstorming buddies—Charlotte Vernaci, Karen Chancellor, Judy Jackson, Linda Tate, Ruth Volk, Cherie Nevin, and Sandy Knight—I not only treasure your friendship but your valuable opinions, which have made this a far better book.

To the Seekers—sisters all—when it comes to talent, humor, and support, you ladies rock! I am so glad you have my back.

To Gabriella Dawn Smith and Alli Moser—two of my very favorite reader friends after whom I've named two of my favorite characters in this book. Thank you not only for your tireless support and encouragement but for going above and beyond in my newsletter contest to have a character named after you. I smile every time I see your names in Katie's story.

To my precious prayer partners and best friends, Joy Bollinger, Karen Chancellor, and Pat Stiehr—I would be lost without you.

To my aunt Julie, my mother-in-law Leona, and my sisters, Dee Dee, Mary, Pat, Rosie, Susie, Ellie, and Katie for your love and prayers, and to my sisters-in-law, Diana, Mary, and Lisa—family just doesn't get any better than you.

A special hug to my sisters Ellie and Kate for always being ready to pray, to read, and to lift me up when I'm down—I thank God for putting us together in the birth line.

To my daughter Amy, whose beauty, wit, and endless lists helped shape Katie O'Connor into the woman I wanted her to be, to my son Matt, who possesses all the kindness and compassion of a Luke McGee, and to my daughter-in-law Katie, the best editor/proofreader outside the business—I love you all more than words can say.

To Keith Lessman, the man I love with every fiber of my being—never in all my dreams of romance did I ever believe it possible to feel so cherished and loved. I've said it before, babe, and I'll say it again—I don't deserve you.

And to the God of Hope, Who has taught me that with Him, there truly is such a thing as "a hope undaunted"—I will serve You all the days of my life.

Julie Lessman is an award-winning author whose tagline of "Passion with a Purpose" underscores her intense passion for both God and romance. Author of The Daughters of Boston series, Julie is also winner of the 2009 ACFW Debut Author of the Year and Holt Medallion Awards of Merit for Best First Book and Long Inspirational. She is the recipient of thirteen Romance Writers of America awards.

Julie resides in Missouri with her husband, daughter, son, and daughter-in-law.

Contact Julie through her website at www.julielessman.com.

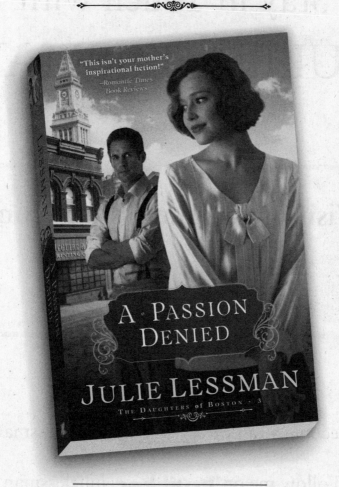

Stay in Touch with
JULIE LESSMAN

Visit www.julielessman.com
to learn more about Julie,
sign up for her newsletter, and
read interviews and reviews.

Become a fan on facebook Julie Lessman

Follow me on twitter julielessman